PRAISE FOR THE NOVELS OF *NEW YORK TIMES* BESTSELLING AUTHOR
DALE BROWN

"Brown puts readers into the cockpit. . . . Authentic and gripping."
New York Times

"The novels of Dale Brown brim with violent action, detailed descriptions of sophisticated weaponry, and political intrigue. . . . His ability to bring technical weaponry to life is amazing."
San Francisco Chronicle

"Dale Brown is a superb storyteller."
W.E.B. Griffin

"Brown's devoted fans recognize him as one of this country's leading military-fiction writers, and his latest will do nothing to change their minds."
Booklist

"Nobody does it better."
Kirkus Reviews

Also in the Dreamland Series

(with Jim DeFelice)

Titles by Dale Brown

DALE BROWN
AND
JIM DeFELICE

DRONE STRIKE

A DREAMLAND THRILLER

HARPER

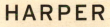

An Imprint of HarperCollinsPublishers

This is a work of fiction. Names, characters, places, and incidents are products of the author's imagination or are used fictitiously and are not to be construed as real. Any resemblance to actual events, locales, organizations, or persons, living or dead, is entirely coincidental.

HARPER

An Imprint of HarperCollins*Publishers*
195 Broadway
New York, New York 10007

Copyright © 2014 by Air Battle Force, Inc.
ISBN 978-0-06-212282-7

First Harper premium printing: June 2014

10 9 8 7 6 5 4 3 2 1

Dreamland Whiplash: Drone Strike

Key Players

Americans

Breanna Stockard, director, Department of Defense Office of Special Technology; Whiplash Director, DoD

Jonathan Reid, special assistant to CIA deputy director and Whiplash Director, DoD

Colonel Danny Freah, U.S. Air Force, commander, Whiplash

Captain Turk Mako, U.S. Air Force, pilot, assigned to Office of Special Technology/Whiplash

Lieutenant Li Pike, U.S. Air Force, pilot, Turk's girlfriend

Ray Rubeo, President and CEO, Applied Intelligence (key consultant and contractor to the Office of Special Technology)

President Christine Todd

Senator Jeff "Zen" Stockard, member of the Senate Intelligence and Armed Services committees (Breanna's husband)

Shahin Gorud, CIA paramilitary operative in Iran

Captain Thomas Granderson, commander of Delta Force special task group operating in Iran

Jeff "Grease" Ransom, Delta Force sergeant, assigned as Turk's personal bodyguard

Iranians

First Air General Ari Shirazi, head of the Iranian Air Force

Captain Parsa Vahid, Iranian air force pilot

Lieutenant Nima Kayvan, Vahid's squadron mate

Colonel Zal Vafa Khorasani, Pasdaran political officer

DRONE STRIKE

MAN BOMB

———

1

Dreamland

They called the aircraft "Old Girl," and not without good reason.

Turk Mako was used to flying planes that had come off the assembly line before he was born. This one had been *retired* two years before he was welcomed into the world.

It was an F-4 Phantom, a tough old bird conceived during the early Cold War era, when planes had more steel than plastic and a pilot's muscles mattered nearly as much as his tactics in a high-g fur ball. So it wasn't surprising that the retirement didn't quite take. Within weeks of being tarped, Old Girl was rescued from the boneyard to run some data-gathering experiments at Nellis Air Force Base. She soon found her way to Dreamland, the top-secret development area still off limits in the desert and mountains north of Nellis.

In the years since, the F-4 had helped develop a wide range of systems, from simple missile-launch detectors to completely autonomous (meaning, no humans anywhere in the decision tree) flight computers. The sheer size of her airframe was an important asset, as was her stability in flight and dependability—the last as much a tribute to tender maintenance and constant small improvements in the systems as the original design. But in truth she was important these days as much for her second seat as anything else—Old Girl could easily accommodate engineers and scientists eager to see the results of their work.

She could also ferry VIPs eager to glimpse Dreamland's latest high-tech toys in action. Which was the case today.

Captain Mako—universally called Turk—checked his altitude, precisely five thousand feet above ground level. He made sure of his location and heading, then gave a quick call to his backseater over the plane's interphone.

"Admiral, how are you doing back there, sir?"

"Fine, son," answered Vice Admiral Blackheart, his voice implying the exact opposite. "When the *hell* is this damn show starting?"

Turk ground his back teeth together, a habit some two hours old. Blackheart had been disagreeable from the moment they met for the preflight briefing. Turk strained to be polite, but he was a test pilot, not a stinking tour bus driver, and though he knew better than to sound off, he couldn't help but wish for deliverance—he, too, wanted the exercise over ASAP.

"Well?" demanded Blackheart.

"Soon as the controller clears in the B-1R,

sir. I believe they're actually running exactly on schedule."

"I don't have all day. See if you can get them moving."

"Yes, sir." Turk had never met a man whose personality was better suited to his name. But he *had* to be polite. Blackheart wasn't *just* a vice admiral—he happened to be in charge of Navy technology procurement. He was therefore a potential client of the Office of Special Technology, Turk's military "employer." Special Technology was a hybrid Department of Defense unit originally chartered to operate like a private company, winning contracts from the different service branches to supply them with new technology. Which meant Blackheart was potentially a critical client, and he had to suck up to him.

Or at least not offend him. Which, he had been warned repeatedly, was ridiculously easy to do.

Turk clicked his talk button, transmitting to the controller. "Tech Observer to Range Control One. Requesting approximate ETA of exercise."

"Perpetrator is at the southern end of the range and preparing to initiate exercise," said the controller, who was sitting in a bunker several miles to the south. He repeated some contact frequencies and general conditions, running down flight information Turk already had. By the time he finished, the B-1Q was in visual range, making a low-altitude run from the south at high speed. Turk nudged Old Girl's stick, banking slightly to give his passenger a better view. The B-1Q was flying at two hundred feet above the flat sand of the glasslike desert range. Old Girl was about a half mile from its flight path, and would keep that distance for the duration of the demonstration.

Like Old Girl, the B-1Q was a flying test bed. She, too, had undergone extensive refurbishing, so much so that she now belonged to the future rather than the past. Having started life as a B-1B Lancer, the plane had been stripped to her skeleton and rebuilt. Her external appearance and performance were similar to the B-1R; like the updated Bone, she was capable of flying well over Mach 2 for a sustained period and carrying armloads of both air-to-air and air-to-ground weapons. But the B-1Q's electronics were very different than those in the B-1R model, and her internal bomb bay held something more advanced than any of the missiles other bombers could unleash.

Turk glanced at the B-1Q as the bomb bay door opened. A gray cloud spewed from it, as if she had been holding a miniature thunderstorm in her belly. The cloud grew black, boiling, then dissipating. Black hailstones appeared, rising and falling around the airplane, until it was enveloped in a loose black cocoon.

"That's it?" said the admiral. "Looks like a net."

"In a way. Sure," said Turk. It was the least cantankerous comment the admiral had made all morning.

"Interesting."

The admiral remained silent as the cloud and the B-1Q continued downrange. Turk tipped the Phantom into a bank, easing off his stick as he realized he should keep the g's to a minimum for his VIP.

Old Girl bucked with a bit of unexpected turbulence as she moved through the turn. Even she seemed a bit fed up with tour bus duty this morning.

The B-1Q started an abrupt climb. As it did, the black cloud began to separate. Half of it stayed with the bomber. The rest continued forward, forming itself into a wedge.

"So that's the swarm," said the admiral. Not only was he not complaining, he sounded enthusiastic.

"Yes, sir," said Turk.

"You're going to follow it, aren't you? Yes? You're following it?"

"Yes, sir. I, uh, I have to keep at a set distance."

"Get as close as you can."

"Yes, sir. Working on it." Turk was already as close as the exercise rules allowed, and wasn't about to violate them—hot shit pilot or not, that would get him grounded quicker than pissing off the admiral. He tilted the aircraft just enough to placate the admiral, who remained silent as the Phantom followed the black wedge.

The wedge—aka "swarm"—was a flight of twenty nano-UAVs, officially known as XP–38UVNs. Barely the size of a cheap desk calculator, the small aircraft looked like a cross between lawn darts and studies for a video game. With V-shaped delta wings, they were powered by small engines that burned Teflon as fuel. The engines were primarily for maneuvering; most of their flight momentum came from their initial launch and gravity: designed to be "fired" from space, they could complete complicated maneuvers by altering the shape and bulges of their airfoil. Though their electronic brains were triumphs of nanotechnology and engineering, the real breakthroughs that made them possible were in the tiny motors, switches, and actuators that brought the skeleton to life.

Dubbed "Hydra," the nano-UAVs stood on the threshold of a new era of flight, one where robots did the thinking as well as the doing. They could be preprogrammed for a mission; their collaborative "brains" could deal with practically all contingencies, with humans in the loop only for emergencies. It was a brave new world . . . one that Turk didn't particularly care for, even if as a test pilot he'd been an important cog in its creation.

Cog being the operative word, as far as he was concerned.

The nano-UAVs headed for a simulated radar complex—a vanlike truck with a dish and a set of antennas transmitting a signal that mimicked Russia's Protivnik-GE mobile 3D L-Band radar. The L-Band radar was generally effective against smallish stealthy aircraft, including the F-35. The exercise today mimicked a deep-penetration mission, where a B-1Q and its swarm would cut past enemy defenses, clearing the way for attack planes to follow.

As a general rule, L-Band radars could detect conventional UAVs, even the RQ-170 Sentinel, because their airframes weren't large enough to create the proper scatter to confuse the long wavelength of the radar. But the Hydras were *so* small and could fly so low, they were dismissed by the radar as clutter. Once past the calculated danger zone, the individual members of the swarm suddenly bolted together, becoming a literal fist in the sky as they pushed directly over the trailer housing the radar's control unit.

"Looks like an air show," said the admiral. "Or a school of fish."

"Yes, sir."

"So they scored a direct hit on that antenna, by the rules of the encounter?"

"Yes, sir."

"And the van?"

"Yes, sir."

"Narrow target, that antenna."

"Yes, sir."

"Hard to hit from the air?"

"Well, um . . ."

Actually, taking out a radar antenna or van was child's play with even the most primitive bomb, and a heck of a lot cheaper: the nano-UAVs cost about roughly $250,000 per unit; a half dozen would have been used to take down the antenna and another half dozen the van—a $3 million pop. In contrast, a five-hundred-pound Paveway II bomb, unpowered and outmoded but incredibly accurate under most circumstances, cost under $20,000.

On the other hand, as air vehicles went, the individual units were relatively cheap and extremely versatile. Mass produce the suckers and the cost might come down tenfold—practically to the price of a bomb.

Hell of a lot cheaper than a pilot, Turk knew.

The flock that had attacked the radar climbed and reformed around the B-1 as it neared the end of the range. The big bomber and its escorts banked and passed the Phantom on the left; Turk held Old Girl steady and slow, giving his passenger an eyeful. Having exhausted a good portion of their initial flight energy, the Hydras now used their tiny motors to climb in the wake of the B-1, using a wave pattern that maximized their fuel as they rose. The pattern was so complicated that Turk, who had controlled the UAVs during some early testing, would never have been able to fully master it without the aid of the nano-UAVs' flight computers. As one techie put it, the pattern looked like snowflakes dancing in a thundershower.

As the Hydras closed around the B-1Q, Turk did a quick twist back, putting the Phantom on track as the second part of the demonstration began—two F-35s flew at the bomber, preparing to engage. When they were about twenty miles apart, the F-35s each fired a single AMRAAM-plus2, the latest version of the venerable medium range antiaircraft radar missile. The missiles were detected on launch by the B-1Q; a second later a dozen UAVs peeled off, forming a long wedge above the mother ship. As they continued flying straight ahead, the B-1Q rolled right and tucked toward the earth.

"Missiles will be at two o'clock," said Turk. "Watch the swarm and you'll see them come in."

The electronics aboard the UAVs were marvels of nanoengineering, but even so, space aboard the tiny craft was at a premium. This meant that not every plane could be equipped with the full array of sensors even Old Girl took for granted. One might have a full radar setup, another optical sensors. The different information gathered could then be shared communally, with the interlinked computers deciding how to proceed.

All of the units contained small radar detectors, and while their power was limited, the size of the swarm allowed them to detect the radar at a fair distance. Thus, the UAVs knew that they had been locked on even before the antiaircraft missiles were fired. They remained in formation as the missiles approached, in effect fooling the AMRAAMs into thinking they were the B-1. Then, just as it looked as if the AMRAAMs would hit the swarm, the Hydras dispersed and the missiles flew on through them.

The radio buzzed with a signal meant to simulate the warheads exploding in frustration.

"Nice," said the admiral.

Turk cranked Old Girl around the range as the demonstration continued. The UAVs were now put through a series of maneuvers, flying a series of aerial acrobatics. They were air show quality, with the little aircraft darting in and out in close formation.

"Impressive," said Blackheart as the show continued. "Nice. Very nice."

Thank God, thought Turk to himself as the aircraft crisscrossed above their mother ship. The

admiral seemed soothed and even enthusiastic.
Breanna would be happy. And tomorrow he could
get back to real work.

Bᴿᴱᴬᴺᴺᴬ Sᴛᴏᴄᴋᴀʀᴅ ʀᴇꜱɪꜱᴛᴇᴅ ᴛʜᴇ ᴜʀɢᴇ ᴛᴏ ᴘᴀᴄᴇ
behind the consoles of Control Area D4. As head
of the Department of Defense Office of Special
Technology and the DoD Whiplash director,
she knew very well that pacing made the people
around her nervous. This was especially true of
project engineers. And those in Dreamland Control Bunker 50-4 were already wound tighter than
twisted piano wire.

Someone had started a rumor that the fate of
the nano-UAV program they'd been working
on for the past five years depended on whether
the Navy bought in. To them, this meant their
dreams and careers depended entirely on the ty-
rannical Admiral Blackheart.

Breanna knew that the situation was considerably more complicated. In fact, today's test had
nothing to do with the long-term survival of the
program already assured, thanks to earlier evalu-
ations. But if anything, what was at stake today
was several magnitudes more important.

Not that she could mention that to anyone in
the room.

The demonstration was going well. The feed
from the Phantom played across the large screen
at the front of the command center, showing the
V-winged Hydras cascading around their B-1
mother ship. The maneuvers were so precise,

the image so crisp, it looked like an animation straight out of an updated version of *Star Wars*: snip off the fuselage, extend the wings a bit, and the nano-UAVs might even pass for black-dyed X-Wings.

Almost.

In any event, on-screen they looked more like animated toys than real aircraft. It was for precisely that reason that Breanna had insisted on putting the admiral in the Phantom—if he didn't see it with his own eyes, the cynical bastard would surely think it was complete fiction.

The bunker, part of the Dreamland facilities leased by the Office of Special Technology from the Air Force, was about four times too large for the small staff needed to run the demonstration. That seemed to be an intractable rule of high-tech development: despite the growing complexity of the systems developed here, the head count only went down. Soon, Breanna mused, she'd be running the entire show herself from her iPhone.

Walking down to the UAV monitoring station, she checked on the large radar plot that showed where all the aircraft were on the range. Turk was doing a good job in the F-4. Flying the plane was the easy part; keeping his mouth free of wise-ass remarks was surely harder. But with the stakes high, she wanted a pilot familiar not only with the program but with combat in general, available to answer whatever question the admiral thought to ask.

Unfortunately, Turk had seemed somewhat moody of late. There was no doubt about his flying abilities, or his adaptability—whether flying an F-22 Raptor, an F-16 Block 30, or the mostly automated Tigershark II, he handled himself with equal aplomb. A bit on the shy side, he lacked the outsized ego that hamstrung many up-and-coming officers; he might even be considered humble, at least for a test pilot. But like a good number of his peers, Turk had a tendency to snark first and think later.

This tendency had increased since he returned from Africa, where he'd spent time as a substitute pilot with an A-10E squadron. Even though they'd been greatly upgraded since their original incarnation, the planes remained intense mudfighters at heart. Perhaps working the stick and rudder of the old-style aircraft in the middle of combat had woken something deep in Turk's soul. He seemed frustrated by his taste of combat; Breanna sensed he wanted more.

"Almost done," said Teddy Armaz, looking up from his station. His right leg pumped up and down. Breanna wasn't sure if this was a sign of nervousness or relief.

"Good distribution on the computing," said Sara Rheingold, working the console next to Armaz. Rheingold's team had built the distributed intelligence system that flew the nano-UAVs. In essence a network of processors aboard the Hydras, it was the most advanced artificial intelligence flight system yet, an improvement over even the system used in the Air Force's new Sabre UAVs, which were still undergoing field testing.

And which had so recently given Whiplash considerable difficulty in Africa.

The Hydras evidenced no such problems. Rheingold began talking about some of the performance specs, quickly losing Breanna in the minutiae. She nodded and tried to sound enthusiastic. Meanwhile, she noticed that the two men working the flight control board were punching their screens dramatically. A second later they called her forward to their station.

"They just had an event over on Weapons Testing Range Two," said Paul Smith, acting flight liaison. His job was to coordinate with Dreamland control, monitoring what was going on elsewhere at the massive test center.

"Does it concern us?"

"It may," interrupted Bob Stevenson, the flight controller. "It sent a magnetic pulse out across the range."

"I have some anomalies," reported Armaz behind her.

"Me, too," said Rheingold. "The root connection to the mother ship is off-line."

"Restore it," said Breanna.

"Working on it," said Armaz, hunching over his console and tapping his foot more violently than ever.

"Knock it off! Knock it off!"

The radio transmission came as a complete surprise. Turk steadied his hand on the stick of Old Girl, holding the plane on course at the eastern end of the test area.

"Knock it off," repeated the B-1Q pilot. "I have

a complete system failure. My control panel is blank. Repeat—I have no panel. Is anyone hearing me?"

The tower acknowledged, clearing the B-1Q to proceed to the main runway. But the malfunction aboard the B-1Q had an effect on the radio as well; the pilot could broadcast but not hear.

"Tower, this is Tech Observer," said Turk, interrupting the hail. "I'm about three hundred meters behind Perpetrator, five thousand meters above him. He doesn't seem to have any damage."

"Roger, Observer. We copy. He's not hearing our transmissions. Can you get close enough for a visual to the cockpit?"

"Attempting."

Turk nudged his stick and throttle, putting Old Girl into a gentle dive, warily drawing closer to the bigger plane. He let the Phantom get ahead of the B-1Q's cockpit, making sure the pilot of the bomber knew he was there before sliding close enough to signal him.

"Do you have eyes on pilot?" asked the tower.

"Working on it," answered Turk.

Old Girl balked a bit as he slid closer. A buzzer sounded, and Bitching Betty began complaining that he was too close.

"What are we doing, Captain?" asked Admiral Blackheart.

"We're going to lead him down," said Turk. "But first I want to make sure he can land. His gear is— *Shit!*"

Turk pushed the Phantom onto her left wing as a black BB shot past his windscreen. For a moment he was back in Africa, ducking bullets from rebel aircraft.

That was easy compared to what happened next. As Turk came level, the nano-UAVs began buzzing Old Girl, flitting back and forth within inches not just of the plane but the canopy.

"Control, I need an override on the swarm," said Turk. "They're looking at me like I'm an intruder. They're in Divert One. Get them out of it."

Divert One was a preprogrammed strategy, where the nano-UAVs would force another aircraft down. The Hydras would continue to push him lower and in the direction of a runway designated by the mother ship. Given the B-1Q's malfunctions, however, Turk couldn't be sure where the aircraft thought they were going—and in any event, he had no intention of complying. He banked into a turn, aiming to get away.

The UAVs continued to buzz around him. Damn things were staying right with him—he saw a small orange burst from one; apparently they still had plenty of fuel aboard.

"Tech Observer, state your intentions," radioed Breanna Stockard from the control bunker.

"I'm trying to lead Perpetrator in. The swarm seems to have a different idea."

"Negative, Whiplash. I want you to divert to Emergency Runway Three. We have two chase planes moving to escort Perpetrator home."

"Uh—"

"Not a point for discussion, Captain."

"Acknowledged. But, ma'am, I have the swarm

on me. They're in Divert One and they want me to land."

"We copy."

"How's their fuel?" he asked.

"No less than three-quarters," she told him.

Turk knew the nano-UAVs could touch roughly a thousand kilometers an hour if they went all out. While Old Girl had been around the block a few times since she was built, she could still push Mach 2, twice the speed of sound and approximately 1,236 kilometers an hour. But if he accelerated away, he would risk losing the robot planes over the range. And besides, they were more an annoyance than a threat.

He tacked north, toward the airstrip. There was a possibility, he reasoned, that they might land with him.

"What's going on?" asked the admiral from the backseat.

"I'm being directed to an emergency landing," Turk said. "The B-1's on its own."

"What's with these aircraft?"

"They're following a program intended to make an intruder land if they're in a restricted airspace."

"They're awful damn close."

"Yes, sir. That's their job."

"This isn't part of the demonstration, is it?" asked the admiral.

"Negative, sir."

Breanna dropped to her haunches between Armaz and Rheingold. "Can we get them back?"

"The systems in the B-1Q are completely shut down," said Armaz. "If I could communicate with them, I might be able to walk the mission specialist through a restart—it might be all we need. But at this point I'm getting no telemetry from them, let alone radio. That magnetic pulse knocked them out good."

Breanna glanced down at the controller. Dreamland Control had just declared a total range emergency, stopping all flight operations. The problem had originated in a weapon designed to fire small magnetic pulses at cruise missiles, destroying their electronics and therefore their targeting ability. It appeared to be more effective than its designers hoped.

Breanna turned back to the computer station. "Jen, what do you think?"

"Are you talking to me?" asked Sara Rheingold.

"I'm sorry. Yes." Breanna realized her mistake: Jen was Jennifer Gleason, who had held a similar position years before. It was a kind of Freudian slip she made only in times of stress, under exactly the kind of conditions that Jennifer had dealt with so effectively.

Ancient history.

"We may be able to take them back from the ground station," she said. "I'm trying the overrides."

"We'll take this in steps," said Breanna. "Let's get Old Girl down first, then we'll work on the Hydras."

"Can Turk land with them buzzing around him?" asked Rheingold.

"That's why he gets the big bucks."

Turk HELD THE STICK STEADY AS THE SMALL AIRCRAFT buzzed around him. It was like flying with a swarm of angry bees in the cockpit. The tiny aircraft darted every which way in front of him. Even though he knew they were programmed to get no closer than a foot, the psychological effect was intense.

"Control, the UAVs are still with me," Turk radioed. "What's their status?"

"We're working to recapture them," the controller said.

"Do you want me to land?"

"Negative at this time. Stand by."

His altitude had dropped to 3,000 feet. He was lined up perfectly on the runway, a long, smooth strip marked out in the salt bed a few miles away.

"Tech Observer, can you remain airborne for a while longer?" asked the controller when he came back.

"Uh, affirmative—roger that. What's the plan?"

"Turk, we want the B-1 to land first," said Breanna. "We have a chase plane guiding him in. We think we can take over the UAVs when he lands."

"Sure, but you know they're still trying to force me down," said Turk. "They're pretty damn annoying."

"Do you need to land?"

"Well, 'need' is a strong word. Negative on that."

"Your passenger?"

Turk glanced behind over his shoulder, then selected the interphone.

"Admiral, they want us to stay up for a while more. That OK?"

"Do what you have to do, son. As long as these things don't hit us."

"Yes, sir." Turk went back to the radio. "We can stay up."

The B-1 was still without radio communications and, presumably, the bulk of its electronic gear. About half the nano-UAVs had stayed with it, flying behind the wings as it approached Dreamland's main test runway. Turk caught a brief glimpse of it descending, wings spread, wheels down, as he began an orbit over Emergency Runway 3. He didn't see much: the UAVs continued to pester him, buzzing in his path.

"What are these damn things trying to do?" asked the admiral from the backseat.

"They want us to land. The controller thinks they'll break off when the B-1 puts down."

"What do you think?"

The question caught Turk by surprise. "Not really sure, Admiral."

"Are we in trouble?"

"Oh, negative, sir. It's annoying, but I've seen this dance before. They're actually programmed to fly *very* close, twelve inches close, but they won't actually hit us."

"This is a preprogrammed routine?"

"The command is, yes." Turk explained that while the nano-UAVs used distributed intelligence—in other words, they shared their "brains"—the individual planes could also rely on a library of commands and routines, which was happening then. The first versions of the Flighthawks—much larger combat UAVs originally launched and controlled from EB-52s—had made use of similar techniques.

"So if it's programmed, won't the enemy be able to learn it and defeat it?" asked the admiral.

"They can be programmed for the specific mission," said Turk. "And this—it's kind of like a football team calling signals. They know they have to keep a certain position and get a certain result, which they all react to."

"They seem angry," said the admiral.

"Oh yes, sir." Turk straightened the aircraft. "Definitely pissed off."

The B-1 landed. If that had any effect on the UAVs, it wasn't obvious.

"Control, what's our status?" Turk asked when five minutes had passed.

"Still trying to get the connection broken, Whiplash."

"Maybe I can break it myself," offered Turk. "I'll point my nose up and go afterburners. We'll stay over the range, so if they drop into Landing Three Preset, they'll come back to you."

"Negative, Whiplash. Negative," said Breanna sharply. "You have a passenger."

"Roger that." Turk toyed with the idea of explaining the situation to the admiral and asking what he thought—he suspected Blackheart, who was undoubtedly listening in, would approve—but decided he'd better not.

The controller guided him through a series of turns as they did whatever they were doing from the ground station, all to no avail.

As he continued to circle, Turk guessed that the engineers were trying to figure out what would happen when he landed—would the UAVs land with him, as they were programmed to do when landing with the B-1? Or would they reform and fly on their own? If that happened, there was no telling what they might do next.

Which explained the flight of F-22s from nearby Nellis air base that were being vectored to the north side of the range. The radars that worked the Dreamland defense lasers were also tracking them.

"Whiplash Observer, how much fuel do you have left?" asked the controller.

"We're good for another half hour or so," he told the controller, looking at Old Girl's gauges. The instruments were still old-school clock-style readouts. "Add twenty to that in reserve. You know. Give or take."

"Give it another ten minutes, then plan to land. The Hydras will be low on fuel by then."

"Gotcha." Turk clicked off the mike, then remembered the admiral. "Roger that, Control. Copy and understood," he added in his most official voice.

"We're landing?" asked the admiral.

"Affirmative, sir. The swarm is just about out of fuel. Sir."

"You knock off all the sirs, Captain." Blackheart's voice sounded just a hint less gruff.

"Thanks, Admiral."

Turk took a few more lazy turns, circling and finally lining up on the runway for his final approach. Emergency vehicles were waiting a respectful distance—nearby, but not so close as to imply they didn't think he'd make it.

BREANNA FOLDED HER ARMS, WATCHING THE LARGE screen as the Phantom made its way toward the long stretch of cement. They had switched the video feed to a ground camera mounted in an observation tower near the runway. From a distance, the F-4 seemed to have a black shroud above its body.

"They should be staying at altitude, shouldn't they?" Breanna asked Armaz. "Why are they descending with him?"

"I'm not sure. They may not think it's the right altitude."

"You still can't get them back, Sara?"

"I keep trying," Rheingold said. "Short of sending another shock through the range, I don't know what else to try."

"Bree—Dreamland Control wants us to keep Old Girl in the air," said Paul Smith, turning from his console. He was practically yelling. "They want to recover their tankers first. They're worried the nano-UAVs will attack them."

"For crap sake? Why didn't they tell us that five minutes ago?"

"Ma'am—"

"Bob?"

"On it," said the controller.

TURK EYEBALLED HIS INSTRUMENTS QUICKLY AS HE continued on course for the emergency runway, then unfurled his landing gear. He tensed, then felt his breath catch—he'd been worried the UAVs would object somehow. But they seemed content to let him land, adjusting their own speed as he slowed.

"Tech Observer, abort landing," said Stevenson, the controller. "Go around."

"I have to ask why," he said tersely.

"Dreamland has a couple of tankers they want to get down first," said Breanna, breaking in. "They're not sure what the UAVs will do when you land."

"Well, in theory, they'll land with me, right?"

"We agree, Whiplash," said Breanna. "They're just concerned. Can you go around, or should I have the tankers divert elsewhere?"

"Negative, negative, I'm good. Going around." Turk tamped down his frustration as he clicked into the interphone. "Admiral—"

"I heard. Do what you have to do, son."

"Will do. Thanks."

Turk pushed his throttle and cleaned his gear, restoring his wheels to their bays. The aircraft's speed picked up immediately. The UAVs started to scatter, momentarily left behind.

In the next moment, he heard a faint clicking noise on his right. It was an odd sound, something like the click a phone made over a dead circuit. He filed the noise away, too busy to puzzle it out.

Two seconds later a much louder sound on the right got his attention—a violent pop shocked the aircraft, seeming to push it backward.

And down.

Turk struggled to control the plane, hands and feet and eyes, lungs and heart, working together, moving ahead of his brain. By the time his mind comprehended what had happened, his body had already moved to deal with it, trimming the plane to concentrate.

"Captain, is there trouble?" asked his passenger.

"Slight complication, Admiral. We're good." Turk's mouth was suddenly dry. His chest pushed against the seat restraints—his heart was pounding like crazy.

He was at 1,500 feet, 1,300. The nano-UAVs were still around him, though at least part of one was in the left engine, or what remained of it.

Like a bird strike, he thought. *Deal with it*.

"Whiplash Observer?" asked the control tower.

"I'm landing."

"You're on fire, Whiplash," said the controller.

Ordinarily, that would have been the cue to pull the ejection handle. But Turk worried that his passenger wouldn't fare well—they were low, there wasn't much margin for error, and it was doubtful the admiral had ever parachuted from a plane.

And besides, he could land the damn plane with his eyes closed.

Come on, Old Girl, he thought. Let's take this

easy now. You've seen harder challenges than this.

He took the plane into a turn, realigning himself for a landing as quickly as he dared. Just as he straightened his wings, something popped on the right side. A shudder ran through his body, the rattle of a metal spike being driven into a bed of shale. He began moving his feet, pedaling, pedaling—he was three years old, trying to get control of a runaway tricycle plummeting down the hill of his parents' backyard. The dog was barking in the distance. The world was closing in. Rocks loomed on either side; ahead, a stone wall.

"Stand by. Landing," he said tersely.

Landing gear deployed, Turk felt his way to the strip, steadying the plane as she began drifting to the right. His nose started coming up; he fought the impulse to react too strongly, easing the Phantom down. The seconds flew by, then moved slowly, excruciatingly—the wheels should have touched down by now, he thought.

The nano-UAVs dispersed just as the rear wheels hit the smooth surface of the runway. He was fast, and little far along the runway, but that was all right—he had another 10,000 feet of marked runway to stop, and miles of salt flat to steer through if necessary. The emergency vehicles were speeding up from behind . . .

Turk's relief vanished as a flame shot up from under the right side of the plane. The first nano-UAV had hit the belly, rupturing the tank there and starting a small fire.

He popped the canopies as the F-4 braked to a stop. Undoing his restraints, he pushed himself up from the ejection seat, helmet still on and oxygen still attached. He ripped off the gear and hopped onto the wing, leaning back to grab Admiral Blackheart. Black smoke curled around them.

"Out of here, Admiral, let's go," said Turk, grabbing the admiral under his left arm and lifting him out of the plane. He took a step back but slipped, falling backward onto the wing. The admiral fell onto his chest.

A cloud surrounded them, enveloping the two men in a toxic blackness.

"Almost home," Turk told the admiral, struggling to get up. He reached his knees but the smoke was so thick he couldn't see the tips of his fingers as he fished for a grip. He finally hooked his fingers into the admiral's soft biceps. Turk pulled him to the edge of the wing, then tumbled with him to the ground. Blackheart's head hit his chest as they landed, knocking the wind from him. Struggling to breathe, Turk turned to his belly and pulled up his knee, levering himself up and pulling the admiral with him.

The smoke drenched them both in inky soot, covering their mouths and poking at their eyes, a caustic acid. Turk pushed and pulled and pushed, finally getting his balance and then his breath. He had the admiral under him like a messenger bag, moving forward until finally the sky cleared and it was bright again, the sky a faultless blue.

There were trucks. A jet streaked overhead.

Someone grabbed him. Someone else took the admiral from him.

"I'm all right," protested Turk.

"Move back," said the airman who'd grabbed him. He was a parajumper, an Air Force special operations soldier trained as a medic. "Come on now. Get in the ambulance."

"I'm OK," said Turk. He turned back to look at Old Girl. As he did, one of the fuel tanks exploded, sending a fireball nearly straight up into the sky. Flames erupted from the fuselage, and two more fireballs shot from the sides.

"Old Girl's going out with a bang," he muttered, turning to find the ambulance.

2

Iran

CAPTAIN PARSA VAHID RAISED HIS ARMS UPWARD AS he walked between the two mounds of sand, stretching his upper body in a vain attempt to unknot the kinks coagulating his muscles. He had been sitting in his MiG on high alert for hours, waiting to fly. It was a ritual he had repeated for weeks now, the government worried that the Americans and Israelis would finally carry out their threats to attack Iran.

Or more specifically, the secret bases in the area of Qom, which lay many miles to the north. The fact that work on a nuclear bomb was being conducted was perhaps the worst kept secret in the world.

Vahid had never been to Qom itself. In fact, though his unit was specifically charged with protecting it, he hadn't so much as overflown it—the government had laid down very strict rules some months before, closing an Iranian air base there and warning that any aircraft in the vicinity was likely to be shot down.

Besides, given the shortage of jet fuel plaguing the air force, Vahid rarely got to fly at all these days.

Qom was an ancient city, dwarfed in size by Tehran but still among the ten largest in Iran. More important than its size was its history. It was sacred to Shi'ites, long a center for religious study, and a site for pilgrims since the early 1500s. Though he was a Muslim, a Shi'ite by birth, Vahid did not consider himself devout. He prayed haphazardly, and while he kept the commandments, it was more for fear of punishment than belief in afterlife or even earthly rewards.

His true religion was flight. Vahid had dreamed of flying from the time he was three. Becoming a pilot had been a pilgrimage through the greatest difficulties, his barriers even higher because he had no connection with either the service or the government. His love had not diminished one iota. Even today, with the service's chronic fuel shortages, problems with parts, poor repairs, bureaucratic hang-ups, and political interference—Vahid could put up with them all as long as he got a chance to get in the air.

The pilot paused at the crest of the hill. Two hours would pass before the faithful would be called to prayer with the rising sun. The words would stretch across the bleak, high desert air base, with its dusty hangars and dorms.

"Captain, you must be careful," said a voice in the darkness. "You are very close to the perimeter."

Startled, Vahid jerked back. A soldier was standing nearby, rifle at the ready. Vahid stared, then realized it was Sergeant Kerala, a man whom he knew vaguely from an earlier assignment. His Farsi had the accent of the South.

"I hadn't heard you," said Vahid. "But why are you working at night?"

"I made the wrong comment to someone."

"Ah." Vahid nodded. The wrong remark heard by any one of the half-dozen political officers assigned to the base, and the consequences could be quite severe. "I was just taking a walk. My legs are stiff."

"Do you think there will be an attack?"

Vahid was taken off guard by the question. His first thought was that it was a trick, but there was little chance of that.

"I don't honestly know," he told the sergeant. "We are ready for whatever happens."

"I don't think the Americans will be so insane," said Kerala. "The Israelis, them I am not sure about."

"We will defeat them. Whoever it is," Vahid assured him. "We're ready. I'm ready."

"Yes," said Kerala. "We will have a great battle if they are foolish enough to try. God willing."

3

Washington, D.C.

Pʀᴇsɪᴅᴇɴᴛ Cʜʀɪsᴛɪɴᴇ Tᴏᴅᴅ sᴀᴛ ᴅᴏᴡɴ ᴏɴ ᴛʜᴇ sᴍᴀʟʟ settee in the passage off the Cross Hall of the White House, listening to the hushed murmur of guests arriving in the State Dining Room a short distance away. Todd was hosting a dinner to honor the heads of several museums, part of a recent initiative to expand awareness of American history. It was a subject dear to the President's heart, and she was especially looking forward to talking to the curator of a recent Smithsonian exhibit on George Washington. But history was hardly the only thing on her mind tonight.

"Decision made?"

Todd looked up at her national security advisor, Michael Blitz. Blitz looked like a walrus in his tuxedo—a gruff and grim walrus.

"Still working on it," she told him.

"The Israeli ambassador is inside already."

"Mmmm." Todd patted the bench, signaling for Blitz to sit. Blitz's voice had a tendency to carry, and she didn't want any of the guests overhearing.

"There really are only two options," said Blitz. "Let Iran have the weapon, or attack now. Stop the process."

"But for how long, Doctor?"

Blitz had a Ph.D. in international affairs, but Todd tended to use the honorific sporadically.

He'd told her several times that he took it as an indication of how she was feeling about him and his advice: if she used "Mister," he was on thin ice; if she used "Doctor," he was sunk.

"If we strike, we stop it for *at least* a year," said Blitz. "Maybe as long as five."

"Your staff estimated less than twelve months."

"That's too pessimistic. Even the Secretary of State thinks it will be halted longer than that."

Todd glanced toward the hall, where one of her Secret Service agents stood, making sure no one wandered down the wrong way. A light scent of food wafted in; the *amuse bouche* maybe, or else a figment of Todd's hungry imagination—she'd skipped lunch.

"We need two years before the ABM system is fully operational and can protect Israel," said Blitz. "Iran knows that. That's why they're trying to move so quickly."

"If there was a guarantee of success—or even a probability," said Todd, "then the decision would be easier."

"The Israelis will attack if we don't. The result of that will certainly be war—declared or undeclared. And as I said this afternoon, the probability of Iran actually using the bomb at some point goes up to one hundred percent in that scenario. Bad for your second term."

Todd managed a smile.

"If you're concerned, we should move ahead on the covert plan first." Blitz himself preferred that option, and had in fact been pushing it. Todd saw the attraction, but didn't like the odds.

"A twenty percent chance of success?" She sighed. "And that's if we're not discovered."

"Better odds than anything else out there. Has Blackheart checked back with you?"

"No. I expect he'll be positive. But I doubt the odds will change." Todd heard her husband clunking down the stairs. She rose just in time to see him step out from the landing. His eyes twinkled as they caught hers—all these years, and she still felt her heart kick up a few beats.

"We'll talk," she told Blitz, holding her arm out for her escort.

Two hours later Todd found herself in a corner of the formal dining room, listening to a museum trustee describe funding problems. It was a litany she had heard many times in the past, and while she was sympathetic, there was little she could do about it. Her next budget—sure to be declared dead on arrival in Congress in any event—held arts appropriations steady from the year before. This in effect was a decrease, given inflation, but it was far better than Congress was likely to do. Even the defense budget would probably be cut in the coming year, something Todd was adamantly opposed to.

She listened for a while longer, then politely excused herself, deciding she would check in on her husband and work an early exit. She spotted the Israeli ambassador across the room, and turned to her right: she had artfully avoided conversing with him all evening, and aimed to keep that record intact.

She bumped into a short, thin man in his mid-thirties, who managed—barely—to avoid dropping his drink or, worse, spilling it on her dress.

"I'm sorry, Madam President," he said, clearly embarrassed.

"Oh no, dear, I'm sorry. I turned without looking." She smiled, trying to remember who he was.

"Mark Tacitus," said the man. He held out his hand. "I, uh, I'm the son-in-law of—"

"Oh yes, yes, I'm sorry I didn't recognize you." His father-in-law was Simon Rockwell, a member of the Metropolitan Museum Board of Trustees in New York and one of her *biggest* contributors in the Northeast. "So—the last time we met, you were working on a book."

"Finished. Yes." He smiled awkwardly. "The book on Nimitz."

"Of course."

"He was an interesting man," said Tacitus noncommittally. He seemed to think she was only making polite conversation.

"Do you still think the *Nautilus* was his most difficult decision?" Todd asked.

"Well . . ." The author flushed, probably trying to remember their last conversation. The submarine *Nautilus* became the world's first nuclear powered vessel of any kind, and the decision to build it was extremely controversial. "I think in a way it was his hardest. There were a lot of decisions we could single out. Some good, some bad."

"A lot good." Todd caught sight of her husband. "Though not always obvious at the time, even to him. We'll have to talk more in depth sometime," she told Tacitus. "I was interested in what you had to say about his wife."

"You read the book?"

The President laughed. She *had* read the book, lingering over the war chapters, where she admired how Nimitz had persevered, taking calculated risks but always sticking to his vision.

Set a course, and move ahead. Good advice for anyone, even a President.

Delay Iran by whatever means. Short-term risks that could pay big dividends were better than no risk that offered none. That was what Nimitz had to say to her.

"We will talk," she said, patting Tacitus on the shoulder and starting across the room. "Thank you. One of my people will get in touch."

Her husband was waiting. "Calling it a night?" he asked when she arrived.

"I'm thinking of it. There was a curator I wanted to see."

"Sandy Goldman, in the blue dress over there. George Washington expert."

"You read me like a book."

"Thank you, Madam President."

"I think I'll have someone sneak her up to the library for a little chat. What do you think?"

"You're the President."

"Could you whisper in her ear? I have to talk to Blitz for a minute."

Her husband slipped away. Blitz was only a few feet away, talking with two men from the Dallas Museum of Art. As President Todd walked in his direction, Blitz excused himself. They stepped aside.

"I'm sorry to interrupt you," she told him.

"Not a problem."

"It should move ahead."

"What made you decide? The Israelis?"

"I haven't talked to them about it, and don't intend to."

"What then?"

"Admiral Nimitz."

Todd cherished the confused look on Blitz's face all the way upstairs.

4

Dreamland

Even though the engineers had reached a tentative conclusion about what happened within minutes of the B-1Q and UAVs touching down, the mission debriefing lasted well into the night. Two of the UAVs had been destroyed and a third damaged when they were unable to anticipate the Phantom's last second landing abort. The others returned to the airstrip where their mother ship had landed, landing in perfect formation and taxiing behind it. Analysis of the computing logic was still ongoing, but it appeared to have followed the proper protocols and decision trees—except for the switch to the intercept. That signal had apparently been inadvertently ordered by the B-1Q's control unit when the pulse hit: a flaw in the B-1Q controls or perhaps the human overseeing them, not the UAVs.

Breanna ducked out after an hour to see to Admiral Blackheart. She was shocked to find him not only in good spirits but almost giddy about the prospect of the Navy using the nano-UAVs.

"You have a hell of a lot of work to do," said the admiral. "But those things have promise. The Navy *wants* to be involved. The technical people are right—this is the future."

If the admiral was enthusiastic about the UAVs, he was even more impressed by Turk.

"Your pilot did a hell of a job saving the plane. Write up a commendation; I'll sign it."

Breanna summarized what they had found so far and offered to let the admiral sit in on some of the debriefing session; he wisely demurred.

She saw the admiral to his Pentagon-bound aircraft, then took a quick detour to pick up a salad. She stopped at her office to double-check e-mail, then headed back to the briefing room. Her secure satellite phone rang as she was about to open the door. The number display told her it was Jonathon Reid, codirector of the Whiplash project.

"Jonathon?"

"Breanna. I heard you had an incident."

"There was a magnetic pulse problem on the range. A new weapon. We think the Hydras themselves were fine. But the pulse affected the antenna of the B-1Q. That project may be set back."

"I see."

She heard ice cubes clinking in the background. It was well past five back in D.C., but still, she was surprised that Reid was actually at home—he would never drink at either the Agency or in the Whiplash center.

Old school to a fault, Reid retained a certain professional distance with Breanna, even though they had come to know each other over the course of the past year and a half working together. When they started, Reid was a special "consultant" to the CIA; he had soon been named a special assistant to the deputy director of operations. Now, with the Agency in turmoil and under political pressure, he was rumored to be in line for the director's job. But he refused to discuss it.

"The President spoke with Admiral Blackheart," he told her. "She wants Roman Time to proceed."

"OK. But—"

"From what I understand, Blackheart described the incident very briefly to her. We're satisfied that the Iranians don't have anything like the weapon that caused it."

"Of course not."

"So it's not a factor."

"No. But I think—I think it mandates having a trained pilot in the loop, as we've said all along," she told him. "And a review of the programming systems. But because the routes on Roman Time would be already set out, I don't think it would be a problem. Of course—"

"There is a complication," interrupted Reid. "The timetable has to be accelerated."

"By how much?"

"Greatly. We have, at best, a matter of a few weeks."

"That's too short to train any of the Delta people."

Breanna knew what Reid was going to suggest before he said anything else. "Captain Mako is the obvious choice."

"He's too valuable," Breanna said.

"Given the target, I'd say that's not true. Not at all."

"He's a pilot, not a snake eater."

"Who else, then?" asked Reid.

There was no one else. Aside from Turk, the only people who had flown the nano-UAVs were civilian engineers. Even if they were to volunteer, all but one was well into his forties and not exactly in the best physical shape.

The lone exception was eight months pregnant.

"Turk has to volunteer," said Breanna.

"And then what do we do if he doesn't decide to go?"

"I don't know. But I can't order someone to take a mission with such long odds on survival. This isn't the sort of thing he signed up for. It's ordering him to his death."

"If he doesn't volunteer, you may have to."

5

Dreamland

TODAY WAS GOING TO BE A GREAT DAY, TURK MAKO decided as he rolled out of bed. Or at least as great a day as you could have without flying.

Heck, he *might* get some flying in. His only officially scheduled duty was to sit through a boring engineering session on the nano-UAVs. Then he was officially off-duty, free, liberated, unchained, for seventy-two hours, which would be spent in the delicious company of Li Pike, his girlfriend.

She was flying in this evening. Li, an Air Force A-10 pilot attached to a unit Turk had hooked up with in Africa, had managed to wangle leave from her own unit so they could be together.

Which reminded him—he had to check on the hotel reservation. And the car.

He couldn't cruise Vegas with the Office of Special Technology Malibu he'd been assigned as personal transportation. A vintage Mustang convertible would be *much* more like it.

Dinner reservations. He needed to make dinner reservations. A quiet place, not too far from the hotel, but not *in* the hotel. He didn't want to seem too anxious.

Turk turned the coffeemaker on and headed for the shower. The "single occupancy/officer/temp duty" apartments at Dreamland dating from the late 1990s were drab and boring. Worse, they had paper thin walls. Not appropriate for how he hoped the night would go.

Turk's good mood was threatened a bit when he emerged from the shower to find that the coffee machine had malfunctioned, sending a spray of liquid and grinds around the counter area. He managed to salvage a single cup, which he downed while cleaning up. No big loss, he decided: there was always better coffee in the engineering bunkers. The geeks might not be much to look at, but they brewed mean java.

Turk's spirits remained high as he approached the guards to the Whiplash building. He waved his credentials at them, then submitted to the mandatory fingerprint and retina scan set up just inside the door. Cleared, he sauntered down the long ramp to the main floor, pausing at the small coffee station near the elevator. He'd just finished helping himself to an extra-large cup when Breanna Stockard called to him from down the hall.

"Turk? Can we talk for a minute? In my office?"

"Sure boss, but, uh, I got a meeting downstairs."

"This won't take long." Breanna ducked back inside the doorway to her office.

Turk topped off his coffee and went on down the hall. While Breanna was generally at Dreamland at least once a month, her office there had a temporary feel to it, and was radically different from the high-tech command center she used on the CIA campus. Even her Pentagon office, which was modest by command standards, seemed spacious if not quite opulent compared to the Dreamland space.

"You're not going to make me pay for Old Girl, are you?" said Turk, plopping down into one of the two stiff-backed wooden chairs in front of her desk.

"Pay?" Breanna asked as she closed the door.

"Just a little joke."

"You did a great job. The admiral wants to give you a medal."

"Really? The tight-ass admiral?"

"*Turk.*"

"I didn't call him that to his face." Turk retreated quickly. Blackheart actually had one of his aides buy him a drink, so he wasn't all bad. For an admiral.

"I need you to be serious, Captain." Breanna was sitting ramrod straight.

"Yes, ma'am." Turk took a sip of coffee and copied her posture.

Breanna had an entire mental script memorized and rehearsed, but for some reason couldn't seem to get it started. She looked into his face, found his eyes, and forced herself to talk.

"We . . . have a special assignment. It's very dangerous," she started. "It involves . . . flying the nano-UAVs."

"Flying them?"

"Directing them. As a backup, actually. But as you saw yesterday, we still need someone in the loop in an absolute emergency."

"Yup."

"I need a volunteer. I— You're probably the only one qualified."

Probably the only one? Breanna silently scolded herself: she hadn't planned on saying that at all.

"Where is this assignment?" he asked.

"I have to tell you—it's very dangerous."

"Great. I'm in."

"Uh—"

"It's combat, right? I want in. Definitely."

"It's . . . it is a combat operation," said Breanna, surprised by his enthusiasm, though she realized now she should have expected it. "I can't give you many details until—unless—you decide to do it."

"I already decided. Where am I going?"

"It's in Iran," she said. "Are you sure you want to do this?"

"Iran? Hell, yes. Hell, yes."

"You'd have to start training right away. It'll be intense."

"Right away when?"

"We have a site in Arizona. We'd need you there as soon as possible. Tonight, preferably."

"Tonight?"

Finally, she thought, he was listening with his brain rather than his heart.

"You can still back out," she told him.

"No, no. It's just, I kinda had plans for this weekend."

"It's not a question of being brave," said Breanna, not quite parsing what he said. "This is voluntary. I mean that. Walk out of my office and I'll have forgotten the whole thing."

"No, I'm doing it. It's tonight, though. That's all I need. The night. I'll report first thing in the morning."

Breanna recognized the furrowed eyebrows and locked mouth—Turk had dug in, afraid that in some bizarre way his manhood was being questioned. She'd seen that look on the face of practically every male pilot she'd ever dealt with, including her husband's. Once set, there was no way for them to back down.

But he did genuinely want to do it. She could read that as well.

"You can report tomorrow?" she asked gently.

"Deal." He jumped to his feet and held out his hand to shake. "Thanks, boss."

Breanna rose. His handshake was firm and enthusiastic.

"I'll have Lisa make the arrangements," she told him. "You'll have a civilian flight to Arizona—the tickets will be in your e-mail queue by this evening."

"Thanks."

Oh God, she thought as she watched him leave. Did I do the right thing?

TURK KICKED HIMSELF ALL THE WAY DOWN THE HALL. He could have gotten the entire seventy-two hours off if he'd been smart about it.

But he wanted to get back into the swing of things. Feel the adrenaline he'd felt over Libya. He wanted to get back into combat.

Li wasn't going to be happy about the timing, though. They'd planned this for weeks—months, since they'd met.

But he'd be back in the thick of things, flying.

Controlling the nano-UAVs meant he'd be in the air close to them.

And Iran—this was going be something *real*.

Turk met Li at the baggage claim. Her lips were softer than he remembered, her hug more delicious. Oblivious to the crowd passing on both sides, they wrapped themselves together, merging their bodies in long delayed desire.

By the time their lips parted, Turk felt more than a little giddy. He was tempted to blow off the dinner reservations and go directly to the hotel, but Li's appetite prevailed. Halfway through dinner at the fancy rooftop restaurant the glow on her face convinced him he'd made the right choice.

But it also made it hard to tell her that he had to leave in the morning.

It got harder with every minute that passed. Turk ordered himself another beer, then a glass of rye whiskey when she ordered dessert.

"It's a beautiful view," said Li, glancing toward the window. With the sun down, the rooftop patio was no longer oppressively hot, and when she suggested they have a nightcap at the bar there, Turk readily agreed. Words were growing sparser and sparser, and yet he knew he had to talk—had to tell her what was up. But he felt paralyzed.

Every day at work, testing planes or in combat, he made dozens of decisions, immediately and without hesitation. His life, and often those of others, depended on it. He'd learned long ago that worrying too much about whether a decision was right or wrong was worse than making no decision at all. You were always going to do something somewhere sometime that *might* be wrong; you did your best to keep those numbers down, but you didn't obsess. Otherwise you did nothing.

And yet he couldn't move now.

Just blurt it out, he thought. And yet that seemed impossible.

The alcohol was just enough to make him a little sloppy; he held Li's hand awkwardly as they sat at a small wooden table near the edge of the roof, staring at the city spread out before them.

"Great night," said Li.

"Definitely."

"It's still early."

"The hotel is pretty close."

"Is it?"

Her smile made it impossible to say anything else. Turk paid the bill and led her to the car, and a half hour later they were in bed. Time had completely disappeared, and conscious thought as well—for Turk there was only her skin and her scent, her hair and the inviting softness of her breasts.

He drifted off, only to wake with a start an hour later. He still hadn't told her. Li was sleeping peacefully. Turk got up, pacing the hotel room—he had to tell her, but to wake her up?

He didn't even know what time he had to leave. He turned on his laptop, angry with himself—what a fool, what an absolute idiotic, ridiculous fool. A damn teenager. An imbecilic middle school kid.

As he tapped his password into the screen, he suddenly found himself hoping the mission had been called off. When he didn't see the e-mail among the first few entries, he nearly yelped with joy: maybe he had a few days reprieve. Even twenty-four hours, even twelve, would suffice.

But there it was, down at the very bottom, between a nudist site link a friend had sent and an advertisement for car insurance.

PLANE LEAVES AT 0705. BOARDING PASS ATTACHED. CIVILIAN DRESS.

Turk took a beer from the minifridge and paced back and forth through the room. He had to tell her, and he had to wake her up. And God, how was he going to tell her?

He could lie and say it had just come up. He just got the e-mail—not in itself a lie, actually.

Technically.

"What are you doing?" Li asked from under the blankets.

He looked at her. Her eyes were still closed.

"I, uh—damn." Turk sat in the chair opposite the bed.

Li opened her eyes. "What?"

"I . . ." He knew he was only making it worse by delaying. He ordered his mouth and tongue to speak—better to blurt it out. "I have to leave in the morning on an assignment. It, um, just came up."

"Huh?" She pushed herself up, propping her head with her right hand. "What's up, Turk?"

He hated himself. If he was a braver man, he'd leap out the window and disappear.

"I have—something came up today, something important."

For a moment he thought he would lie—just show her the e-mail and say nothing else. But he couldn't lie to her. Something in her eyes, in the look she was giving him: it wasn't disappointment entirely; there was more—loss and vulnerability. He was hurting her, and lying would only make that worse, much worse. Because he didn't want to hurt her. He loved her, though he'd never used that word.

"I've been putting off telling you. They need me to do something really important. I have to leave for Arizona in the morning. I'm sorry. I should have told you, but I couldn't. I didn't want to ruin the night."

Li slipped out of the bed, naked. She walked across the room and put her fingers to his lips.

"It's OK, Turk. I understand. I know it must be important."

She kissed him, and they folded their bodies together, hers warm, his cold. They went back to bed and made love, though their thoughts were already both moving far apart.

6

Arizona, three days later

THIS WAS *NOT* WHAT HE HAD IN MIND. NOT AT ALL.

Turk kept his head down as he ran through the scrub at the foot of the hill. Two men were following him, but he was more concerned about what lay in the hills. The curve ahead looked like a perfect place for an ambush.

When Breanna told him that he'd start training right away, he assumed she meant working with the nano-UAVs. But he hadn't seen the aircraft, or *any* aircraft, since arriving at the "camp" in the Arizona scrubland. Instead, training had been more like SERE on steroids.

SERE—Survival, Evasion, Resistance, and Escape—was the Air Force survival course designed to help prepare pilots who bailed out over enemy territory. It had never exactly been his favorite class. He'd taken the course twice at Fort Bragg, and nearly washed out both times.

This was a hundred times worse. He'd been here five days and trained the entire time; no breaks. The sun beat down relentlessly during the day. Nighttime temperatures dropped close to freezing. The ranch covered thousands of acres, with hills of all sizes and shapes. There was a dry streambed, an almost wet streambed, and a raging creek. Name a wild beast and it was most likely hiding behind a nearby crag.

The remains of ranch buildings abandoned

some thirty or forty years before were scattered in various places. Turk had visited them all, running mostly, occasionally under live fire. For a break the first day, he'd spent two hours on a target range with rifles and pistols nearly as old as he was. That was fun, but as soon as his trainers saw that he was a comparatively good shot—he'd won several state marksman competitions as a Boy Scout—they replaced the gun instruction with more survival training.

They were very big on running, especially from armed pursuers, as he was doing now.

Turk slowed as he reached the crease of the hill, trying to catch his breath and listen. He needed to keep moving, but he didn't want to fall into a trap.

It was morning, or so he thought—his watch had been taken from him upon arrival. Assuming it in fact was morning, he put the sun over his shoulder and faced what he reckoned was north. His objective lay in that direction.

As he turned, he thought he saw something flickering on the ground in the pass ahead.

A trap?

He couldn't retreat; the two men chasing him were no more than five minutes behind. Going straight over the top of the hill and trying to ambush whoever was hiding probably wouldn't work either; he'd been caught in a similar situation the day before, ambushed in his own ambush by a lookout.

Turk stooped and picked up a few small rocks. Then he slipped along the face of the slope, moving as quietly as possible. When he was within three feet of the point where the side of the hill fell off, he tossed two of the rocks down in the direction of the trail. Nothing happened for a moment. Then the barrel of an AK-47 poked around the side of the hill, eight feet below him.

He waited until a shoulder appeared, then launched himself.

The gun rapped out a three-shot burst. Turk's ears exploded. His fist landed on the side of the man's face and both of them went down, Turk on top. He punched hard with his right fist and felt the other man's body collapse beneath him. Turk gave him another punch, then leapt for the rifle, which had fallen to the ground.

He had just reached the stock when something grabbed his leg. He flailed back with the gun, gashing the man he'd jumped hard on the forehead. Blood began to spurt. Turk got to his feet as the man collapsed, horrified yet satisfied as well.

"Hey!" Turk started to yell, his shout was cut off by a thick arm that grabbed him around the throat and began choking. He kicked, then remembered one of the techniques he'd been taught on day two. He grabbed at the elbow with both hands, pushed his chin down, then tried to hook his leg behind his enemy's, turning toward the arm holding him. But his attacker anticipated that and managed to move around with him. Turk kept trying, shrugging and pulling his shoulders as the other man tightened his grip. Finally, the uneven ground became an ally—they fell together. Turk tried rolling away but the other man's arm remained clamped to his neck.

"Knock it off! Knock it off!" yelled Danny Freah, appearing above them. Freah was the head of Whiplash's special operations ground unit and ostensibly in charge of the training, though Turk had only seen him on the first day, and then for about thirty seconds. "Knock it the hell off! Now!"

Turk's attacker gave him one last squeeze, then pushed him away. Turk coughed violently as he caught his breath. Meanwhile, two men in black fatigues ran out from behind the hill and began attending to the man Turk had bloodied. The man was sitting upright, his entire face a thick frown. As soon as the medics saw he was OK, they started teasing him.

"Pilot beat the shit out of you good, Jayboy," said one.

"The geek owns your ass now," said the other.

"Fuck yourself," said Jayboy. He was in green and brown digi-camo, like the man who'd been choking Turk. "Both of you."

"I'd say you gentlemen are doing a good job." Danny put his hands on his hips. "An excellent job. A *Delta Force* job."

Jayboy grumbled a curse under his breath. Turk offered his hand to the man who'd been choking him. The soldier frowned and brushed past, joining the knot of soldiers who'd been trailing him and were just now catching up.

"Hey, Grease, no hard feelings," Turk yelled

after him. "You taught me that release. I almost got it."

Grease—Jeff Ransom—didn't answer. That wasn't uncharacteristic, and in some ways was even an improvement: the six-six Delta Force sergeant first class was generally openly antagonistic. But it peeved Turk—in his mind, he'd fought to a draw against big odds. That meant he had gotten the better of his trainers, finally, and the soldiers ought to admit it. They'd sure ranked on him when they had the advantage.

Jayboy—his real name was Staff Sergeant Jayson Boyd—knelt with his head back now, clotting the bleeding in his nose. Turk went over to him and apologized.

"I'm sorry I bashed you," said Turk.

"Forget it," grunted Jayboy.

"I'm sorry."

"Yeah."

"I'm getting better, huh?"

"Fuck you, Pilot."

"Turk, you're with me," shouted Danny. "Everyone else, knock off for the day. We're done."

Finally, thought Turk. Playtime is over. Now I get to fly.

Tired and sore but floating on a wave of triumph, Turk fell in behind Danny. He walked as fast as he could manage but quickly lost ground. His clothes were sopping with sweat and every muscle in his body ached.

He'd considered himself in good shape until this week. The Delta trainers had ragged him about that: "Come on, Pilot. You're in good *Air*

Force shape. Now it's time to live with *real* stand-ards."

Pilot.

It was the first time Turk had ever heard that used as a slur.

When Danny reached the Humvee, he waved the driver out of the vehicle and got in behind the wheel. He backed the Humvee into a U-turn and waited for Turk.

"I see you're getting the hang of things," Danny said as Turk climbed in.

"I didn't mean to bash him so hard."

"Hell no, hard is good." Danny smiled as he put the Humvee in gear and sped away. They skipped the turnoff for the cafeteria—a barn that had been very slightly modified—and headed toward the county highway that divided the property in half.

Maybe we'll get lunch someplace nice, thought Turk. But when they reached the road, they went straight across, driving along a scrub trail.

"Pretty country," he told Danny.

"Very nice."

"So I guess you're going to tell me what's going on soon, right?"

"We'll be there in a few."

Minutes? Hours? Danny didn't say. Turk knew better than to press the colonel any further, and contented himself with gazing out the window, looking for the rabid coyotes the Delta boys had warned him about. The parched scrubland became somewhat greener as they drove south along the trail, the hilly land husbanding runoff in underground aquifers. About halfway through the pass, the road narrowed and the sides of the hills sharpened. A week before, Turk would have looked at the etched sandstone and thought how pretty it looked; now he saw it as a perfect place to ambush someone.

The Humvee kicked up a good cloud of dust as they came through the pass. Danny turned to the right, leaving the trail and driving through a flat piece of land. Boulders were sprinkled amid the thigh-high grass; Danny veered left and right to avoid them, navigating to a dry creek bed. Here he turned right, following up it a hundred yards before finding a trail on his left; the trail led to a road, dirt but hard-packed and relatively smooth. Finding the going easier, he sped up.

A sharp curve took them to the head of a valley. A house spread out along the crest of the hill ahead rested like a giant with its arms saddling the rocky top. The sun, now almost directly overhead, glinted off the massive window at the center, the rays pushing aside the massive wooden beams that framed the facade and held the green steel roof and its solar panels in place. The exterior was all glass and logs, though the place could not be called a log cabin without a great deal of irony.

The road stopped about a third of the way up the hill. Danny turned right across a stretch of rough rock bed, bumping his way up a slight incline and around another bend until he came to a driveway of red gravel. This led him toward the house in a series of switchbacks, until at last the back of the structure appeared. An immense portico shaded a cobblestone driveway that circled around the entrance.

Danny parked in the center and got out. Turk followed him into a wide hallway, where they were met by a man in black fatigues. Though imposingly large, the man had no visible weapons, not even a sidearm; he gave Danny an almost imperceptible nod as they moved through a small room and into a narrower hall, passing steps on either side and a pair of bathrooms before entering a large great room faced by the windows Turk had seen from the Humvee.

Four massive couches with attendant armchairs and tables failed to fill the room. The floor's large flagstone tiles, irregularly shaped and each covering at least five square feet, were overlaid by hand-woven rugs. A pair of fireplaces, each large enough for a man to stand up in, flanked the sides of the room.

Ray Rubeo stood in front of the fireplace on the left, arms folded, staring at the tangle of unlit wood in the iron pit.

"Hey, Doc," said Danny, walking toward him.

Rubeo turned slowly, apparently lost in thought. The scientist headed a private company, Applied Intelligence, one of the Office of Special Technology's prime contractors. It was responsible for the AI that guided the Hydras, but that was far from its only contribution to either the command or its Whiplash subcomponent. Rubeo had personally worked on a number of projects Turk had been involved in, including the Tigershark II and the Sabre unmanned attack plane. He was an austere man, peculiar in the way geniuses often are. He was also, as far as Turk knew, rich beyond his needs. But the scientist seemed deeply unhappy, constantly frowning, and acerbic even when generous levity would have been more appropriate.

Rubeo stared at both of them for another few seconds before finally offering a greeting.

"Colonel." He nodded. "Captain. Have you eaten?"

"I haven't," said Turk. "I'm famished."

"We have a tight schedule," said Danny. "Things have been pushed up."

"Yes," said Rubeo, in his usual withering tone. He was the only man Turk had ever met who could make *yes* sound like a curse word. "You can eat while I talk," Rubeo offered. His tone was nearly magnanimous, certainly in contrast to what had come before. "Let's see what Wendy can make for you, and then we'll go downstairs."

RAY RUBEO HAD ASKED IF THEY WANTED FOOD AS A way to delay the briefing, if only for a few moments, but now as he watched Turk Mako eating the turkey sandwich he couldn't help but feel worse, as if he were watching a condemned man's final meal.

At least in that case the man would have deserved his fate.

"How much have you figured out on your own, Captain?" asked Rubeo, walking to the side of the basement conference center, a secure area dug deep below the main floor of the house. The building belonged to one of Rubeo's companies, as did the range where Turk and the Delta team had been practicing. Occasionally used by Special Technology to test out equipment, the property was mainly leased to Delta and SOCCOM, the U.S. Special Operations Command, for various training and practice exercises. It had once been three separate ranches; Rubeo bought them all and merged them to make a property large enough to keep the curious far at bay.

"I've been too busy to make guesses," said Turk. "They've been running me nuts. But if we're talking Iran, I assume we're going to strike their nuclear facilities."

"One facility," said Rubeo. "Just one."

"This one is special," said Danny. "It's hard to get to, and it's their newest facility. We need to move quickly, while we still have a chance. Even more quickly than we anticipated a week ago."

"OK, sure," answered Turk.

Rubeo rubbed his earlobe. There was a small gold-post earring there, its tiny surface smooth from his habit of touching it whenever he encountered a difficult moment, large or small. He waved his hand in front of a small glass panel on the side wall. The lighting dimmed and the wall at the front of the room turned light blue, a presentation screen appearing as lasers in the floor and ceiling created a visual computer screen that took up most of the space. "This should answer most of your questions. It will show the target and the general theory. Please wait until it has finished to ask questions."

"OK." Turk took another bite of his sandwich.

Rubeo folded his arms as the video presentation began. There was no sound; he supplied the running narrative.

"The target is accessible through a set of air shafts, utility conduits, and hallways. The main obstacles are at the mouth and a pair of air exchange mechanisms about fifty meters into the facility. Once you navigate past those, the rest becomes easy."

The screen showed a louvered metal air scoop about three feet high by eight feet wide. The next image showed a mesh screen behind the louvers; this was followed by a schematic.

"We haven't actually seen the face of these," added Rubeo, hitting pause by pointing at the lower left corner of the screen. An infrared camera read his gestures. "Due to some technical problems with detecting fine mesh. That means it's possible there will be no screen. But we are planning for a screen."

He lowered his finger and the video continued.

"The first thing you'll do is blow a hole through the screen," said Rubeo. "There are no electronics in the area of the intakes, and we assume therefore that there are no detection devices, and the explosion will go unheard. In any event, it's doubtful that there are any measures they can take to stop the attack."

"I'm hitting it with missiles?" Turk asked.

Rubeo halted the show and glanced at Danny.

"The nano-UAVs," said Danny.

"That's why you're here," said Rubeo. "Why did they say you were chosen?"

"The Hydras are still being tested."

"They're the only weapon that can destroy the bunker," said Rubeo. "Because of the configuration. You're going to fly them right into the deepest part of the facility and blow it up."

Turk left the rest of his sandwich on the plate as Rubeo continued. The mission he was outlining was radical in the extreme. A small group of nano-UAVs would enter through air shafts hidden in a cave. After breaking through an air exchanger and flying down a series of conduits, they would enter the work space and find a room with the targeted equipment. When they ignited, they would set off a large explosion, weakening and hopefully destroying the entire structure.

There was an incredible amount of intelligence behind the presentation Rubeo was moving briskly through. The amount of detail on the air shafts was stunning—dimensions, material, even details on soldering flaws. Turk could see that the operation must have been in planning for months.

Even so, the intelligence had not been perfect. Danny made it clear they were pushing up the timetable.

"What am I flying these from?" Turk asked. "The Tigershark?"

"No," said Rubeo. "That's too risky. You'll get a helicopter in Iran."

"A helicopter? I can't fly one. I mean, I can learn—"

"You're not going to fly it," said Danny. "We have a team in place to help you."

"It's regrettable," interrupted Rubeo, "but the UAVs have a very limited control range, as you know. In a few months, we will have that solved. But for now . . ."

He shook his head.

"I have to fly them into the facility?" asked Turk.

"You are not actually flying them, Captain. Your only function is to guide them if there is trouble. You are the override." Rubeo's lips curled in a smirk. "Their roles and routes will be pre-planned, but if there is a problem, or a contingency we haven't planned for, we will need you there. You have done this before."

"I've done more than that."

"You'll have to get within five miles of both sites," said Danny, interrupting. "A Delta team is already in-country to help assist you. They've been scouting the sites."

"Five miles is the absolute limit of your range," said Rubeo. He looked over at Danny. "Closer would be better. May I continue?"

Danny nodded. Neither he nor Turk interrupted again.

RUBEO SPOKE MOSTLY ABOUT THE CONTROL UNIT AND how the modified UAVs differed from the ones Turk had worked with. The technical aspects were far from Danny's domain, and he felt like a bystander. And in fact he was, removed from even the actual attack itself.

The plan was the latest of a long campaign to

thwart Iran's dogged efforts at building a nuke. It was the most recent variation in a line of contingencies aimed at taking down the hidden installation. It was better protected than any of the others involved in the Iranian program, deeper and more cleverly constructed. The team inside Iran hadn't been sent to plot the nano-UAV strike; they were actually in place to assess the effects of a nuclear strike if the President ordered it to proceed. This attack was a recent brainstorm; it had been proposed by Rubeo after he was asked to consult on the analysis of some of the Iranian equipment detected at the site.

Because of that, the ground operation remained a Delta Force show. That meant there would be no Whiplash people at all on the mission. Danny had no doubt about Delta's professionalism or capabilities; while by design Delta avoided publicity, its handpicked members represented the elite of the world's military. He himself had worked with Delta on several occasions, with very good results.

However, he had also witnessed some culture clashes when different units worked together. In this case, the fact that the ground unit would be working closely with an Air Force officer they didn't know could potentially be a problem. Turk would have to quickly earn the team's respect. Danny wondered if that was doable.

It wasn't that Danny didn't think the pilot was a good warrior; on the contrary, he'd already proved himself in battle. But those battles had been in the air, where Turk was a real star. The ground was something different. Even Danny, who as an Air

Force officer was constantly dealing with pilots, had trouble dealing with some of their egos. If the head didn't match the hat, so to speak, there was bound to be trouble.

If everything went as planned, the men would have relatively limited contact with Iranian civilians, and none at all with the military. But nothing ever went as planned.

"All right, I think I have the gist of the thing," said Turk finally. "When do we start practicing?"

"There's not going to be any practice," said Danny. "We have new intel from Iran. We have to move ahead immediately."

"Right now?"

Danny nodded.

"You shouldn't have to take over the aircraft," said Rubeo. "We have maps and other data prepared. You'll be able to study them on the plane to Lajes."

"Lajes?" asked Turk.

"In the Azores," said Danny. "You'll fly from there to Iran. Direct."

"Direct? What kind of commercial flight is it?"

"It's not a commercial flight. It's a B-2. You'll parachute in a man bomb."

7

Lajes Field, Azores

SOME TEN HOURS LATER TURK STOOD IN THE LIGHT rain outside a hangar at Lajes Field, trying to shake out the charley horse that had taken hold of his leg. He'd spent nearly the entire ten hours studying the data on the nano-UAVs and the mission. Contained on a slatelike computer, the information was considered so secret that the program displaying it automatically changed its encryption scheme every ten minutes; Turk had to reenter his password each time and press his thumb against the print reader to unscramble it.

The password was the same as his "safe word"— Thanksgiving. He was supposed to work the word into a conversation if there was a question about his identity.

He had never been on a mission where he needed a safe word. Whiplash command had various ways of identifying him, including a special ring on his finger that marked his location to within a third of a meter when queried through a satellite system. Thinking about the contingencies where the system might not suffice was somewhat unsettling.

He was wearing a plain khaki uniform, a bit frayed at the cuff and worn at the knee. He guessed it was an Iranian-style uniform, though he hadn't bothered to ask.

A half-hour before, a Gulfstream had dropped

him off in front of a hangar where an officer waiting in an SUV rolled down the window and said
two words: "Wait here." Then the truck sped off,
leaving Turk completedly alone. The rain started
a few minutes later. Fortunately, the hangar was
open, and he'd waited at the doorway, just out of
the storm. Even so, the spray seemed to weigh
him down, washing away the surge of confidence
that had built on the way there. He didn't doubt
that he could direct the nano-UAVs—it wouldn't
be much harder than any of a dozen things he'd
done in the past two months. But surviving on
the ground—was he really ready for that?

The whine of jet engines nearby shook away his
doubts, or at least postponed them. Turk stepped
up to the corner of the hangar doorway as an
SUV approached. Right behind it he saw a C-17
cargo plane, a big, high-winged transport. He
folded his arms, admiring the taxiing behemoth.
He'd once shared the typical fighter jock prejudice against transports and their drivers, thinking the big planes were little more than buses
requiring little skill to guide. A few stints in the
cockpit of an MC-17R undergoing testing had
disabused him of that misperception. On his first
flight, the commander had made a turn tighter
than a Cessna 182 might have managed on a good
day, plopping down on an airfield that looked to
be about the size of a bathtub. From that point on
he had nothing but respect for Air Mobility jocks
and their brethren in general.

Turk moved toward the hangar wall as the plane
neared. The C-17 stopped about twenty yards past

the hangar. The rear cargo bay opened and the ramp descended slowly, the four "toes" at the end unfolding to the ground. With the engines continuing to whine, two men trotted to the tarmac; both were armed with automatic weapons. The one closest to Turk eyed him quickly, then touched the side of his helmet and began talking into the headset. Meanwhile, a crewman checked the ramp and the sides, making sure they were secure. Moments later what looked like a fat torpedo came down the ramp, propelled by electric motors at the wheels and controlled by a crew chief holding a wired remote. He stopped at the base of the ramp, looked around quickly, then shouted something to the two men with the guns. One of them did something with his hand—a signal to proceed—and the torpedo began making its way to the hangar, flanked by the two guards.

Another man came down the ramp then, a rucksack on each shoulder. He was tall, and silhouetted in the light looked almost like a science-fiction robot rather than something of flesh and blood. Turk stared at him as he approached, then realized he'd seen the saunter before—it was Grease, the Delta Force sergeant he'd trained with. The sergeant ignored him, walking into the hangar behind the cart.

"Grease," said Turk coming over.

"Captain." Grease turned back and inspected the cart and its cargo.

"Here's our chariot, huh?"

Grease's expression was somewhere between contempt and incomprehension.

"You use the man bomb before?" Turk asked, trying to start a conversation. Danny had already told him that Grease had used the contraption three times.

"Idiotic nickname. Don't call it that," muttered Grease.

The man bomb—officially, SOC Air Mobile Stealth Infiltration Non-powered Vehicle JH7-99B—sat on its skid upside down, exposing the belly and a clamshell door. The outer skin was covered with radar absorbing material. If Turk were to touch it—neither he nor anyone else was supposed to do so unnecessarily—it would have felt like slick Teflon.

"We gonna fit in that?" Turk asked.

"One of us will."

"Just one?"

Grease didn't answer. The man bomb was designed to hold one person, but it could in a pinch hold two. The pressurized container fit into the bomb bay of a B-2 Spirit, once the aircraft's Rotary Launcher Assembly was removed.

Contrary to the nickname, the device was not dropped from the aircraft. Instead, its passenger (or in this case, passengers) fell from the container when its target area was reached. After falling a sufficient distance they opened their parachutes and descended to their target in a standard HALO jump, if any High Altitude, Low Opening free-fall could be termed "standard."

Turk had parachuted and was in fact officially qualified for HALO jumps, though he did not have extensive practice doing so. But because of

the importance of the mission, the limited avail-
ability of B-2s, and the dangerous area they would
be jumping into, the mission planners had decided
he would jump in tandem with his Delta guide—
Grease.

A tandem jump basically tied both jumpers together in a single harness. This was a fine practice
when leaving a plane; there was plenty of room
to maneuver to the doorway, and any feelings of
paranoia because someone was standing over your
shoulder were literally blown away by the rush of
the wind as you stepped off. But the man bomb
hadn't been designed with tandem jumps in mind.
The two men would have to cradle in each other's
arms during the flight, which even at best speed
would take close to eight hours.

Grease dropped his packs a short distance
from the hangar and hulked over their transport.
He opened the top of one and took out a large,
T-shaped metal key, which he inserted into a
panel near the front of the man bomb. He turned
it and the claw doors opened. He took out two
large packs—their parachutes—and some bags of
gear from the interior. Satisfied that everything
was there, he turned to Turk.

"You have briefing data?" he asked.

"In here." Turk patted his ruck.

"Hand it over."

Turk gave him the slate computer. Grease went
back to his packs. He took out what looked like a
large padded envelope, put the computer inside,
then walked to a trash barrel just outside the
hangar.

"Hey!" managed Turk as Grease dropped the bag into the can.

Fire shot from the top of the barrel. Turk ran over to rescue the slate computer, only to be grabbed by Grease before he got near. He was pulled back as the can rumbled with an explosion.

"Can't risk it," Grease told him. "Had to be destroyed."

"You gonna blow up the controls, too?"

"Not yet," said the trooper.

FORTY MINUTES LATER THE TWO MEN SNUGGLED UN-comfortably together as the man bomb was twisted upside down and then locked in the bay of a freshly fueled B-2. Turk had never felt so claustrophobic in an airplane before.

"Get sleep now," said Grease as the plane began to move. "We ain't gonna have much chance once we're in Iran."

"Pretty hard to sleep like this."

Grease made a snorting sound. They were both in flight suits, wearing helmets and oxygen masks. Their sound systems were hooked into the plane's interphone system; the crew could hear every word, so they were not supposed to talk about the mission.

"You do enough of this," said Grease finally, "you learn to sleep anywhere, even on your feet."

It was good advice, but Turk couldn't take it. The bumps and the whine of the plane as it taxied, the sudden g forces as they rose, the strange sensation of being in a flying coffin—it all offended his innate sense of what flight was all about. He should be at the stick, and if not there, then at least able to sit upright and look around. He felt he needed to control some part of his destiny. Here, he was no more than a soon-to-be-dispensed part.

Turk tried to clear his mind as they flew, but this was futile, too. His thoughts drifted from the mission to Li, then back to the mission. He hadn't quite memorized the maps; he didn't realize they'd be destroyed.

As Grease slept, Turk felt as if he'd been packed into a bear's den, and was stuck through hibernation season. The only thing worse than sleeping, he thought, would be waking up.

A HALF HOUR FROM THE DROP POINT THE PILOT SPOKE to them for the first time since takeoff, asking if they were awake.

"Yes," said Grease, his voice thick and groggy.

"Captain Mako?"

"Uh—yeah." Turk had drifted into a kind of fugue state, awake but not focusing his thoughts in a conscious way. He mumbled something in response, then began struggling to get his mind back in gear.

"We're ready," added Grease.

"Release point in twenty-nine minutes," said the pilot. "We're on course."

"Thanks."

"You sound cheery," Turk told Grease. He meant it as a joke; there was no emotion in

Grease's voice. But Grease took it literally, and his voice sounded more enthusiastic than Turk could remember.

"I'm ready. We'll do it."

The next twenty-eight minutes passed so slowly they felt like days. Then time sped up. Turk braced himself as the bomb bay doors opened. The aircraft bucked—and then there was a whoosh, air rushing around him. His arms flexed involuntarily; Grease folded his own around him, cocooning Turk with his body as they fell.

"Arms out," Grease reminded him.

Turk struggled to get his arms into the proper position, jerking them against the wind. It was as if something was holding them back—they were cramped and compressed, his muscles atrophied by the long wait in the hold of the plane.

"Just relax," said Grease.

"Trying."

"Do it."

Opening the bay door made the B-2 visible to some radars, and while the flight plan had been designed to minimize the possibility of detection, there was still a chance that the bomber would be picked up by an alert Iranian crew. The plan, therefore, was to avoid opening the parachute until the plane was a good distance away. In effect, this meant waiting. And falling. It was dark, and stare as he might, Turk could not see anything on the ground, not even the little pinpricks of light the briefing had suggested he would see.

The altimeter on his wrist said they were at 17,000 feet.

"We using the chute?" he asked Grease.

"We're not there yet."

Turk closed his eyes, waiting.

Finally, it came: a sharp tug back into Grease's chest as the chute deployed and the straps pulled him tight. His groin hurt where one of the straps pulled up sharp. He told himself it was better than the alternative, and tried to shift to relieve the pressure.

Now they were an airplane, flying to their drop spot. Turk was a useless passenger again, trying to stay as neutral as possible as Grease steered the chute with his togs.

There were lights in the distance, many lights. A city.

They turned in the other direction. Turk thought back to the satellite images of the landing zone, trying to see it in his mind. They were supposed to fall into a valley, right along a rarely used road.

Be just my bad luck to land when a car is coming, he thought.

But that didn't happen. They hit the ground a fraction of a second sooner than he thought they would; he fell off to the side and Grease followed, thrown off by his passenger's disarray. The sergeant quickly unbuckled the harness that held them together, unlatched the bags they'd jumped with, then began gathering up the chute.

By the time Turk had taken his helmet off, Grease had the nylon wing bundled and ready to hide. With their packs, they walked toward a rock outcropping about thirty yards from where they'd touched down. Turk remembered it from the satellite image—Grease had come down within millimeters of the planned spot.

As they started to dig, Turk heard a vehicle approaching in the distance.

"Our guys?" he asked Grease, clutching for the pistol in a holster under his jumpsuit.

"Should be. Stay behind the rocks." The sergeant opened one of the large packs and took out a pair of rifle sleeves. He handed one to Turk. "AK. Don't shoot me."

The gun was an AK-47 assault rifle. The external furniture, folding paratrooper stock and all, was old and authentic; the guts of the forty-year-old weapon, however, had been refurbished with precise replacements.

Turk took the gun and ducked behind the rocks. He pulled off his jumpsuit, exposing his Iranian fatigues. The vehicle was still a decent distance away, coming from the south. It was a truck.

Not Delta, he thought. Not our guys. So relax. Just relax. It's not real until our guys get here.

But it was very real. Grease perched near the road, gun ready. The truck's lights swept the valley to Turk's left as it came down the curve. It was a troop truck, an army transport of some sort, slowing as if the driver had seen something.

Turk's finger tensed against the trigger guard.

The truck's lights blinked as it approached. Grease stood up and ran to the vehicle. He spoke to the driver, then hopped on the side as the truck turned off the road and headed toward Turk.

Maybe it's all been an exercise, Turk thought.

Just a rehearsal, to make sure I'm ready. We aren't really in Iran. We aren't really in danger. I'm back in Arizona, still being tested.

He'd half convinced himself of that by the time the truck pulled up. Grease jumped off the running board and jogged over to him to get the packs. A man wearing plain green fatigues opened the passenger side door and hopped down.

"You're the pilot?" he asked, holding out his hand to help Turk hook his left arm into the strap of the bag that had contained the guns; it was light now, filled only with ammo. He pulled the ruck for the control unit onto his other arm.

"Turk Mako."

"Dome." He said it as if it were the sort of name everyone used. "You're right on time. Good work. I'll take your packs."

"No, no, I got them." Turk had been told not to let the control unit out of his possession, and he wasn't giving it up for anyone. His own gear was with Grease in a smaller ruck. He started walking slowly toward the truck.

Dome pushed him gently.

"Come on, we gotta run. Don't want to sit out here too long. Iranians got a little training unit just up the road. Sometimes the Guard does night maneuvers."

"Revolutionary Guard?"

"Yeah, well, not the Coast Guard, right? You're wearin' their uniform," Dome added. "We all are."

Grease got in the cab while Dome helped Turk to the back of the truck, which was empty. They lifted the bags in, then scrambled up after them. The inside of the truck smelled like cow manure.

"Nice flight?" asked Dome.

"I had better."

"Grease is a lot of fun, huh?"

"Cracked jokes the whole way. Are you two the only guys on the team?"

"The others are watching us, don't worry."

They drove for about a half hour. Turk used the time to check his pistol—an Iranian SIG-226 knockoff, known in Iran as a PC-9 ZOAF, with authentic furniture and substituted parts like the AK—then filled his pockets with ammo from his personal ruck. But otherwise the time passed like sand slowly piling up on a beach. His legs had stiffened during the long flight and now felt like they were going to seize up. He flexed them back and forth, then got up and walked around the back of the truck, trying to keep them from turning into steel beams.

"Getting spasms?" asked Dome.

"Yeah."

"You oughta do yoga. Helps."

"Really?"

"Shit, yeah. Every morning. Dread's got some muscle relaxers if you need 'em," he added. "Tell him."

"Who's Dread?"

"Petey Rusco."

"How come he's named Dread?"

Dome shrugged. "Not sure. Just is."

"How come you're Dome?"

"I used to shave my head. Plus my first name

is Dom—Dominick Sorentino. Turk's your real name?"

"Yup."

"I thought all you Air Force guys had names like Macho and Quicksilver Hotshot and like that."

Turk smiled. "Turk's enough."

"Yeah," said Dome. "Call me anything. Just as long as it's not asshole."

CAMP WAS A SMALL FARM IN THE SIDE OF A HILL SOME twenty miles south of where they had landed. Two soldiers met them near the road and guided the driver as he backed into a ramshackle barn. Dome introduced Turk around, then got him some food.

The team consisted of seven men. All but one was a member of Delta Force, though they never identified themselves as such. It was obvious from their easy camaraderie that they'd trained and operated together for some time; Turk knew they'd been in Iran for several weeks.

The seventh man, Shahin Gorud, didn't announce his affiliation, but Turk guessed he was CIA. His beard was longer and thicker than the others', and he was at least ten years older than the next oldest man, David "Green" Curtis, a black master sergeant. Turk couldn't speak Farsi—sometimes called Persian, Iran's primary language—but he guessed Gorud was fluent.

"You speak Russian?" asked Gorud warily when they were introduced.

"Yes," said Turk. "A little. My mother was from Russia."

Gorud said something quickly; it sounded like, *Where did she come from?*

"Moscow."

"Say it in Russian."

Turk did so, then added, in slightly hesitant Russian, that he didn't remember much of the language.

"You'll do. You know more than the Iranians. Just keep your mouth shut unless I say to talk."

"How did you know I spoke Russian?"

Gorud smirked.

Green was the father figure of the team, and while not technically the highest in rank, was the de facto leader, the first one the others would look to for direction. The officer in charge, Captain Thomas Granderson, was surprisingly young, just a year or two older than Turk. He spoke Farsi and Arabic fluently, though a notch less smoothly than Gorud and Grease. Dread—Petey Rusco—was one of two advanced combat medics on the team. The other was Tiny—Sergeant Chris Diya—who in time-honored style was the exact opposite of "tiny" at six-eight, even taller than Grease. While in a pinch all of the men were capable of doubling as medics, Dread and Tiny could have done duty as doctors in any emergency room on the planet.

Red—the truck driver, whose hair (now dyed black) gave him the nickname—was a sergeant from Macon, Georgia, and sounded like it, too, at least when he spoke English rather than Farsi. The last member of the team, Staff Sergeant Varg

Dharr, was a pudgy soldier who did much of the cooking, and was responsible for the spiced goat that Turk devoured after arriving. All of the men looked at least vaguely Iranian, and all but two had Middle Eastern roots on at least one side of their family.

After he'd eaten, Turk got rid of his jumpsuit, then checked his personal gear. There wasn't much: aside from a change of underwear and socks, he had an off-the-shelf GPS unit, water, and first aid essentials. Most important was a satcom unit that looked like a standard Iridium satellite phone but was programmed with a more advanced encryption set. He shouldn't need much more: the reason he was here was the larger rucksack he kept close at hand, which contained the control unit, its antenna, and a backup battery. If all went well, they'd be back home in three days; five tops.

Turk took out the control unit and ran it through its diagnostics, making sure it hadn't suffered during the trip. The controls consisted of three pieces—a nineteen-inch flat screen, a sending unit, and a panel that held the actual flight controls. This looked like a miniature version of a Flighthawk, with a few extra joysticks attached to either side. A standard keyboard sat in the middle; at the top was a double row of function keys, whose purpose changed depending on the situation and the program. Two touch pads sat at the bottom; these were similar to the touch pads on a standard laptop. Dedicated keys on the right controlled the general flight patterns and swarm commands; three extender keys on the left changed the function of each. The joysticks were flightsticks or throttles, as designated by the user. In theory, up to eight nano-UAVs could be directly guided at any one time, though it was impractical to override the computer for more than a few moments if you were flying more than two.

Even one was difficult to work at all but the slowest speeds. If he had to take over, Turk knew he would designate the course and allow the computer to fly the plane along it. Assuming, of course, there was time.

Granderson and Gorud squatted down on the floor next to him as he finished his tests.

"You're ready?" asked Gorud.

"Yes."

"They want us to go into action tomorrow night," said Granderson. "There are two windows, one starting at eleven, the other at three. I'd like the eleven. Gives us a lot more room to maneuver. But the schedule will be tighter getting to the airport where we'll meet your ride. We'll have to travel while it's still daylight. Just for an hour or so, but still."

"It's not a problem," replied Turk. "Not for me."

"Good."

The "windows" were times when an X-37B delivery vehicle would be in the vicinity overhead and in range to launch the nano-UAVs. The X-37B was an unmanned space shuttle. While the X designation was supposed to indicate it was experimental, in fact the shuttle had been flying missions since 2011. Just over twenty-nine feet long and nine and a half-feet high, there was more than enough room for the three dozen nano-UAVs in each spacecraft's cargo bays. The X-37Bs had been launched about the time Turk was landing in the Azores.

"So where's my helicopter?" he asked.

"We're meeting it in Birjand," said Gorud. He took a piece of paper from his pocket, unfolding it stiffly. The paper was thick and stiff, treated with a waxy substance that would make it burn quickly. The map printed on it was a hybrid of a satellite image and a more traditional road map.

"Why?" asked Turk.

Gorud gave him a look that told Turk he was not used to being questioned. Turk had seen that look before, from Nuri Abaajmed Lupo, the lead CIA officer on the Whiplash team. It must be common to all CIA employees, he thought, implanted when they got their IDs.

"Because it's convenient," said Gorud. "The security there is also nonexistent. It's close enough to where we have to go that we won't stretch fuel reserves. And it's the way I drew it up. Enough reasons for you?"

"Do they teach that look in the Agency?" retorted Turk.

"What?"

"I asked a simple question. You don't have to get all shitty about it."

Grease clamped his hand on Turk's shoulder, attempting to calm him. Turk brushed it away.

"It's already arranged," said Granderson quietly. "The helicopter's going to be waiting."

"What is it?" asked Turk.

"A Russian Mi-8. It's leased to a Russian company. It will fit with your cover story, if that's ever needed."

"How far is it from Birjand to the target?" He looked at the map. Turk wasn't a helicopter pilot, and far from an expert on Russian helicopters like the Mi-8, an old workhorse that came in dozens of variations. But he knew helicopters in general, and he knew that the distance between Birjand and the target area would test the chopper's range.

"Roughly four hundred and fifty miles," said Gorud. His tone remained hostile. "Yes, it's far. We'll carry extra fuel, and refuel halfway. The flight itself shouldn't be a problem. The Russian oil exploration company that uses it makes that flight through the area all the time. We get it at 2000 hours, refuel by midnight, begin the operation at 0100. Then we fly on to the farm near Dasterjad, wait out the day, and leave."

"Disney World after that," said Granderson. He got a few smiles, but no laughs.

Turk visualized the map he'd half memorized on the flight out to the Azores. The target was a hidden complex in Abuzeydadab northeast of Nantz, which itself held a major facility, though its existence had been made public by the West years before. Abuzeydadab's had not. The Iranians believed the U.S. didn't know about it, and had studiously avoided anything that would draw attention to it. That gave the operation certain advantages; chief among them was the absence of serious air defenses or a detachment of troops.

They'd have to worry about shoulder-launched weapons—MANPADS, or Man Portable Air Defense Systems—and grenade launchers, but if things went well they wouldn't be close enough for those to be a problem.

The actual penetration of the plant and the final attack were preset with the computer, so assuming nothing went wrong, Turk believed the toughest part of the job would be "picking up" the nano-UAVs as they descended. This was as much a matter of being in the right spot as pressing the proper buttons when they needed to be pressed. When prompted, the control unit broadcast a lower-power signal for the aircraft to home in on. But to make sure he got the connection, he'd have to start broadcasting well before the UAVs were due to arrive, and stay within a two-mile-square box. Once the assault began, two UAVs would circle above the attack area, relaying the signals to the rest of the swarm. They would self-destruct when the last signal from the swarm members was lost, a security precaution hard-wired into the units and that could not be overridden.

Two miles sounded like a large area, but a helicopter flying in the vicinity for nearly twenty minutes as the mission unfolded was certain to attract attention. Fortunately, the area to the east of Abuzeydadab was desert and largely empty. Even if they were heard, it would presumably take the Iranians a while to respond.

"Problem!" said the man at the door of the barn. "We got a car coming down the driveway."

"Lights," said Granderson, even as they were doused.

Grease grabbed Turk by the arm and began tugging him toward a window at the back. "Stay close to me."

"Who's in the car?"

"Just come on."

Turk tried to object, but it was useless—Grease pushed him to the ground, smothering him with his body as gunfire erupted at the front of the house.

ADVENTURER

———

1

Iran

By the time Grease let Turk up, the gunfire had stopped and the barn was empty.

"All right, let's go," said Grease, pointing. "Through the window."

Turk pushed the control unit back into its pack, took his rifle and followed Grease to the window. He went out first, waiting while Grease jumped through.

"What's going on?" Turk asked.

"Don't know. We'll find out soon enough. Keep your gun ready. This way."

Grease led him across the flat yard to a small out-building that the team had agreed earlier would be a first regrouping area if they were attacked. Grease checked around the building, then had Turk kneel next to him on the side farthest from the road.

"Uh, thanks for watching out for me," said Turk as they waited.

Grease didn't respond.

You have to be the coldest son of a bitch I've ever met, thought Turk.

Sergeant Major Curtis trotted toward them a few moments later, followed by Dome. The younger man was carrying an M-240 machine gun.

"We're clear," said Curtis. "We move out as soon as the captain gives the signal." He looked at Turk. "You OK, Pilot?"

"I'm good."

"Careful with that rifle, all right? Especially if that safety is off."

Turk realized he was pointing it at Curtis. "Sorry."

"Someone told me you were a good shot." Curtis smiled. "So you don't need to prove it."

Dome laughed.

"I'm all right," said Turk defensively. "Not as good as you guys, I'm sure."

"Don't worry. Your job isn't to shoot," said Curtis mildly. "Wait for the truck."

Curtis and Dome left, circling around behind the house as they checked the perimeter. Two troopers were moving near the front of the barn; Turk asked Grease what they were doing.

"Dunno. Probably hiding the bodies."

"Shouldn't we be getting out of here?"

"Relax, Pilot. We'll get you where you got to go."

They waited in silence until the truck emerged from the barn a few minutes later. Then Grease wordlessly nudged Turk into motion, trotting alongside him as the truck moved up to the front of the house. The others were waiting there in a semicircle, standing by a Toyota sedan.

"In," said Grease, pointing to the truck.

"Where are we going?"

"We'll find out when they tell us."

2

CIA campus, Virginia

DANNY FREAH PAUSED FOR A SECOND, WAITING FOR the computerized security system to recognize him by his biometrics, then continued through the large, empty basement space surrounding the "Cube"—Whiplash's secure command center on the CIA headquarters campus in McLean, Virginia. He walked directly toward a black wall, which grew foggy as he approached. The wall was actually a sophisticated energy field, which allowed him through as soon as he touched it and was recognized by the security system.

He went down the hallway—these walls were "real"—to the central command center, where Breanna Stockard, Jonathon Reid, and six specialists were monitoring the Iran operation in a small, theaterlike room. Three rows of curved console tables, arranged on descending levels, sat in front of large screen. The floor, chairs, and tables moved, allowing the room to be reconfigured in a half-dozen ways, including a bowl-like arrangement that reminded Danny of a baseball stadium. While the designers had hailed the flexibility, it turned out the room was almost exclusively used as it was now, in a traditional "mission control" layout.

Paul Smith looked up at Danny from the back bench. Smith was a military mission coordinator "borrowed" by Whiplash from the Air Force's Space Reconnaissance Command. He'd worked as the liaison with Dreamland on the nano-UAVs, and was now the primary communications link to the command center with Turk and the ground team. Like the others in the room, he generally handled a variety of tasks, often all at once.

"He's in-country," Smith told Danny.

"Any trouble?"

"Not with the jump. They had to move, though. One of the owners came to the house where the Delta team had hidden. Just one of those things. Murphy's Law."

"Were they compromised?" Danny asked.

Smith shook his head. He wore civilian clothes to fit in with the rest of the team; only Danny was in uniform. "Bad luck for them."

Smith meant for the people who had undoubtedly been killed, though Danny didn't ask.

Luck, good or otherwise, was the wildcard of life. It was also the one ingredient of every operation, covert or conventional, that could never be fully factored in. Things happened or didn't happen; you planned for as many contingencies as possible, then thought on your feet.

As it happened, the team's presence at the farm was already part of a contingency plan—they'd moved from what had been an abandoned warehouse complex when workmen showed up suddenly to start tearing down the place. But then the entire operation was a cascading series of contingencies, revamped on the run.

"They have another site about two miles farther north," added Smith. "They have two guys there who've been watching it from a hide nearby. They should be OK there."

"Danny, do you have a minute?" asked Breanna, rising from her seat at the front. She came up the stairs slowly, obviously tired. Danny guessed that she hadn't slept the night before. "Just in my office. Coffee?"

"No thanks. Too much on the plane."

Danny followed Breanna as she detoured into the complex's kitchenette. The smell of freshly brewed coffee tempted him.

"How was he?" she asked.

"He looked good. He nearly beat one of the trainers to a pulp."

"There's yogurt in the fridge," she told him, going over to the coffeepot. "Good for your allergies."

"Haven't been bothering me lately. Desert helped."

"How was Ray?"

"A sphinx, as usual."

A smile flickered across Breanna's face as she brought the coffee to one of the two small tables and sat down. She put both hands around her coffee cup, funneling the warm vapors toward her face.

"Cold?" asked Danny.

"A little," she confessed. "It's sitting in one place, I think. What did Sergeant Ransom say?"

"Sergeant Ransom knows his duty," Danny told her.

"I wish we could have trained someone else for the mission. The timetable just made it impossible. It wasn't what we planned."

"I think it'll be better this way. Easier to train Turk to get along with the snake eaters than to have one of them try and figure out the aircraft."

"But—"

"They'll make it out," Danny told her, reading the concern on her face. "I would have preferred it if it were our team," he admitted, "but they were already there. They'll do fine."

"God, I hope you're right." Breanna's whole body seemed to heave as she sighed; she looked as if she were carrying an immense weight. "The second orbiter will be launched tomorrow night. Once it's in place so we have full backup, we'll proceed. Assuming nothing happens between now and then."

"Sounds good," said Danny.

Breanna rose. "I don't think it will be necessary. I think they'll make it out."

"So do I," answered Danny. "I'm sure of it."

3

Iran

THE NEW HIDING PLACE WAS A COLLECTION OF CRAGS at the back end of what had been a farm in the foothills. It hadn't been tilled in years, and the two men who'd been watching it reported that they hadn't seen anyone nearby since they'd arrived some forty-eight hours before.

"We're near a road the Quds Force uses to truck arms from the capital to the Taliban in western Afghanistan," said the captain, leading Turk and Grease to a shallow cave where they could rest. "That's good and bad—good, because we're likely to be left alone. Bad, because if someone spots us, they're likely to be armed. And there'll be a bunch of them."

"We'll be ready, Cap," said Grease.

"Probably never come. Pilot, you should get some rest." The captain took a quick look around. "I'll wake you when it's time to go. You got about eight, nine hours."

Turk set the control pack down against the back wall of the cave, then leaned against it. There were no blankets or sleeping bags—they would have been dead weight on the mission.

Better bullets than a pillow.

One of the trainers had said that in Arizona. Not Grease. But who? And when? The sessions, so intense at the time, were now blurred in his memory. Everything was blurred.

He should sleep. He needed to be alert.

"What'd they do with the car?" he asked Grease.

"They'll get rid of it somewhere."

"Were they civilians? The people who came to the house. It was a civilian car."

"I don't know who they were. Would it matter, though?" added Grease. "We have to do this. We have to succeed. If we don't do it, a lot more people are going to die. A lot."

Turk didn't disagree. And yet he was disturbed by the idea that they had killed the civilians.

"Rest easy, Pilot," said Dome, checking on them. "You got a busy night ahead of you."

"Is that my nickname now?" Turk asked.

"Could be. There's a lot worse."

Turk shifted around against the backpack, trying to get to sleep. As his head drifted, Turk remembered falling asleep with Li the night before he left. He relived it in his mind, hoping it would help him nod off, or at least shift his mind into neutral.

4

Washington, D.C.

"I'VE NEVER SMOKED IN MY LIFE." PRESIDENT TODD rose from the chair, defiant, angry, ready to do battle. "Never."

"I know." Amanda Ross raised her gaze just

enough to fix the President's eyes. Dr. Ross had been Todd's personal physician for nearly twenty years, dating to Todd's first stay in Washington as a freshman congresswoman. "I'm sorry. Very sorry."

"Don't be sorry." Todd folded her arms and tried to temper her voice. They were in the President's Sitting Room on the second floor of the White House, used by Todd as a private, after-hours office, a place she could duck into late at night while her husband slept in the bedroom next door. Now it was two o'clock in the afternoon, and with the exception of the Secret Service detail just outside the door, the floor was empty, but Todd didn't want to broadcast her condition to even her most trusted aides. "Just give me the details plainly."

"It's a relatively . . . well not rare, but lesser, um . . ." The doctor stumbled for words.

"Lung cancer," said Todd, a little sharper than she wished. "Yes."

"I'm sorry, Chris. Madam President."

"Chris is fine. We've known each other long enough for that." Todd reached her hand to the doctor's arm and patted it. "I do want to know everything. And I'm not blaming you."

"I know."

Todd squeezed the doctor's arm, then sat back down in the chair. "Tell me everything you know about large cell undifferentiated carcinoma. I won't interrupt until you're done."

"I'M NOT RESIGNING." PRESIDENT TODD POINTED HER finger at her husband. For just a moment he was the enemy, he was the cancer.

"Resectioning your lung, followed by chemo? *Chris*-tine."

The way he said her name, dragging it out so that it was a piece of music—it took her back in time to a dozen different occasions, all difficult and yet somehow happily nostalgic now. She loved him dearly—but if she didn't stay hard, if she didn't stay angry, she would crumple.

"I did not take my oath only to give up two years into my term."

"Three, I think." He looked over his reading glasses. He was sitting up in bed, reading his latest mystery novel, as was his bedtime habit for all the years she'd known him. "And don't think I haven't counted the days."

"In any event, I'm not giving up."

"Jesus, it's not giving up, Christine."

"I have a responsibility to the people who elected me. To the country."

"Not to yourself?"

"The office comes first."

"Well maybe you should think about the sort of job you'll be doing when you're vomiting twenty-four/seven from the chemo."

Her lip began to quaver. She felt her toughness start to fade. "You're so cruel."

Daniel Todd put the book down and got out of bed. He glided across the room, forty years of wear and tear vanishing in an eye-blink. He reached down to the chair and pulled her up, folding her gently in his grasp. He put his cheek next to hers. She smelled the faint sweetness of the bourbon he'd drunk earlier in the evening lingering in his breath.

"I love you, Chris. I'll stand by you, whatever you decide. But honestly, love, just for once, could you please think about yourself? Your health. The Republic will survive."

"I know it will, Dan."

The President bent her face toward his shoulder, wiping away the single tear that had slipped from her eye.

And then she was over it, back in control.

"I get to the point where I can't carry out my duties, then, yes, yes, then I will resign. But the doctor assures me—"

"Now listen—"

"The doctor *assures* me that it is at an early stage. There's hope. A lot of hope. And a plan to deal with it."

"I know there's hope."

Todd rested against her husband's arms for another few seconds, then gently pushed him away. She took his hands, and together they went and sat on the edge of the bed.

"When are you going to go public?" he asked.

"I'm not sure yet."

"You can't keep it a secret."

"I realize that. But there's a lot going on at the moment."

"Chris-tine. There is always a lot going on."

"I think what I'll do is announce it right before the surgery. That's the most appropriate time."

"Says you."

"Yes, but I'm paid to make that decision." She smiled at him; Reid was always telling her the same thing. "Besides, there's no sense worrying people beforehand."

"You won't tell your staff?"

"I will. But doing that is almost a sure guarantee that it will go public."

"What about your reelection campaign?"

"That—That is a problem."

"You're *not* running for reelection."

"No. I agree." Todd had given it a great deal of thought. Even if things did work out right—and she was sure they would—she didn't think the public would vote for someone who'd had lung cancer. True, attitudes about cancer were changing, but they weren't changing that much. Todd herself wasn't sure whether she would give someone a job knowing he or she had cancer that would require aggressive treatment. So the best thing to do would be not to run. She'd been on the fence anyway; this just pushed her off.

"I'll avoid the issue for a while," she told her husband. "If I make myself a lame duck, Congress will be even more of a pain."

"Avoid the issue, or put off a decision?" asked her husband.

"The decision is made, love." She let go of his hand and patted it, then moved back on the bed. Her nightgown snagged a little; she rearranged it neatly.

"They'll hound you until you say something, once the news about the cancer is out."

"True. But I'm used to that. The big problem is lining up a successor."

"You're going to line up a successor?"

"If I can, yes."

"How?"

"With my support. I have my ways."

"Not Mantis?" He meant Jay Mantis, the vice president.

"Don't even think it." Privately, Todd called him the Preying Mantis, and it was anything but a compliment. He was the most duplicitous person she had ever met in politics, and that was saying a great deal.

"Who then?"

"I'll tell you when I've made up my mind."

"I have some ideas."

"I'll bet you do." She pulled back the covers and pushed her feet under. "I have more immediate problems to worry about over the next few days."

"Chris."

"Don't be a mother hen."

"A father hen."

Todd let her head sink into the pillow. Her health would wait; she had to deal with the Iranian mess first. Which meant a few hours nap, then back to work.

"Feel like going to sleep?" she asked her husband.

"To bed, yes. Sleep no."

"That sounds a lot like what I was thinking. Let me turn off the light."

5

Iran

BY NINE O'CLOCK TURK HAD GIVEN UP ALL ATTEMPTS at sleeping and lay on his back, eyes open, staring at the ceiling of the cave they were huddled in. He was ready for the mission, ready to succeed. But time moved as if it were a man crawling across the desert inch by inch.

He got up and left Grease sleeping to see what the others were doing outside. Dread, the medic who had looked him over, was pulling a radio watch, manning the communications gear with Gorud, the CIA officer.

"How we doing?" Turk asked Dread. The main com gear was a surprisingly small handheld satellite radio-phone that allowed the team to communicate with Whiplash and its parent command. Dread also had a separate device to talk to other team members who were working in Iran, including two-man teams watching the target. There was a backup radio, much larger, in a pack.

"We're all good," answered Dread. "I thought you were sleeping."

"Can't."

"I have some sleeping pills. Like Ambien, but stronger."

"I heard that stuff will make you sleepwalk."

"Not this. Puts you down and out."

"Then I might not get up. You got any coffee?"

Dread shook his head. "Can't cook here. Might

see the smoke or the flame. Or maybe smell the coffee. If we had any."

"None?"

"Got something that's basically Red Bull. You want it?"

"No, maybe not."

"Caffeine pills?"

"Maybe I'll try to sleep again in a little while." Turk sat down next to him, legs crossed on the ground. "Any sign that we were followed?"

"No. That house hadn't been lived in for at least three months," added Dread. "Don't know what they were up to. Came to buy it or maybe have sex. Two guys, though."

"Weird, being in somebody else's country."

"What do you mean?"

"I just—nothing. They don't seem to know it's a war."

"It's not a war. We don't want one. That's why we're here, right?"

"Are you ready to do your job?" asked Gorud. His voice sounded hoarse.

"Yeah," answered Turk.

"Then worry about that."

"I don't have to worry about that. I can do it," added Turk, feeling challenged.

Turk stayed away as the Delta team traded shifts. Around noon he had something to eat—a cold MRE—then tried once more to sleep. This time he was successful; nodding off after nearly an hour, he slid into a dull blackness.

The next thing he knew, Grease was shaking his leg back and forth.

"Time to get up," said the sergeant.

Turk rolled over from his back and pushed up to his knees. His neck was stiff.

"We're leaving in five," said Grease.

"Got it."

"We'll get food at the airport."

"OK." Turk unzipped the control backpack and checked it, more out of superstition than fear that it had been taken or compromised. Satisfied, he secured the pack and put it on his back.

It was three o'clock. He wished it was much later.

"Car's here," said someone outside.

Turk was surprised to see the civilian Toyota from the night before making its way up the rock-strewn trail. He thought they'd gotten rid of it.

"The three of us will use the car to get to the airport," said Grease. "We'll be less conspicuous. The rest of the team will be in the troop truck a short distance away. Put the backpack in the trunk."

"I don't want the control unit out of my sight."

"You're not going to leave the car."

"It stays with me." Turk's only concession was to take it off his back and put it on the floor between his legs.

"If we are stopped at a checkpoint, you are Russians," said Gorud after Turk and Grease climbed into the backseat. Gorud was at the wheel and a Delta soldier named Silver took the front passenger seat; his accent was old New York, so thick it could have been a put on.

"We are all Russians," repeated Gorud, making

sure they knew their cover. "We are looking for new oil fields and business opportunities."

"Right," said Turk.

"You all speak Russian," answered Gorud.

"*Da*," said Silver.

"Yeah," said Grease, who then added a phrase that translated to the effect that Gorud could perform several unnatural acts if he had any question of the sergeant's abilities.

Gorud scowled but turned to Turk. "Captain?"

"*Ya govoryu na russkim dostatochno khorosho?*" answered Turk.

"Tell me that you're an engineer."

"I don't know the word."

"*Inzhenr.*"

Gorud worked him through a few different phrases. Turk couldn't remember much—it had been years since he'd spoken much Russian, and then it was mixed with English as he spoke with his aunt and grandmother. But any Iranians they met were very unlikely to speak any themselves, and in any event, the CIA officer had told him he shouldn't talk at all.

"For once we agree," said Turk.

"Use a *Ruuushan* accent with your *Enggg-lish*," said Gorud, demonstrating. "You speak like this."

"I'll try."

"Say 'I will' instead of 'I'll.' Do not use slang. You are not a native speaker. You don't use so many contrac-*shuns*. Draw some syllables out. Like Russian."

Turk imagined he heard the voices of his relatives and their friends speaking in another room, then tried to emulate them. "I will try to remember this," he said.

"Hmmph," answered Gorud, still disappointed.

Turk folded his arms, leaning back in the seat. The CIA officer passed out passports and other papers that identified them as Russians, along with visas that declared they had been in the country for three days, having landed in Tehran. Among his other documents was a letter from a high ranking official in the Revolutionary Guard, directing that he be admitted to an oil field for inspection; the letter of course was bogus and the oil field far away, but it would undoubtedly impress any low ranking police officer or soldier who was "accidentally" given it to read.

The euros they were all carrying would impress him even more. Or so Turk believed.

He felt the vaguest sense of panic as a car approached from the opposite lane. It eased slightly as the car passed, then snuck back despite the open road ahead. It was hours before dusk; Gorud was vague about how long it would take to get to the airport, and not knowing bothered Turk.

Gorud's attitude bothered him more—the CIA operative ought by all rights to be treating him with respect, and as a coequal: without him, there was no mission.

A pair of white pickup trucks sparked Turk's anxiety; similar trucks were used throughout the Middle East and much of Africa by armies and militias. But these were simply pickups, with a single driver in each. Turk closed his eyes after they were gone.

"Just get me to the damn helicopter," he muttered.

"What?" asked Grease.

"I just want to get on with it. You know?"

"It'll be here soon enough. Don't wish yourself into trouble."

The rugged terrain around them was mostly empty, though occasionally a small orchard or farm sat in a sheltered arm of a hill along the highway. They passed a small village to the west, then passed through a larger collection of battered buildings, metal and masonry. Sand blew across the lot, furling and then collapsing on a line of concrete barriers, which were half covered in sand dunes.

"Old military barracks," said Silver. "Abandoned a couple of years ago."

"Glad they're empty," said Turk.

Gorud raised his head and stared out the window as they came around a curve at a high pass in the hills. The city lay ahead, but he was looking to his left, past the driver. Turk followed his gaze. He could see a rail line in the distance and tracks in the rumpled sand. What looked like several revetments lay a little farther up the hills. A large dump truck sat in the distance, the setting sun turning its yellow skin white. There were more beyond it.

"What's going on here?" Silver asked.

"Good question," said Gorud. "There are mines—but . . ." His voice trailed off.

"*But?*"

"Missiles, maybe," he said. "Or something else."

A reminder, thought Turk, that the problem they were dealing with was vast, and might not— would not—end with this operation.

The airport appeared ahead, a crooked T of tarmac in the light red dirt and lighter sand. They turned with the road, skimming around an empty traffic circle and then toward the terminal complex, driving down an access road four lanes wide. It was as empty as the highway they'd come down on. An unmanned gate stood ahead, its long arm raised forlornly. They passed through quickly.

The troop truck with the rest of their team continued on the highway, driving around to the south of the airport. They were on their own now; any contingency would have to be handled by Gorud, by Silver, by Grease, by himself—he touched the butt of his rifle under the front seat with the toe of his boot, reassuring himself that he was ready.

Immediately past the gate the road narrowed. Tall, thin green trees rose on either side; beyond them were rows of green plants, studded between sprinkler pipes. Two white vans sat in front of the parking lot in front of a cluster of administrative buildings. The buildings themselves looked empty, and there was no traffic on the access road that continued past the largest building and went south. Just beyond the building, they turned and drove through the lot to another road that ran around the perimeter of the airstrips. This took them past a truck parking area on the outside of the complex, beyond a tall chain-link fence. Turk caught a glimpse of their truck moving on the highway, shadowing them.

The access road took them to the front of the civilian passenger terminal, dark and seemingly forgotten. They turned left and drove around the building, directly onto the apron where the aircraft gates were located.

"Nothing here," said Silver as they turned. "No plane."

"I see." Gorud looked left and right.

"What do you want me to do?"

"Keep going."

"Onto the runway?"

"No. Onto the construction road at the far end. We'll take it back around."

"If it's sand we may get stuck."

"Chance it. We don't want to look like we took a wrong turn if we're being watched. We're examining the airport—we would fly equipment in through here. We're all Russian. Remember that."

"Problem?" asked Grease.

"The Israeli and the helicopter should have been at the terminal," said Gorud. "I don't see it."

"What Israeli?" said Turk. "Is that who is bringing the helicopter?"

Gorud said nothing. He didn't have to; the expression on his face shouted disdain. Belatedly, Turk realized that "the Israeli" could only be their contact. He also guessed that the man was likely a Mossad agent or officer; the Israeli spy unit would have numerous agents studded around the country, and they would surely cooperate with the U.S. on a mission like this.

But it was also quite possible the man wasn't Mossad at all. Everything was subterfuge—they were Russian, they were Iranian, they didn't even exist.

"Place looks abandoned," said Grease.

"It is," replied Gorud. "More or less. Most airports outside Tehran look like this with the sanctions. Even if they have an air force unit, which this one doesn't."

"There was an aircraft on the left across from the terminal as we came in," Turk said. "I didn't get much of a look. Maybe that was it."

"Was it an Mi-8?"

"I don't think so. It looked a little small for an Mi-8."

"We'll go back."

"Can you call your contact?" Grease asked.

Gorud shook his head. Turk guessed that he was afraid the missed connection meant that the man on the other end had been apprehended. Calling would only make things worse—for them.

"We can do it by ground if we have to," Turk said. "If we have to."

Silver took them across the dirt roads at the side of the terminal. A half-dozen excavations dotted the surrounding fields; all were overrun with dirt and sand that had drifted in. There were construction trucks on the other side of the entrance area, parked neatly in rows. As they drove closer, Turk saw that they were covered with a thick layer of grit. They'd been parked in the unfinished lot for months; work had stalled for a variety of reasons, most likely chief among them the Western economic boycott.

They had just turned back toward the administrative buildings when Turk spotted a light in the sky beyond the main runway.

"Something coming in," he said.

"Take the right ahead, bring us back to the edge of the terminal apron," Gorud told Silver.

Turk craned his head to see out the window as they turned and the aircraft approached.

"It's not a helicopter," he told them. "Light plane—looks like a Cessna or something similar. No lights."

"What should I do?" asked Silver.

"Keep going, as I said," snapped Gorud.

They parked at the edge of the terminal road, across from the gates and close enough to see the runway. The plane was a high-winged civilian aircraft, a Cessna 182 or something similar. The aircraft taxied to the end of the runway, then turned around quickly and came over to the terminal apron.

"Wait here," said Gorud, getting out.

"Something is fucked up," muttered Silver as the CIA officer trotted toward the plane.

Turk continued sketching an alternative plan in his head. In some ways it would be easier to work from the ground, he thought. His part would be easier: there'd be no possibility of losing a connection, and he wouldn't have to worry about the distraction of working in a small aircraft. It'd be harder to escape, of course, but that was what he had the others for.

The key would be getting there. It was a long way off.

Gorud ran back to the car.

"It's our plane," he said. "Only two of us will fit. Come on, Captain."

Grease put his hand on Turk's shoulder. "I go where he goes."

"You won't fit in the aircraft," said Gorud.

"Then you stay on the ground," said Grease.

Turk pushed out of the car, leaving Gorud and Grease to sort out the situation themselves. The man in the right front seat of the aircraft—the copilot's seat—got out to help him. He pushed his seat up and nudged Turk into the plane.

"What happened to the helicopter?" Turk asked as he got in.

The pilot shook his head.

"You speak English?" Turk asked.

Another head shake. The cockpit smelled like a locker room after an intense basketball game: sweat, and a lot of it. Perspiration ran thick on the back of the pilot's neck. His shirt was drenched.

Grease slipped in next to him.

"Let's get the hell out of here," said the Delta sergeant. "Come on."

The man who'd gotten out of the plane climbed back in. Turk assumed he was the Israeli.

"What happened to the helicopter?" asked Turk again.

"Contingency," said the man. "This will have to do. Gorud is not coming?"

"Not unless he sits on your lap," said Grease.

"Too much weight anyway," the man said as he slammed and secured the plane door. The plane moved fitfully back toward the runway.

"I'm Turk," said Turk, reaching toward the front.

"No names," said the Israeli.

Turk slipped back and looked at Grease. "At least I know now I'm on the right plane," he muttered.

The faintest of smiles appeared on Grease's lips.

6

CIA campus, Virginia

"SPACECRAFT TWO IS SIXTY SECONDS TO TARGET area," said Colonel Schaffer, the Air Force liaison tracking the X-37B. "They need a final go to launch."

Breanna glanced at Jonathon Reid, then back at the screen showing where Turk was. The pilot was wearing a small ring that allowed the Whiplash network to locate him at all times.

"Has Gorud sent the signal?" she asked Reid.

"Still waiting," he replied, his voice so soft she could barely hear it over the whisper of the air conditioner. It was a habit of his—the more tense he felt, the quieter he made his voice. Undoubtedly it had served the old CIA hand very well when he was in the field.

Gorud was supposed to signal that the operation was proceeding by calling a prearranged number in Egypt that they were monitoring. The number belonged to an Iranian who spied on the West, a nice little piece of misdirection cooked up by Gorud himself. They expected the call when they boarded the helicopter, but though Turk was clearly aboard and moving, there had been no signal.

Breanna stared at the screen, watching as Turk moved away from the airport. They didn't have real-time visual of the operation, having decided that even a stealthy UAV might give them away if something went wrong. Iran, using Russian technology, had already demonstrated the ability to track American drones.

There was something wrong about the way the aircraft was moving—it didn't seem like a helicopter.

"Is the X-37 close enough to Birjand to pick up that aircraft?" Breanna asked Schaffer.

"Negative. Not even close. Is there a problem?"

"Turk's supposed to be in a helicopter."

"What's wrong, Breanna?" asked Reid.

"I'm pretty sure Turk's in a plane, not a helicopter as planned."

"Maybe they had to change their arrangement," said Reid. "Will he be able to control the UAVs?"

"He should. The question is whether they can stay in the area, and do so without attracting too much attention."

"Maybe Gorud thought the plane would be less noticeable," said Reid.

At one of the original briefing sessions on the planning, someone had mentioned that there were often helicopter flights in the area; she remembered quite clearly because she'd asked a question about it.

"I'm not trying to second-guess their operation," she told Reid. "I am concerned because we haven't confirmed that it is our aircraft. Gorud hasn't checked in."

"Understood."

"Ma'am." Schaffer cleared his throat. "If you want a launch, you need to authorize. The window on this pass is only forty-five seconds."

If she authorized the launch and Turk wasn't in a position to "catch" the UAVs, the mission would be aborted and the aircraft lost. The operation would have to wait another twenty-four hours, and the margin of error would be cut in half.

Breanna looked again at the screen plotting Turk's location. He might be heading for the target. Or he might be going to Tehran—the logical place to bring a prisoner.

Something her father had told her years before popped into her head: *There are always reasons to put off a mission, Bree. A lot of them, and they're always good ones. Going ahead is always the lonelier way. But it's almost always the better choice.*

"Launch," she told Schaffer.

7

Iran

TURK BRACED HIMSELF AS THE CESSNA BANKED sharply. It turned nearly 270 degrees in what felt like a half second, dropping at the same time. His stomach felt as if it had hopped up to his eyeballs.

"What the hell are we doing?" he demanded as the pilot leveled off.

"We have to avoid being detected," said the man in the right front seat. While Turk labeled him the Israeli because of what Gorud had said earlier, his accent sounded Eastern European. But then those two things were not necessarily a contradiction.

"You haven't told me what happened to the helicopter."

"This will have to do," said the Israeli.

"What happened?" snapped Turk.

"It's immaterial," said the Israeli. "This is what we have. Do the job."

"Listen—"

Grease patted him twice on his leg, silently trying to calm him. The pilot started speaking quickly in Farsi.

"Let's all relax," said Grease, first in English, then Farsi. He turned to Turk. "You OK?"

"He's going to have to stay very close to the site," Turk said. The plane dipped sharply. "And he's going to have to fly a hell of a lot better than he's flying."

"He's a good pilot," said the Israeli.

"And I'm a good truck driver."

They leveled off, the plane steadying. They were flying fast and low, and it was possible that the pilot was just jittery because he was a little nervous—the Israeli didn't exactly put people at ease. Even a light plane, if unfamiliar, could be a handful. Turk tried to give him the benefit of the doubt, leaning back in his seat and recalculating the mission in his head, rearranging what he would have to do.

As long as they stayed in the general area, they'd be OK. He'd have the Cessna fly a long, continuous circuit as close to the target as the pilot dared. Once he acquired the UAVs, things would happen pretty fast.

Turk checked his watch. They were four hours from the rendezvous time. The mission plan had called for the helicopter to take about two hours getting to the refuel site; the target area was another hour and a half away.

"Are we stopping to refuel?" Turk asked.

"Nonstop," said the Israeli. "Straight line."

Turk leaned forward, checking the gauges. The pilot had the throttle at max; they were pushing 140 knots.

"Set your speed to 110 knots," Turk said, calculating their flight time. "One hundred and ten knots."

The pilot made no move to comply.

"Tell him to drop his speed to 110 knots," Turk told the Israeli. "Or I'll strangle him."

Grease glanced at Turk, then took out his pistol.

The Israeli said something to the pilot. The pilot disagreed, and they started to argue.

"Look, we don't want to get there too soon," said Turk. "If 110 knots is too slow for the aircraft, then we'll have to change course and fly around a bit. But he's heading straight for the target area. I don't know what you've told him, or what you think we're doing, but we don't want to get there too soon. Do you understand? This isn't a race. We have to be there in a precise window of time."

"He says we have to maintain speed," said the Israeli harshly.

"The pilot does exactly what the captain says," Grease announced, raising the Iranian-made Sig and nudging it against the edge of the pilot's neck, "or he dies."

The pilot glanced back nervously. The plane edged with him, reacting to his hand on the yoke.

"Don't be a fool," hissed the Israeli. "You'll kill us all."

"He's going too fast," said Turk. "Tell him to relax. Tell him I'm a pilot, too. I know what I'm talking about."

"He knows where he has to go and when to get there," said the Israeli, only slightly less antagonistic. "He wants a cushion."

"We can't afford a cushion. This isn't a transport. Tell him there's a penalty for getting there too soon."

The Israeli frowned.

"Does he know what we're doing?" Turk asked. "Do you?"

"He knows the very minimum he needs to know. As do I."

The pilot said something. His voice was high-pitched, jittery. A thick ribbon of sweat poured down the side of his face. Turk thought of finding a place for them to land and taking over flying the plane. But he couldn't do that *and* guide the UAVs.

"Tell him I know that he's nervous, but I trust that he can fly the plane," said Turk. "Tell him I'm a test pilot. And I like his skills. Tell him to relax, just relax and fly. He's a good pilot. A very good pilot."

The last bit was a lie—a rather large one—but Turk's goal was to get the man to trust him, and accurately evaluating how he was flying would not do that.

The pilot nodded, though there was no sign that he relaxed.

"Tell him that we'll be flying a low figure eight when we get to the area," said Turk. "Even if we get there when planned, we'll have to do that for more than a half hour. That's a long time. We don't want to be detected. The longer we're there, the more chance of that—that's why we want to slow down. And it'll conserve fuel."

"I want him to know the minimum necessary," answered the Israeli. "Telling him he has to orbit for a half hour isn't going to calm him down."

"Tell him whatever the hell you want," said Grease, "but make him do what Turk says."

"I think we should all calm down," said the Israeli. "There's no need for excitement."

"Then let's follow the captain's game plan. To the letter," said Grease.

8

CIA campus, Virginia

"THE CALL HAS BEEN MADE," SAID REID, RISING. "That's their plane."

Relieved, Breanna looked at the large area map of Iran projected on the front wall. They had hours to go; she knew from experience the time would alternately drag and race, as if her perceptions were split in two.

"Breanna, could we speak?" said Reid, touching her elbow.

"Sure."

Breanna got up and led Reid down the hall to her office. The lights flipped on as she entered. She saw the small clock on the credenza at the back, thought of her daughter, and wondered what subject she would be studying now.

Just starting English. They always did that before lunch at eleven.

Breanna stopped in front of her desk, standing at the side of the room. She'd been sitting too long; she felt like standing.

"Gorud made a call from the airport," said Reid. He stood as well. The gray-haired CIA veteran seemed a little more tired than normal, but there was good reason for that. "After the plane took off."

"Plane?"

"There was a problem and they had to substitute. There wasn't enough space in the aircraft. Gorud opted to stay on the ground. It was either him or Grease."

"I see."

"He decided it was important enough to break the planned protocol. That's why it took so long. I just wanted you to know. I've got to go back over to the big building," Reid added, using his slang for the Agency's administrative headquarters across the way. "I have to run back for a quick meeting. I'll be here again in time for the actual show."

"OK."

"You'll alert the President?" said Reid.

"Of course. I better get back inside. The WB-57 will be launching from Afghanistan soon."

9

Iran

Turk ran through all the tests a third time, receiving one more confirmation that everything was in top order and ready. The main screen on the controller, which resembled a laptop, was currently displaying a situation map, with their location plotted against a satellite image. He tapped the window to the left, expanding it and then selecting the preselect for the target area. The image that appeared looked at first glance like a sepia-toned photo of capillaries crisscrossing a human heart. Only after he zoomed the image did it start to look something like it was: a synthesized image of the target bunker, taken in real time.

The image was being provided by a WB-57, flying at high altitude just over the border from Iraq. Owned by NASA but currently being flown by an Air Force pilot, the WB-57 was a greatly modified Cold War era B-57 Canberra. Originally designed as a bomber, the high-flying, ultrastable plane had proven adept at reconnaissance from the earliest days of its career. After their retirement from the bomber fleet, the planes continued to do yeoman's service during the Cold War, snapping photos of missile sites and other installations. When no longer useful to the Air Force, a handful of planes were taken in by NASA, which made them into high-flying scientific platforms, gathering data for a number of scientific projects.

This WB-57 had been borrowed from NASA for a more ominous assignment. Inside its belly was an earth-penetrating system that could map deep-underground bunkers in real time. The gear would be used to monitor the nano-UAVs as they penetrated the target.

Related to the technology developed for the HAARP program, the complex monitoring system used the auroral electrojet—a charged-particle stream in the ionosphere high above the earth—to send a burst of dispersed ELF, or extremely low frequency waves, into the bunker. The WB-57 tracked the waves, using them to draw pictures of what was happening beneath the earth's surface. The angle and direction of the waves meant the WB-57 could stay a considerable distance away from the bunker.

Even at 60,000 feet the plane was vulnerable to all manner of defenses, from Iran's recently acquired Russian S-200s and even older Hawk missiles left from the Shah's era. And while it could provide detailed images of what was underground, its sophisticated equipment could not provide even the fuzziest picture of the ground's surface. For that Turk knew he would have to look at the video provided by the Hydras as they approached the target.

He fiddled back and forth with the screen configuration, trying to decide how much priority to give the optical view of the lead UAVs. He tried his favored arrangement for the Sabre UAVs, dividing the screen into two unequal parts, the right side about three times as large as the left. He then created a pair of panels on the right, with an area plot at the bottom and the larger, forward video feed at the top. The left panels were split into four equal boxes, each to receive a feed from a different UAV. That would make it easier to switch as the mission progressed.

The control unit bounced on Turk's knees as the Cessna jerked upward. They were flying in a mountain range, at roughly 8,000 feet, which left a hundred feet and sometimes far less between their wings and the nearby mountaintops. The pilot was even more nervous than he'd been when they took off, and on top of that appeared physically exhausted. He kept glancing to his right as he flew, checking on the Israeli in the right seat but rarely saying a word.

The Israeli said even less. His attitude made the severe Gorud look like a carnival clown high on laughing gas. Turk had begun thinking of him as the Grim Reaper, but *grim* barely described his demeanor.

"This shows where we are, right?" Grease asked, pointing at the lower map on the control unit.

"Not exactly," answered Turk. "It shows where the target area is. Then when I add this, we get a GPS indicator to show that we're in it. But I don't want to query too often, on the off chance that the Iranians will monitor the signal."

"Is that likely?"

Turk shrugged. It wasn't, but at this point the fewer chances the better.

"So we're close?"

"We're a little ahead of schedule."

"That's not good?" Grease said, reading Turk's frown.

"We'll have to keep flying around. I'm afraid of being seen. There are radars all along this area, and a major antiaircraft site here at Natanz. Not that they'd need much to shoot us down."

The antiaircraft sites had all been marked on a special map in the briefing files, which were destroyed when Grease torched the pad computer. But in truth the location was immaterial—the Cessna was already well within their range. The success of the plan hinged on staying low, near the mountaintops. As long as they did, the radars associated with the missile batteries were unlikely to see them.

"You're going to have to hold the plane a lot steadier once we reach the target area," Turk told the pilot as the aircraft bucked. "We'll be there in ten minutes."

The pilot didn't answer.

"Tell him," Turk told the Israeli.

"He knows."

"Tell him anyway."

He did. The pilot replied curtly, apparently not agreeing with whatever the man said.

"He suggested I fly the plane myself," said the Israeli.

Turk laughed. It was the first time the man actually sounded like a pilot.

He reached forward and patted the man on the shoulder. Then he took the folded map on the board clipped to the instrument panel.

"This is where we have to stay," he said, drawing the safe area within five miles of the target. He showed it to the pilot and then to the Israeli. "We fly a steady figure eight and hold altitude. We're on the west side of the mountains. We have to stay steady until I say we go home. It'll be a while."

The Israeli explained. The pilot nodded.

"When he comes over the peak ahead, tell him

to bank southward," Turk told the Israeli. "Take it south gently, and stay in the area I've outlined."

As bright as the stars were, the ground was pitch-black, with no lights visible anywhere nearby. The city of Badroud lay some twenty miles beyond the peak, off their left wing. Turk expected to see a yellow glow in that direction as they turned. When he didn't, he checked their position again. The GPS locator in the control unit had them exactly twenty-two miles from Badroud, as did his handheld unit. They were precisely on the course.

Early, though—the UAVs wouldn't be in range for twenty-two more minutes.

"We're looking very good," he announced, deciding to look on the positive side. "Just keep flying the way we planned, and everything will be fine."

10

Omidiyeh, Iran

CAPTAIN PARSA VAHID TOOK HIS HELMET IN THE CROOK of his arm as he got out of the Khodro pickup truck, balancing the rest of his gear in his right hand as he reached for his briefcase with his left. Then he spun and kicked the door closed, walking toward the front of the ready hangar. The nose of his MiG-29 sat just inside the open archway. The aircraft was armed and fueled, sitting on ready-standby in the special hangar.

The pilot who'd been on watch until now was standing on the tarmac outside the building. He shook his head as Vahid approached.

"You're late, Parsa," said the pilot.

"Five minutes," insisted Vahid. "I needed to eat."

"You're so busy in the day that you couldn't eat earlier?"

Vahid shrugged. "If there had been a call before now, it would have been yours."

"Phhhh. A call. The dead will rise before we fly in combat," said the other pilot disgustedly, starting for the pickup truck. "The Israelis are cowards."

"And the Americans, too?"

"Worse."

"Good evening, Captain," said Sergeant Hami, the night crew chief. "We are ready to fly tonight?"

"Ready, Chief. My plane?"

"Ho-ho," said Hami, his jowls shaking back and forth. "We are in top shape and ready to fly when the signal comes."

"So it's tonight, then?"

"With God's will."

Vahid walked over and put his gear down on a table at the side of the hangar. A pair of metal chairs flanked the table; he and Hami would customarily play cards there for most of the watch. But first he would inspect the aircraft.

"A nice night to fly," said Sergeant Hami, waiting as he set down his helmet and personal gear. His accent was thick with Tehran, reminding Vahid of the city's many charms. "You will shoot down some Americans, yes?"

"If I have the chance."

The nights were always like this: bravado and enthusiasm at first, then dull boredom as the hours dragged on. The first night, Vahid had sat in the cockpit, waiting to take off in an instant. Even the base commander now realized that was foolish. The U.S. forces in the Gulf were paper ghosts, strong in theory but never present. They kept well away from Iranian borders.

Of course, the same might be said of the Iranian air force, even Vahid's squadron. The four MiG-29s, the most advanced in the Iranian air force, had been moved to Omidiyeh air base six weeks before. The base had been largely abandoned in the years following the Iran-Iraq war; while still theoretically open for commercial traffic, the only civilians Vahid had seen were the members of a glider club, who inspected but did not fly their planes the first week of the squadron's arrival. Since then the base had been empty, except for military personnel.

He began his walk-around at the MiG's nose, touching her chin for good luck—a superstition handed down to him by his first flight instructor. The instructor had flown in the Iran-Iraq war, where he had served briefly as a wingman to Jalil Zandi, the legendary ace of the Iranian air force.

Even without the connection to greatness, Vahid would have venerated the instructor, Colonel One Eye. (The nickname was not literally accurate, but came from his habit of closing one eye while shooting on a rifle range.) The colonel could fly everything the Iranian air force possessed, from F-86 Sabres, now long retired, to MiG-29s. Like Zandi, One Eye had flown Tomcats during the war against Iraq, recording a kill against an Iraqi Mirage.

Vahid stopped to admire the plane. The curved cowl at the wing root gave it a sleek, athletic look; for the pilot, it evoked the look of a tiger, springing to the kill. The export-version MiG was one of thirty acquired by Iran in the mid-1990s; the air force now had just over a dozen in flying condition.

A siren sounded in the distance. Vahid froze.

A fire?

No.

No!

"The alert!" yelled Sergeant Hami. "The alert!"

Vahid grabbed his helmet from the table, then ran to the ladder at the side of the plane. As he climbed upward, a van with the rest of the ground crew raced across the concrete apron, jerking to a stop in front of the hangar. Hami helped Vahid into the cockpit, while the arriving crewmen began pulling the stops away from the plane and opening the rear door of the hangar.

Two nights before, a false alert had gotten Vahid out of the hangar, but he was called back before reaching the runway, some 1,000 meters away: the radars had picked up an Iranian passenger flight in the Gulf and, briefly, mistaken it for an American spy plane. He expected this was something along the same lines. Still expecting the flashing light at the top of the hangar to snap off, he powered up the MiG, turning over one engine and then quickly ramping the other. Hami, back on the ground, shook his fist at him, giving him a thumbs-up.

Vahid began rolling forward. The tower barked at him, demanding he get airborne. Ignoring them for a moment, he took stock of his controls. Then, at the signal from Sergeant Hami, he went heavy on his engines. The plane strained against her brakes. The gauges pegged with perfect reads. The MiG wanted to fly.

"Shahin One to Tower, request permission to move to runway," said Vahid calmly.

"Go! Go!" answered the controller.

The MiG jerked forward, overanxious. At the other end of the base three pilots were running from the ready room. Their planes would be a few minutes behind. It was Vahid's job to sort things out before they were committed to the battle.

"Cleared for immediate takeoff," said the controller.

Vahid didn't bother to pause as he came to the end of the runway—there were no other flights here, and it was clear he was under orders to get airborne immediately. Selecting full military power, he started the MiG down the runway. The screech of the engines built to a fierce whine. He felt himself starting to lift.

Airborne, he made a quick check of his readouts, then cleaned his landing gear into the aircraft. The MiG leapt forward, rocketing into the night.

Moments later the local air commander came over the radio, giving him his instructions directly.

"You are to fly north by northeast," said the general, "in the direction of Natanz. There are reports of a low-flying airplane near the Naeen train station. We will turn you over to Major Javadpour for a vector."

"Acknowledged."

Vahid had to look at his paper map to find Naeen. It was a dot in the mountains north of the city of Nain, a small town camped at the intersection of several highways that transcribed the Iranian wilderness. He was some five hundred kilometers away.

Major Javadpour directed Vahid to the west of the sighting—he wanted him to fly close to Natanz, one of the country's main nuclear research sites.

Gravity pushed Vahid against the seat as he goosed his afterburners. At full speed he was just over ten minutes away.

"We have no radar contacts at this time," said Javadpour.

"No contacts?"

"We have two eyewitnesses who saw and heard planes. But no radar."

"What sort of aircraft did they see?" asked Vahid.

The controller didn't answer right away, apparently gathering information. Vahid pictured a flight of American B-2 Stealth Bombers, flying low over the terrain. They would pop up before the attack.

He might be too late to stop them. But he would surely destroy them. He had two R-27 air-to-air medium-range missiles and six R-73s, all Russian made, under his wings. The R-27s were radar missiles; he had been told they would have trouble finding B-2s unless he was relatively close, but this didn't bother him at all. The B-2 was slower than his plane, and far less maneuverable. As for the R-73s, they were heat-seekers, very dependable when fired in a rear-quarter attack.

They might have escorts. If so, he would ignore them—the bombers were the far more important target.

Vahid continued to climb and accelerate.

"We still have no contacts at this time. Negative," said Javadpour, coming back on the line. "The eyewitnesses describe a small plane, possibly a drone, very low to the ground."

"A *small* plane?"

"Single engine. It may be civilian. That's all the information I have at this time," added the controller. "Maintain your course. I show you reaching the area in six minutes."

Damn, thought Vahid, another false alarm.

11

Iran

Turk watched the train of triangles as they flowed steadily from the northwest. They were two minutes from the target, traveling at nearly Mach 4, gliding with the momentum of the ship they'd launched from.

He looked up. Grease was sitting stone-faced next to him. The Israeli and the pilot in the front were silent, staring straight into the darkness. They were just over three hundred feet above the nearby slope, with the target area six miles away off the right wing.

"Keep the plane steady," Turk said softly, picking up the small headset. "The words I say will have nothing to do with us, unless I address Grease directly. Grease, if you need me, tap on my leg. But don't need me."

He turned his attention back to the screen, hunching his head down to isolate himself from the others. He was used to distractions, used to splitting himself away from his immediate surroundings to concentrate, but this was a challenge even for him.

The small plane tucked up and down as it came across the mountain slope, buffeted by the wind and twitching with the pilot's nervous hand. A light beep sounded in the headset.

"Ten seconds to acquisition range," the computer told him.

A quick kick of doubt tweaked Turk's stomach: *You can't do this. You haven't trained properly. You will fail.*

You are a failure.

Red letters flashed on the screen before him.

"Establish link," Turk told the computer calmly.

Doubt and fear vanished with the words. The UAVs, still moving with the momentum of their initial launch and the gravity that pulled them to earth, came into his control in quick succession.

It wasn't exactly control. It was more like strong influence. He could stop them or turn them away, goose them ahead or push them down, but for the most part now he was watching as the thirty-six aircraft, each the size of the sat phone sitting in his pocket, plummeted toward the air exchanger hidden in the cluster of rocks on the hillside.

Turk tapped his screen, bringing up the status window where he quickly checked the roster of aircraft. Two were flashing red—the monitors had detected problems. He tapped the names, opening windows with the details. The computer highlighted the difficulties. Both had abnormal heat sensors, suggesting their shields had failed. That would likely degrade the solid Teflon propellant, though with the engines not yet ignited, it was impossible to tell what the actual effect would be.

The most likely effect was incomplete propulsion—they'd lose power too soon to complete the full mission.

"Aircraft 8 and Aircraft 23 forward," Turk said. "Eight and 23 to lead."

"Calculating. Confirmed. Complying."

Turk watched the Hydras shuffle. Moving the problematic aircraft to the front would give them the role of blowing through the grill in the air exchange; their engines wouldn't matter, since they wouldn't be used.

Until this moment the UAVs had been barely guided missiles, with steering vanes rather than wings. Now the computer popped the vanes into wings, extending them and banking the robot planes in a series of circles, separating them into mission clusters and slowing them to a more controllable and maneuverable speed.

More red on the screen. Aircraft 5 was not responding.

Lost. Turk mentally wrote it off. The UAV would dive into the hills, exploding on impact.

Tapping the target area on the sitmap, he looked at the image of the bunker provided by the NASA plane. A small flag appeared at the side; he tapped the flag, and was presented with a three-dimensional wire-frame drawing in the center of the screen. He enlarged it with his index finger.

"Compare infrastructure to known. State deviations," he told the computer.

"Congruency, one hundred percent."

Nothing had changed since the mission was drawn up. They were good to go.

The computer provided an assortment of data on the bunker. One set of numbers in particular caught his eye: there were 387 people in the facility.

Turk hadn't expected that many; the briefing

had indicated a skeleton crew of guards, at best, given the hour. The number seemed very high, but there was no time to double-check it.

The UAVs dropped in twos and threes from the oval path they'd been flying, diving for the air exchanger opening. They were subsonic but still moving incredibly fast, just over 550 knots on average. He saw them in his mind's eye falling above his shoulder, shooting stars on a fateful mission.

"Proximity warning," buzzed the computer. "Control unit moving out of range."

Turk jerked his head up and yelled. "Pilot, get the plane back into the right parameters. Put us where I told you. Now!"

12

Iran, near Natanz

CAPTAIN VAHID CHECKED THE LONG DISTANCE RADAR scan on his MiG-29 a second time, making sure it was clean before contacting his controller.

"No contacts reported," he said. "I am zero-two minutes from Natanz."

"Copy, Shahin One. You have no contacts reported."

It took a moment to process the controller's simple acknowledgment. Obviously excited, his Farsi had a heavy southeastern accent, and the words jumbled together with the static in Vahid's headset.

Natanz was under blackout conditions and the pilot couldn't see the faintest shadow of the facility to his left as he approached. Nor could he see any sign of its several satellites, or the support facilities arrayed around the region. Shrouded in literal darkness, the vast infrastructure of the country's nuclear arms program Vahid was tasked to protect was as much a mystery to him as it was to most Iranians.

Vahid didn't think much of the program. To him, it was a needless waste of resources—the air force could be greatly expanded with a hundredth of the funds, the navy could gain more submarines, the army strengthened. All would provide Iran with weapons that could actually be used, as opposed to the bomb no one would dare unleash, lest the retaliation result in the country's death sentence.

And there would be money left over for food and gasoline, in chronic short supply these past few years.

Vahid was careful not to share these opinions. Even Jalil Zandi, the legendary ace and great war hero, had been jailed twice for saying things that contradicted the ayatollahs.

The controller called back with further instructions, alerting Vahid that he was sending two of the other three MiGs that had scrambled after him farther north. The third would patrol around Natanz.

So it was definitely a wild-goose chase, Vahid

thought. But at least he was flying. The MiG felt especially responsive tonight, as if anxious to prove her worth.

"You are to proceed east in the direction of the original sighting," added the controller. "Other aircraft are being scrambled. Await further instructions."

Acknowledging, Vahid shifted to the new course. The air force was using a lot of its monthly allotment of jet fuel tonight, he thought; they'd pay for it in the coming weeks.

Banking toward Nain, his long range radar picked up a contact. It appeared only momentarily, the radar confused by the scattered returns of the hills. Vahid changed modes but couldn't get it back.

Still, there had to be something there: very possibly the light plane he had been scrambled to find. He altered course slightly and readjusted the MiG's radar to wide search. Reaching for the mike button, he was about to tell the controller that he'd had a contact then thought better of it. Send out a false alarm and he would be quizzed for hours about why he failed to turn anything up. Better to wait until he had something more substantial than a momentary blip.

13

Iran

THE PROXIMITY WARNING STAYED ON AS THE FIRST nano-UAV hit the mesh screen, the Cessna's pilot fighting a rogue air current in the foothills to get back in the proper position. But Turk didn't need to take over the swarm: the Hydra struck within two millimeters of the programmed crosshair, exploding perfectly and blowing a hole through the outer filter assembly. Two seconds later the second UAV hit the large grate positioned three meters deep in the shaft. The thick blades of steel crumbled, leaving the way clear for the rest of the swarm.

The proximity warning cut off a second later. By then the control unit had switched the video feed to UAV 1 inside the airshaft. Turk saw the seams whip by like lines on a highway pavement, the aircraft dipping down the five-hundred-meter tube that led to a Z-turn and the air exchanges.

There was no way Turk could have piloted the craft through the turn, even though its speed had slowed considerably. The computer puffed the nano-UAV's wings, fired the maneuvering rocket, and spun the Hydra through the Z. Two more aircraft followed, forming an arrow-shaped wedge that hit the interior fan assembly like a linebacker barreling into an ill-protected quarterback. They blew a hole through the exchange mechanism large enough for a bus to squeeze through.

Unfortunately, they did their job a little too well: there was a hairline fissure in the wall directly below the fan assembly. Weakened by the shock of the explosion, the wall began to collapse within seconds.

Ten UAVs made it through, though two were damaged by debris. And now Turk went to work. He managed to save two Hydras that had not yet entered the complex. The rest were caught in the landslide as the upper portions of the bunker began to implode.

By the time he turned his attention back to the lead aircraft, it was within seconds of the targeted chamber in the basement of the complex. Maneuvers and air friction had slowed the aircraft below ninety knots, but that was still incredibly fast. Finishing a straight run nearly two miles into the heart of the complex, the lead Hydra slammed into the grill of an air vent and exploded, opening the way to a hallway in the cellar of the complex. This time there were no fatal flaws in the workmanship, and no debris to stop the nine aircraft that followed. Turk caught a glimpse of something on the ground as the next feed snapped in—an Iranian scientist or engineer had been close to the vent when it exploded; blood was pouring from his head onto his white lab coat.

There were people in the hall—he saw heads as the UAVs dashed down the corridor into an open space. There was metalwork ahead, the large, circular gridwork he'd memorized as the sign that they had reached the target room. The target itself was the cluster machinery below.

The UAVs orbited above, forming another wedge to strike.

And then there was nothing, the feed switching back to the two aircraft above.

Nothing?

God. We've failed, he thought. I failed—I lost it right at the end. Damn. Damn!

And then, trying to think what he would do next, how he might retrieve the situation somehow with only two aircraft and a blocked passage, he saw a puff of smoke in the right corner of the feed from Hydra 35. He grabbed the joystick and took control of the aircraft. As he did, the smoke blossomed into a vast cloud and then ocean. The ground in the distance shook. The earth seemed to drop, imploding with a vast underground explosion.

They hadn't failed. They had succeeded beyond calculation. The bunker exploded and the ground swelled, then collapsed with a tremendous explosion.

Turk forced himself to concentrate. The mission wasn't finished—he had two more aircraft to take care of.

"Thirty-six, trail leader 35," he said, then put his hand over the microphone. "We're done," he told Grease. "We're good. We're good."

A warning blared in his ear. An aircraft near UAV 36 was using its radar.

A Russian air-to-air radar. The nano-UAV's radar detector identified the signal tentatively as coming from a Russian N-O19 unit, meaning it could be anything from an ancient MiG-23 to a much more capable MiG-29. But that really didn't matter—anything the Iranians had would be more than a match for the unarmed Cessna.

"Get us out of here," Turk told the pilot, looking up. "Get low and stay low. There's a fighter in the air five miles west of us."

14

Over Iran

THE ANALOG RADAR IN THE MIG WAS FAR FROM STATE of the art, but it was all Captain Vahid had ever known. The fact that his contact flickered on and off in the display didn't alarm him, nor did he jump quickly to any conclusions about the unidentified aircraft he had on his screen. It was flying low and it was going very slow. The profile fit a small, civilian-type aircraft, but what would one be doing here and at night?

Most likely it was a drone, he thought, but there was also a (distant) possibility that it was a Stealth Fighter flying a very erratic pattern, its radar signal disguised.

He heard his breath in the oxygen mask. It was all in a rush; he must be close to hyperventilating.

Vahid slowed his breathing down, tried to conjure One Eye's voice in his headset: *Stay calm. Stay on your plan.*

His eyes hunted for the enemy. It would be

close, the return confused by the stealthy characteristics of the aircraft. A black shape floated by his right, about where the contact should be. Then there was another, and another—he was seeing and chasing shadows.

"UP! UP!" SCREAMED THE ISRAELI IN ENGLISH. THE Cessna's nose jerked almost ninety degrees, the wings jostling as the windscreen filled with shadows of black and brown. Wings fluttering, the light plane cleared the barely seen peak, just missing disaster.

Turk flew the UAVs toward the Cessna, looking for the fighter. The sky was dark, but both planes were equipped with infrared sensors as their viewers. He saw a ridgeline ahead of Hydra 35. A cross rose from the rocks, a good hundred feet above the tip.

The Cessna.

"You have to stay low!" said Turk as they continued to climb. "We're being followed by a MiG."

"Any lower we'll be dead," muttered the Israeli before translating.

VAHID'S RADAR FOUND THE AIRCRAFT ONLY FIVE MILES away, rising through the mountain ridges on his left. He began a turn, planning to lock up the aircraft and fire one of his radar missiles. But the light plane disappeared from his radar, once more lost in the clutter of the reflected radar waves.

Vahid came level out of his turn, then reached

to the armament panel and selected the heat-seekers. It would be easier to use the infrared system to take them down.

He found nothing for a few moments, then he realized what must have happened—he misinterpreted the other plane's direction. It wasn't flying toward Natanz at all; it was going east, flying away from the scientific site.

Unsure how to interpret this, he called the controller and reported the contact as he brought the MiG back to the point where he had first seen the other plane. The controller bombarded him with questions. Most of them were unanswerable.

"The contact has been extremely intermittent," Vahid told the major. "I can't get a good radar fix in the mountains—he's very low."

"Are you using your infrared?"

"Affirmative. Weapons are charged and ready. Do I have permission to fire?"

"Affirmative. You are cleared to fire. I thought I made that clear."

"Affirmative. Do I need to visually identify it? If it's a drone and—"

"Just shoot the damn thing down," said the controller.

THE LITTLE PLANE JERKED FEROCIOUSLY AS THE PILOT yanked at the yoke, once more missing the side of the mountain by a few feet. Turk knew their luck wasn't going to hold much longer. If they couldn't get the MiG off their backs, they would either pancake into the side of the sheer rocks all around them or be blasted out of the sky by an Iranian air-to-air missile.

As they had just demonstrated, the small UAVs could fly a precise, preprogrammed course. But freelancing was a different matter entirely. They generally relied on outside radar to guide them to a target. Without that he would have to rely on their native sensors—which meant they would have to stay close to the Cessna until the MiG showed up on the infrared.

By then it might be too late.

Turk hit on the idea of widening the search area by putting the two aircraft into a long trail—the first UAV, 36, could stay within four miles of the Cessna, and 37 could stay four miles away from 36. That way they'd see the MiG before it got too close to escape.

Hopefully.

Several minutes passed as the Hydras stretched out behind them. Their air speed was starting to become critical.

There was the MiG, two miles from UAV 36.

A MiG-29 Fulcrum. Iran's best.

"Control," said Turk, putting both hands on a control stick and flying the planes simultaneously. "Designate unidentified contact oh-one as target."

The computer complied, marking the Iranian with that legend. The computer analyzed the aircraft, using the library in the control unit—essentially the same database used by the Sabres and Flighthawks. It ID'ed two R-27 air-to-air medium-range missiles and six short-range heat-seeking R-73s.

The MiG was moving south about 5,000 feet above them, only a mile to the west. Their direction, eastward, was almost exactly abeam of it. Apparently it couldn't see them.

Yet. It was only a matter of time.

The nano-UAVs were at 10,000 feet. He pushed both noses downward.

"Show intercept," he told the computer. "Fuel full use."

The computer plotted the course. Turk nudged the trail plane to the right, but otherwise he was dead on.

"Intercept in thirty seconds," predicted the computer as the speed of the small aircraft increased.

As the MiG turned left, the computer began recalculating. Turk altered course as well, then realized why the MiG had made that maneuver.

"He sees us!" yelled Turk, raising his head as he yelled at the pilot. "Turn west. Tell him to turn west!"

"OK, OK," said the Israeli, starting to speak in Farsi.

Turk ducked back down. "Contact range critical," the computer told Turk.

"Complete intercept," Turk told the computer. "Autonomous."

The Hydra engines slammed to life. As UAV 36 twisted toward the MiG, Turk saw two flares light under the MiG's wings, then two more. They'd just been fired at.

"Two missiles launched. Repeat missiles launched," Vahid told the controller. "I—"

He heard a sharp snap behind him. In the next moment the plane seemed to fall away from him, the left wing veering down. Vahid forgot about everything else—the aircraft he was pursuing, the nuclear research facility, the missiles he had just launched—and fought to recover the plane.

The dive sent him earthward so quickly that he felt light-headed. His breathing was shallow and sharp, reverberating in his head.

One Eye spoke to him from beyond the grave, advising him to roll out, to get his nose attitude right and keep his power up. He recovered from the unexpected roll as if he'd planned it all along, except of course he would never have planned to go down to just barely 2,000 feet, lower than most of the peaks around him. He turned back west and felt the plane thumping. There was something wrong, definitely wrong.

Vahid cut his speed and adjusted his trim. It wasn't clear what the problem was. He craned his head upward, staring down the side of the aircraft. He saw only jagged shadows.

"I have a flight emergency," he told the controller finally. "I need to return to base."

"What happened to your target?"

"I—I'm not sure. I need to land immediately."

The first missile missed spectacularly, flaring in the sky more than a mile away, its final arc a fiery, flamboyant semicircle above a nearby mountain.

They weren't as lucky with the next.

The pilot turned sharply into a box valley as it approached. The missile continued straight, temporarily lost, then veered to follow. Either the maneuver caused a malfunction or the circuitry sensed a near miss and the warhead exploded, sending a small stream of shrapnel into the air.

Some of the spray hit the Cessna's left wing, tearing jagged holes in the skin. Worse, bits of the shrapnel flew into the side of the fuselage. Two large pieces of metal struck the engine. A third barely grazed the windshield, etching a jagged line across a third of it, yet somehow leaving it intact.

Two more went through the pilot's window, striking him in the head and neck. He slumped; as he did, his body hit the wheel and pushed the plane downward.

Half realizing what was happening as the plane tipped, Turk dropped the control unit and reached forward, grabbing the pilot's shoulders and pulling him back against the seat.

"Hold him back, hold him back off the stick," Turk told the Israeli. "Help me."

As the other man pushed the pilot back, Turk tried leaning over him to grab the yoke. The plane was still nosing down, though not as dramatically. The ground closed in. This wasn't going to work.

"Pull him out of my way," said Turk, trying to squeeze into the seat as the Israeli pulled the pilot away.

Taking hold of the control yoke, Turk pulled

back against the momentum of the plane as he struggled to get the nose level. The Cessna was not reluctant; she wanted to stay in the air, and finally pulled her chin up to comply with her new master's commands. But the loss of the engine and closeness of the ground were a problem neither she nor Turk could fully solve. He struggled to keep the wings level as the plane continued. She was steady and tough; if there'd been a runway ahead, the approach would have been near perfect.

But there wasn't a runway ahead.

"Brace!" yelled Turk. "Brace!"

MISSIONARY

———

1

Iran

THE CESSNA STAYED LEVEL TO THE LAST SECONDS, HER wheels touching the earth nearly together. A great deal of speed had already bled off with the destruction of the engine and subsequent descent, but she was still moving at a good clip, racing forward with no brakes to help slow her.

The only piece of luck was the fact that they had cleared the last of the low hills, coming to ground in the desert behind them. Baked by the sun and scraped by the wind, the ground was hard if not perfectly smooth, and they bumped along for a few hundred feet until the right wing found a patch of loose dirt. The plane pitched and turned sharply, skidding along for another hundred feet before tipping back the other way. The left wing snapped; the Cessna dug into the earth for a few yards, then teetered back upright, as if the laws of physics had decided to give the occupants a break.

By the time the aircraft stopped, Turk had been tossed around like stone in a polishing machine. He was dizzy and his nose felt as if it was broken;

his face, neck, and shirt were covered with blood. He'd fallen or been dumped into the narrow space between the rear and front row of seats, wedged sideways against one of Grease's legs. Unfolding himself upright, he flexed his arms, surprised that though disoriented, he still seemed intact. He coughed, and felt as if he was drowning— the blood from his nose having backed into his sinuses.

Grease grabbed Turk's arm and pulled him in his direction, yanking Turk across the folded forward seat and out the passenger side.

The Israeli stood a few feet away, waving an AK-47. "Come on. We have to get out of here," he yelled at them.

Turk turned back to the plane, not quite comprehending where he was or what had happened. He put his hand to his lip, then his nose.

"Damn!" He cursed with the pain.

"Your nose," said Grease, next to him. "You have to stop the bleeding. You have a handkerchief?"

"I need the control unit," said Turk.

He took a step back to the plane but Grease stopped him.

"I'll get it," said the sergeant, handing him a patch of cloth—his shirt sleeve, which he'd cut off with a knife. "Put your head back and stop the bleeding. You've already lost a lot of blood."

Turk's nose felt numb until he pushed the wadded cloth against the nostril. The pain ran up the bone ridge and into the space between his eyes, as if he'd taken an ice pick and plunged it there.

"Let's go," said Grease, remerging with the control unit stuffed into Turk's rucksack.

"Where's the pilot?" managed Turk through the wadded cloth.

"Dead," said Grease.

"Aren't we going to bury him?"

"No time. They'll be looking for us."

"It's a mercy he's dead," said the Israeli. "I would have had to kill him myself when we landed."

THEY DEBATED BRIEFLY WHETHER THEY SHOULD SET the plane on fire, but decided that whatever small advantage it might have in making it harder to get information about them was more than counterbalanced by the fact that it would make it easier to find. Grease squared away the plane as well as he could, hoping to make it less obvious that there had been passengers, but there was nothing he could do about the blood splattered around the interior in blobs both big and small in the back. They set out east, walking along a wide plateau that sat like a ledge above the valley to their right. Had they settled down a few hundred yards in the other direction, or perhaps stayed in the air for another mile, they would have all died in the crash. It was luck or Providence, take your pick, but Grease clearly was awed, giving Turk complete credit for their survival.

"You did a hell of a job," he told him. "It was a great job."

It was the first time Grease had said anything

positive to him, and yet Turk felt he had to be honest: he hadn't really done much.

"I just held the nose up, the plane did the rest," he said, then asked where they were going.

"Train line runs to Naneen," Grease told him. "We'll parallel the road and the train tracks. Our guys will pick us up where and when they can."

"You talked to them?" asked the Israeli.

"They'll know. I have the GPS. We just have to get there."

"We blew it up," said Turk. "The whole place—I wonder."

"What?" demanded the Israeli.

"The explosion was huge."

"Nuclear explosions usually are. Even underground."

"It was a bomb?" asked Turk incredulously. He'd been told they were blowing up machinery.

"Why else would they send you on such a suicide mission?" asked the Israeli, trudging onward.

2

CIA campus, Virginia

Breanna Stockard rubbed the tears away from her cheeks. They were tears of relief, if not outright joy—the indicator on the map was moving in a way that what the computer declared meant Turk was still alive.

She pushed her hand away quickly; she didn't want the others to notice her emotion.

"I've transmitted the information to the ground team," said Danny Freah. "Gorud just acknowledged."

"Good." Breanna glanced away for a moment, collecting herself. "How long before they get there?"

"Hard to say. They were already up near the original rendezvous point." Danny looked at the three-dimensional holographic display in front of him, tracing the area. "It's a couple of hundred miles back east. And they'll have to go south to avoid patrols and whatever else the Iranians put out there."

"Will they make it in time for tomorrow night?" Breanna asked.

"I can't even guess. Not at this point."

"I have preliminary numbers," said Jonathon Reid from his station. "Just under four megatons. On par with Chagai Two, roughly, at least. Given that the device wasn't completely ready. It was a close call. A good, good mission."

Reid rose. Chagai II was an early Pakistani atomic test. Though Western experts continued to debate the matter, it was generally regarded as something of a failure, since it didn't yield anywhere near the explosion that was intended, which was at least eighteen megatons. (The blast yield of the bomb dropped on Hiroshima measured between thirteen and eighteen megatons.) The final measure would take some time to determine, using instruments that would provide different data sets, including the magnetic distortion—while the underground explosion did not yield an electromagnetic pulse effect like a high-altitude bomb would, even the extremely slight disruption it produced could be analyzed. In any event, while the yield of the bomb was relatively small, it was still large enough to do considerable damage, and contaminate the area where it was used for decades to come.

"I told the President we would give her a more complete update at the half hour," Reid told Breanna. "We won't have visual imagery for another few hours, but the seismic data should be quite enough."

"We can take some of the video from the WB-57," Breanna said. "It's quite impressive."

"Agreed."

"Have the Iranians said anything yet?"

"They know something is up—the communication lines went down with the explosion. But it should take them a while to realize the extent of it. They may fear the worst. We're monitoring the local communications with ferret satellites, so we'll know pretty much as soon as they do."

"Mr. Reid, you better look at this," said Lanny Fu, a CIA analyst tasked to monitor current intelligence from sources outside the operation. "The Iranians just made a status request for all facilities under the Qom directorate."

"Right on time," said Reid as he turned back to Breanna. "They fear there's been an accident or an attack. Their procedure now will be to ask each one to check in, and in the meantime they'll send someone to the targeted facility."

"Sir," interrupted Fu. "The significance here—there's a code number for a facility on the list that we have no record of."

"What?"

"I believe there may be another bunker somewhere."

"I'm sure you're mistaken," said Reid. "They have been well calculated. Double-check."

"I already have," said Fu. "The analysts have been alerted. We're working on it."

"Another lab?" said Breanna.

"I doubt that," insisted Reid. "I strongly doubt it."

3

Omidiyeh, Iran

IN THE FIRST FEW MOMENTS AFTER HIS AIRCRAFT WAS struck, Captain Parsa Vahid thought for sure he would have to bail.

Rather than setting off a panic, the knowledge calmed him. It also saved the plane.

Vahid, like many well-trained pilots, became in the crisis a logical, methodical engineer. He worked through a long list of procedures and directions necessary to save the aircraft. If one thing didn't work—if too much fuel was leaking from one tank, if a control surface didn't precisely respond—he switched to another, then another, and another, moving on down the checklist as calmly as an accountant tallying the numbers of a sale.

Even when he landed the plane, he confined his thinking to a very narrow checklist. He taxied to the maintenance area, trundling past the white skeleton of a transport that had been battered by an Iraqi attack some twenty-five years before. He shut down the plane and then, finally freed of his life-or-death lists, rose in the cockpit and took the deepest breath of fresh, desert air that he had ever managed.

He was met on the tarmac by the base commander, who asked with a grave face how many of the American B-2s he had seen.

"There were no B-2s," said Vahid. "There was a small plane, a light plane. My missiles shot it down."

"There must have been B-2s," said the general. "They have blown up Natanz."

"What?"

"There is no contact with one of the plants. We were asked to try, and failed."

"There was no B-2. I shot down the only plane."

The commander shook his head. Stunned, Vahid walked slowly to the nearby transport vehicle. Rather than taking him to his squadron room, where he ordinarily would debrief, he was driven to a bunker at the far end of the military complex. The colonel in charge of intelligence met him outside the entrance and led him downstairs to his office.

"I'd like to change from my gear," Vahid objected when they arrived.

"You will change when we are done."

The room smelled of fresh concrete. It was much larger than the squadron offices upstairs. Two long tables, twice the size of normal conference tables, sat at the middle of the room. There were only chairs, but each was a well-padded armchair.

The interview began as soon as he sat down.

"How long after takeoff did you encounter the enemy bombers?" asked the colonel. He was tall and thin, with glasses, a beak nose, and a brush moustache above a thin and close beard. In the harsh light he looked as if he were a cartoon character, a caricature of an officer created as a foil for a popular hero.

"I never encountered enemy bombers, or any bombers," said Vahid. "I will tell you what happened."

"First answer my questions," said the colonel. He lifted his glasses higher on his nose. "How many bombers did you encounter?"

"You keep talking about bombers. There was one aircraft, a light plane. Maybe a Cessna. A small trainer at most."

"It was more likely an American Predator," suggested the colonel.

"I—"

"You shot it down."

"I believe I shot something down," answered the pilot. He had never encountered the American UAV known as the Predator, but he was naturally familiar with the profile, and the plane he had encountered bore little resemblance to the drone. "But I think it was—"

"I think that is what you encountered," insisted the colonel. "A Predator."

"You'll see when you recover it, then," said Vahid. He was trying to keep his temper in check, but couldn't help the note of sarcasm that crept into his voice.

"How many other planes were there?"

"None. I saw none. Check my video record."

"Sometimes those are not complete."

"Yes, at times there are things not recorded," said Vahid, finally surrendering. It was foolish to resist; the man was trying to help him. His goal was probably to spare the commander and the air force in general, but to do that most effectively, he had to help Vahid as well.

There would soon be other interviews, much more difficult.

"Men in the heat of battle do not know everything that is going around them," said the colonel. "They cannot fly that way. They have to focus on the immediate threat."

Vahid nodded. "What happened at Natanz?" he asked.

The colonel stared at him.

"The Americans attacked it?" the pilot prompted. "But the facilities are many miles beneath the ground. No one could attack them. Unless they used a nuclear bomb. Did they use a nuclear bomb on us?"

"You are not the one to be asking questions. You know absolutely nothing, beyond the fact that you did your duty. You shot down a plane."

"Yes."

The colonel folded his hands in a tight cluster in front of him, pressing them down on the table-top as if he might try and bend it toward the floor. Finally, he took a small tape recorder from his pocket and put it on the table.

"We will start from the beginning of your flight," he said. "Recount everything from your takeoff. Leave nothing unmentioned, however trivial. Remember what the end result is."

4

White House situation room

"THEIR RESPONSE INDICATES THEY DON'T KNOW WHAT happened, not yet, anyway." National Security Advisor Blitz frowned as he assessed the situation for President Todd. The operation had gone extremely well—a good thing, since the Iranian bomb program appeared to have been much further ahead than anyone had believed. "It's been three hours now and they're only just starting to seal off the site. Or what's left of it."

"Was it totally destroyed?" Todd asked. She and Blitz were sitting alone in the room. The President had decided she would have no witnesses to the discussion; even her Secret Service body-guards were in the hall, none too happy at having been summarily ordered to stay outside the door, a rare Todd decree.

"Our satellite won't be passing overhead for another two hours, and we don't want to risk a plane," Blitz told her. "But the images of the explosion and its aftermath from the NASA aircraft show the tunnels and entire underground complex were completely wiped out. It's history."

Several hundred workers had died along with it. Regrettable, but necessary.

Blitz's phone vibrated in his hand. He glanced quickly at the face.

"Ms. Stockard and Mr. Reid are ready for the video conference," he said.

The President turned to the console as Blitz flipped it on. Breanna and Reid appeared on a split screen, their faces projected from the Whiplash command center at the CIA complex.

"I understand congratulations are in order," she said. "Job well done."

"Thank you, Madam President," said Reid.

"Have we recovered our team yet?"

"We're working on it," said Breanna. "But there has been—there is a complication." She turned to her right, evidently looking toward Reid in the center.

"There's new information," added Reid. "We're still compiling it. But there appears to be another facility that we haven't known about until now. And it's possible—very possible, I'm afraid—that there is another nuclear device there, waiting to be tested."

"How is this possible?" Todd felt her chest catch.

Her lungs acting up? She ignored the pain and continued.

"The facilities were examined in great detail before I approved the mission," she said. "Well before."

"I know, Madam President," said Reid. "I can't make any excuses. There does seem to be another facility. We have a code name, a radio address, really. We're trying to match it up to a physical plant. At the moment, we have two different possibilities. Both were closed two years ago. At that time we believed one was completely shut down because of an accidental explosion there; the other housed centrifuges that were no longer needed. Our best theory is that one or both may actually have been kept open and developed—it's the same pattern they used for the lab we targeted."

"Which we found."

"Thanks, actually, to the Israelis." Reid was very big on giving credit where credit was due, even if it went to a competitor; he'd even been known to laud the Defense Intelligence Agency, something most CIA officers and nearly every Agency bureaucrat would never do. "In any event, we're working to determine what is going on at those facilities. Whatever it is, the Iranians have gone to great lengths to keep their status secret. Given that, we believe it's very possible— likely—that one may be another bomb assembly area. Because the amount of fuel in the explosion is about half of what we projected, worst case. And now, well, worst case seems to have been too conservative, given the state of the bomb we destroyed."

Christine Todd was famous for keeping her

temper. She prided herself on being able to control her emotions: all of them, but her temper especially. As a little girl, her mother had said she had the famous "Irish temper" of her ancestors.

You are easygoing in your needs, Mother often declared, *but let someone fall short of their job or responsibility, and there's hell to pay. 'Tis a flaw, Christine Mary, a flaw that will make people dislike you, friends especially.*

By the time she was out of her teens, Todd had learned to control herself—and more important, learned that everyone was human, most especially herself. The Golden Rule—*Do unto others as you would have them do unto you*—had become something more than just a biannual theme for a fifteen minute sermon at Sunday mass.

But every so often the forces that she'd chained deep in her psyche reasserted themselves.

"Why in the name of all that is holy," she demanded, "was this site not found earlier?"

Reid didn't answer.

"Jesus, Mary, and Joseph, Jonathon," she continued, her Irish-American heritage asserting itself with the mild profanity. "How many times did I go over this with your agency?"

"I don't have control over the analysts," he said mildly.

"We believe we can deal with the problem," said Breanna, stepping in. "We've drawn up a tentative plan for a second strike tomorrow night."

Breanna. Good job. God bless Magnus for recommending you.

"Why tomorrow night?" Todd asked.

"It's the soonest the assets will be in place," said Breanna. "We want to strike quickly, obviously."

"Before I say anything else, let me note that I expect better information, more timely, from the intelligence community," said Todd.

"Understood," replied Reid.

How could he argue?

This was one more reason to fire the head of the Agency—not that she needed any more.

And replace him with Jonathon?

Hmmph.

"You can determine which site it is?" asked Todd sharply.

"Yes, ma'am," said Reid. "Or we'll hit both."

"Prepare for a second mission," Todd said. "I want updates on the hour, and I want you, Jonathon, *personally* to vouch for the final briefing, and *personally* available for questions if the need arises."

"Yes, ma'am."

"Very good." Todd hit the switch and dismissed them.

"It was an intelligence failure—unacceptable," said Blitz. His face was red.

"That, Dr. Blitz, is an understatement." Todd glanced at her watch. It was later than she thought—she was due to speak with the Secretary of State upstairs in five minutes; there was a full National Security Committee session slated immediately afterward. "Your staff will have to explain itself as well. We'll deal with the immediate problem, then worry about Monday morning quarterbacking."

"In this sort of situation," said Blitz, "failure—this is why we need a change of leadership from the top at the Agency. You've given everyone concerned more than enough time to fail. And now, this will be—"

"Failure is not acceptable," snapped the President, standing. "Get the Joint Chiefs ready—I want a plan to take out the remaining site. They are to report to me in an hour. Less, if possible."

5

Suburban Virginia

THE TV DRONED ON IN THE OTHER ROOM. ZEN, HOME early and hungry, barely paid attention as he made a sandwich with leftovers from the fridge. He wheeled himself back and forth between the refrigerator and the counter island at the center of the kitchen, which was set at wheelchair height to make it easier for him to work. He was just trying to decide whether to add prosciutto to the leftover roast pork and marinated sweet peppers when the word "Iran" caught his attention. He left his sandwich and wheeled over to the family room. The late afternoon talk show had been replaced by an announcer, who according to the flashing red legend at the top of the screen was presenting "Breaking News."

". . . an isolated area in Iran north of the capital,

Tehran. The area where the earthquake struck includes at least one known Iranian atomic research facility, raising the question of whether an accident occurred there. However, the Iranian government immediately denied there had been any human activity in the area that could have led to the earthquake . . ."

Zen listened as the reporter described the earthquake, saying that preliminary data estimated that it was in the "high fours or very low fives," which while causing shaking would only damage very poorly built structures. This section of Iran was often subject to earthquakes, added the announcer, and it was too early for information about casualties.

"Interesting," said Zen to himself, wheeling toward his bedroom, where he'd left his cell phone turned off. Sure enough, he'd missed a dozen calls in the last ten minutes. He scrolled through the list, then selected the number of Jenny Shapiro, one of the staff members of the Intelligence Committee.

Shapiro answered on the first ring. "Senator Stockard, have you heard the news?"

"Earthquake in Iran?"

"Atomic explosion in Iran," said Shapiro. "More P waves than S."

"That means something to you, I'm sure."

Shapiro gave Zen a brief explanation of the type of shock waves generated by explosions and earthquakes. While every event had its own particular "fingerprint," scientists generally had little difficulty differentiating between earthquakes and man-made explosions by the overall pattern of the shock waves. In this case, said Shapiro, one of the committee's technical experts, there seemed little doubt that this was some sort of event—almost surely an accidental explosion of a nuclear device.

"Why accidental?" asked Zen.

"A couple of reasons. For one thing, the epicenter wasn't set up as a test area, or in a known facility." Shapiro's Boston accent got quicker and quicker as she spoke. "But if I had to make a guess, I'd say they were putting a device together for testing elsewhere and somebody made a very big mistake."

"Or they were helped."

"You said that, Senator. I didn't."

"And we don't know about this facility?"

"If the epicenter of the waves is where the scientists say it was—"

"What's the word from the White House?"

"No word is the word. NSC staff say, 'Evaluating.' State is preparing a statement on 'the Iranian earthquake.' That's what I know," she added. "Are you going to be available for the special meeting?"

"Which is when?" Zen glanced down at the list of callers. Two were from the secretary in charge of arranging the Intelligence Committee's meetings.

"Fifty-two minutes and counting."

"On my way," he said.

6

Iran

THE STARS FADED EVER SO SLIGHTLY AS THEY WALKED, as if they were pulling back from the earth. Turk's thigh muscles burned with fatigue, but there was no time to slow or complain. He wasn't afraid of being caught but of being left behind. The Israeli and Grease had moved at the same steady pace since they'd started, and even if he hadn't been exhausted he would have had trouble keeping up. But he had to keep up, because the alternative was being left in Iran, and being left in Iran was unacceptable, was impossible.

Turk's confidence wavered under the weight of his fatigue. He was back to being a pilot—competent, more than competent, in the air; nearly useless on the ground.

When they first set out for the train tracks, he thought they would arrive within minutes. To keep his brain occupied, he amused himself by picturing his arrival home, back in Las Vegas, back in Li's arms. He felt her arms and smelled her perfume; he remembered the way they'd lain together in bed.

Now he thought of nothing and simply walked.

"Up there," said Grease, stopping ahead and crouching.

Turk walked up to him. Grease put his hand on his shoulder and pushed him down. "Sssssh," said the soldier.

The railroad tracks were about fifty yards away on the right, just on the other side of a hard-packed dirt road. The ground sloped gently from their position to the tracks, then fell away a little steeper. The cover was sparse, large clumps of stiff grass and clusters of low bushes.

"What are we waiting for?" asked Turk, hoarse.

"Ssssh," said Grease, this time sternly.

The Israeli started ahead, then suddenly flattened himself.

"Come on," hissed Grease, moving on his haunches to a nearby bush.

Turk lost his balance as he got up. He managed to push and fall forward, half diving and half crawling into position behind Grease. Under other circumstances it might have been hilarious, but Turk was not in the mood to laugh at himself, and Grease seemed congenitally averse to humor of any kind. Neither said anything.

A hum grew in the air, vibrating stronger and stronger. Turk didn't realize it was a train until it burst in front of him. There were no lights on either of the two diesel engines in the front, nor were there any on the two passenger cars and a half-dozen freight cars that followed, or the flat-cars with trucks and tanks. The train melted into a brownish blur, leaving a film of dust floating in the air in its wake. The scent of half-burned diesel fuel was so strong Turk thought he would gag.

"They're sending troops to cordon the area off and find out what happened," said Grease. "There'll be patrols."

"Yeah."

Turk remembered the image of the ground as it imploded. He wasn't sure what the radioactive effects would be. Would the entire area be poisoned for years?

Was five miles far enough way to avoid the effects? A slight twinge of paranoia struck him—maybe his fatigue was due to radioactive poisoning.

Unlikely. He was just exhausted, plain and simple.

They both rose, Turk unsteadily, Grease as solid and smooth as ever. The Israeli trotted toward them.

"There's a truck at the other side of the intersection," he said when he reached them. "I think it is your people."

A FEW MINUTES LATER TURK WAS SITTING IN THE BACK of the truck, wedged between Gorud and Grease. The other members of the team were spread out along the floorboards, sitting or leaning toward the back, watchful. The Israeli had gone up front with the driver.

Gorud had been emotionless when Turk reported that the mission was a success. Turk wondered at his own peculiar lack of elation as well—they'd just struck a tremendous blow against Iran, probably prevented a war or at least a wider conflict, and yet he didn't feel particularly elated. He didn't feel anything, except the aches and pains of his bruises, and the heavy weight of his eyelids.

"We'll be there soon," said Gorud, checking his watch. "Granderson and one of the men are already there. It should be safe until morning, or beyond."

"Why are we waiting there?" asked Grease.

"They didn't explain," said Gorud as the truck bounced along the dirt road. "They just want us to stand by for further instructions."

"We should be getting as far away as possible," said Grease.

Turk completely agreed. There were still a few hours before dawn. They ought to use every one of them to get closer to safety.

Several plans had been drawn up for their "exfiltration." The preferred one had been by airplane from the airport where they were supposed to meet the helicopter. But that option had apparently gone by the boards when they were shot down.

"I don't disagree," said Gorud. "But this is what they said. Maybe they know something we don't."

"Right," sneered Grease.

A few minutes later the truck slowed to a stop. One by one they got out. Dread helped Turk down, easing him onto the ground as if he were an old man. Turk was mildly amused—until his legs went rubbery on him after a step or two. He stood stock-still for several seconds, regaining his composure.

They saw what looked like a large construction area, with bulldozed sections and piles of dirt, sand, and gravel. Captain Granderson, waiting here with one of the troopers in the car they'd "borrowed" earlier in the evening, said the area had been used by the Iranian army for maneuvers some years before. There were buildings across the road to the east. They were abandoned, but Granderson had decided to avoid them.

"We've been monitoring the radio," he told Turk. "There's been an announcement of an earthquake. But the military has been put on alert. They have aircraft all over the place."

"Probably looking for us. We were shot down."

"You were shot down?"

"Yeah. I managed to get it in, more out of luck than anything else. The pilot was killed."

"Damn."

"Did you hear anything about a MiG?" Turk asked. "I went after it with the nano-UAVs. I don't know if I got it down."

"I haven't heard anything. It's not always easy to understand what they're saying, though."

"What are they talking about, you think?" Grease asked, nodding toward Gorud and the Israeli. The two appeared to be arguing.

"Don't know. Gorud doesn't like him, though."

"He said that?"

"You could just tell." Granderson stared at the two men as if he could read their lips in the twilight.

"Does he trust him?" asked Grease.

"I don't think like and trust are related," said Granderson.

"If he didn't trust him, he wouldn't have let us go with him, right?" said Turk.

"He's Mossad?" asked Grease.

"I don't know. I think he's actually a Russian who's paid by Mossad," said Granderson. "Based on what he was cursing about."

"How do we get out of here?" Grease asked.

"At this point, go north through the mountains to the Caspian," said Granderson, understanding the question to mean the country, not the pit where they were hiding. "We have two stash points along the way, and there should be two guys near the water waiting for us. There's also a SEAL unit that's a quick reaction force, more or less, that can help us once we're farther north." Granderson seemed almost matter of fact, but he was proposing they travel through rough mountains. "But we can't do anything until I get the OK from the States."

"You think we can sit here all day without being sighted?"

"If we have to."

7

Washington, D.C.

"THE WHITE HOUSE POSITION THAT IT'S AN EARTH-quake is untenable," said Shapiro, the Senate committee aide who was an expert on, among other things, the Iranian nuclear program. "Even if they are just referring everyone to the Iranian government. Every scientist looking at the data will know it's false. They're not going to be quiet about it. Already someone from MIT was quoted in a Web report saying it must have been related to their nuke program."

Zen leaned his head back, gazing at the ceiling in the closed conference room. He could think of exactly one reason why the White House wouldn't want to confirm that it had been a nuclear accident: the explosion was the result of a U.S. operation which was still under way.

Senator Brown, the chairman of the committee, gave him a sideways glance as Shapiro finished. He seemed to have come to the same conclusion.

Not that this necessarily made the President's silence right.

"So am I correct that the members are not comfortable with the lack of information coming from the White House?" said the chairman mildly. He of course knew he was, and waited for only the briefest moment before proceeding. "What we want is an up-to-date, no-holds-barred, closed-door briefing. Do I have that correct? I'll set about getting one."

Brown tapped his gavel lightly before anyone could answer. Zen rolled backward from the table, trying to make a quick escape.

He didn't make it.

"Jeff—Zen—if you could hold on a second," said Brown. "I just need a word."

Zen smirked as if he was a grammar school kid caught trying to leave class via the window. He backed himself against the wall and nodded to the others as they filtered out in twos and threes.

"You want me to talk to the President," he said to Senator Brown when they were alone.

"Exactly."

"You don't think that's the chairman's job?"

"I'll definitely call her, but it'll be next year before she returns the call."

"I doubt that."

"Will you talk to her?"

"All right. But I don't expect her to say more to me than she's willing to say to you or the committee as a whole."

"We're supposed to be informed."

Zen nodded.

"If this is the start of a war," added Brown, "there'll be hell to pay. Impeachment maybe. She's got plenty of enemies around here."

"Maybe she's trying to stop one."

"Either way," said Brown, "the result may be the same."

8

Washington, D.C.

As far as President Todd was concerned, there was no choice—she had already committed herself to destroying the Iranian bomb program. If there was another site, or even ten more sites, they had to be eliminated.

Far better to do it with the tiny and apparently

undetectable Whiplash aircraft. But the B-2s and B-1s were ready. If the team inside Iran couldn't pull this off, she'd send the bombers in. She was not about to do what her predecessor had done and leave the problem for the next shift.

An overt attack by the U.S. was sure to have dire consequences. The Iranians couldn't strike the U.S. directly, but they would surely unleash wave upon wave of terrorists. They might also take another shot at blocking the Persian Gulf.

Todd expected Secretary of State Alistair Newhaven to use that as part of his argument against an attack. But he surprised her, telling the packed conference room in the White House basement that he thought the attack must be pressed.

"I think it's not a matter of debate," said Newhaven, gesturing with the back of his hand at the map on the display screen at the front of the room. "In for a penny, in for a pound, as the old saying goes. The real question is what the Iranians will do. If I'm them, I push up my timeline. A lot."

"If they're capable," said the Secretary of Defense Charles Lovel. "We don't have enough data. Frankly, it's not even clear whether they would go ahead with a test."

"We have to assume that they have the capability," said National Security Advisor Blitz. He studiously avoided looking at the head of the CIA, who sat glumly at the side of the table, all but wearing a dunce cap. "They have been ahead of every estimate. Consistently."

"If they do test the bomb, they'll have no material for another," added Lovel. "We've wiped out their centrifuge arrays."

"They'll build more," said Blitz. "We'll have a twelve month to three year window."

"I'll take that," said Todd. "In any event, that isn't the issue at the moment. We'll have time to analyze the situation further once we have more intelligence."

She took a quick poll on a second attack, going around the room; it was unanimous. As was her custom, Todd let the others think that she was undecided until they had given their opinions; as usual, her mind was already set.

"We will continue the campaign," she said, rising. "Covertly if possible, overtly if necessary. I expect a second strike within twenty-four hours. Our official posture, until then, will be as it has been: an earthquake. No leaks. Absolutely no leaks—lives are on the line here. And I don't mean those of just our operatives."

"Congress," said Blitz. "The intelligence committee has been screaming—"

"I'll deal with Congress," said Todd.

ZEN WAS A LITTLE SURPRISED WHEN THE WHITE HOUSE called back so quickly, but the "invitation" to join the President for an early dinner did catch him off guard. When he hesitated before answering, the President's chief of staff came on the line personally and told him that "Ms. Todd really wants to talk to you as soon as possible, and if you can't make supper—"

"I can certainly get to the White House right away," said Zen. "And I'd love to have dinner with the President. Should I bring my wife?"

"Actually, it's supper, not dinner. And while I happen to know that the President thinks very highly of Mrs. Stockard, the invitation is for one only. Would you like us to send a car?"

"I'll drive my van over," said Zen. "I'm leaving now."

CHRISTINE TODD LIKED TO WALK AROUND THE WHITE House kitchen, not because she felt the urge to cook or check on the staff, but because it was a refuge from the formal business of the rest of the house. The people doing their jobs here—chefs, cooks, assistants—could have been anywhere in the world. They were naturally circumspect and on their best behavior when she walked in, but even so, the hint of the world beyond the bubble she lived in was welcome.

She wondered how they would take the news of the cancer. Certainly they'd feel bad for her. Would they feel that she betrayed them by not mentioning it?

Maybe she should arrange to tell them first. Or not first, but very soon in the process. Personally.

It was still too theoretical to contemplate. She had too many other things to do.

"Our guest enjoys his beer," she told the head steward as he came over to greet her. "Anchor Steam is one of his favorites, as I recall. I believe you have that."

"We'll look after Senator Stockard, ma'am. Not a problem."

The President walked around the steel-topped prep island, glancing at the stove and the young cook watching the gravy.

"Very good, very good," Todd announced. "Wonderful, actually. Thank you, everyone. It smells delightful, as usual."

One of the chief of staff's aides intercepted her in the hallway; he had the latest update on the Iranian situation—the strike unit was standing by in Iran, waiting for the next target. The backup set of nano-UAVs were being programmed for the attack. The intelligence agencies were scrambling for more data on the possible target—still unsure which of the two former sites it was.

The update, ironically enough, had come straight from Breanna Stockard. The President had no doubt that Zen knew nothing about the operation, at least not from Breanna.

What an interesting household *that* must be, she thought as she headed to the family dining room where Zen was already waiting.

She entered the room with her usual bustle, greeting Zen and going straight to her chair. He moved his wheelchair back as a sign of respect.

"Senator, so nice to see you. I hope I haven't kept you long."

"I just got here," said Zen politely.

The residence dining room—occasionally known as the President's Dining Room or the Private Dining Room—was one of three in the building (not counting the formal room), and when she was dining with someone, Todd chose the room depending on the tone she was trying to set. This was the most intimate, less ornate than the Family Dining Room and less work-oriented than the Oval Office Dining Room. At least that was how *she* thought of it.

"I'm glad you could make it," said Todd, pulling out her chair. "Especially on short notice."

"I don't get invited to the White House very often," said Zen. "Especially without my wife."

"Yes." She turned to the attendant who was waiting nearby. "Perhaps the senator would like something to drink. A beer? Maybe an Anchor Steam?"

"That'd be fine," said Zen. "Just one, though—I'm driving."

"I'll try one as well, and some water," Todd told the attendant. She turned back to Zen. "I never understood—what's the difference between regular beer and steam beer? Or is that just something for marketing?"

Zen elaborated on the difference in brewing styles. The beer arrived before he finished.

"It's very good," said Todd, taking a sip. "Crisp."

"I'm guessing you didn't invite me over to discuss beer styles," said Zen.

He drank heartily, very much like her husband, Todd thought.

"No, though it has been educational."

Todd studied him. He would make a good President: sure of himself, easygoing yet intelligent, with sound judgment—usually. An excellent service record, a decorated hero, which in some ways made him virtually unassailable.

Then again, she'd seen more veterans than she could count chewed up by the political naysayers. Washington was a place where real achievements meant much less than the dirt others could throw at you.

Todd felt an urge to tell him about her condition, and what it meant, and would mean, for the future. She wanted suddenly to suggest he run for President. But she couldn't do that. Too many questions, too many complications. And that wasn't why she had called him here.

"My invitation came after I called on behalf of the Intelligence Committee," prompted Zen.

"Yes." Todd pulled herself back into business mode. "Your committee is wondering, no doubt, what's going on in Iran."

"Exactly."

"You and I, Senator—occasionally we have disagreed."

"More than occasionally," admitted Zen.

"Even so, I consider you one of our finer senators."

"I'm flattered."

"We're wondering what's going on in Iran ourselves."

Zen raised his eyebrow.

"Of course, there are situations when we—when I—cannot tell everyone precisely all that I *suspect* about things that go on in the world," said Todd, using her most offhanded tone. "I'm always faced with the question: will what I say jeopardize other people?"

Zen nodded. "I imagine it must be difficult to make that call. I think I may have even said something like that to the committee earlier."

"Are you here personally?" she asked. "Or as the representative of the committee?"

"Both, I guess."

"What is it that you *personally* want to know, Senator?" asked Todd.

Zen had pushed his wheelchair sideways—the table was a little higher than what would have been comfortable. He leaned his right elbow on it, finger to his lips, thinking.

"I would not want any information that would jeopardize anyone's lives," he told her.

"That's good, because you won't get any."

"What I would want to know is that the administration is aware of the implications."

"Absolutely."

"I'm told that the signature of the earthquake is not the sort of signature that one sees in earthquakes."

"Interesting." Todd reached for her beer and took another very small sip.

"I think that news is going to be public knowledge pretty soon," added Zen.

"Well, it is a fact that the area contains a number of nuclear research centers," said Todd, choosing her words as carefully as he had.

Zen glanced toward the door. The steward was approaching with their dinners.

"Meat loaf," said Todd. "One of your favorites."

"It is," said Zen, sounding a little surprised.

"You must have mentioned it somewhere," said Todd. "The staff doesn't miss much."

"I bet they don't."

"I like it, too," she confessed. "Especially the gravy. But it's very fattening."

They ate in silence for a while.

"Very good meat loaf," said Zen.

"I think a full and candid report is in order for your committee," said the President. "As soon as it can be arranged."

"How long, do you think, before that can happen?"

"It may be twenty-four hours," said Todd.

"That's quite a while," said Zen. "There are a lot of historical precedents with much shorter time spans."

"Hmmm."

The Constitution gave Congress the power to declare war, of course, but the operation was far short of that. Current law called for the President to "consult" with Congress about the use of force, but even that was a gray area here. The previous administration, and the two before that, hadn't felt the need to inform Congress of *every* covert operation being undertaken, and in fact had even been rather "loose" when talking about specific programs.

On the other hand, this was an extremely volatile issue, and the dire consequences could certainly include war. Todd knew she needed to keep Congress on her side, and alienating the Intelligence Committee would not help her meet that goal.

"I think we should have enough information for a thorough briefing by then," she said. "But there's always a possibility it will take longer."

"I would think that if something was going to happen that involved a great deal of resources," said Zen, "a lot of resources, then consultation would have to take place before those resources were ultimately committed."

Todd took that to mean the committee wanted to be informed before she sent the bombers in.

"I don't know that that would be possible," she parried.

"Possible or not, I would guess that would be the sentiment of the full committee."

"So the volume of resources makes a difference?" said Todd.

"Well, I don't know how one measures that," said Zen carefully. "I do know that, personally, I draw a line somewhere. But if there were, well—to speak theoretically—if there was a sizable commitment, something so large that the press couldn't help but notice—there are a lot of members who naturally, and rightly, would press for an explanation."

Todd didn't answer. Zen wasn't necessarily demanding that she inform Congress before she attacked, but he was certainly telling her that if she didn't, there'd be consequences. But then, she was already aware of that.

"In the meantime, I'd like to schedule that briefing from NSC or the Agency," said Zen, meaning the National Security Council or CIA staff. "Can we say first thing in the morning?"

"I think that's premature."

"The afternoon?"

"I don't know that I could commit to that."

"An entire day." Zen's voice more than hinted disapproval. "That's a long time under the circumstances. A lot may happen by then."

"I know some on the committee thinks the intelligence services are overstaffed," said Todd, her tone matching Zen's. "But I'm sure you don't share that feeling."

Zen only smiled. They ate for a while longer, each concentrating on the food, until Todd broke the silence with a remark about the Nationals, who had unfortunately just lost five games in a row. Zen responded with some thoughts about how soon the hitting might come around. Dessert arrived in the form of a peach cobbler, but Zen took only a few bites.

Todd skipped hers completely. She had a great deal of work to do; the staff knew to save it as a midnight snack, when it would get a fresh dollop of ice cream on the side.

"Tell me one thing," said Zen as he got ready to leave. "Was it a success?"

Todd studied him. He *would* make a good President, she decided; his only problem would be the wheelchair. Were people ready to vote for someone with such an obvious handicap, even if it had been "earned" while in the service?

"Good night, Senator," she said finally. "Best to your wife."

Iran

Turk slept deeply, his mind plunging so far into its unconscious layers that he had no memory of dreams when he woke. He was disoriented for a moment, unsure where he was. Then he saw the boulders at the side of the dugout space where he'd bedded down. He rolled onto his back and saw blue sky above.

"Come on," said Grease. He was a few feet away, hastily grabbing gear. "We have to go."

Turk rose to a sitting position. "What time is it?"

"Oh-seven-twenty. Come on. We have to move."

"Did you wake me up?"

"Yeah. Come on."

"What's happened? Were we spotted?" asked Turk.

"No—they have a new mission for us. For you."

"Huh?"

"We're not done yet," added Grease, walking out around the sand pile.

Turk shook out the blanket he'd slept on and folded it up. The control gear and his rifle were sitting next to him. He checked the pack, made sure everything was there, then shouldered it and went to find the others.

Gorud, the Israeli, and Captain Granderson were standing near the hood of the car, bent over a paper map. Not one of them looked anything less than disgusted.

"Here's the pilot now," said the Israeli. "Let's ask him."

"We have to get up beyond Qom without being seen," said Granderson. "We have to be up there before midnight. They want you to launch another strike. And they won't tell us where it is until we're in place."

"How can we go somewhere if we don't know where we're going?" asked Turk.

"Even the pilot is baffled," said the Israeli darkly.

"It's not his fault," answered Gorud. He slid the map around to show Turk. "We'll backtrack up this way, and go the long way around, across the mountains, then come down through the desert. This way, we avoid the area they hit altogether."

"Back up a second," said Turk. "How are we going to attack the place again? It blew up."

"It's another facility," said Gorud. "They didn't know it was there. But they're not sharing details at the moment. This is roughly where we're going. It's north of Qom."

Qom—rendered sometimes on maps as Q'um, Qum, or Ghom—was located about a hundred miles south of Tehran, and at least two hundred by air from where they were. Qom was a holy city, with hundreds of seminaries and universities. It housed a number of important sites sacred to the Shi'ite branch of Islam, and served as the general locus of several nuclear enrichment plants.

"We have to go north," said Granderson. "Stay

as far away from the crash site as possible. Then we'll cut east. We don't want to be stopped, if at all possible."

"What do we do if we are?" asked Grease, peering over Turk's shoulder.

"Deal with it, depending on the circumstances."

WITH THE CAR AHEAD OF THE TROOP TRUCK, THEY drove northward through the desert on a barely discernible road. They risked the lack of pavement to cut an hour off their time and avoid the highway, which one of the scouts said had been heavily traveled by military and official vehicles since dawn. The scrub on the hillside gradually became greener as they drove, and soon they saw a small patchwork of narrow streams and ditches, with an occasional shallow pond.

Turk, sitting in the back passenger seat of the car, passed the time by trying to imagine what sort of people lived here and what their lives were like. Farmers of some sort, though most seemed to have given up tilling some years before. The handful of buildings they passed—always very quickly—looked abandoned.

As they wound their way down on a road that led west, they passed a high orchard whose fruit trees were fed from a shallow but wide creek along the road. Two men were inspecting the trees. Turk slid down in the seat and watched them stare as they passed.

A few minutes later they found the road blocked by a dozen goats ambling passively down the hill.

The goatherd was in no hurry to move, even when the Israeli, impatient in the driver's seat, began to use the horn. The goatherd cast an evil eye at the car and the truck behind it, slowly guiding his charges off the road.

"You think he knows we're foreigners?" Turk asked Grease when they finally cleared the obstruction.

"I think he doesn't like the government or the army," said Grease. "Common out here."

A few minutes later, as they approached the heart of the valley, Gorud spotted a pair of Iranian soldiers near the side of the road. They were about a half mile outside of a small hamlet that marked the intersection of their trail and a wider road that led to a local highway north.

"There'll be a roadblock," said Gorud over the team radio to Granderson and the others in the truck. "You're escorting us away from the earthquake zone. We're under orders from the oil ministry to report to Kerman by noon."

Kerman was an administrative center, sufficiently big and far enough away that it should impress whoever stopped them.

Sure enough, a checkpoint appeared two bends later. Two soldiers ambled from the side of the road as they approached. The men, both privates and neither old enough to grow more than a loose stubble on their chins, raised their arms to stop the car.

"I talk," said Gorud. "You can mumble in Russian, but it's best if you don't say anything."

He rolled down the window as Dread eased

on the brakes. Rather than getting out, Gorud climbed up so that he was sitting on the ledge of the door, talking over the roof to the two soldiers. He waved papers at them, speaking in rapid Farsi.

An officer walked out from behind the small clump of trees. His body language said he had a long day in front of him and didn't want it to start badly.

Gorud took full advantage, and began yelling at the man before he even reached the road. He slipped out from the window, papers in hand, and began walking toward him, still yelling. The officer finally put up his hands apologetically, then waved at the driver to continue. The two privates stepped back and Gorud got in the car.

"Go, go, go, go," he said softly. "Let's get out of here."

Turk relaxed and leaned his head to the right, looking past Gorud to see what lay ahead.

The sharp crack of rifle made him start to turn his head. There was another shot a second later, then automatic rifle fire and a light machine gun, but by then Grease had grabbed him and pushed him down toward the floor to protect him.

10

CIA campus, Virginia

Rᴀʏ Rᴜʙᴇᴏ ᴛᴏᴜᴄʜᴇᴅ ʜɪs ᴇᴀʀ ʙᴇғᴏʀᴇ ʀᴇᴘʟʏɪɴɢ ᴛᴏ Breanna's question—a bad sign, she realized.

"You might have enough vehicles to strike both plants," he told her.

"From what you've seen of the three-dimensional map," said Danny, "do you think it's possible?"

"Possible, Colonel, is one thing. Just about anything is possible. But *will* it happen? That is another question."

"Your best guess, Ray. Will it work?"

Rubeo frowned, and crossed his arms. The body at the front of the conference room appeared *almost* real—if Breanna squinted, she would have sworn that Rubeo was actually standing there. But in fact he was speaking from his home out West; his image was a hologram.

"I think it's the sort of gamble we can only decide to take when we have *all* the target data," said Rubeo.

"What if we don't get any more?" asked Breanna.

"Then it becomes a computing problem. A difficult one."

"All right, thank you," she said. "We'll be in touch soon."

The holographic projection disappeared.

"He's in a particularly upbeat mood," said Danny.

"What do you think?"

"Unless the Agency develops more information in the next few hours, I think you have to split the forces," said Danny. "You only have a few hours left."

"I'm not even confident they can get the best route figured out by then," confessed Breanna. "There's so little data on the sites."

She swung in the chair and picked up the phone to call Jonathon Reid, who was over in the CIA main building.

"We're still working on it," said Reid when they connected. "By eight A.M. our time, I hope to have a definitive word on which of the two sites it is. New images from the 57 would be helpful."

"If we send the aircraft now, it won't be ready to support the assault," said Breanna. The problem was not the plane but the gear—it had to be carefully reprogrammed and calibrated before the mission.

"Understood."

"If we can't get more data, we'll find a way to strike both sites," she said. "It's our only option to make the President's deadline."

11

Iran

TURK STRUGGLED TO GET UP FROM THE FLOOR OF THE car, but it was impossible with Grease holding him down. The car whipped up the road, fishtailing and taking several turns before straightening out.

"What the hell is going on?" he asked when Grease finally let him up.

"I'm keeping you alive," said Grease roughly.

"I mean with the gunfire."

"They just started shooting."

They drove another five minutes before pulling over. Gorud hopped out. Turk reached for the door but Grease stopped him.

"No chances." Grease shook his head. "Stay in the car."

"Come on, damn it. I'm not a fuckin' kid."

"It's safer in here, and it won't be a minute. Two guys got shot up pretty bad," added Grease.

"So you want me to just sit here while the CIA and Mossad figure out what to do?" asked Turk, reaching for the door handle to his left. "No thank you."

This time Grease didn't stop him. Turk slammed his door and stalked back to the truck. Gorud stood talking to the Israeli at the passenger side of the cab. Captain Granderson, grim-faced and blood splattered, came out from the back.

"What the hell is going on?" demanded Turk.

Both men ignored him. Turk grabbed Gorud by the shoulder and turned him around with such ferocity that he surprised even himself. Taken off guard, the CIA officer stumbled back against the side of the truck, dropping the paper map he had folded in his hand.

"I said, what the hell is going on?" demanded Turk.

"We're trying to figure out how to get north as quickly as possible, without too much risk," said Gorud. He straightened, trying to recover his composure.

"You were talking about the Caspian," said Captain Granderson.

"He was," said Gorud, gesturing at the Israeli. "Not me."

"My mission here is complete," said the Israeli. "You can do what you want. I am leaving."

"Then start walking," snapped Turk.

The Israeli looked as if he'd been slapped across the face. He turned to Gorud and said something in Farsi. Gorud didn't respond.

Turk looked at Granderson. "What happened back there? Why did they shoot?"

"I don't know. They just started firing as we drove up. They must have seen something about the truck. We killed them all. I don't think they had time to radio, but we won't have too much of a head start once someone checks with them and they don't answer."

Turk reached down and picked up the map. They were at the edge of high desert, land that on the map seemed empty, but he knew from the satellite images that it would be studded with small settlements.

"This spot here—this is where the fuel rendez-vous was to be with the helicopter, correct?" He pointed out the mark to Gorud.

"That's right."

"Let's take the road that leads to it, sweep north, and then back west."

"It will add hours of travel time," said Gorud. "Better to go directly. Our gas is limited."

"There's a town here," said Granderson, point-ing to Khur. "We can get gas there."

"We may be questioned," answered Gorud.

"We'll be questioned everywhere. Let's go—we need to move."

"I agree," said Turk. "Let's do it."

He turned and found Grease standing so close to him that he nearly collided with him.

The Israeli started to object. "This doesn't make sense."

"It's what we're doing," said Turk. "Like I told you, you can always walk."

THE SIXTY MILES BY AIR TO THE REFUEL SITE WERE easily doubled by the switchbacks and curving roads that took them there. In several places the road was only theoretical, a fictional notion on the map describing a path that had been brushed away by a surge of wind-driven dirt and sand.

At least they weren't being followed. Turk kept expecting aircraft to appear overhead, but the only ones he heard were well to the south.

It was nearly noon by the time they reached the abandoned strip mine where the fuel for the helicopter had been hidden. Waiting about a half mile south for a two-man scouting team to make sure the area was clear, Turk considered what he would do if it turned out to be an ambush. He checked and rechecked the AK-47 and pistol.

I'll save the last bullet for myself.

A fine, romantic thought. But almost impossible to carry out, he suspected. In the heat of battle, who was going to count bullets?

He would gladly exchange the pistol or rifle, for that matter, for an airplane. On the ground he was nothing. Put him in the air and he could take on anyone.

"It's clear," said Gorud, touching his earphone as the radio transmission came in. "Drive in slowly. We don't want too much dust."

The hiding place was a man-made horseshoe canyon, with the two arms squeezed together at the southwest, away from the road. They went in slowly, but still kicked up so much sand that Turk couldn't see when he got out of the car.

The supplies had been tucked into a crevice at the side of the right arm, where the site had been quarried and workers created or enlarged a small cave. Besides the fuel drums, there were emergency supplies including water and packaged food.

Green, the Delta top sergeant, opened up one of the food packages and passed out the contents. Turk ate with abandon. The Delta troopers took theirs and then fanned out into protective positions outside the perimeter. Grease stayed with Turk; Granderson and Green huddled near the barrels, whispering together. Gorud and the Israeli, meanwhile, sat together in the car, silent.

Ironically, the two Delta men who'd been wounded were the designated medics. Tiny was by far the worse. Semiconscious, he'd lost a great deal of blood from two bullet holes in his thigh, and a third at the top of his hip looked nearly as bad. The other man who'd been hurt was Dread; his shoulder was shot up and he had a graze wound to his cheek.

"Chick magnet," he told Turk, pointing to the bandage. "Scar'll get me laid for the rest of my life."

Doc was less cheery about Tiny's wounds. "Medevacking him out would be a good idea."

"Yeah," was all Turk could say. They both knew it was impossible.

Granderson had dropped off two of his men a few miles south to make sure they weren't being followed. They checked in every few minutes, reporting that the road remained deserted. But they could see a good amount of activity at a town just two miles to the east, a patch of green in the chalky hills.

Set in the shadow of a Z-shaped hill, the town was crisscrossed by green fields divided into small rectangles flanking the shallow valley. There were maybe two hundred houses on the outskirts of the fields.

What looked like army barracks were located directly across from a group of large barns. They appeared to be empty, save for a single pickup truck baking in the middle of the courtyard.

"I'd like to take that truck," said Granderson, relating to Turk what the men had seen. "If we did, maybe at some point we could get rid of this one. The hole in the windshield is a pretty obvious giveaway."

"You think you can grab it in the middle of the day?" asked Turk.

"Why not? If it's just sitting there."

"Be a good idea to use their gas as well," said Grease. "Give us more of a reserve."

"True."

Green had quietly listened to the discussion. Now he stepped forward. "If they have med supplies, that would be even better. If we can get some plasma for Tiny, it might make the difference. Might."

"Unlikely they have plasma," said Grease.

"Worth a try," said Granderson.

"If we're going there, then it makes sense to look," said Green. "That's all I'm saying."

"What's Gorud say?" asked Turk.

"I wanted to get it straight with you first," said Granderson.

The captain was trying to get his votes together, as it were, before confronting Gorud and the Israeli with what he assumed they would think was a risky venture. Turk guessed the Israeli would be opposed, but he wasn't sure what Gorud would do.

"Do you think you could pull it off?" Turk asked.

"Yeah," said Granderson without hesitation. "We could."

Turk looked at Green. The soldier nodded, then at Grease. His stone-faced expression gave nothing away.

"I'll back you," Turk said to Granderson. "Let's talk to Gorud."

They walked over to the CIA officer and the Israeli. Turk spoke first.

"The Delta boys think they can get a truck in town," he said. "They can get medicine for Tiny, too."

"Plasma," said Granderson.

"There's a set of army barracks that are deserted," continued Turk. "It's a little out of town, isolated—we could get in and out."

"At the barracks?" asked Gorud.

"Place looks empty," said Granderson. "Or I wouldn't suggest it."

"Risky." Gorud looked at Turk. "Your mission is our primary concern. We're not even sure where we're going yet."

"Understood." Turk noted that Gorud's attitude toward him had subtly changed. He wasn't deferential, exactly, but he was at least treating him with more respect. "And I know it's a gamble, but it might help us get there easier. And we might be able to save our guy."

Gorud frowned. He took the paper map from his pocket and examined it, as if the answer were written in the topographic lines that waved across the landscape, or the symbols at the bottom of the page.

"If we can get in and out of the compound without trouble," he said finally, "it would definitely be worth it."

THEY SET UP A PERIMETER, MEN WATCHING THE BACK and sides of the compound as well as the road, and then they went with a plan both simple and audacious—they drove directly to the buildings. Granderson leapt from the truck, followed by Dome and Meyer; they ran and began clearing what they assumed was the barracks. Gorud and the Israeli took the second building.

Meanwhile, Grease and Turk went to the pickup. Grease pulled it open, intending to jimmy out the ignition wiring with his combat knife. But the key was in the ignition. He hopped in and started it up while Turk watched anxiously with the rifle.

"Full tank," said Grease. "Your luck is holding."

A burst of automatic weapons fire sent Grease scrambling from the cab as Turk ducked behind the rear tire. Two more long bursts followed. Turk felt a twinge of self-doubt—he'd argued that coming inside with the others was as safe or safer than staying outside. Now he wasn't so sure.

Grease put his hand to the radio headset. "It's just them," he said. "They're good. Come on. Get in."

Turk jumped into the back of the truck bed as Grease got behind the wheel. He drove the pickup to the door of the building, backing around so they could load it easier. Meanwhile, the troop truck was driven across the way to the fuel pump at the end of the compound. One of the troopers hopped out and began filling it with fuel.

"We can get fresh uniforms," said Gorud, appearing. "Help."

Turk shouldered the AK-47 as he ran into the building, Grease close behind. The structure looked at least a hundred years old. The clay bricks leaned toward the interior and the ceiling hung low. Turk ducked through the door and entered a long hallway that ran along the front of the building. It had been modernized during the seventies or eighties; ceramic tile lined the floor, and the walls had faded to a dirty gray.

Meyer waved to Turk from the far end of the hall. Turk passed two empty barracks rooms on the left; a body lay on the floor of the second in a pool of blood. Two more lay at the intersection at the far end, just to the left of Meyer.

"Medical room at the back." Meyer thumbed down the other hall. "They're getting supplies. There's a computer in that office," he added, pointing to the first doorway down the side corridor. "We'll take that, too. Grab any clothes you can find."

Turk stepped over the bodies. One had a pistol in his hand; another gun, an older rifle with a wooden stock, lay on the floor. As he stepped into the office, he saw movement out of the corner of his eye and spun right; he jerked around, ready to fire, only to discover it was a small oscillating fan, moving left and right.

Shaking his head, he went to the computer. It

was an American-made Dell with an Internet Explorer browser open to an odd porn site: it featured a virtual game where the characters were in the process of disrobing each other.

There were several other tabs open. One was for what looked like a news site in Tehran; the lettering was Persian, and he had no idea what it said. Turk clicked on the video player at the middle of the page and footage of a desert began to play—it appeared to be a report on the "earthquake" that had struck Natanz.

The footage showed rows of demolished houses. He stared at them for a few moments, amazed at the damage, wondering if it was real.

"That's Badroud," said Gorud, coming into the room behind him. "They didn't know they were sitting on an atomic bomb. Excuse me." After gently pushing Turk aside, he took the mouse and started fiddling with the browser, first checking the history and then opening the Favorites folder.

"You can read this?" Turk asked him.

"You think I'd be here if I couldn't?" Gorud frowned at him. "I want to make sure they didn't get an alert out," he added, his voice less antagonistic. "Doesn't look like it."

"Do they know what happened?" Turk asked.

"The news, at least, believes it's an earthquake." Gorud straightened. "Or that's what they say. Come on. We gotta go."

He pulled the wires from the back without turning the machine off. Granderson and the others were already outside. They'd found plasma and were treating Tiny. Turk peeked into the back and saw the soldier lying comatose, his skin so pale it looked like a sheet of paper. He was about to ask if the man would make it but thought better of it.

"We better get moving," said Granderson, hopping off the back. "Let's go."

The pickup went first, driving out of the compound and back to the helicopter rendezvous point. There, some of them changed out of their uniforms, with Turk and Grease putting on a set of civilian clothes that had been found in one of the rooms. They were tight on Grease, loose on Turk. Then the team rearranged themselves in the vehicles—the Israeli in the car with Grease and Turk, who went back to posing as Russians; the captain and Green in the pickup, with their hired bodyguards, Gorud, and the others in the truck, in theory their Iranian escort.

"How you doing back there?" asked Grease from the front seat.

"I'm good." Turk was alone in the back.

"You're so quiet, I thought you were sleeping."

"No."

"You might try. You're going to be awake all night. And you have to be alert."

"I'll be all right. This area we're driving through," he said to the Israeli, "what are the people here like?"

"Iranians."

Grease scoffed.

"That much I knew," said Turk.

"They live at the edge of the desert. They

scrape by," said the Israeli. "If you think too much about them, you'll have trouble doing your job."

The comment effectively ended Turk's try at conversation. He slumped back in the seat.

How many people had died in the nuclear explosion, or been buried by the resulting tremors? It was the Iranian leaders' fault, he told himself, not theirs, and certainly not his. If anything, he had saved thousands, millions. Destroying the weapon meant it couldn't be used, and even the crudest math would easily show that the damage here was far less than if the weapon had been.

But though he didn't feel guilt, exactly, Turk felt unsettled. He was uneasy—uneasy with the way the world was, unsettled by reality. In a perfect world, no one would kill, no one would threaten to exterminate a race. It was disappointing to be reminded that the world was far less than perfect.

"Farmers," muttered Grease. "Right side."

Turk leaned back against the seat, watching from the lower corner of the window as they passed. Two men were doing something to a tractor; they didn't look up as the trucks passed.

A few miles later they turned westward, following a road that was little more than a trail down the side of a ridge. Probably flooded with water during the rainy season, he thought, when the rare but heavy rain washed through the area, the road now dry and wide. Its surface consisted almost entirely of small stones and pebbles, but the dirt below was soft.

Before long they started bogging down. The Israeli tried to compensate by building his momentum, but the car refused to cooperate, sliding to one side and then the other as he struggled to keep it under control. Then they spun around in a 360, jerking to a stop when the front wheels slid into a deep layer of soft sand.

The Israeli began cursing in Russian. Turk, a little dizzy, got out and fell to the ground, tripping in the loose dirt. Grease pulled him up.

The pickup stopped a short distance away, the troop truck stopping right behind it.

"We're going to have to push it out," said Grease as Granderson and Gorud ran up. "Going to have to push it this way."

"If it will come loose," said the Israeli.

"The question is whether we can get it any farther," said Granderson, looking down the path in the direction they were to take. "Nothing that way looks much better than this stretch."

Most of the men had gotten out of the truck to stretch their legs. Turk walked over and leaned in the back. "How's Tiny?" he asked.

Dread looked at him but said nothing.

Turk understood what that meant. He put his lips together. "How's your shoulder?" he asked.

"It's OK."

"We'll get home soon," offered Turk.

"Yeah."

A few awkward moments passed. Turk felt as if he should be able to offer something to the others, consolation or something. He felt responsible for Tiny. He'd been killed protecting him, after all. But there was nothing to say, nothing that wouldn't sound bizarrely stupid.

He asked Dread for water, but the trooper was listening to something else.

"Truck," he said, grabbing his pistol with his good hand. "Couple of them."

A funnel of dust appeared down the ridge.

Grease was staring at the vehicles when Turk reached him.

"Three Kaviran tactical vehicles, and a pair of two-and-a-half-ton trucks," Grease told him. The Kaviran were Iranian Land Rover knock-offs. "Two miles off, maybe a little more. They're coming right up this way."

12

Washington, D.C.

Zen stared at the number on his BlackBerry phone. It looked vaguely familiar, but he couldn't place it or the name above: DR. GROD.

He looked up from his seat in the stadium box. The National Anthem was still about five minutes off.

What the hell.

"Excuse me," he told his guests, a pair of junior congressmen from Florida who had supported one of his bills in the House. "I guess I should take this. It's on my personal line."

He wheeled himself back a few feet and hit the talk button.

"This is Zen."

"Senator Stockard?"

"This is Zen. What can I do for you?"

"It's Gerry Rodriguez from the Vegas clinic. Remember me from Dreamland? I know it's been a while."

"Gerry." Zen closed his eyes, trying to associate the name with Dreamland.

"I had interviewed you as a follow-up to the experiments that followed, well, what the press ended up calling the 'nerve center experiments.' The cell regeneration group."

"Right, right, right." The experiments he remembered; Gerry he didn't.

"You asked if I ever came up with anything . . . about regenerating the spinal tissue. If there was a project—"

"Sure." Zen glanced toward the front of his box. The two congressmen were rising; the National Anthem was about to begin.

"I'm going to be in Washington tomorrow, as it happens. And I'd like to talk to you. If, uh, we could arrange it. I know your schedule is pretty tight, but—"

Zen got requests like this all the time: scientists looking for direction on how to get funding— and often specifically handouts. Standard Operating Procedure was to fend them off to one of his aides.

"Come around to the office and we can discuss it then," he told his caller.

"Um, when?"

"Whenever. I don't have my appointments

handy. Tomorrow, the next day. See Cheryl. She'll take care of you."

"Great. I—"

"Listen, I'm sorry. I have to go." Zen hit the end call button and rolled toward the front of the box just as the music began.

13

Iran

THE IRANIAN MILITARY COLUMN WAS TOO CLOSE FOR them to simply avoid. Granderson decided their best bet was simply to play through—keep moving along the road, moving with purpose, and hope to pass the column without hassle.

It almost worked.

With the car in the lead, the American caravan quickly set out, moving along the scratch road as quickly as it could. As they approached the lead Kaviran, the Israeli tucked as far to the side as he dared, the wheels of the car edging into the soft dirt. The Kaviran kept going. Turk, who had his head back against the car seat, caught a glimpse of the driver, eyes fixed on the road ahead, worried about getting past the pickup and truck. The next Kaviran thumped by. Turk saw the passenger in the front of the third Kaviran turn toward them, craning his neck to see inside.

"Faster," muttered Grease.

But the Israeli was struggling to keep the vehicle simply moving. The two troop trucks hogged the road, and the only way to pass them was to swerve onto the loose gravel at the side. The Israeli waited until the last possible moment, then pitched the car to the right, drifting precariously toward a drop-off on the other side. They held the road, though just barely. Turk grabbed the handle of the door next to him as the car slipped around, the back wheels sliding free on the gravel.

Clear of the last truck, they had just started to accelerate when Turk heard a loud pop behind them. It sounded a little like a firecracker or a backfire, not a bullet, and he at first couldn't make sense of it. In the next second, Grease barked at the Israeli to keep going and get the hell out of there. Turk turned around, trying to see what was going on, but all he saw was dust swirling everywhere, a massive tornado of yellow edged with brown. Reaching to the floor, he retrieved his rifle. By the time he got it, Grease had leaned over from the front and was pushing down on his shoulders, yelling at him to stay down.

"We have to help them," protested Turk.

"Just stay the hell down."

The next few minutes passed in a blur, the Israeli going as fast as he could up the road, Grease holding Turk down while he tried to get the rest of the team on the radio. The jagged hills played havoc with the low-intercept; he kept calling to the others without a response. Turk struggled to free himself even as he realized there was little he could do.

By the time Grease let go, the Israeli had started braking. They came around a curve in the mountain, swerving into a descent and two switchbacks until finally coming to a flat piece of land. He pulled over behind a tumble of rocks.

"Where are our guys?" demanded Turk.

"Easy," said Grease, letting him go. "You're more important than all of us combined. We'll sort it out."

Turk's legs shook when they first touched the dirt. He took a few steps toward the road before Grease caught him, the Delta trooper's thick fingers clamping hard into his arm.

"Where the hell do you think you're going?" Grease demanded.

Turk spun toward him. Their faces were bare inches apart. "I'm not going to stay back while our guys are getting pounded."

"Our job isn't to save them."

"Screw that."

"No," said Grease firmly. "Your mission is more important than their lives. Much more important. If you fail—they fail. They don't want you hurt."

Flustered, Turk opened his mouth to speak but couldn't.

"Listen," said the Israeli. "Something's coming."

They ran back to the rocks, Grease dragging Turk with him. Turk took a knee and peered out, trying to sort his feelings. Grease was absolutely right—and yet he felt responsible for the others. In his gut he knew he had to help them, no matter the cost.

The curve of the hills muffled the noise at first,

and it wasn't until the pickup appeared that Turk was sure the vehicles were theirs, and only theirs.

Granderson leaned out the passenger-side window of the troop truck. The truck had been battered, the windshield and side window completely blown out, and half the front fender hung down. "What the hell are you stopped for?" he yelled. "Go! *Go!*"

"Are you OK?" Turk shouted.

"Just get the hell out of here!" yelled the Delta captain. "Just go, go go! Damn. *Grease!* Get the hell out of here."

"We're going," he said, practically throwing Turk into the car.

THEY STOPPED A HALF HOUR LATER, IN THE SHADOW OF the foothills, within sight of Jandagh, a small city that commanded one of the north-south valleys at the edge of the desert. Old archeological digs, long abandoned, sat nearby. Windswept sand pushed across low piles of rocks; the outlines of forgotten pits spread before them in an intricate geometric pattern, disturbed by an occasional outlier.

The troopers had blown up the two trucks with grenade launchers they'd taken from the barracks but were still badly mauled; the only one in the truck who hadn't been hit by bullets or shrapnel was Granderson, who miraculously survived without a scratch. Green was the worst; he'd taken shots in both legs and lost considerable blood. It was small consolation, but they'd killed all of the Iranians.

The back of their stolen troop truck had been

turned into a makeshift rolling clinic. Turk climbed up, talking to the men as Grease watched from below. Dread tried to make a joke about seeing the "beautiful Iranian outback," but it fell flat. The canvas top had been punctured by bullets, but the air inside still hung heavy and fetid, smelling of blood and cordite.

Granderson came back from the pickup to get Turk and figure out what to do next. Turk had been lingering with Green. It seemed impossible that the solid old warrior could be wounded, as if his body was made of steel and concrete, yet his legs and fresh green uniform blouse were covered with blood.

"I'm good, Pilot," he kept muttering. "I'll be all right."

There was nothing Turk could do for Green, or any of them. He slipped out and walked around the side with Granderson, who was explaining what had happened.

"The passenger in the front of the first troop truck jumped out with a handgun and tried to wave down the pickup," Granderson told him. "We didn't stop. When he started to fire, Gorud and the troop truck ran him down, but the second truck swerved to block us. We fought it out."

It hadn't taken too long—three minutes, five— but Granderson was worried that they got off a call for help; one of the command vehicles had disappeared before they could fire at it.

"Hills are so bad Grease couldn't even hear your radios," said Turk. "Probably, they couldn't get anything out."

"Maybe." Granderson turned and pointed to the troop truck. "We won't get far with this. It's pounded to crap. And the pickup's not too much better. We'll have to steal something from Jandagh."

It was just visible in the distance, off to the right. Turk rubbed the sand off his face and looked at the dunes scattered between them and the small city. Yellow buildings floated below a wavy haze. Patches of green appeared like bunting amid the parched landscape and distant bricks.

"We'll never get a truck out of there during the day without being seen," said Gorud, walking over with the Israeli. His left arm was wrapped in a thick bandage. "Assuming we find one."

"Sitting here is not a good idea," said the Israeli.

They studied the GPS and the paper map. They were roughly two hundred miles from the target area, and that was if they went on a straight line. Even the best roads would add another hundred miles.

"Maybe the best thing to do is split up," Gorud suggested to Granderson. "Take the pilot west for the mission. You wait until dark, then take the truck and go north to the escape route. Route 81 is nearby."

"We're not leaving without you," said Turk.

"Gorud is right," suggested the Israeli.

"It's not going to happen," said Turk. He glanced at Grease. The soldier's stone face offered no hint about what he should say or do. "What if we wait until nightfall?" he asked. "Then we slip into the city and take what we need."

"Not with wounded," said Granderson.

"What other cities are there along the way?" Turk asked. "We could go a little distance, stretch it a little bit, then steal something."

That seemed promising, until they examined the map. The desert west of Jandagh was mostly dunes; the car probably wouldn't make it and the pickup might not either. So the only route possible was north, where about eighty miles of travel would take them to a cluster of hill cities and oases. If the truck made it that far, it could go the entire way.

Before they could make a decision, Turk heard helicopters in the distance. As they scrambled back to the vehicles, he had an idea.

"We'll go back up the hill," he yelled. "We'll make it look like we're investigating what happened."

He spotted the helicopters a few minutes after the car pulled onto the road. There were two, both Shabaviz 2-75s, Iranian reverse-engineered variants of Bell's ubiquitous Huey series. They looked like Bell 214s, with a thick, rectangular-shaped engine box above the cabin. Dressed in drab green paint, they were definitely military aircraft. They flew from the north, arcing over the sand in the general direction of the gunfight, though about two miles from it.

"They going to be close enough to see what happened there?" Turk asked as they drove back up the road. They were going as slow as the Israeli could manage without stalling the car.

"Absolutely," said Grease.

The helicopters continued southward for a half minute, then turned in a circle and headed toward the vehicles. Grease radioed a warning to the others but got no response, even though they were within a few hundred yards of each other.

Turk fingered his rifle as the helicopters approached. They appeared unarmed, but someone inside the back cabin with a machine gun could do a hell of a lot of damage.

On the other hand, if the choppers did land, the crews might be overpowered.

Turk didn't know how to fly a helicopter, but he certainly had every incentive to try.

The helicopters skipped low near the side of the mountain, passing near the vehicles. They flew over the car and the small caravan and promptly banked away, back in their original direction.

The sound of the rotors grew steadily softer. The Israeli continued for a short while and found a place to turn around. They passed the pickup as it started into a three-point turn.

The troop truck wheezed up the road, then just stopped as they drew near. Granderson got out and started to climb underneath. As he did, the truck lurched backward. Granderson froze, then looked underneath gingerly as Dome pressed hard on the brake.

"Oil case is dinked all to hell," the captain told them. "There's mud all across the top of the chassis. Must be from the fluid leaking."

"We can back it down to the spot where we were," suggested Turk.

There wasn't too much question now. They

needed another vehicle. They were going into Jandagh.

14

Jandagh, Iran

IF THEY WEREN'T GOING TO WAIT UNTIL NIGHTFALL, Gorud suggested, then the best approach would be to drive straight in and attempt to buy—or steal—an extra vehicle. And in that case, the most likely candidates were Gorud and the Israeli, since they both spoke the language well and were reasonably familiar with the country. But Gorud was wounded and wouldn't be much in a fight, so Turk suggested that he go in his place, which would have the advantage of leaving behind a guide in case something went wrong. Grease, his shadow, would go with him.

No one else liked the idea, but it didn't take long for them to see it was the most practical alternative if they weren't going to wait until night. They worked out a cover story on the way—they were Russians, one of their vehicles had broken down, and they wanted to buy or lease another to make it across the desert to the town where they were supposed to meet an official from the oil ministry.

Jandagh, like many Iranian cities, had a broad but only lightly used main street. It was anchored by two roundabouts on the southern end. Trees lined both sides of the road, though their short branches provided little shade. Beyond them to the west, wind blew the loose sand off the dunes, driving it toward the white walls of the houses. It hadn't been exactly cool in the hills, but now the heat built oppressively, overwhelming the car's air conditioner and drawing so much sweat from Turk that his white button-down shirt soaked through, graying with the flying grit.

They saw no one on the street until they neared the second traffic circle. Two children were standing in the shade of a doorstep, staring at the car. Farther on, a small knot of men sat on some boxes and leaned against the facade of a building that looked to Turk like an old-fashioned candy shop. A police car sat opposite the end of the circle, its lone occupant watching from behind closed windows.

They passed it slowly, then continued along the road, which was divided by a center island of trees, these in slightly better condition than the others. Turk guessed that there might be a dozen people walking or standing in front of the buildings on either side of the next quarter mile of road. On the right side the buildings were separated by long alleys in a perfect if small grid; from above they would look like a maze for learning disabled rats. The buildings on the other side were larger and more randomly arranged. Most met the public with plain walls of stuccoed stone.

"See anything worth taking?" Grease asked the Israeli.

"Nothing."

Another large intersection marked the end of the quarter-mile main street. The Israeli passed through it cautiously. The buildings surrounding them were residential, and there were more vehicles on the side of the street—many more, including several vans that Turk thought they might take.

"Easy enough to find once the sun goes down," said the Israeli. "There are too many people around to try it now."

They avoided the old city and fort area on the hill, turning left and heading toward the highway. Here, there were more vehicles, including several tractor trailers parked around a large open space at the side of the highway. An array of small shops stood at the city end of the space; they were family-run restaurants. Men stood in most of the doorways, bored touts who perked up as soon as they saw the car, but then slouched back when it became obvious it wasn't stopping.

"There was a junkyard just where we first turned," said Grease when the road opened up. "There were some cars and a pickup or two. We might try there."

The Israeli turned around.

The junkyard was actually a garage, the finest not only in Jandagh but the best in any desert in the world, according to the gap-toothed man in his seventies who ambled over to greet them when they got out of the car. The Israeli gave him a brief version of the cover story, but the old man didn't seem too interested in why they were there. He had several vehicles they would be interested in, he said, urging them toward a group parked in front of the ramshackle buildings on the lot.

None of the cars was less than a decade old, and a few appeared to be missing significant parts, ranging from a fender to an exhaust system. The prices, as best as Turk could tell, were commensurate; the highest was only 50 million rials—$2,500, give or take. The Israeli haggled over the prices, but it was all show; none of these vehicles would suit their purposes.

Turk saw one that might—a school bus, parked next to a pair of vans and a panel truck at the far end of the lot. The Israeli saw it as well, but he worked the owner like a pro, meandering around, arguing, dismissing, obtaining a price for everything and committing to nothing. Eventually, he settled on one of the vans next to the bus, going back and forth on the price and requirements—he wanted new seat cushions, which the dealer couldn't do, and a full tank of gas, which would have come close to doubling the price of eight million rials. Feigning frustration, he pointed to the school bus and asked how much that was.

One hundred million Rials, with some diesel thrown in.

Too, too much. The Israeli went back to the van.

"I'm going to get him to help me buy my next car," Turk whispered to Grease.

Grease didn't answer. He was gazing across the empty lot at the side, to the far road. The police car they'd seen earlier had driven over and parked nearby.

"Watching us?" said Turk when he saw it.

"That or they're thinking of upgrading."

The Israeli spent a few more minutes haggling before the lot owner gave up in frustration, deciding that he was just a tire-kicker.

"We'll come back," whispered the Israeli, walking over to them. "I think we can steal the bus."

"Cop's watching us," said Grease under his breath.

"I see."

They got into their car and drove a short distance to a small restaurant. The Israeli did all the talking here, ordering an early dinner and filling the server in on their backstory—Russians, visiting sites that promised to yield oil, and how bad was the earthquake? The story was intended for the policeman, who had followed but stayed outside; surely he would come in and question the owner if he didn't stop them himself. Turk and Grease played along, exchanging bits of Russian while the Israeli chatted up the waiter, who turned out to be the owner of the place.

The man's face grew worried when pressed for details about the earthquake. He had heard rumors, he said, that it wasn't an earthquake at all, but an attack by American stealth bombers. If so, there would be hell to pay, he predicted; the Americans would be wiped off the face of the earth.

The Israeli pretended to translate all of this into Russian, then translated their "responses," agreeing with the Iranian that the Americans were the worst people on earth, always ready to stir trouble. Absolute devils.

No, said the shop owner, it was just their government that was bad; he had met Americans several times, and always they were polite and even generous. It was a shame that their leaders were so horrible.

Grease grinned when the Israeli relayed this after the owner disappeared into the back. The dishes came out shortly—rice and vegetables covered with a thin sauce. The sauce had a curried taste, which ordinarily would have turned Turk's nose if not his stomach, but he was hungry, and he finished his small plateful quickly.

They spent just under an hour in the café. During that time, they could have been tourists or even the Russian oilmen they claimed to be, oblivious to the dangers both of their mission and Iran in general. But reality confronted them as soon as they emerged—the policeman who'd been watching them earlier had been joined by a companion. They were now camped on the front bumper of their car.

They'd obviously searched the vehicle—the two AK-47s they'd left under the seats as a precaution were on the hood.

"I'll handle it," whispered the Israeli. "Stay back a bit. They just want bribes. Speak Russian only."

The Israeli stormed toward them, yelling in Russian that they were thieves and waving papers in their faces. The Iranians wilted under the pressure of his complaints, backing toward the car and gesturing with open palms.

Grease casually positioned his hand at the back of his right hip, ready to grab the pistol hidden in the small of his back. Turk's pistol was at his belt, under the baggy shirt—harder to grab. He stood with his arms crossed, trying to rehearse grabbing it in his mind. All he could think about was an infamous case a few years before back in the States, where a football star accidentally shot his leg while grabbing a Glock from his waistband.

The Israeli modulated his tone, and it was clear they were now negotiating the price of a "fine." Turk started to relax, until he saw Grease's mouth tighten. He followed Grease's stare out to the highway, where another police car was just turning toward them.

"Getting expensive," said Turk.

"Let's hope that's all it is."

Grease took a small step toward their car, then another. Turk realized what he was doing—he wanted to be as close as possible to the rifles if there was trouble. Turk decided to take a more direct route; he walked over to the Israeli as if listening in. The Israeli swatted the air, waving him off; Turk slid back against the fender of the car. Grease joined him.

The policeman the Israeli had been negotiating with suddenly stopped talking, noticing the other police car for the first time. He yelled something at the Israeli and pushed him back, his fist suddenly in the Israeli's chest.

The other officer went for his gun.

Grease got his first, firing two shots into the man's chest. Turk grabbed both AKs and ducked behind their car as Grease fired at the policeman they'd been negotiating with. The police car that had come off the highway, meanwhile, sped toward Grease and the Israeli. Turk rose and began firing, riddling the passenger compartment with gunfire as the car careened across the lot toward Grease. The sergeant leapt out of the way at the last moment, but the Israeli was caught by the back end of the police car as it fishtailed. He fell back, just barely missing being pinned as one vehicle smashed against the other.

Turk had backed away from both vehicles, but the impact drove the police car against the front of their car and pushed it all the way to where he was standing, knocking him onto his back.

"Turk, Turk!" yelled Grease.

"I'm good, I'm good."

He struggled to his feet, the rifle still in his hands. Grease made sure the policemen were all dead, then went to the Israeli, who was bent over the hood of the second car.

"I'm all right," said the Israeli. "We have to get out of here."

Turk looked into the police car. His bullets had shattered the heads of both men inside; the interior was full of blood. He pulled open the door, then pushed the driver toward his companion.

"What are you doing?" Grease asked as he got in.

"I'll back it up."

The car had stalled. Turk turned the key but nothing happened. The smell of blood and torn body parts started to turn his stomach. As calmly as he could, he put the car in park, put his foot on the brake, and tried the ignition again. The car started; he backed up.

Grease helped the Israeli limp back to the vehicle. Though in obvious pain, he remained silent, moving stoically. Turk backed the police car out of the way, then got out and ran to the others.

"We better get the bus now," Turk told Grease. "They'll look for it."

"You don't think they'll look for this?"

They drove over to the lot. The man who ran the garage must have seen or at least heard the gunfire, but he was nowhere to be seen. Turk pulled near the school bus and got out. Unsure how to work the exterior lock—it was a handle that turned on the front part of the cab—he forced the door open with his rifle, then dashed up the steps.

The key wasn't in the ignition. He dashed back down, running toward the small building where the office was. The door was locked. Turk put his shoulder against it twice but failed to budge it, so he took the rifle, put it point-blank against the lock and fired. The gun jerked practically out of his hands, but the burst did enough damage that the door swung open. He pushed in, expecting to see the owner cowering inside, but the place was empty.

A large board with keys stood by the door. Turk tossed the ones that were obviously car keys, but that still left him with half a dozen to try.

Outside, Grease had lifted the Israeli into the bus, then gone to work jumping the ignition wires. He had the bus running by the time Turk appeared with the keys.

"Take the car and follow," he yelled. "Let's go. Back to the others."

15

Omidiyeh, Iran

CAPTAIN VAHID SPENT THE MORNING AFTER THE ATTACK in an administrative "freeze." While the rest of his squadron conducted a patrol around the scientific research area, the pilot was told to prepare a personal brief for the area air commander. That meeting was scheduled for 8:00 A.M.; it was postponed twice, then indefinitely "delayed." He sat the entire time in a vacant room next to the squadron commander's office, waiting with nothing to read or do. The only furniture were two chairs, both wooden; one was sturdy but uncomfortable, the other so rickety that he didn't dare to use it even as a foot rest.

A pair of plainclothes guards from the interior ministry stood at the door. He wasn't under arrest, but he wasn't allowed to leave either. He wasn't given anything to eat.

Vahid had reviewed his mission tapes, and knew that what he had shot down was some sort of light plane, not a drone and certainly not a B-2. It seemed impossible that the plane had made any sort of attack itself, or been involved in one. He had a host of theories, but they boiled down to this: either there had been a genuine earthquake, or the nuclear program had a major accident.

He favored the latter.

Vahid sat in the uncomfortable wooden chair until his butt was sore, got up and paced around until he tired of that, then sat back down. He repeated the ritual until after two in the afternoon, when one of the squadron commander's aides appeared in the doorway to tell him that the general was finally on his way.

Vahid straightened his uniform. In the days of the Shah—long before he was even born—the Iranian air force was a prominent organization, equipped with the finest fighters in the world—F-14s and F-4 Phantoms. They trained with the Americans, and while the larger Israeli air force might claim it was better, many rated the Iranians just as good. The branch was an elite part of the Iran military and its society.

The overthrow of the Shah hurt the air force tremendously. An order for F-16s was canceled. Needed parts became almost impossible to get. Worse, though, were the questions, innuendo, and accusations leveled at the pilots and the service in general. The air force had supported the Shah to the bitter end, and in the Revolution's wake, many of the officers were shunned, purged, and worse.

The service regained a measure of respect with the blood of its members during the Iran-Iraq war, where its aces shot down a number of Iraqis and carried out many successful bombing missions. But some thirty years later, the air force continued to be viewed with suspicion by many, especially the government and the Revolutionary Guard, which was jealous of any entity that might have a claim to power and influence.

Politics had always been a distant concern for Vahid, who joined the air force only because he wanted to fly. But the longer he sat in the little room with its bare walls and blue-shaded fluorescents, the more he came to realize that he was a pawn in something he didn't understand. So when the door opened and General Ari Shirazi—the head not of his wing or subcommand but the entire air force—entered, Vahid was far less surprised than he would have been twenty-four hours before.

The general studied him for a moment.

"You're hungry," Shirazi said, more an order than a statement. "Come and eat."

Vahid followed him from the room, falling in behind the general's two aides and trailed by a pair of bodyguards. They walked out of the building to the cafeteria, where the VIP room had been reserved for the general. Two sergeants were waiting near the table, already stiff at attention, as the general entered. Shirazi ignored them, gesturing to Vahid to sit before taking his own chair. He folded his arms, worked his eyes slowly across the pilot's face, then turned to one of the sergeants.

"Get the captain some lunch," said the general.

"Sir, for you?" asked one of the sergeants.

"I am not hungry."

The general placed his hands on his thighs and

leaned forward. Energy flooded into his face, and determination.

"Tell me, in your own words, everything that happened," said the general. "Hold nothing back. Begin with the alert."

"I was with my plane . . ." started Vahid.

He spent the next thirty minutes relaying every detail he could, ignoring the food that arrived. The general listened without interrupting; when Vahid paused too long, he gestured with his index finger that he should go on. Finally, Vahid was back on the ground, taxiing to the hangar area. He recounted the debriefings quickly, adding that he had not had a good look at the damage to the plane himself.

"Do you have the identification of the ground unit that fired at you and struck your plane?" asked the general.

"No, sir. I—I'm not even sure if it was a ground unit."

"What else would it be?"

"I wondered if an airplane had been far above and fired down from a great distance, random shots, or a missile that went undetected—"

Vahid stopped. The theory was too ridiculous to be credible. The way he remembered the incident, he had been struck from above. But it was impossible. His mind surely had been playing games.

"We've looked at the damage," said the general. "Multiple shots from larger caliber antiaircraft weapons. There is a Sa'ir battery south of Natanz. The weapon was fired; undoubtedly that was your assassin. Fortunately," he added dryly, "the battery is a Sepāh unit."

Sepāh was the shortened term for the Sepāh-e Pāsdārān-e Enqelāb-e Eslāmi, the Revolutionary Guard. The general's implied slur would have been daring in a lesser man; Shirazi was obviously sure of his position—or planning to have the pilot executed shortly.

Vahid was not sure which.

"You will leave us, and close the doors," the general told the servers. They quickly ducked back into the kitchen. He glanced at the guards and his aides; they stepped out, too.

"There was an accident at their facility," the general told Vahid. "It is clear from the seismic data. But they are trying to cover it up. That is impossible. Scientists are already explaining about their information. There are some near the president—"

The general stopped abruptly, considering his next words very carefully.

"Some members of the project are claiming that the Americans blew up the facility," said the general. "They have no evidence for this, of course. On the contrary, we know that was impossible—there were no bombers in the air, or missiles. They would have been on our radar. And you would have seen them."

"Yes, General."

"The reports of B-2s—you saw none."

"None. Yes."

"You're sure."

"Yes." Vahid nodded. And then he thought:

This is odd. It's the truth, and yet saying it feels like a lie.

"Clearly, it was an accident," continued the general, "but those jackals will do anything to keep themselves alive. They take no responsibility. Nothing. None."

The general's face reddened, blood flowing with his anger. It happened in a flash, as if he were a computer image changed by the flick of a button. Vahid lowered his gaze to the table. He was helpless, really, trapped by powers that regarded him as little more than an ant.

With the grace of the one true God, thought Vahid, they will shoot me and I will die quickly.

"I am going to make use of this incident, son, as others will. I tell you this because I want you to have confidence—others will pressure you to change your story. But you will stick to the truth. Because if you do stick to the truth, you will have a powerful protector. Do you understand?"

"I think I do."

"Just stick to the truth. To what you saw."

"Yes, General."

"Once an announcement is made, then that will be the government's position," continued the general, his tone now heavy with sarcasm. "There will be questions for you. Simply trust that I will watch out for you. And that your career will proceed accordingly."

Vahid faced a truly Faustian bargain. If he did what the general said, he could well be targeted by the backers of the nuclear program, including the Guards. Shirazi, so confident in an air force base, might not be nearly as powerful out in the wide world. Hitching his career, and more likely his life, to the general could prove disastrous.

On the other hand, what was the alternative? Going against Shirazi was simply impossible.

I just want to fly, thought Vahid. I don't want to be in the middle of this at all.

"Are you OK, son?" asked the general.

"Yes, General."

"We're agreed?"

"Of course. I can only tell the truth."

Shirazi leaned back from the table. "You're feeling well, now that you've eaten?"

"Yes, sir."

"So, why are you not back in the air, then?" asked the general.

"I . . . was waiting to speak to you, sir."

"Good, very good."

The general started to rise. Vahid shot to his feet. "Sir—the plane?"

"Which plane?" asked the general.

"The light plane that I encountered."

"Ah. A spy for the Israelis—delicious—a member of Sepāh. The plane was stolen from Isafahan. It flew south, then to the Esfahan region, southeast of the Natanz complexes. A body has been recovered. You don't think he was trying to bomb the plant, do you, Captain?"

It would make a great propaganda story, thought Vahid, and he would be the hero, as he had shot down the aircraft. But anyone with any knowledge of aircraft and their capabilities would scoff and point to a thousand inconsistencies.

"No," said Vahid.

"Good. Because there were no bombs or evidence of any aboard. There may have been a passenger. We're searching. As are the Pasdaran." The general gave him a fatherly pat on the shoulder. "Get back in the air, son. The sooner you fly, the better you will feel."

16

Iran

THE BUS'S BODY WAS BATTERED, BUT ITS DRIVE TRAIN was in top condition; Turk had trouble keeping up as they drove back to the site where the rest of the team was holed up. The troopers accepted the appearance of the bus without comment, as if they'd been expecting one all along. Turk told Granderson all that had happened as they carried Green into the back of bus. It started in disconnected bits, punctuated by gasps of air. Even to Turk it sounded unreal.

"Was it just a cock-up?" asked Granderson. "Or were they looking for us?"

"It might have been—I don't know."

"Doesn't matter now."

They got the wounded inside the bus, then took off, Granderson in the lead at the wheel of the school bus, followed by the Israeli alone in the pickup, and Gorud, Grease, and Turk together in the car. They let the bus get a little ahead, figur-ing it would be what the Iranian authorities would be looking for; the others would close the gap if there were trouble.

Gorud had plotted a route east of the city over mining and desert roads that would keep them away from most towns. But the roads were nearly as treacherous as driving through the town would have been. Soon after they started, they hit a long stretch of hard-packed pavement completely cov-ered with sand. Even though the bus and truck passed over it without a problem, Gorud lost trac-tion for about twenty yards until the front wheels found the hard surface again.

"Maybe one of us should drive," suggested Turk, noticing that Gorud's injured arm had given him problems.

"Yeah," said Grease.

"Let me," added Turk. "You can watch with the gun."

"I'm OK to drive," protested the CIA officer.

"It's better this way," said Turk, tapping him on the shoulder. "Come on."

They changed places. Turk, too, had trouble with the loose sand. Once on the highway, the car steadied and he settled down a bit. He didn't relax—his heart still pounded like a racehorse nearing the finish line. But his view expanded, the cloud of fear lifting slightly. It was as if the horizon had pushed back—he could see farther out and plan before reacting.

Then, almost imperceptibly, either seeking

relief from the present or simply lulled into a relaxed moment, his mind began to wander. He thought of Li and their last moments in the hotel room. He ached to see her. He felt her weight against his shoulder. He wanted to brush his fingers across her breasts.

Grease's voice interrupted his thoughts. "You getting tired of driving?"

"No, I'm good."

"Careful where you are on the road."

Turk steered back to the lane gently, trying to stay in control. He glanced over his shoulder; Gorud was dozing in the back. He was tempted to ask Grease if he thought they'd get out of this, but the question seemed too defeatist, as if it implied he'd already decided they wouldn't.

"They're looking for a place to change the bus," Grease said after talking to the others by radio. "I don't know if we're going to reach your target area by tonight."

"Yeah, I was thinking that myself."

"You have to talk to them, don't you? You haven't checked in."

"Oh, God."

"Keep driving. They'll wait."

Turk hunched forward, leaning toward the wheel as if that would help him focus. He needed to use his pilot's head—he needed to be clear and precise, not dreamy, not distracted. Being on the ground unhinged his concentration.

No more thinking of Li. No more thinking, period. Except for the job.

"Road," said Grease.

This time Turk jerked back. His fingers gripped the wheel so tightly they started to cramp.

"I'm thinking maybe we just abort," said Grease, his voice almost a whisper. "Go straight north while we still can."

Shocked, Turk jerked his head. "No fuckin' way."

Grease stared at him for half a moment, face blank. Then, though the rest of his face hinted at sadness, the ends of his lips peaked upward ever so slightly. "You've been hanging around with us too long."

THE FIRST PLANE PASSED NEARBY ABOUT AN HOUR later.

They were south of Sar-e-Kavir, a small town in the shadow of the desert hill where Highway 81 connected with the east-west highway they needed to take. Turk couldn't see the aircraft, but from the sound he knew it was propeller-driven, something small, very likely similar to the aircraft they had crashed the night before. It didn't linger, but that was small consolation; for safety's sake they had to conclude they had been spotted.

Not that they had many options.

Granderson turned up a mountain path about two miles from the town. The steep and rocky path turned out to be a driveway to a pair of small farms dug into the rock outcroppings. Both had been abandoned some years before, though when they first drove up they didn't know that, and they spent ten minutes checking and clearing the dilapidated far buildings on the larger of the two properties. Sure they were secure, they took the bus into the barn, where there was just barely enough room amid the clutter of old crates and a dilapidated trailer to hide it.

They parked the pickup under a lean-to roof shed at the side; the rear poked out a little, but it would be hard to see even directly overhead. Turk drove the car fifty yards down the hill to what had once been a grove of pomegranate trees but was now mostly a collection of dried stumps. Here and there green shoots and a leaf struggled from the twisted gray trunks, nature refusing to give up even though the underground spring that once supplied the crisscross of irrigation ditches had dried to bone.

He got out of the car and walked a short distance away before using the satellite radio to check in.

Breanna Stockard herself answered. "Turk, are you OK? Where have you been? Why haven't you checked in?"

"We had a setback in Jandagh," he told her. "The police—there was an incident in town. A lot of our guys are hurt. We escaped with a bus."

"The mission tonight, can you—"

"We won't make it in time."

Breanna went silent.

"I'll be in place tomorrow," said Turk. "Tonight's going to be too tough. We're still pretty far away. And we're pretty banged up."

"All right. All right. Listen, I know where you

are. We have intercepts from the Iranian police and the interior ministry about a stolen bus in one of the towns where you spent time. Is that you?"

"Must be."

"All right. Stand by."

Turk heard another aircraft in the distance. This was another propeller plane, but larger; two engines, he thought.

"The report concerning the bus stolen in Jandagh talks about terrorists," said Breanna. "They're looking for Russians."

"That fits with our cover. Do they mention the other vehicles?"

"Negative. The descriptions are vague: three Russian males. Some of these communiqués claim it's a robbery." Breanna paused, obviously skimming through screens of data. "They haven't made a connection with the attack."

"OK."

"Turk, what kind of condition are you in?"

"I'm fine. Not a scratch."

"Your team?"

"Very shot up," he said. "Only Grease, me, and Granderson are really at full strength. We have two guys—no, three now—who are just immobile. Coming in and out of consciousness. Everybody else is hurt to some degree, though they can still fight."

"Have you considered aborting?"

"No."

"You've already completed the mission you were sent on."

"We . . ." Part of him wanted to say yes, they

were through; it was time to go home, time to bail.

But the larger part wanted desperately to complete the mission—the next phase. Because the object was to stop the Iranian weapons program. If there was another site, they had to hit it.

So much of a sacrifice, though. For all of them. Was it worth it? Couldn't they just send in bombers and be done with it?

There was no guarantee they'd make it out alive in that case either. Better to go ahead. Better to do his duty.

At such a cost.

"I can do this, Bree," Turk insisted. "We just have to get to the other side of the desert. And if they don't really know what we're up to—"

"I can't guarantee that they won't," Breanna told him. "The reaction force can't reach you that far deep in Iran."

"It's all right. I've done harder things."

In the air, perhaps, but not on the ground. Definitely not on the ground. But Breanna didn't call him on it.

"I want you to contact me at the top of the next hour," she told him. "Do you understand?"

"I will if I can. Sometimes—"

"No. You are to check in every hour. I need to know you're still alive."

"I will call you if I can," he said, hitting the end call button before she could respond.

17

CIA campus, Virginia

Breanna turned to Reid as soon as the transmission from Turk ended. "They've taken heavy casualties. I think we should pull them out."

"It's not our decision, Breanna."

"They're all shot up."

"He's not."

"Let the bombers go in. If they stay, it's suicide."

"It already is suicide." Reid picked up the phone and told the computerized operator to get him the President.

Twenty minutes later Breanna and Reid were on Lee Highway, speeding toward the White House. As a security precaution, the driver had always to follow a different route; at four in the morning traffic was not a particular concern, and for once they were going on a relatively direct route.

Reid stared out the darkened window at the cars passing in the distance. The lights in the parking lots of the buildings and on the signs and streets melted together in a blur.

He would tell the President that they should continue. It would inevitably mean the death of his officer, Gorud, of the Whiplash pilot, and whoever remained from the rest of the team. The Israeli operative, a deep, valuable plant with an impeccable cover. And a family.

But Reid knew absolutely that this was the right thing to do. The nano-UAVs had done a perfect job on the first strike; they would succeed here as well. The result would be far more desirable than a missile strike. No matter what the Iranians did, the scientists who rebuilt the program would never be sure whether there had been an attack or a critical flaw.

Delaying the strike twenty-four hours would increase the odds of success. Even if the analysts didn't identify which of the two sites was the one with the bomb—or if they decided both had enough material to be a threat—the delay would give Rubeo and his people more time to work on the programming for the mission.

The scientist had demurred when asked for a prediction about the outcome of a split attack. The first strike had been heavily modeled. This one was still being calculated.

"Lovely night," said Breanna. It was first time she'd spoken since they got in the car.

"It is." Reid forced a smile. He had grown to like the younger woman, though he felt at times she was too easily influenced by her Pentagon superiors. "Though it's almost morning now."

"Technically, it is morning."

"How's the senator?"

"Still stubborn as ever," said Breanna. "And still swooning over the Nationals. Their losing streak has him in the dumps."

"I hear there's talk he might run for President."

"God help us."

The words were so emphatic that Reid didn't

know how to respond. He remained silent the rest of the way to the White House.

PRESIDENT TODD HAD MANAGED BARELY AN HOUR OF sleep, but she felt a surge of energy as Breanna completed briefing the current situation, ending with a PowerPoint slide showing the general vicinity of the two possible targets.

Charles Lovel, the Defense Secretary, opened his mouth to speak. Todd cut him off.

"The question comes down to this," said the President. "If we wait twenty-four hours, do we guarantee success?"

"There are no guarantees for anything, ever," said Blitz, the national security director.

"The odds will be greatly improved," said Reid, sitting next to Breanna. "Getting our pilot in place helps if there is a problem with the units. True, they were impeccable in the first strike, and compensated well. But I think, as Ms. Stockard said, the human factor increases the chances of success. Plus, we may be able to narrow down the possible targets. At a minimum, we'll have a better plan for dealing with both facilities."

"I don't know that we can afford to guess which of the sites is the real target," said Blitz. "Not at this point."

"On the other hand, the odds of the ground team being discovered will also be higher," said Reid. "And if they're discovered, we lose them."

"We may lose them anyway," said Lovel.

"The Iranians may close the sites," said the Secretary of State, Alistair Newhaven.

"Twenty-four hours is not enough time to do that," said Reid.

"If the attack fails—"

"If it fails, we go ahead and we eliminate both sites with B-2 attacks," said the President, cutting in. "That's an easy decision."

"I would vote to launch a B-2 attack now," said Lovel. "Why wait?"

"Nothing has happened at that site—at either of the possible sites," said Reid.

"We were *rushing* to strike tonight," said Lovel, "because we needed to hit quickly. Now we're going to delay another twenty-four hours. The sooner we get this over with, the better. For everyone."

"Not for our people," said Breanna. "If we strike, if the bombers go in, we're writing them off. Because they'll know that the first attack was launched by us, and they'll be on the alert."

"I agree it increases their risk," said General Maximillian Fresco, the head of the Joint Chiefs of Staff. Fresco had only been on the job for a month, and was still feeling his way—a disappointment to Todd, who had selected him because he seemed determined and, like her, prone to err on the side of hawkishness rather than caution. But maybe he would come around.

"They are already at considerable risk," said Reid dryly. "No matter what."

"I think we should pull them out," said Breanna, her voice quivering. "Then send the bombers in."

Todd was surprised. She looked at Reid. His expression showed he clearly disagreed. Ordinarily, they were in lockstep; she couldn't remember a time when they had offered even slightly different opinions.

"Our best chance, overall, is to use the nano-UAVs," said Reid. "We know they work. We haven't seen the bunker busters yet. This is our best chance."

Fresco started to object, but Reid cut him off.

"The Hydras work. They leave no trace of our involvement; they raise no moral or ethical questions if there is a mistake. They limit the casualties strictly to those involved in the program." Reid sounded like a college professor, summing up a semester's worth of instruction. "The benefits are obvious. At worst, we have the bombers in reserve."

Todd agreed. She saw from the corner of her eye that the Secretary of State was going to say something—probably, she thought, questioning Reid's statement about moral questions: they were, after all, setting off a nuclear explosion, even if it was the Iranian's own bomb.

There was no need for that debate now.

"I think I've heard enough," she said quickly, raising her hand. "We will delay for twenty-four hours. After that, the bombers will be authorized to attack."

IN THE CAR ON THE WAY BACK TO THE CIA CAMPUS, Breanna fiddled with her personal phone, thumbing through text messages from the past several days, even though she'd read them already. She longed to talk to Zen about the operation but couldn't.

Her only acceptable alternative was Reid, and she didn't want to talk to him about anything.

"Why did you change your mind?" asked Reid.

Breanna looked up. "I'm sorry?"

"You're opposed to the operation now. You weren't earlier."

"I'm not opposed."

"You sounded like you are. Your tone was negative. Even in the presentation."

"No. I was trying to be neutral. My concern—I just want to get our people out. I feel responsible for them."

Reid looked at her, his old-man eyes peering into her soul. He was beyond retirement age, and at times like this—deep into an operation, under heavy stress—he looked even older.

He reminded her of her father, once commander of Dreamland, now a virtual recluse.

"Your guilt is misguided," said Reid.

"I don't feel guilty." The words spit out quickly, beyond her control. They weren't true. "Why would I be guilty?"

"You're not. That's my point."

"I'm responsible for my people. It's my job to think of them."

"We are," said Reid softly. He turned his head toward the driver in the front seat, separated by a thick, clear plastic barrier that made it impossible for him to hear. "But our first responsibility is to the mission. The nano-UAVs are clearly the best choice."

"Yes," said Breanna reluctantly. "I can't disagree."

18

Iran

Walking down from the barn into the aban-doned grove, Turk checked his watch, then took out the sat phone. He was a few seconds early, but there was no reason to wait.

"This is Breanna."

"I'm checking in."

"Good. What's your status?"

"Same as it was forty-five minutes ago."

"We have approval to push the operation off until tomorrow night," said Breanna. "Twenty-four hours. And then it's on."

"Thank you."

"Turk, we've been speaking with WARCOM. The SEAL command landed the recovery team from the Caspian. They're not going to be able to reach you before the attack. We're sending as much support as we can, but—"

"I know, I know. It's all right. We're good. Don't worry about me."

Turk felt a little annoyed—first at Breanna, then at himself for sounding like a teenager fend-ing off an overanxious mom.

"We have a plan," he added. "We'll execute it."

He heard the sound of another aircraft in the distance. It was flying quickly, moving in their direction.

One engine. Loud. The plane must be low.

"Listen, I have to go," he said to her. "I'll check back at the top of the next hour."

He clicked off the satcom, then took a few steps toward the barn before realizing that he would never make it before the plane was overhead. The closest thing to cover nearby was an empty irrigation ditch; he jumped into it. Grease, his constant shadow, followed. They crawled a few yards to a spot where the sides were nearly horizontal and the shadow was thick.

It was another light civilian aircraft, a Beechcraft Bonanza, a later model with a conventional tail instead of the trademark V. Turk saw it flying from the northeast, paralleling the other side of the highway. It looked to be at about eight hundred feet.

He ducked his head, as if believing that if he didn't see it, it wouldn't see him.

The plane made another pass, this time to the north. Turk remained prone until the sound sunk into a faint and distant drone.

"I don't think he saw us." Turk stood and stretched the muscles in his back, then his legs. He leaned against the soft dirt of the ditch and kicked his toes into the other side. "He would have circled a few times."

"Maybe," said Grease, noncommittal.

"When do you think Granderson will be back?" Turk asked. He and the Israeli had taken the pickup into town, hoping to find another vehicle to either buy or steal.

"Soon."

"I was wondering—maybe it would be better if just you and I went and finished this. Let them take care of their wounded."

"They're never going to leave you, Turk. To the last man. They'll crawl along and bleed out before they let that happen. Every one of them."

"That wouldn't make much sense."

"It's their mission. It's their job and duty. Their honor."

"Together, we attract more attention than if we were on our own. Way more."

Grease shook his head.

"We could take Gorud," said Turk. "Because he speaks the language. But we don't need escorts. I don't really even need you. No offense."

"Not happening."

Turk started to laugh, but Grease's grim expression warned him off.

"Let's get inside," he said instead.

GRANDERSON AND THE ISRAELI RETURNED NOT FIFteen minutes later, the latter driving an open farm truck. The truck had been parked in the town center, in front of a small building. They'd driven up in the pickup, spotted it, jumped out and walked over. The keys were in the ignition.

"Pretty quiet town," the captain told Turk as they checked it over. "If anybody saw us, they didn't say anything."

"You sure you weren't followed?" asked Grease.

"If we were, they'd be here by now, right?"

Gorud thought they should leave the school bus in the barn, but Turk suggested that it might work better as a decoy—if the planes they'd seen and heard earlier were part of a search party, making the bus easier to find would give them something to do. By the time they spotted it and then checked it out, it would be nearly nightfall, maybe later. He volunteered to drive it himself down along the highway.

"I'll get rid of it while you're organizing to go," Turk said. "I'll point it south on the highway."

"You're not going," said Grease.

"You sound like my mother. It's better than waiting around."

"I'll follow you in the pickup," said Grease.

The ride back to the highway was longer than Turk remembered, and bumpier; he didn't reach it for a good fifteen minutes. When he did, an SUV approached from the direction of Sar-e-Kavir; Turk sank behind the wheel, hoping whoever was in the vehicle wouldn't get a good glimpse of his face. The SUV continued south, moving at a good pace; Turk drove out cautiously, starting to follow. His speed gradually picked up, the bus accelerating slowly but steadily. After about five minutes Grease sped up in the pickup and began flashing his headlights. Turk slowed, then pulled off.

"I kept it running," he told Grease when he reached him in the truck. "If they find it with the motor on, it'll be a mystery. Maybe it will buy us more time."

"Wishful thinking," said Grease.

"It's all we got," replied Turk as they headed north to join the rest of the team.

19

Iran

Back in the flight rotation, Captain Vahid found himself assigned to a late afternoon patrol, flying what was in fact a combat air patrol mission over the area of the atomic lab, though officially the mission was written up as a "routine observation flight." Given the air force's fuel woes, the fact that it was being conducted at all meant it was hardly routine, but that was the least of the official lies involved.

Vahid was not allowed to overfly the epicenter of what was officially termed the earthquake area; he had to maintain a five mile buffer between the ostensible fault point at all times. He tried avoiding the temptation to glance at the area, though he couldn't help but notice the roads in the vicinity were empty. Checkpoints had been established; rescue teams were supposedly heading in to help relieve victims, but there was no surge of aid. Clearly, the state and national authorities were still confused about what to do.

Vahid accepted that what General Shirazi had told him was correct; it made the most sense and fit with what he himself had observed. He wondered if the facts about what had happened would ever come out. It would be much easier to blame the Americans or the Israelis than to admit that the project had suffered a catastrophic setback. On the other hand, blaming the Americans or the Israelis would be tantamount to admitting that the Iranian nuclear program was not aimed at producing a peaceful source of energy rather than a weapon.

Everyone knew, of course, that it *was* aimed at making a bomb. But admitting that it was a lie before the bomb was completed would be a great loss of face. Only when the weapon was completed could it be revealed. Then the lie would not be a lie, but rather a triumph against Iran's enemies.

Vahid knew this the way he knew that one plus one equaled two, as every Iranian did. "Truth" was a subjective concept, something directly related to power; one accepted it as one accepted the fact that the sun rose and set.

With General Shirazi as his backer, he knew his future was bright. Squadron commander was in his sights. Wing commander would not be an unattainable goal. There were already signs of his improved standing: he had been assigned the squadron's reserve jet and given the most sensitive area to patrol.

Vahid ran his eyes around the gauges, confirming that the aircraft was operating at spec, then checked his six, glancing briefly in the direction of his wingman, Lieutenant Nima Kayvan, who was flying off his right wing and about a half mile behind. Their box north of the Zagros Mountains was clear of clouds, as well as enemies. The flight had been completely uneventful—another sign to Vahid that the Americans had not struck the lab, since they would surely be conducting reconnaissance and perhaps a follow-up raid.

The ground controller's adrenaline-amped voice caught him by surprise.

"Shahin One, stand by for tasking."

"Shahin One acknowledges." Vahid listened as the controller told him there had been a terror attack in Jandagh; he and his wingman were to head west and join the search for a school bus.

"So now we go after auto thieves," said Kayvan on the squadron frequency as they changed course. "What would the Jews want with a bus?"

Kayvan certainly had a point, but Vahid chose not to answer. The wingman was an excellent flier, but his mouth would one day land him into much trouble.

Jandagh was some three hundred kilometers away, across a series of high desert mountains and a mostly bare landscape. Vahid immediately snapped to the new course, tuning to the contact frequency he'd been given for the Revolutionary Guard unit assigned to coordinate the reaction. He tried for several minutes but couldn't get a response to his hails.

"We'll go down to three thousand feet," he told Kayvan. "Look for anything moving."

"Goats and sandstorms included?"

They saw neither. The ground appeared as

empty as the sky. Kayvan did see something moving near a road about two miles west of their course north, and they made a quick pass, only to discover a pair of dump trucks and an excavator working a gravel or sand pit. Swinging back toward their original vector, the commander of a local militia unit contacted Vahid on the radio and asked him to help check a vehicle a civilian had spotted south of Sar-e-Kavir.

"We have another unit to rendezvous with," Vahid told him.

"I am making this request at the order of the special commander," explained the officer, saying that the colonel who originally requested the air support had now delegated him to use it. The radio garbled the name of the commander—it sounded like Colonel Khorasani—but as the officer continued, Vahid realized the special commander was a member of the Pasdaran—the Revolutionary Guards—assigned to investigate the "earthquake." The fact that there would be an investigator had been mentioned by the intel officer at the preflight briefing: alienating the Pasdaran was a greater danger than American F-22s.

"That's over a hundred kilometers away," said Kayvan, once again using the short-range squadron radio so his disrespect wouldn't be overheard. "They don't have other planes?"

"You'd rather sit on the ground?" snapped Vahid.

"I would rather see the girl who will be my bride. And we do not have much fuel."

The wingman was right. Vahid did a quick calculation, and figured that once they reached Sar-e-Kavir they would have about ten minutes of linger time before having to head back to their base.

"We'll make the most of it," he said. "Stay on my wing."

"I do not plan to disappear."

Vahid found Highway 81. The road climbed over the desert ridges, paralleling a route once used by silk traders; well before that, it had over-looked the edge of a vast lake. Now the area was largely desolate. Barriers lined long sections of the road to cut down on the sand drifts.

Passing over a pair of white four-door pickup trucks heading north on the road, Vahid angled his jet toward a collection of ruins ahead on his left. He descended quickly, thinking he might catch a glimpse of anyone hiding amid the old clay brick walls and foundations. But he was by them too quickly to see anything other than shadows and broken earth.

As he nudged back toward the road, he spotted the bus about two kilometers ahead. Slowing to just above stall speed, he leaned toward the canopy, getting a good view of the road and the vehicle. It was facing south, off the road on the shoulder. The old highway was to the right.

"I have found a bus," Vahid told the local ground commander. "Stand by for the position."

The commander took the information with great enthusiasm. Vahid's description seemed to match the bus that had been stolen. The only problem was it was facing in the wrong direction—toward the town where it had been taken. But that didn't seem to bother the ground commander, who asked Vahid to take a low pass and see if there were enemies nearby.

"Vehicle looks abandoned," Vahid radioed the ground unit. "The area around it is empty."

"Acknowledged, Shahin One," said a new, more authoritative voice. It belonged to Colonel Khorasani, the Guard officer who had been assigned to investigate the situation. He was handling his communications personally. "I have ground units en route. They should arrive in zero-five minutes."

"Acknowledged. We're going to spin around the area and see if we can find anyone."

"Police units are coming down from the north," added the local ground commander. "They will arrive quickly."

"Acknowledged."

Vahid and his wingman began a slow, spiraling rise above the area.

"Farm building to the north on the side of the hill," said Kayvan. "Maybe they are there."

"Make a run," Vahid told him. "I'll follow you."

Vahid climbed out and changed positions with his wingman, so that Shahin One was now trailing Shahin Two. The buildings were on a small, nearly flat tongue of land. Just below, he saw an abandoned orchard, its trees parched stubs.

A crooked road ran from the highway to the farm, then petered out. Neither Vahid nor the wingman could see any other vehicles, let alone people.

"Shahin One, what's your status?" asked the Pasdaran colonel.

"We're waiting for ground units to arrive. We have no contacts."

"We have a report of a vehicle stolen from Sar-e-Kavir. A farm vehicle. We believe there may be a connection."

"Do you have a description?"

"Stand by."

20

Iran

THEY TOOK A SHORTCUT ACROSS THE RIDGE, DRIVING on a hard-pack road that got them out in front of Granderson and the others. Grease had been studying the maps and gotten advice from Granderson; there was an Iranian army barracks about twenty-five miles ahead on the highway. Once past that, they should have an easy time north; they could cut south of the cities of Semnān and Sorkheh, then follow the highway west for another two hours or so before veering once more onto narrower roads in the mountain foothills. At this point they would pick up one of the trails the Delta team had scouted as an alternate route to the target area, aiming for a hiding place originally planned as part of the escape route. Ironically, it was within a half-hour drive of their new target area. They would stay there through the next day, achieve their objective, and leave.

It was easy when you laid it out step by step that way. Simple and direct.

Turk leaned into the back, grabbing one of their last two bottles of water. He took two sips, then put it back.

"Rationing yourself?" Grease asked.

"Yeah."

"There should be more water at the place where we stop. A team went in and set it up two weeks ago."

"What if it's been found?"

"Nobody'll find it."

Turk folded his arms. "I hope you're right."

"Granderson and the truck are two miles ahead," said Grease. "Pickup's about a half mile ahead of that. Gorud's driving. The Israeli swapped with him in the troop truck."

"Why?"

"His leg's pretty screwed up. Didn't you notice?"

"I thought he was all right."

Grease shook his head. Badly battered when they encountered the police, the Israeli's knee had locked; most likely there were torn ligaments and cartilage damage as well.

"You think Green and the others are going to make it?" Turk asked.

Grease thought for a moment before answering. "Yeah. Probably."

"Probably or maybe?"

Another pause as he weighed his estimate. "Probably," he announced at last.

"That's what everybody has to say, right?" asked Turk, suddenly oppressed by the weight of what they had to do. His energy had completely drained, taking his optimism with it.

"You know what will help?" asked Grease. "Focus your mind on the next checkpoint, the next step along the way. If you try to keep the whole mission in your head, it may wig you out. But if you go from A to B to C, it'll be much easier. It's a fact."

Turk's ears perked up—he heard a jet nearby, low. Two of them.

"Somebody's looking for us," he told Grease, thumbing above.

FIVE HUNDRED METERS ABOVE THE GROUND, VAHID rode Shahin One up over the ridge, banking easily to the west. There was a car ahead, white and fairly new—probably a government official, Vahid thought, maybe even someone from the interior ministry. As he nudged a little lower, he saw a glint in the distance—another vehicle three or four kilometers farther along the highway.

In normal times this would hardly have been unusual, but today there was so little traffic it couldn't help but pique his interest. Vahid steadied himself at three hundred meters and waited for the vehicle to appear.

It was a pickup truck. Just as Vahid was about to turn off, he saw the top of another vehicle just descending a low hill. This one was larger, another truck.

"Shahin Two, do you see the vehicle beyond the pickup?"

"Confirmed."

"Looks like it could be a farm truck. I'm going to get a closer look."

"On your six."

Vahid pushed even lower, dropping through three hundred meters. The truck matched the description—a green farm vehicle with slat sides—but it had a canvas top, which hadn't been described.

"Two, radio the Pasdaran colonel and see if you can get a definitive description," said Vahid. "I'm going to take another pass."

TURK FELT THE MUSCLES IN HIS STOMACH TIGHTEN AS the MiGs turned ahead. They were definitely interested in something on the highway, and since there was no other traffic nearby, that meant them. He bent forward to the dashboard, trying to get a glimpse as the planes flew by.

"Only air-to-air missiles," he said as the lead plane thundered past. The wingman was higher and offset to the south; hard to see, but Turk guessed he would be equipped the same.

"What's that mean?" asked Grease.

"Means he won't be able to bomb us. But he'll have a cannon he can use if he decides to shoot."

Turk opened the car window and leaned out,

trying to see where the planes were. He wished them away far to the east. Instead, he saw them turning in the distance behind them.

"Coming back for another look," he told Grease.

"Captain, you seeing those airplanes?" Grease asked over the team radio as Turk slid back down. The sun was just setting; the red glow on the horizon might make it tough for the pilot to see.

Not tough enough, though.

VAHID ASKED THE COMMANDER TO REPEAT WHAT HE said.

"You are ordered to stop the farm truck," said Colonel Khorasani. "Destroy it."

"Colonel, it appears to be a civilian vehicle."

"It is a vehicle filled with Israeli commandos."

The colonel's voice was completely rational, and soft rather than loud—which chilled Vahid even more. "It is a little different than you described when you radioed me earlier."

The colonel was silent for a moment. "Should I call your commander?"

"Of course not," said Vahid. "I want to make sure I understand your requirements. My fuel tanks are close to empty."

He was, in fact, about sixty seconds from bingo, the calculated point where he would have only enough fuel to get home. He considered using that as an excuse not to shoot up the truck, but what was the point? Already two other members of his squadron were flying northward; they would destroy the truck if he didn't.

And going against the Pasdaran colonel was not a wise move, even if General Shirazi was his patron.

But to kill civilians?

Surely they were thieves. As unlikely—as *impossible*—as it must be that they were Israeli commandos, they still had no right to steal a truck. So it was Allah's punishment that he was meting out.

"Shahin Two, you're on my wing," he told Lieutenant Kayvan, glancing at the armament panel to make sure his gun was ready.

"We're going to shoot up the truck?"

"We're going to stop it, yes."

Turk HEARD THE RUMBLE OF THE JET ENGINES AS THE MiGs came up the road behind him. Once more the muscles in his stomach clenched. He pushed back in the seat, waiting as the car began to shake.

"Shit," he muttered as the plane shot overhead, then rose into a quick turn.

"Tell them to get out of the truck!" Turk yelled. "Tell them he's coming in to fire! He's firing!"

As Vahid PUSHED THE MiG's NOSE DOWN, THE FARM truck seemed to fly into the pipper. He gave the trigger a gentle squeeze before breaking off. The rounds missed, flying into the pavement well ahead of the vehicle.

Which was what he intended. In his mind, an

innocent civilian would see the bullets and realize something was wrong. He would pull off the road and run from the truck.

"Shahin Two, did he stop?" Vahid asked.

"Still moving."

"Stay clear."

"No fun for me?"

Vahid ignored his juvenile wingman, moving into position to destroy the truck. He rode the MiG through five hundred meters before tucking his left wing toward the highway. He leveled the wings and found the vehicle speeding ahead.

It started to weave left and right. He pressed the trigger.

A GRAY GEYSER OF SMOKE ERUPTED AHEAD.

"Shit, shit, shit!" yelled Turk. He pounded the dashboard as the gray turned black. A funnel of red appeared from within, like a volcano.

They rushed toward it as the cloud shifted downward, folding itself across the road. Turk had shot up trucks himself a few months before, pouncing on them from the air. Now he was seeing things from the other side, from underneath and inside out.

The truck was on the right, off the road, completely destroyed, smoldering.

Two bodies, black, lay between it and the road.

"You're not stopping!" Turk yelled at Grease.

"I know that."

"You gotta stop!"

"We can't."

"Grease! Grease!"

Turk grabbed for the door handle. Grease reached over and grabbed him with his hand, holding him in place even as he accelerated away from the wreckage.

SUPERMAN

1

Iran

CAPTAIN VAHID FLEW OVER THE WRECKAGE OF THE farm truck one last time, making sure nothing was moving. The vehicle had been split into five different pieces by the MiG's cannon. Only one, a segment that included part of the cab, was still on fire.

The pickup truck and then the white car he'd seen had passed by quickly. The pilot wondered at that: he could understand the pickup, but why the car, which he assumed belonged to a government or perhaps a Guard official. Wouldn't they have been curious?

They must have been afraid. People seemed to have an unnatural ability to shut everything else out when they felt themselves in danger.

Did they think they were next?

And really, why wouldn't they? As far as they knew, he had just destroyed a civilian truck, a poor man's vehicle at that.

Vahid banked, aiming for another pass over the highway.

"One, I am at bingo fuel," said Lieutenant Kayvan.

"Acknowledged, Two. Set course for base."

As Vahid clicked off his mike, another transmission came, this one from Colonel Khorasani, asking what their status was.

"The truck has been destroyed."

"Are there confederates? Are there other vehicles?"

"It doesn't appear so."

Vahid slowed, edging toward stall speed, so he could get another look at the truck. While he'd splashed some targets in training, he had never blown up a "real" truck before, certainly not one that was moving.

At the moment he fired he felt joy—that was the word for it, *joy*—but already his feelings were complex. There was great satisfaction at having achieved his objective, but there was something empty about it as well.

He flew past the lingering black curl of smoke, accelerating before climbing out. Vahid felt a flush of anger—he should hit the car. The men were cowards to go by without stopping to help.

How would he explain?

Easily—Khorasani had just given him an excuse. The men were compatriots. They'd been close to the truck when he blew it up.

Kayvan radioed to ask if they were leaving.

"Go ahead, Two. Return to base."

"I'm staying with you, Lead," said the wingman.

Strike the government vehicle? But they would

find out eventually that it wasn't connected. And there would be repercussions.

It was not his job to punish cowards.

Vahid radioed the Pasdaran commander. "The truck is a complete wreck. No survivors. We are low on fuel. We need to return to base."

"Go. One of my units will be at the site in a few minutes."

He thought of giving the colonel a sarcastic answer to the effect that he was welcome for the assistance—the colonel hadn't so much as thanked him. But he thought better of it. With the Pasdaran, it was always better to keep your mouth shut.

2

CIA campus, Virginia

Breanna sat stoically as Turk recounted their situation. Gorud's arm had been injured but he was all right to drive. Grease was fine, as was Turk.

The rest of the team, including the Israeli spy, had been killed. Turk and the others were traveling toward Hoz-e-Soltan Lake and the vast, empty salt desert north of Qom and east of their target. He estimated they would be at the hiding place in two more hours.

Breanna had read the translated Iranian communications relating to the strike soon after the truck was destroyed. Captured by a U.S. elint satellite and forwarded by the NSA after translation, the script was succinct and depressing: the Iranian air force officer, though clearly concerned he was firing on civilians, nonetheless followed orders and killed them.

Breanna knew from the locator data that Turk was still moving. But she suspected from the description that the truck was theirs. And even if it hadn't been, the savagery of the decision was chilling.

She glanced to the end of the table where Reid was sitting. His face was pale, as if the long night had bled the blood from his body. There were times when he looked ancient, and other times beyond age. This was one of the former. Reid's eyes darted from the map screen to the blank transmission screen—there was only audio, no visual. The rest of his body remained stone still, as if he were a projection.

Breanna leaned forward in her chair. "Turk, I want to ask you a question. I need a candid answer. Do you feel you can carry out the mission?"

"Yes." He said it quickly, without hesitation.

"You're going to have difficulty getting out of the country."

"It'll be no harder then than now."

"We're confident you will succeed," Reid told him.

"Yes," said Breanna, trying to inject enthusiasm into her voice. "Check in when you reach the cave."

"Yup."

He signed off. Breanna rose. Reid remained sitting, staring at the map, his thoughts obviously far off.

"Coffee?" Breanna asked him.

"The SEAL element that was coming down from the Caspian," Reid said. "They've run into resistance. They are going to have to withdraw."

Reid continued to stare at the map. One of the suspected sites was five miles northeast of Fordow, the other a few miles west. The area was near a Guard base established at a former Iranian air force installation. It would be heavily patrolled, especially now.

"It makes no sense to get them out," said Reid finally. "Even to try will be suicidal, and possibly expose the operation."

"Of course it makes sense." Breanna felt her face flushing. "Gorud is there, too—what are you saying?"

Reid didn't answer.

"I'm *not* ordering Sergeant Ransom to kill him after the attack," said Breanna.

"He's already under orders, Breanna."

"We need a backup if the SEAL team has to withdraw. We need Kronos."

"It's too late to revive Kronos," said Reid. "And it was vetoed for a reason."

"I understand that. But—"

"Kronos calls for assassination."

"Escape *or* assassination. And I think he can get them out. I've always thought that."

"We may end up losing him as well."

Now it was Breanna's turn to be silent.

"Very well," conceded Reid. "We had best attempt to move it forward. Do you want to talk to Colonel Freah, or should I?"

3

Iran

THE SMELL OF DEATH STUNG COLONEL KHORASANI'S nose as he got out of the Kaviran. It was metallic, with the slightest hint of salt.

He disliked it. He disliked death completely. How ironic, then, that it had become so intimately entwined with his profession.

"We count six bodies, Colonel." Sergeant Karim made a sweeping gesture toward the truck. "An entire team of Mossad."

Khorasani said nothing, continuing across the soft ground to the burned out farm truck. The charred remains of automatic weapons had been discovered in the back, but that hardly meant that the occupants were Mossad, or even foreign agents. Khorasani in fact worried that they were Pasdaran—some of the local units had not yet reported to their commanders, and this could easily be a group of men who'd been on the way to their barracks.

He could deal with that, if it turned out to be the case. It would be far easier to explain than letting saboteurs get away.

The colonel continued his circuit around the vehicle. He'd been on his way to the destroyed lab when the report of the stolen school bus was relayed to him. Khorasani had decided to follow a hunch, joining the investigation personally. It was risky on many counts. But it did allow him to say he was pursuing his leads with vigor.

And vigor was the word he would have to use for the pilot: he had followed his orders well. The vehicle had been utterly demolished.

Good, perhaps, if there were questions.

"A phone," said Private Navid, pulling at a brick of melted plastic and metal that had melted to one of the bodies. "Or a radio."

It was tangled with other material—cloth and hair, skin and a bone that snapped as easily as if it had been a brittle twig. Navid handed it to him.

The phone would have fit easily in Khorasani's hand, but the debris that had melted to it was two or three times as large. Khorasani turned it over, unable to discern anything from it.

A satellite phone, maybe? An Israeli would have one.

Or a cell phone, which a member of the Guard would have. The remains were too mangled to tell.

"Colonel, the ayatollah wishes to speak." Khorasani's communications aide had walked up unobtrusively. He handed him the secure sat phone.

It was twice the size of the one in the wreck. Khorasani handed the melted mess back to Navid and told him to put it in his staff car.

"Reverence," he said, putting the phone to his ear.

"What progress have you made?" asked the ayatollah.

"We have found the men who stole the bus. They are dead."

"All of them?"

"Yes, your excellency."

"They were responsible for the explosion?"

Khorasani hesitated. Saying yes would simplify things for him, but it could also come back to haunt him as well.

"I have no evidence yet. The Israelis are very clever and would do much to disguise themselves."

"But you are sure they were responsible."

Khorasani considered what to say.

"Be honest," the ayatollah reminded him before he made up his mind.

"I have no indication that any outsides were near the facility," confessed Khorasani. "I am only starting my investigation. This seemed like a good lead, but to be frank, I see nothing at the moment that connects it. And my aides—the preliminary inquiries would suggest an accident. Everything we have seen suggests no one was aboveground when the explosion occurred."

"You are saying it could have been a quake."

"I've been told that is . . . unlikely."

The ayatollah, who was a member of the ruling council, had undoubtedly been told the same. He let the matter drop. "Have you spoken to the pilot who shot down the plane?" he asked instead. "Find out what he saw. Perhaps it was a B-2."

"That is on my agenda, your excellency." The wreckage had been recovered; it was a light plane, flown by a man tentatively identified as an Iranian. Perhaps he was a spy, but more likely an unfortunate smuggler bound for Iraq. Considerable money could be earned ferrying certain people and items from the country. But pointing that out would not be useful at the moment.

"Report to me. Speak to no one else."

The line went dead. Khorasani handed the phone back to his aide. "Tell Major Milanian that I wish to speak to him as quickly as possible. He will need to investigate this site. It would be best if he could get here before it is much darker."

"Yes, Colonel."

"The pilot—the one who shot the plane down last night. Find out where he is stationed. I wish to speak to him."

"I believe it is the same squadron that responded to the vehicle," said the aide.

"Really?"

"They were given responsibility for this area."

"Excellent. Find his name," said Khorasani, walking to his vehicle.

4

Washington, D.C.

"SENATOR, HE INSISTS IT'S PERSONAL. HE'S NOT HERE for funding, or legislation. He really emphasized that."

Zen frowned at the intercom. It was his own fault, though; wanting to get Rodriguez off the phone when he'd been at the baseball game, he invited him to come in person whenever he wanted.

Even that would have been acceptable had the Nationals not proceeded to give up six runs in the top of the first.

"All right. Send him in." Zen wheeled out from behind the desk. By the time Cheryl knocked and opened the door, he was sitting a few feet from the door.

"Senator." Rodriguez, visibly nervous, extended his hand.

"Gerry. How are you?" Zen shook his hand. The night before, he thought he vaguely remembered Rodriguez. Now he couldn't place him at all. "It's been too long."

He nearly bit his tongue. He hated being a BS artist—it was the normal political crap: *beentoolong, howareya, goodtaseeya, wereallymustgettogethermoreoften.*

Trivial phrases, meaningless, expected, but using them made him feel like a phony.

"I wasn't sure you'd remember me," said Rodriguez.

"I don't," admitted Zen. "Not well, anyway. Dreamland seems like a million years ago."

"I know. It was, um, well, the experiments didn't go that well. So, um . . . I guess I've changed quite a lot."

Rodriguez—the friendly junior doctor who'd worked out with him pre-experiment?

Yes.

"Sure—you jogged with me while I used my chair, right? Or maybe it was a fast walk."

"Definitely a jog," said the scientist. "If not a run."

"You've gained a little weight, Jersey," said Zen, suddenly remembering Rodriguez's nickname. "You're not running anymore, I'm guessing."

"I do, but a lot less than I should. And, uh, a hernia operation a couple of years ago slowed me down." He gently patted his stomach. "Put on about twenty pounds I haven't been able to get rid of."

More like thirty or forty, thought Zen, but now that he knew who Rodriguez was, he felt more comfortable. "So what have you been up to?"

"Well, I left Nevada for a few years, to work at Stanford. Then I came back with the Spinal Cell Clinic. I, uh, well, I helped start it. I'm one of the partners." Rodriguez shifted in the chair. "I— we've been doing very interesting, very important work over the past few years. I guess, well maybe you saw the piece on *60 Minutes* the other night on Mark Huntington." Rodriguez sat.

"He was one of your cases?"

"Yes, as a matter of fact. As you saw, he can walk now."

"I met him," said Zen. "I met him right after his accident at the bowl game. And I saw him again a few weeks ago. You're right. He can walk. It's a phenomenal story."

"There's a lot of hope for the procedure."

Zen glanced quickly at his watch. It wasn't a dodge; the Iranian "earthquake" had greatly complicated his schedule. "Doc, I have a lot of things I have to do today, including getting down to the floor in ten minutes. You've sold me. You have my backing. Tell Cheryl what you need. To the extent that I can help—"

"I'm not looking for backing. Or money. We're funded through the next decade. And, to be honest, the patents—we may actually, um, stand to make a considerable amount of money."

"Well, why are you here?"

"We want to try the process on someone who was injured at least ten years ago. Someone in good shape, willing to put the time in. Someone we already had a lot of baseline information on. You'd be the perfect candidate."

5

Washington, D.C.

ONCE UPON A TIME, MARK STONER HAD BEEN A CIA paramilitary officer. He had been a good one. Even exceptional. Paras, as they were often called, were *all* highly accomplished, but Stoner stood out as a man of great skill, courage, and flexibility. He had worked with some of the best operators in the Agency's clandestine service, and in other agencies as well, including the secret Air Force units that operated out of Dreamland.

Stoner had no memory of any of that. He had

seen all of the records of his missions, scant as they were; none were familiar. On the bad days he could feel the echo of long-ago wounds he'd suffered. But he could make no link between the aches and pains and whatever had caused them.

His mind was a blank when it came to his past. He had no retained memory of anything beyond the past few months. He couldn't remember his elementary school days, his high school years, college. He didn't know the names of his teachers or the faces of his best friends. He could close his eyes and think of his childhood home and it wouldn't be there. He couldn't remember the faces of his mother and father—long dead, he was told—not even with the help of photographs.

The doctors who treated him sometimes said it would be better that way.

Stoner had been through an extremely rough time. Captured after a horrendous crash in Eastern Europe, he had become a human experiment. Designer drugs and steroids were pumped into his body to rebuild his muscles and erase his will. He'd been made into an assassin, controlled by a criminal organization in the dark recesses of the old Soviet empire.

Better not to know, said the doctors. Even his friend Zen Stockard agreed.

Stoner didn't have an opinion, particularly. Opinions belonged to a realm beyond him, housed in a metaphysical building some towns away. The only thing he cared about now were his present surroundings—a gym on a quiet campus of a federal prison. Stoner wasn't a prisoner, exactly; he just had no other place to go, at least not where the government could keep an eye on him.

For his own protection, the doctors said.

Stoner looked at the boxing gloves on his hands, checking the tape. Then he began hitting the weighted bag. It gave slightly with each punch, though never so much that he felt as if he were a superman.

Jab-jab-punch. He danced left, jabbed some more, then moved right. He wasn't a boxer. He could box, but he wasn't a boxer. He just hit the bag for something to do.

"Hey, Mark. How's it going?"

Stoner stopped in mid-jab and looked behind him. Danny Freah was standing near the door next to two of Stoner's doctors—Dr. Peralso and Dr. Rosen. Rosen was the case doctor; Peralso was the head of the psychiatric section responsible for him.

Both men were afraid of Stoner. It was obvious from the way their eyes darted when he approached.

Danny wasn't afraid. He was a friend. But his eyes betrayed a different emotion: pity.

Stoner greatly preferred fear.

"Danny, hi." He turned back and began pounding the bag again.

As he continued to wail away, he heard the three men walking across the large gymnasium floor toward him. His senses of hearing and sight were greatly improved, thanks to the ordeal he couldn't remember. Or so the doctors said.

Stoner slammed his fists against the thick

canvas. It didn't really feel good, but it didn't feel bad. It just was.

Finally, he turned toward Danny.

"Business?" he asked.

"Yeah." Danny nodded. "A couple of weeks ago you told me you wanted something to do. Well I have something. It's not easy. Actually, the odds are against success."

Stoner shrugged. "Sounds good."

DANNY FOLLOWED STONER AND THE DOCTORS DOWN the long hallway. His friend's reaction was exactly what he had expected. There'd be no joy or disappointment, no excitement, and no fear. He wondered if Stoner really understood.

The doctors, though they didn't know the actual outlines of the mission, clearly suspected it was suicidal, because they began peppering Stoner with objections from the moment he agreed. They were still at it now, talking about "treatment modalities" and "long-term rest."

Stoner ignored them, continuing to his room. He pressed his index finger against the reader at the lock, then raised his head so the laser reader embedded above the door could measure his face. The biometric check took only a few seconds. The door snapped open as the security system recognized him.

The room was as spare as a Buddhist monk's. A bed covered with a single sheet sat in the middle of the room. There were no blankets, no pillows. An orange vinyl chair sat in the corner. Stoner's clothes, the few he had, were closeted behind a set of folding doors opposite the bed. Having removed his gloves while walking down the hall, he pulled the last bit of tape from them and dropped it in a nearby wastepaper basket. He put the gloves on one of the shelves, then started to change.

"Do you want privacy?" Danny asked.

"Why?"

Danny backed out of the room anyway. The doctors stayed. He guessed they were continuing to argue with Stoner about not going.

Danny didn't mind. Part of him agreed with them.

Stoner emerged from the room, dressed in jeans and a black T-shirt.

"Is that all you're taking?" Danny asked.

"Do I need anything else?"

"No. I guess not."

Stoner glanced at the two doctors, who had fallen silent.

"I don't know when I'll be back," he told them.

They walked together to Danny's car, neither man talking. Danny got in, but hesitated before turning the key to the ignition.

"This may be a suicide mission," he said, staring straight out the front window. "Assuming it's authorized, you'll be dropped into Iran. It's doubtful they'd keep you alive if you are captured."

"OK."

"You have to locate someone," added Danny. "An American. He may be in custody by the time the mission is approved. If so, the mission will continue."

"OK."

"He can't be allowed to tell the Iranians any-thing."

"OK."

Danny turned to look at Stoner. The former CIA officer was looking straight ahead, as if he were watching a movie. It would have to be a boring movie, as his face was expressionless.

"You'll have to leave promptly."

"Sure."

"Immediately."

"Yes."

"You can say no," Danny told him.

"Understood. Let's go."

6

Iran

THEY HID THE CAR ABOUT THREE MILES FROM THE CAVE that would be their sanctuary, parking it behind a ramshackle cottage off Highway 81 that the advance team had scouted a few weeks before. Grease arranged some threads on the seat as markers to tell them if it had been disturbed— the last of their surveillance devices had been de-stroyed with the truck—and then ran to join Turk and Gorud in the pickup. Grease suggested he'd drive, but Gorud insisted on staying at the wheel. He was better with the language.

Turk, exhausted, slumped in the middle, giving way to fatigue. He drifted into a vague sleep. Li was there, walking with him, talking. They were in Sicily, though not anywhere that he could remember being, even though it felt very familiar.

The beach was made of rocks rather than sand. Surf frothed up, running over their shoes and pants—he was in his dress uniform; Li was wearing shorts and a T-shirt that clung between her breasts.

A truck careened down on the beach. It was the military vehicle the team had been driving when they first met.

Dread was at the wheel, eyes fixed on some destination beyond them, in the water. When the truck drew near, Grease leapt from the back. The truck burst into flames as it reached the water's edge.

It exploded. Li ran. Turk turned and saw Grease coming at him, an AK-47 aimed at his skull—

"Hey, come on. You're too damn heavy to carry."

Turk bolted from the dream back into reality. Grease was standing outside the truck, leaning in and shaking him. They were in the cave.

Turk shook his head, as if that might shake off the horrible image that lingered.

"You're drooling," said Grease. "I hope she was worth it."

Turk wiped his mouth as he got out. There was a faint bluish glow to his right. He walked toward it, cautious at first, worried that he was still in the dream.

He found a turn and was nearly blinded by the flood of late afternoon sun. Gorud, an AK-47 cradled in his arms, knelt on one knee behind some rocks ahead. The mouth of the cave was another fifty feet away, up a gentle slope.

"How long did I sleep?" Turk asked the CIA officer.

"A bit."

"I don't remember getting here."

"Uh-huh."

"This place is bigger than I thought it would be."

Gorud said nothing. A pair of binoculars sat on the rock right in front of him.

"Mind if I take a look?" asked Turk, reaching for them. Gorud didn't stop him.

From their vantage point they had a good view of the countryside, speckled with more green than the area they were in the day before. A wide expanse of concrete sat in the distance; he focused the binoculars, moved them around, then finally satisfied himself that he was looking at a runway. He couldn't see any planes, except for the glowing white carcasses of two old trainers—Texans, he thought, though from this distance it was impossible to tell.

"That's an airport?" he asked Gorud.

"Was. They only use it to fly equipment and VIPs in and out now," said the CIA officer.

"We could use it to get out."

"There are no planes there. The standing orders direct that any air force plane attempting to land there be shot down. If the pilot survives, he's to be shot summarily. We thought of using it," added Gorud. "Too risky getting in with anything smaller than two full companies. Didn't work."

Turk nodded, though he continued to stare at the runway. It was long, in perfect shape except for a patched wedge at one side.

"How are you feeling?" Gorud asked.

"I'm good."

"You should get some sleep," Grease said from the shadows behind them. Even after all this time, the fact that he was hovering nearby surprised Turk.

"I just slept. You go." He looked at Gorud. "Where are we?"

"Within ten miles of both possible targets," said Gorud. "Site Two is that way. One is a little farther away, on the left, down."

Turk looked in the direction of the second site. "There's a village."

"It's about a mile farther on."

"People." He couldn't see past the village. The uneven ground blocked his view. "It's probably not the right one."

"They say it's more likely."

"What kind of idiots would put a plant so close to people?"

Grease snorted in derision; to him the answer was obvious: that was exactly where they would put it to make the Americans less likely to attack.

Turk put the glasses down and walked back into the cave to the pickup. The space was about three times as wide as the vehicle was long, though it narrowed the deeper he went. The top and the side on his right were jagged, but straight lines ran down the wall on the left. He guessed they were left from drilling and explosives; the cave had clearly been widened before it was abandoned.

If that was so, he soon found a possible reason: he could hear the sound of water dripping in the distance. He walked toward it, gradually losing the light until he had to reach to the wall to make sure of where he was.

"Careful," said Grease when he stumbled. The Delta sergeant flicked on a small light. "There's a pool of water ahead."

The beam caught the edge.

"Salty in here," said Turk. "Like being at the sea."

"Must've been part of the ocean a couple of million years ago." Grease shone the light to the right. "There's a passage up around the water. Come on."

He led Turk to a narrow, slippery ledge. As they started to walk, Turk slipped. Grease grabbed him and pushed him hard against the rocks to keep him from falling in.

"Easy," said Turk. "I can swim."

"We're not sure how deep it is," said Grease. "But it's more than a hundred feet."

"Really?"

"This was originally cut for a bunker."

Sobered, Turk clung to the wall but kept going. The path extended another thirty feet or so. After that, the ledge became more of a walkway, wide enough for two people. Twenty feet farther, it widened into a large hall. Grease led Turk to a pile of rocks, playing the light on it. There were packs and boxes just beyond them.

"Backup gear," he said. "MREs, ammo, more guns. Spare radios."

"Damn, I forgot to check in," said Turk.

"I did it."

"You did it?"

"You were sleeping. I didn't want them worrying."

"You should've woken me up. Did they say anything?"

Grease shook his head.

"Did you ask about extraction?" asked Turk.

"No."

"Did they say anything?"

"I didn't ask."

"They're not going to come for us. The reaction team. The SEALs were pulled back." Grease knew as much. Turk was just telling himself, needed to state reality so it was clear to him. "If something screws up, they're not going to come for us. We're on our own."

"Something did screw up," said Grease. "The mission changed. Come on with me this way. I'll show you the back exit. There are some rocks that have to be taken out of the way so it can be used."

7

Omidiyeh, Iran

Tᴵʀᴇᴅ ᴀꜰᴛᴇʀ ʜɪꜱ ʟᴏɴɢ ꜱᴏʀᴛɪᴇ, Vᴀʜɪᴅ ꜱᴋɪᴘᴘᴇᴅ ᴅɪɴɴᴇʀ and headed straight for his quarters, a room on the second floor of the squadron dormitory. He lay down on the bed, staring at the ceiling; within moments he was asleep.

The next thing he knew, someone was banging on his door.

"Go away," he muttered. "Go."

"Up," said a stern voice next to him.

Vahid opened his eyes and saw two soldiers. One was pointing a rifle in his face.

"How did you get in?" he demanded.

"Captain, it is not a good idea to make Colonel Khorasani wait," said a sergeant near the door. "Get dressed and come with us. You should not be sleeping."

"I was flying. The mission was long and trying."

"That is immaterial. The three of us have worked around the clock to deal with this situation. No one should rest while the Revolution's enemies are free."

Tᴇɴ ᴍɪɴᴜᴛᴇꜱ ʟᴀᴛᴇʀ Vᴀʜɪᴅ ꜱᴀᴛ ɪɴ ᴛʜᴇ ꜱᴍᴀʟʟ ʀᴏᴏᴍ where General Shirazi had found him the day after the attack. He recognized the name of the man he was supposed to see, Colonel Khorasani.

It was the investigator who had ordered him to blow up the truck.

While he didn't like the fact that he had been woken from a sound sleep, he did want to talk to the colonel—he wanted to make sure the men he had killed in the truck were in fact enemy commandos, and not simply Iranian farmers.

But the colonel hadn't come to talk about the truck. After he strode in alone, he got right to the point: "When you saw the airplane the night of the earthquake, what did you think it was doing?"

"I didn't see very much at all," Vahid said, rising. "Is that why you've come?"

"Answer the question fully. What was it doing?"

"I don't know. It was flying south at first, then turned eastward. Maybe it had been off course. I never got very close. I had a brief shadow on radar, then later my IR detected it. I could see there was something there."

"You radioed him?"

"I attempted contact, but there was no answer. By the time I closed in, I was already under orders."

Vahid began describing how the radar would have been blocked by the ground clutter, or even the peaks between them. Khorasani held up his hand.

"It was a civilian plane that you shot down? A Cessna?"

"I believe so."

"The air force has Cessnas?"

"We have a few," admitted Vahid. "But they would have answered the radio or we would have known about it, the command would have known."

"If it wasn't the air force, it must have been flown by a spy. Or it was the air force, and it was a traitor. It may have very well been the air force, since all of the civilian planes in the area have been accounted for."

Khorasani stepped closer to Vahid. He was not a tall man; in fact, he was several centimeters shorter than Vahid, who himself was not very tall. He wore a brown sport coat and an open white shirt, with gray trousers that strained slightly at the waist. He was in his thirties, with a soft face and large hands, and his fingernails were at least a week from a good clipping. But intensity was the colonel's defining characteristic: he leaned forward, his body coiled as he fired his questions, his mouth a cannon more potent than the one on Vahid's MiG. "How would this plane be fitted with a bomb?"

"It wouldn't," said Vahid.

"How would it be done, Captain?"

"You can't put a bomb on a Cessna, or any light plane," said Vahid. "I mean—you couldn't put much of a bomb on it."

"Why not?"

"It can't carry much. A five hundred pound bomb—that would be as much weight as the plane could carry, depending on the weight of the passengers and fuel it needed. And a five hundred pound bomb would do *nothing* to Natanz."

"How do you know how much damage would be done?"

"You're trying to trick me," snapped Vahid.

"How do you know the target was Natanz?"

"I don't know anything. There was an earth-quake near Natanz. Or an accident. That's what I know. Why is the Pasdaran interested?"

That was a foolish question; nuclear program aside, the Guard felt entitled to know about everything that affected Iran in the slightest way.

"How about your plane, Captain?" asked Khorasani. "Could you attack the laboratories near Natanz?"

"How? By bombing them?"

"You tell me."

"They're impervious to attack. And—who would bomb their own country? It was an accident, and you don't want to admit it. You don't want to admit failure."

The colonel said nothing. Vahid stared into his face; Khorasani stared back. Only when Vahid looked down toward the floor did Khorasani turn and leave the room.

THE THEORY HAD NOT FORMED ITSELF UNTIL HE WAS speaking with the pilot, but now Khorasani wondered if that was what really happened: had the air force sabotaged the program themselves?

They were extremely clever. Rather than setting things up to point the finger at the Israelis or the Americans, they had gone about things subtly—a private plane in the vicinity, stolen vehicles. They made it seem as if there were saboteurs on the loose. The clues were a false trail, something for himself and the other investigators to chase. In the meantime the air force said nothing.

And the decoy truck: what a lucky break to be ordered to destroy it. They had provided the perfect villains, unable to defend themselves from any accusation. The destruction had been complete, with no clues to their identities.

Captain Vahid had been the *same pilot* involved in both incidents. That was too much luck for one man.

Or proof that it wasn't a plot. Because no one would have been so obvious.

Khorasani worked the problem over in his head as he walked down the corridor. If the air force was involved—he reminded himself he must keep it theoretical, it was just a wild theory—then General Ari Shirazi, the air force chief, would surely be behind it.

The motives were simple: the air force was jealous of the Pasdaran, and had been from the very beginning of the Revolution.

Would they go so far as to destroy the bomb? That seemed unlikely.

Sergeant Karim met him in the hall.

"Colonel, I have compiled the data we have gathered, including the interviews with the people in Jandagh and at the junkyard. I believe there was a car involved that may have gotten away. I have a description. I've issued an alert to all police departments."

"Good."

"An air search might be useful as well. Even if

it were abandoned, the vehicle might have evidence."

"True."

"The squadron commander volunteered earlier that he would help you."

"No. I don't want their help. No one from the air force. The spotter planes that we used yesterday. Are those still available?"

The planes belonged to the Basiij Resistance Force—the Guard-sponsored militia. They were ancient, but the men could be relied on.

"I believe I can arrange it."

"Do so."

"Jets—"

"Move quickly."

Sergeant Karim knew better than to question his commander further. Still, his raised eyebrow betrayed him.

"It is nothing more than routine security," said Khorasani. "Just routine."

"I'll send the order immediately."

8

CIA campus, Virginia

Ray Rubeo closed his eyes and lowered his head, resting his brows on the tips of his fingers. Numbers and equations spun through his brain, percentages, statistics, possibilities.

In sum: *chance*—the great enemy of necessity.

"Both sites must be attacked," he announced. "Both sites. There simply is no other solution."

He opened his eyes and looked up. The others— Breanna, Reid, Smith, Armaz, the two Air Force analysts, Reid's nuclear expert, three planners detailed from the Air Force chief of staff's office— all stared at him.

"Consider this. Even if we worked the numbers so that the probability is 99.9 percent in favor of Site Two rather than One," Rubeo explained, "the penalty for being wrong is too catastrophic. And we can't get the probability even close to that."

The analysts began making arguments about how good a job they'd done assessing the various indicators, which pointed to Site Two with an eighty-three percent confidence level.

"If you were that good," said Rubeo finally, his tone acid. "You wouldn't have missed the sites in the first place."

Rubeo did not share the others' optimism about the B-2 strikes. His people had conducted a preliminary analysis of the first attack, and concluded that the "flaw" that caused the bunker's upper stages to collapse was not a flaw at all, but rather a fail-safe intended to preserve the material far below. Had it worked, the Iranians would have had to spend six months to a year digging out— but their material, and the bomb they had built, would have survived.

There were additional political concerns, which he didn't give a whit for, though others did. Clearly, the Hydra strike was by far the best alternative, and to guarantee success, they must hit both sites.

Reid put up his hand as the discussion continued.

"I think Dr. Rubeo's analysis is on point," he said. "Even if we do destroy one of those two facilities, we still won't know precisely what is going on in the other. We'll never be given access to determine whether some material remains or not. The second site would have to be hit at some point in any event."

"But you're reducing the probability of success to thirty-seven percent at each site," said Armaz, "which gives us well under fifty percent chance of taking out both. The odds almost guarantee failure."

"I believe that we can use the delay to increase the probability of success to a minimum of eighty-five percent," said Rubeo, "which is essentially where we are now. And possibly more, assuming we still have a human pilot in the loop to make one critical call during the attack."

"Stoner's ready," Danny told Breanna. "He'll be at Vandenberg within the hour. They can launch as soon as you give final approval."

"Very good."

"There's one other thing."

"Colonel?"

"I want to move the Whiplash unit into Iraq so we can support them if necessary."

Breanna studied Danny's face. He knew, as she

knew, that Stoner's mission was almost surely one-way—the odds of getting Turk out alive were infinitesimally low, and Stoner's briefing documents made that clear.

"Your team is still on leave," said Breanna. "You're not in position and this has been a Delta show from the beginning."

"It's not Delta anymore," said Danny. He ducked his head, looking down at his uniform shoes. "I should have been there."

"No, Danny, we discussed this. The mission was not and has not been a Whiplash mission. You've done exactly as you should have."

"You think?" He looked back at her. She knew exactly what he was thinking: He should have been there.

"Put the team into Iraq," she said. "But—"

"I know," said Danny. "We'll get there, just in case."

UNDER RUBEO'S PLAN, HUMAN "INTERVENTION" WAS important at several points. The swarm would make a staggered, piecemeal attack against each site, progressing past each critical part of the installation with just enough units to clear the way. Once the path was open, the final attack would be launched. The controller—Turk—would have to supply some last minute guidance on each attack.

Not only that, but Rubeo's team would have to modify the memory system used by the units, removing some of the basic embedded programs that weren't needed to add mission data. He calculated that they had just enough time to do that. No one openly questioned the scientist's assessment, but Breanna noticed that Sara Rheingold's eyebrows rose significantly when he mentioned what he had in mind.

Breanna studied the large projection of the area around the sites. Turk would have to go very close to a Pasdaran stronghold to get into position to strike both plants. And he'd have to wait there— the ideal orbit for Rubeo's plan wouldn't bring the X45 into position until just past 5:00 A.M. The attack wouldn't be over until six-thirty—a half hour past sunrise.

"It is a problem," conceded Reid. "But overall, this is the best plan. There will be a lot of confusion on the ground, and hopefully Turk can take advantage of it. He has proven quite resourceful to this point."

"I think it's more than a small problem," said Breanna.

"Can you think of an alternative?"

She looked around at the others. With the exception of Rubeo, they were pretending to focus on something else.

Rubeo stared directly at her. As usual, his expression was void of any emotion.

"I can't think of an alternative," Breanna admitted. "I agree, it is our best course."

9

Iran

THEY HEARD THE FIRST AIRCRAFT AROUND NOON. IT was low enough and close enough that it woke Turk. He sat up, hugging the blanket to his chest. The plane rumbled above, passing within a hundred yards of the cave. It passed again, this time a little farther away.

"They must be looking for us," said Grease.

"No. They can't have traced us," replied Gorud.

"Why not?"

"It is a general search. Nothing more."

Turk got up and went to the mouth of the cave. He could see the plane in the distance, circling to the north.

"You're too close to the mouth of the cave," said Gorud, grabbing his arm and pulling him away.

"He's definitely looking at something," said Turk.

"How do you know?" asked Gorud.

"It's obvious. He's circling."

"Is he looking at us?" asked Grease.

"I don't think so. It could be that village to the west. Or maybe the car."

Turk and Gorud studied the map, but it was impossible to say for certain what the plane was focusing on. It made a dozen more circular sweeps, then moved on.

No one slept after that. They kept their shift watches—Grease was up next—but that was just a formality. All three men stayed close to the bend in the cave, back far enough from the entrance to avoid being seen, but close enough to catch a glimpse of anyone coming from the road.

A little after noon Grease went to the supply cache and got lunch. One by one he inserted rations in a flameless ration heater and added water. The heater was actually a bag that contained iron, magnesium, and sodium. A chemical reaction started by the water heated the food.

"Cheese tortellini," said Grease as he handed out the food.

Turk's tongue felt numb. He seemed to have lost the sense of taste, though the aroma of the food that wafted up from the bag was strong enough to provoke memories of his middle school cafeteria. He ate quickly and scraped the side of the bag when he was finished.

"More?" asked Grease.

"Nah."

"Good, huh?" His tone was mocking.

"It was fine."

"You Air Force guys aren't used to eating out of bags, huh?"

"No," admitted Turk.

"How about you?" Grease asked Gorud.

The CIA officer turned to them. "I've eaten out of a lot of things," he said solemnly. "Including a human skull."

No one spoke for quite a while after that.

Eventually Turk's legs grew stiff from sitting.

He got up and walked around the cave. Grease had given him a small LED flashlight from the gear stash, but Turk left it off; the darkness somehow felt more comforting.

Creeping to the edge of the interior lake, he sat and listened to the nearly silent but resonant hush that filled the space. Every so often something would drop from the ceiling. The plunks echoed throughout the cave.

He thought about how he would escape, and worried about having to swim in the Caspian. He wasn't a bad swimmer, but in his vision now he saw the waves surrounding him. Suddenly, he felt claustrophobic in the dark. Hand shaking, he reached into his pocket for the LED flashlight and lit it. Then, heart pounding, he backed away from the edge of the water.

He collided with Grease and fell. A shudder of fear ran through him, dissipating only after the trooper hauled him to his feet.

"Shit," Turk muttered. "I thought you were on watch."

"Gorud's there. I was making sure you didn't try swimming."

"I feel claustrophobic," he told him, without explaining why. To his surprise, Grease told him that he did, too.

"I don't know what it is," added Grease. "Adrenaline builds and then it runs away. It leaves you empty, and you start focusing on stupid things, things that might kill you, but won't in a million years. It's related to tension I guess."

"Yeah," said Turk.

"You feel that when you're flying?"

"Not too much."

"But sometimes."

"A few times," admitted Turk. "Mostly, you're too busy to think about it."

"I know what you mean."

AROUND 3:00 P.M. THEY HEARD HEAVY TRUCKS IN THE distance. Turk crawled to the entrance where Grease was keeping watch and peered out at the highway a half mile to the west. The road was empty, but a cloud of dust rose another mile beyond it, near the outskirts of the small village.

"Be nice to have a UAV over us," said Turk.

"It would show them where to look," answered Grease.

"There is that."

Grease handed over the binoculars. There were three military trucks driving on a desert road near the hamlet, coming up from the south. Two troop trucks and a command vehicle—a patrol of some sort.

"You think they're looking for us?" Turk asked.

"No."

"Why not?"

"You got any evidence that they are?"

"No."

"That's your answer."

"I'd love to hear something more reassuring."

"Me, too."

10

Iran

COLONEL KHORASANI GOT OUT OF HIS COMMAND VE-
hicle slowly. The old building reminded him of
his mother's parents' house in Gezir.

Lovely days. Parties every evening with the
neighbors and relatives. Iran was a different place.
Some of the neighbors were Sunni, and there
would occasionally be long arguments about religion, but with no one thinking of taking some
sort of revenge or turning the others in.

"The truck is in the back, Colonel," said Sergeant Karim.

"The place is abandoned?" asked Khorasani as
he walked with his sergeant.

"For years now. We are checking the local records."

The four-door Toyota had been tucked close
to the house, invisible from the road and much
of the surrounding area, though not from the
air. The pilot who had spotted it had been over
the area the morning after the "earthquake," and
swore he had not seen the vehicle.

A very similar pickup was seen on the road near
the farm truck that had been destroyed; it was
clear in the video from the aircraft. That truck
had a dent in the top rail; this one had an identical mark. The first character in the registration
plate—all that could be seen—was identical.

But this was entirely the wrong place for the

pickup truck to be located. It was closer to the lab, not farther away.

Maybe they were tasked with seeing what had happened. The colonel turned south, gazing in the direction of Fordow, which had a high security plant. There were dozens of others scattered between there and Qom farther south. The precincts were off limits to all but the workers and scientists involved in the bomb's development. Khorasani himself didn't even know the location of all of them.

But perhaps the most obvious explanation for the truck was that it wasn't related at all. Smugglers would use a house such as this to stash their wares. It was empty, but perhaps the airplane had driven them off.

The structure had been abandoned years ago. Part of the wall was missing. Khorasani stepped through, entering what was once a bedroom. All of the furniture was long gone, but there were old photographs tacked to the wall: a family picnic lost now to memory.

The colonel walked through the rooms. Dust was thick everywhere.

Khorasani stood in the middle of what had been the kitchen and stared at the weathered pipes in the wall. He had no other leads. The more work he and his investigators did, the more he came to believe that the "incident," as he called it, was actually an accidental blast caused by the scientists themselves.

That was unlikely to be admitted.

The truck must be linked somehow. Parking

here—maybe they were smugglers, but what if they were spies? What if there were more commandos, eyeing another attack?

Khorasani strode outside. Sergeant Karim was waiting.

"Colonel, it is the captain coordinating the Twelfth Guard unit," said the sergeant, holding the satellite phone out. "He wishes to take his men off alert. They're worried about their families."

"They can worry later," Khorasani snapped. "Tell him the entire area is to stay on alert. Tell him—tell him we are looking for commandos who stole this truck."

"Uh—"

"Sergeant Karim, follow orders," he said, returning to his command vehicle.

11

Iran

Turk HAD TO STAND NEAR THE ENTRANCE TO THE CAVE for the sat phone to work. He was just punching the quick-dial to connect with Breanna when he heard a plane approaching from the north.

"I may have to cut this short," he said as soon as the connection went through. "There's a plane nearby."

"Turk, are you OK?" asked Breanna. He heard concern, even fear, in her voice.

"I'm good. I don't want to take the chance of being seen. The Iranians have been sending airplanes through the region." He leaned back against the side of the cave. The plane wasn't getting any closer. "It should be dark soon. Do we have a target?"

"We have two."

"You still have two? I thought—"

"I have a coordinate for the area we think is safest for you to operate from," she said, cutting him off. "The procedure you're going to have to follow is different than the first strike."

"How different?"

"They're still working on things. It'll be more hands on and you may be making the attack in the morning, near or after sunrise."

"In the day?"

"Possibly. Probably, I should say."

Turk looked out across the valley in front of him, letting the words sink in. They were still figuring out exactly what to do—that wasn't a good sign.

"Turk?"

"Yeah, OK. Those coordinates?"

"I'm sending them via the text system now."

His satcom beeped, signaling that the information had been sent.

"Call when you've arrived. We need you in place by 2200 hours," Breanna added, using the military term for 10:00 P.M. "So we can download everything to your unit before clearing the launch. We're going to use the first orbiter as a relay station; some of your programming has to be changed. There's only a small window to do the download."

"Understood."

"THEY'RE INSANE IF THEY WANT US TO GET TO THIS point." Gorud shook his head. "We'll have to pass two barracks and an antiaircraft site. They're crazy. God."

The CIA officer got up and started pacing. He folded his arms over his chest and began scratching his left bicep frenetically, as if he wanted to tear through the cloth and dig past the skin to the muscle and bones.

Grease glanced at Turk and gave him a look that said, *He's losing it.* Then he took out the paper map of the area that had been stored there and examined it. Turk looked over his shoulder.

The topo map showed a trail they could take from the road toward a narrow hillside ledge, but it ended about a half mile before reaching that point. The topo lines squeezed together, showing a sharp rise. It would be a difficult climb.

Grease studied the area.

"If we could go through this air base, we'd have an easy time," he said, pointing at the map. "Otherwise the nearest road is ten miles here. Then we have to go out this way and back."

"Unless we go through the desert," said Turk.

"We can't—this is the salt lake. It's water out here. There may be patrols on the road."

"There'll be patrols inside the base."

"Not as many as you'd think. Remember the

place we hit the other day? Security is something you do at the perimeter, if there."

"Those are barbed-wire fences, I'll bet." Turk pointed to the parallel fence line on the map. "And they're not going to let us through the gate."

"We can cut through the fences. That's not a problem." Grease studied the map some more. "We'd have to scout it, obviously. A satellite image would be convenient."

"Yeah," said Turk. They weren't likely to get one; the data download was due to take place after they arrived.

"We could take one of their trucks and get right out the front gate. Be less likely to attract attention than ours."

"What are you talking about?" demanded Gorud. "What the hell are you thinking?"

The CIA officer started waving his good arm in the air. He seemed dangerously close to losing control—maybe he already had.

"You don't understand," he said. "They've given us a suicide mission—"

He stopped speaking. Turk stared at him for another second, then looked at the map again. Grease had already turned his attention back to it.

"We can leave the truck about a mile away and walk through this ravine," Grease told Turk. "We get past the fence here, then it's a straight jog to the administrative buildings."

"What if there are no vehicles?" asked Turk.

"It'll work, don't worry," said Grease. "Worst case, we go back. But we won't have to."

"You're crazy!" shouted Gorud. "Both of you! Crazy! We have to leave now! We have to leave now—now! We have to get out!"

Gorud turned and ran toward the deep black of the cave's interior. Frozen for a moment, Turk finally got moving only after Grease jumped to his feet.

They caught the CIA officer at the edge of the underground lake. Turk, whose eyes seemed to have adjusted better to the dark than Grease's, grabbed the back of his shirt and started to pull. Gorud swung around, trying to hit him. Instead they both fell. Grease leapt on Gorud, pinning him to the damp, uneven floor.

Gorud yelled and screamed in pain. Grease leaned against his neck with his forearm while pulling the flashlight from his pocket as the other man squirmed harder.

"Get him a styrette," said Grease. "Morphine."

"God, he's burning up," said Turk. "He's hotter than hell. He's got some sort of fever. His wound must be infected."

"Get the morphine."

Turk stumbled back to the medical kit for one of the morphine setups. When he returned, Grease had spun Gorud over on his stomach and was holding him down with his knee. The CIA officer continued to scream until the moment Turk touched the morphine needle to his rump. Then, as if a switch had been thrown, Gorud looked at him with large, puzzled eyes, shuddered, and began to breathe calmly.

Turk pushed the plunger home.

"I'm going to give you an antibiotic," he said. "And aspirin. You have a fever."

Gorud said nothing. Turk took that as an assent and went back for the drugs. Gorud didn't talk as he plunged the second needle home. He swallowed the aspirin wordlessly, without taking the water Turk offered.

"Don't give us any more trouble, spook," Grease told Gorud before letting him go.

Gorud curled up defensively.

"It's all right," Turk said, reaching to help him up. "We'll get out of here."

Gorud stared but didn't take his hand.

"We need to get back to the mouth of the cave," said Grease. "And we have to be quiet." He spun the flashlight around. "Come on. You, too, Gorud. Let's go. And don't do anything weird."

Turk reached out to help Gorud, but he refused to be touched. He got up on his own.

"We'll be OK," Turk told him. "We'll be OK."

12

Iran

ABOUT A HALF HOUR BEFORE THEY PLANNED TO leave, an Iranian military vehicle drove down the hard-packed road near the cave. It was a Neynava, a new vehicle with a squared cab in front of a panel-sided open bed, the local equivalent of a U.S. Army Light Military Tactical Vehicle, or M1078.

The sun had just gone down, but there was still plenty of light, more than enough to see the lingering dust cloud after the vehicle passed. The rear was empty; the man in the driver's seat concentrated on the road.

A few minutes later it came back up, moving a little slower this time. Turk decided it must have gone to the small hamlet about a mile south and then returned for some reason. It wasn't until the truck came down the road again, this time moving at a snail's pace, that he became concerned. He called Grease over from the pickup, which he'd been loading.

"He's gone back and forth twice now," he said. "The back of the bed is empty."

"Mmmm," said Grease. "Probably moving troops around."

"I don't see any."

"Not yet."

Grease took the binoculars. Turk checked the AK-47, making sure it was ready to fire. He had an extra magazine taped to the one in the gun, and two more in easy reach. Suddenly, they didn't feel like enough.

"If they come up at us," he said to Grease, "do we fight, or try to sneak out the back?"

"I don't know. Depends."

"On?"

"How many there are?" Grease continued to survey the area below. "I see two guys patrolling. They're just walking, though. Heads down. They don't have anything definite." Grease crouched down and moved to his right, angling for a better view. "They're just assigned to check the road. BS stuff, that's what they're thinking . . . It'd be best to sneak out, but then we have to walk. It's a long way."

He didn't say that they'd have to leave Gorud, but Turk knew they would.

"We can wait a while," said Turk.

"Yeah."

Grease moved away, toward the mouth of the cave. Turk stayed near Gorud, who was propped against the cave wall, sleeping.

Leaving Gorud would condemn him to death, he was sure. But maybe he was already doomed.

Leaving him alive here was too risky, Turk realized. They'd have to kill him.

He knew he faced death himself. He didn't think about it, didn't even consider the many times he had, to one degree or another, cheated it. But killing someone else, someone on *your* side, to complete a mission—that was very different.

"I saw two more guys coming down the road," said Grease, returning. "The truck went back up."

"What do you think?"

"I think they're just looking along the road for anything out of place, then they'll leave."

"Are they going to come up this far?"

"The mouth of the cave blends into the rocks. They can't see it. These guys don't look too ambitious."

"So we chance it."

"I guess."

They waited another half hour. Night had fallen by then; Turk heard insects but no vehicles.

"We're going to have go down and see if they've left," said Grease finally. "Otherwise we won't know if it's safe."

"Go ahead."

"I'm not leaving you."

"One of us has to stay with Gorud. I'll be fine. You're the better scout."

Grease said nothing.

"I'll be OK," Turk insisted. "You don't have to look over my shoulder the whole time."

"It's my job."

"One of us scouting is less likely to be seen," said Turk. "And it makes sense that you're the one to do it. You're going to have to trust me."

"It's not a matter of trust."

"I haven't done anything stupid yet," said Turk. "Except get involved in this."

Grease helped Turk put Gorud into the cab of the pickup. The CIA operative was still running a fever, though he didn't feel quite as hot as he had before. It was dark in the cave now, too dark for Turk to see anything more than Grease's shadow as he backed out of the truck and closed the door.

"Stay by the mouth of the cave," Grease told him. "Just stay there. No matter what happens."

"Agreed."

"I'll come back and we'll drive out. Or we'll go the back way."

"Got it."

It was hard waiting. The darkness made it impossible to see. Turk was anxious. For the first time since the mission began he felt very alone—more alone than he had ever felt in his life.

He started thinking about what he would do if Grease didn't come back.

He heard a vehicle in the distance, driving in his direction. He waited, saw the faint arc of the headlamps.

They disappeared. The night fell quiet again.

Ten minutes later he heard someone scrambling across the rocks to his right. He went down on his right knee, brought the rifle up and moved his finger to the trigger, ready to shoot.

"Me," hissed Grease, still unseen outside.

"Come."

"There's a patrol down there," said Grease when he was closer. "They have a checkpoint on the road. My guess is there's another one on the north side that we can't see."

"Can we take them?"

"Going Rambo's not going to help us complete our mission." Grease moved past him to the pickup.

"What are you doing?"

"Watch the mouth of the cave."

Turk hesitated for a moment, then started after him. He didn't catch up to Grease until he'd reached the truck.

"What are you doing?" he asked.

Grease ignored him, working inside the pickup. Turk peered over his back as he jabbed Gorud's side.

"What are you doing?" said Turk again. "Hey."

"Shut up," snapped Grease.

Turk tried pulling him away, but the sergeant was built like a bear and wouldn't be moved. He jabbed twice more.

"Grease, what the hell?" he demanded.

"He's not going to make it."

"You're giving him morphine? Why?"

Grease remained in the truck. Turk pulled at him.

"Just get back," said Grease, voice shaky. He turned and shoved Turk with his free hand. Caught off guard, Turk stumbled back and fell down. He felt powerless for a moment, then gathered his energy and leapt back to his feet.

There was a muffled gunshot. Grease closed the pickup door.

"Get your stuff," he told Turk. "We gotta walk."

13

Iran

COLONEL KHORASANI STUDIED THE MAP. HE HAD made the mistake of reporting the vehicle to General Arfa, the political commander who in ordinary times was his boss. Arfa had immediately seized on the theory that it belonged to saboteurs—defectors, rather than commandos or smugglers—and demanded that Khorasani find them. Khorasani knew he had only himself to blame.

"It is getting rather dark," said Sergeant Karim.

"I'm quite aware of the time, Sergeant," said Khorasani.

"Every house and farm within five kilometers has been searched. The roads are being patrolled. But some of the troops—"

"What about this block here?" asked Khorasani. "These mines. Were they checked?"

"The search area didn't go down that low. And, the map says—"

"I know what it says." The legend declared the hills a special reserve area—in other words, a place owned by the nuclear research projects, though as far as Khorasani knew, there were no labs there.

Mines would be a good place to hide.

"Get Captain Jalol back on the radio. Tell him to have his men begin searching the hills north of the Exclusion Zone, in this area here. There are old mines—check each one. Look for caves in the hills. Each one to be checked. No excuses! And I want a house-by-house search in Saveh. And it's to start *now*, no waiting for morning. If there are questions, have them speak to me."

"There'll be no questions, Colonel," said the aide, gesturing to the communications man.

14

Iran

MOVING THE ROCKS THAT BLOCKED THE BACK EN-
trance of the cave was easier than Turk expected,
and within minutes they were outside, walking
along a narrow ridge and trying not to fall off the
side or start a small avalanche of dirt.

Turk was tense and tired, his nerves raw. He
felt as if his colon had twisted itself into a rat's tail
of knots on both sides of his abdomen. The fresh
air, though, was a relief, a blast of oxygen blowing
away a hangover.

They were on the far side of the hills, away from
the patrol. As the path widened the walking got
easy. Turk felt as if they had escaped into a different country, free of the men who would kill them
on sight. But he soon heard more troop trucks.

They'd made the right decision, even though he
hated it with all his soul.

The gentle slope they walked out to had been
farmed many years before, and in the twilight
provided by the sliver of moon and the twinkling
stars, he could see not only the outlines of a dirt
road but a network of drainage ditches long since
filled in by blowing dirt and neglect. The land
here must surely be among the most difficult in
the country to cultivate, excepting the absolute
desert, and yet people had tried, apparently with
quite an effort.

"Don't lag," said Grease.

"I'm moving."

"We have two hours to go eight miles," said Grease. "Come on."

Past the ridge, they were about three-quarters of a mile from the paved road they needed to take south. They angled westward as they walked, gradually getting closer. Turk saw the lights of one of the checkpoints: headlights from a truck, and a barrel filled with burning wood or other material. Shadows flickered in front. Turk counted two men; Grease said there were three.

Rather than taking the road, they walked along a very shallow ravine that paralleled it. Roughly a quarter mile from the road, the ravine had been formed ages ago by downpours during the rainy months. It was wide and easy to walk along, and at first Turk felt his pace quicken. But gradually the weight of the control pack seemed to grow, and he slowed against his will. Grease at first adjusted his pace, then fell into a pattern of walking ahead and waiting. He was carrying his own ruck, filled with ammunition and medical gear, water, and some odds and ends they might need. They'd changed back into fatigues similar to those the Iranian Guard used, and decided not to take spare clothes. Even so, Grease's pack was heavier than Turk's, and though he offered to take the control unit, Turk refused.

"Pick up the pace, then," muttered Grease. He repeated that every few minutes, and it became a mantra; before long Turk was saying it himself, almost humming it as he trudged. His knees ached and his left calf muscle began to cramp. He pushed on.

After they had walked for about an hour, Turk heard the sound of an aircraft in the distance.

"Jet," he said, without bothering to look.

"Will they see us?" Grease asked.

"Nah. They don't have the gear."

Turk listened as they trudged onward. The plane was low—no more than 2,500 feet above the ground.

"You sure he couldn't see us?" asked Grease after it passed.

"Nah," insisted Turk, though he was no longer sure. How good were Iranian infrared sensors? He didn't remember—had he ever even known?

After about fifteen minutes Grease spotted some buildings that hadn't been on the map. Making sure of their position with the GPS unit, they walked into the open field to the east of the settlement. The area looked to Turk as if it had been soil-mined; mounds of dirt sat on a long, gradual slope southward. They reached the western end and climbed up an uncut hill, then walked along the edge and continued south for about a half mile.

Something glowed in the distance: lights at the shuttered airfield and military base they were aiming for.

"Down," hissed Grease suddenly, punctuating the command with a tug on Turk's shoulder that nearly threw him to the ground.

A set of headlights swept up on the left. They were closer to the highway than they'd thought.

After the vehicle passed, Grease took out his GPS. "That's the base."

"That's good."

"We're behind schedule. It's almost 2100 hours. We'll have to hustle to make the rendezvous point by 2200. If there's no vehicle here, we won't."

"We'll try."

Grease propped himself up on his elbows and looked in the direction of the glow with his binoculars. He studied it for so long that Turk decided he'd given up on that plan and was trying to think of an alternative. Finally, Grease handed the glasses to him.

"There's a dark spot on the far side there," he said, pointing. "We can get past the gate there, get across the runway and then get the vehicle."

"All right."

"It's going to take a while. You better check in."

15

Office of Special Technology, Pentagon

"Answer," said Breanna crisply, ordering the computerized assistant to put the call through. It was from the duty officer at the Whiplash situation room, reporting on Turk. The call had been routed through the Whiplash system to her Pentagon phone. The background noise on the phone changed ever so slightly—from the vague but steady hint of static to one vaguer and intermittent—and Breanna knew the connection had gone through. "This is Bree. What's going on?"

"Turk just checked in," said Sandra Mullen, one of the duty officers borrowed from the CIA to help monitor the operation.

Breanna glanced at her watch, though she knew the time. "He's a half hour early. What's wrong?"

"They're heading toward a patch where they have to go silent com," Sandy told her. "He wanted to check in."

Breanna slid her chair closer to her desk. She'd come to the Pentagon to brief the Chairman of the Joint Chiefs of Staff; she was due in his office in ten minutes. "You're sure he was OK?"

"Safe words and everything," said Sandy, indicating she'd quizzed Turk herself to make sure. "Gorud's dead."

"What?"

"He'd been wounded—they had to leave his body to get out without being caught."

"Oh, God. Does Jonathon know?"

"Yes. There's a possibility they won't make the control point in time for the download."

"They won't make it in time, or not at all?"

"They'll get there, but they may be late. They had to walk out of the cave. They're still pretty far away."

Breanna had already worked out an alternative with Rubeo that would allow them to send the information just before the strike. But that assumed, of course, they did eventually make it.

"What about Kronos?" said Breanna, asking about the plan to send Mark Stoner to Iran.

"The aircraft is in the air and about fifteen minutes from release. Danny Freah is still gathering his team. They'll be in Iran in forty-eight hours."

"Very good."

Sandy continued, filling in little details.

Breanna had an alternative plan for getting the data downloaded, but to utilize it, she'd have to commit to launching the UAVs no later than 2300. If Turk wasn't in position by then, she would have to scratch the mission.

"I know I'm not supposed to second-guess them," said Sandy, her words breaking into Breanna's wandering train of thought. "But—it may be a stretch for them. They're stealing a vehicle from a Revolutionary Guard camp. And even if they get it, to drive that far—it's going to be tight."

Breanna leaned her forehead down toward her desk, cradling her head in her hand. But she managed to keep her doubts to herself.

"It's all right, Sandra," she said. "Let's let them make the moves they think they have to make. Just keep me informed of his progress."

She sat like that for a while, face in her hand, wanting to collapse on the desk and sleep. Not give up; just sleep. She knew she couldn't.

There are always moments of doubt in command. The trick is not to let them stop you. Push on.

That was her father's advice. She played it over in her head, knowing it was good, it was solid, it was what she had to do.

Keep moving forward.

Breanna glanced at the wall, where she had hung a photo of her dad receiving the Medal of

Honor from the President. He had a smile on his face, but it was an uncomfortable smile. He didn't appreciate the fuss, and he didn't think he deserved the medal.

He surely did, that one and many more. But in many ways Tecumseh "Dog" Bastian was a man out of his time, a throwback to the generation that did heroic things and called them their duty.

The phone on the desk buzzed. Her secretary was reminding her that she was due for the private briefing with the Chairman of the Joint Chiefs of Staff. Breanna grabbed the thumb drive from her computer, fixed her lipstick, and set off.

16

Iran

THE FIRST FENCE WAS EASY.

Either some of the men stationed there or black marketeers doing business with them had bent a portion of the bottom away from the ground almost exactly at the spot Grease was aiming. Turk pushed the ruck ahead of him and crawled into the no-man's-land between the two fences. The ground was dry but its scent was salty. His nose itched and he felt as if he were going to sneeze.

Grease crawled through behind him. "Let's go," he said, jumping up and starting to run. "Move."

Turk did his best to keep up. The sergeant led him to the left, crossing from the spot of inky darkness into the outer edge of a dim semicircle of gray shadow. Grease had spotted another bent-up fence here and trusted that the locals knew the safest route.

Turk squeezed the ruck through once again. His shirt snagged as he went under and he had to back up to get loose. He moved forward and snagged again, the edge of the fence digging into his skin. Suppressing a curse, he twisted sideways, then fought his way free.

A truck or a jeep was headed their way. He looked over at Grease, just coming through behind him.

"Yeah, I see it," said the Delta sergeant. "Come on, come on."

They ran for an area of low scrub about fifty yards away. Turk's heart pounded in his chest, and by the time he threw himself down next to Grease, his thighs had cramped. He slipped off his pack and pushed low into the dirt, trying in vain to ignore the pain in his legs.

Headlights appeared to their right, swinging around from the direction of the runway.

"All right. Come on," hissed Grease, rising to a crouch.

He started running straight ahead. Turk grabbed the ruck and followed, thinking they were going to stop behind a second clump of bushes about ten yards away. But Grease continued past it.

In seconds Turk lost sight of him in the darkness.

"Grease?" he hissed.

Not hearing an answer, he dropped on his belly. The jeep was near the perimeter of the fence, to his right. He crawled forward, moving in the direction Grease had taken.

"Here!" hissed Grease a few seconds later.

He was ahead, sitting in a defensive position—a foxhole, dug into the inner ring of defenses. He was pointing his rifle toward the jeep.

"Do they see us?" asked Turk.

"Back to us. I doubt it."

It was a tight fit in the foxhole. Turk shifted himself around, then reached for his pack.

"What are you doing?" asked Grease.

"I'm getting my gun." It was packed into the ruck next to the control unit, the stock folded up.

"Just relax, huh?"

Oh yeah, really, thought Turk, taking it out. Relax.

Two men got out of the jeep and walked in front of the headlights. Turk stared at the haze around them, not sure if he should hope they came toward them—kill them and the truck would be easy to take.

Grease must have read his mind. "We let them go for now. If we shoot them, someone will hear. If there's one vehicle here, there's bound to be two."

Turk hunkered lower to the ground. The shadows of the men grew more distinct. They walked back to the vehicle, got in, and continued around the interior circuit of the base.

Grease started to move almost as soon as they put it in gear.

"Let's go," he said, reaching down to help him up.

They ran toward the hangar buildings just south of the end of the runway. Turk ran as fast as he could, legs growing rubbery; by the time he reached the back of the building where Grease was crouched, he felt barely able to stand.

"Just a little more," said Grease. "Catch your breath."

"OK."

Turk slumped against the wall, trying to will his heart rate back to something close to normal. Grease crawled out from the corner of the building, observing the barracks and administrative areas about fifty yards away.

"It's gonna be easier than I thought," said Grease when he returned. "Two trucks, parked near the fence. We get up over it and take one, disable the other."

"We're going to stop and disable it? How?"

"You're going to get under the hood and pull the wires off. I'll get the other truck going. Pull off anything you can," said Grease. "Ready?"

"Which way and which one?"

Grease made a little diagram with his finger as if they were running a football play. There was a fence; he'd have to climb it as quickly as he could.

"What about the other jeep we saw?"

"We shoot them if we have to. I don't think we'll need to. They went up near the big building. They're probably the night guard or something along those lines. Come on."

Turk managed to keep up all the way to the fence, threw himself against it and began to climb. He couldn't get his boots into the links well. He pulled himself up but his fingers slipped.

He told himself it was the obstacle course where he'd first started training with the Delta boys. He pushed harder, remembering the snarls of his trainers. After what seemed an eternity he managed to get to the top and slid his foot over.

By the time he got back to the ground, Grease had the hood open on one of the vehicles.

"Get the other one," he hissed. "Open the hood. Pull the wires. Every wire you see."

Turk went to the second truck. It was a Kaviran; up close it looked to him like a cartoon version of a Land Rover, its metal squared and thin. He hunted for the release to the hood.

The other truck revved. Turk pulled the hood on his up, then reached in and began pulling wires. When he had pulled everything he could find, he let go of the hood, expecting it to slam, but it was held up by hydraulic arms at the back. He reached up and slammed it down, louder than he should have, then grabbed his pack and gun and walked to the other truck.

"Fucker's a standard," said Grease.

"Can you drive?"

"I got it."

Grease got it moving but had to hunt for second gear, revving the engine too soon as the gears ground and then nearly stalling it. They drove out around the back of the barracks and headed left, turning and driving toward the perimeter fence. Turk stayed quiet, his heart pounding in his chest. They passed a small guard building, its exterior dark, and headed toward the front gate.

"Slide down a little bit in the seat," Grease told Turk. "You look too white."

Turk did as he was told. His fingers curled around the body of the gun as they turned toward the front gate. He tried to slow his breathing, knowing he was gulping air.

"Here we go," said Grease, the truck gathering speed.

As they breezed out the open gate, the Delta sergeant raised his arm in a half salute to obscure his face.

"They left only a skeleton crew," he said as he turned onto the main road. "If that. I bet they're out looking for us. Those assholes we saw up near the cave came right out of this barracks. Funny, huh?"

"Oh yeah. I'm just about dying of laughter."

"We should have gone inside and stolen new uniforms," said Grease. He glanced at Turk. "You got crap all over your face."

"I thought you said I look too white."

"Where there isn't any dirt, sure."

Turk rolled down the window. The breeze felt nice, cooling the sweat at the side of his face and the back of his neck. His shirt was soaked with perspiration.

"All downhill from here, Turk." Grease seemed happier than Turk remembered ever seeing him. "They think we're outside. We're inside. The one place they won't look. All downhill from here."

Iran

THE NEWS THAT ONE OF THE PASDARAN TEAMS HAD found a pickup truck in a cave filled Colonel Khorasani with pride touching on smugness; his hunches had led to the breakthrough. But that quickly dissipated as the next report indicated only one man had been found, and he was dead, shot in the head, undoubtedly by a compatriot.

The man's body was still warm. He looked Iranian, and had papers identifying him as such. That, of course, meant nothing—a smuggler or an Israeli spy could easily have obtained forgeries or hired a local with the promise of enough gold. But Colonel Khorasani felt confident; he was going to solve this mystery. He ordered the units in the region to deploy around the cave, racing men up from the south, where they had been concentrated. And he called the air force to ask for search planes.

As usual, they were uncooperative. The heathens should be shot with the infidels. The local squadron commander refused to take his call; Khorasani finally called General Shirazi himself, invoking the ayatollah's name in a gambit to get what he wanted.

"I need patrols in the area north of Qom," he told the head of the air force. "We believe we may have found saboteurs."

"You are still chasing ghosts? I heard you had

a farm vehicle shot up and killed members of the Guard."

"The occupants were spies," insisted Khorasani. The wreckage had been so decimated by the attack that it was impossible to say who the men were, but admitting this wouldn't help him in the least. "I am tracking their accomplices. We have found a truck. I need air surveillance."

"We don't have the capacity for night searches."

"Your planes can't see vehicles?" Khorasani paused. "What good are they?"

"We do our best with what the government allots us," snarled the general.

"I hear aircraft above. What about them?"

"We are patrolling in case the Americans attack. They won't come by ground."

"Can I tell that to the ayatollah?"

The general didn't answer. Khorasani decided to take a different tack—the general had political ambitions beyond the air force; perhaps those would work in his favor.

"We are all Iranians," said Khorasani, softening his tone. "And cooperation will help us all, no matter the outcome. Evidence that you worked violently against commandos—this would surely be positive in the ayatollah's eyes, and in everyone's."

It took only a moment for General Shirazi to respond. "You will have more patrols. They will be up in two hours."

"I want good men."

"I don't have any who aren't," snapped Shirazi.

"The pilots who shot up the truck. They were skilled." More importantly, they had proven they could follow his orders. But Khorasani didn't mention that. "Get them."

"If they are available, they will fly," agreed the general. "But I expect full cooperation in all things. Now and in the future."

"Certainly," said Khorasani, deciding an alliance with an ambitious general might not be a bad thing.

18

Iran

"ANOTHER TRUCK," SAID GREASE AS THE HEADLIGHTS swept along the highway, moving up the pavement toward them.

Turk slid down in the passenger seat and tried not to stare at the lights as they came close. He saw the vehicle from the corner of his eye as it passed; it was another Kaviran, filled with soldiers.

"Check the GPS," said Grease. "We should be real close to that turn."

"Another mile," said Turk. "It'll be on the left."

Grease found the dried up streambed without any problem. The truck's springs groaned as they left road and navigated past a tumble of rocks, but they found solid, easy ground to drive on before they'd gone more than thirty yards. The ground had been worn down to bare rock; it was slippery in spots, but they were able to move quickly.

"Look for a good place to stash the truck," said Grease.

Turk scanned the silvery landscape. It seemed something like a scene in a movie, lit for impending horror. Grease turned off the headlamps, but the reflected light from the moon filled the air with phosphorescence.

"What's behind those rocks?" he asked, pointing ahead.

Turk stuck himself halfway out the window to see. "Just dirt."

"Too much of a slope," said Grease as they got close.

"It's hilly everyplace."

"Yeah."

The ground became pebbly and loose; the wheels started to slip. Grease put the truck in its lowest gear.

"Those bushes," he said, angling toward a low clump of gnarled shrubs about thirty yards away. "If we can make it."

He stopped just below them, cranked the wheel, then attempted to back up the Kaviran so its nose would point down the hill. Even with the lowest gear and all wheels engaged, they couldn't quite pull the truck entirely behind the brush, but it didn't make much difference—the bushes barely came to the top of wheel well and would not completely hide the truck.

Grease stopped the engine by stalling it, his foot hard on the brake while the clutch was still engaged. He pulled the emergency brake so hard Turk thought he would snap the handle.

"Maybe we get to use it again, maybe not," he said.

Limbs suddenly stiff, Turk got out of the truck and shouldered the ruck. He checked the AK and kept it in his hands as he started to climb behind Grease. It was 2250.

19

CIA campus, Virginia

Breanna perched herself at the edge of the seat, one hand on the seat belt buckle as the helicopter swept down toward the lawn behind the building Whiplash used as its command center. She rarely used a helicopter to get around Washington, but time was of the essence.

The private briefing for the head of the Joint Chiefs of Staff had gone as well as could be expected. Maximillian Fresco was not a big supporter of the Whiplash concept—he was uncomfortable not with the technology, but with the relationship with the CIA—and it seemed clear to Breanna that he had already concluded the operation would fail. That was ironic, given that she had been against using bombers in the first place. But she decided that knowing the President insisted the atomic program be stopped, Fresco had decided war with Iran was inevitable and should be relentlessly pursued.

War might come even if their operation succeeded. It would be pointless and stupid—Iran would certainly be punished severely. But there would surely be a price to pay for all.

Breanna leapt out as the Jet Ranger steadied itself on the ground. As she ran across the lot, two members of the Agency security detail trotted behind her; the escort was more ritual than necessity, as it would have been extremely difficult for a terrorist or other criminal to get onto the CIA campus, let alone near the small facility Whiplash used. Pausing at the entrance to the building, she turned and waved at the men, dismissing them. Then she put her hand on the identity panel, where all five of her fingerprints were scanned, and the door automatically opened. Inside, she gave her password as she entered the elevator; the hidden systems analyzed her biometrics and she was whisked downstairs.

Jonathon Reid was waiting at the door of the secure conference center. The room was empty. The only light came from the glow of the near wall, which was filled with the blank static of the secure video connection to the White House.

"Two minutes to spare," he said. "How did the meeting go?"

"Better that you weren't there," she said.

Reid, a scarred veteran of the political infighting between the DoD and the CIA, gave her a wry smile. Breanna followed him inside. The pitcher of water on the table was draped with perspiration, as if even the inanimate objects understood the gravity of the situation.

"Are you ready for the President?" intoned the deep voice of a White House staff member.

"We are ready," said Reid.

"Ready."

Breanna sat down, wishing she had been able to grab a cup of coffee. She glanced at Reid, who shook his head—Turk had not checked in.

Still waiting for the President to appear on-screen, Breanna tapped a small rectangle on the table. As soon as it glowed green, she spread her hand. A computer screen appeared. After placing her hand flat so the computer could read her prints, she tapped the corner and a menu appeared. She selected the status map; a map of Iran appeared. She zoomed until she found Turk's marker. He was moving in the direction of the rendezvous point, but even without asking the computer to calculate, she knew it was excruciatingly slow.

She switched the underlying image from map to satellite. An image appeared. It was several hours old, taken during the day as a satellite passed, but it was an accurate depiction of the terrain. They were climbing up a rock slide.

President Todd's image flashed on the screen. She was in the White House situation room, sitting at the head of the conference table. Two aides were behind her, leaning against the wall; Breanna knew the room would be filled with NSC staffers and other advisors.

"The Joint Chiefs of Staff will be with us in a second," said the President. "Before they come on, I wanted to speak to you."

"Yes, ma'am," said Breanna, her voice a bare whisper. She reached for Reid's water and took a sip.

"We've taken a lot of casualties," said the President. Her voice was dispassionate, empty of emotion. Reading her expression, Breanna thought she was struggling to remain neutral. "Can we complete the mission?"

"Absolutely," said Breanna.

"And you've taken care of all contingencies following the attack?"

"The SEAL unit had to withdraw. We have another backup plan in place."

The President turned her head, listening to someone else in the room. She frowned and turned back. "Jonathon? Will we succeed?"

"I'm confident we have a good chance of success," said Reid. "But I can't make any guarantees."

"Understood." Todd nodded.

Breanna glanced at the screen on the table. Turk was still some distance from the control point.

"I understand you have to give the final authorization for the attack within ten minutes," said Todd, turning her head back in Breanna's direction.

"It's slightly more complicated than that," said Breanna. "But yes, ma'am, that's the gist."

"Your ground team is not yet in place?"

"They're en route."

"Will they be there by the time you launch?"

"Probably not," admitted Breanna. "They will be there in time for the assault."

"Can the mission be completed without them?" Todd asked.

"It would be difficult," admitted Reid. "Without a good bit of luck."

"Ms. Stockard?"

"Madam President, they *will* be in place," said Breanna. "This mission will succeed."

Breanna expected a nod, or some other sign of acknowledgment. Instead, Todd's expression turned even more grim, her lips pursing together.

"Bring the chiefs on-line, please," the President told her communications aide.

SEVERAL ROOMS AWAY IN THE WHIPLASH BUNKER, Ray Rubeo stared at a screenful of numbers. Technically, they described a parabola, a line following the plane section of a cone. In this case, they described one movement in the flight path the last nano-UAV would have to take to breach the final research chamber at Site One. The flight path was trivial for the computer. The problem was fitting the instruction into the limited memory of the small aircraft. Rubeo's team had been working for hours on what at first seemed a trivial problem. But math was an unyielding master, and in the end the numbers simply would not yield. There was not enough space in the onboard memory to fit the instructions.

The only possible solution was to have the pilot take over and fly the last leg.

To the people down the hall, Breanna and Reid included, it would seem a trivial matter: the pilot was there precisely to guide the aircraft. But to Rubeo the difference was immense—he would *fly* the last few planes, not *tell* the computer how to fly them.

Human error would greatly distort the probability equation.

But there was no choice. The scientist sighed, then clicked the screen to review the instructions he would give.

Breanna glanced at her watch. She had to authorize the launch in exactly three minutes.

If the President decided to abort the mission, what would she do?

Tell Turk to get the hell out of there; a war was about to erupt.

He was as good as dead already. They'd never make it to the border without being detected, and Sergeant Ransom was under orders to kill him if they were in danger of being captured.

If the mission hadn't changed, if they had only gone for the one site and left, maybe he'd be in the Caspian by now.

"All right, gentlemen and ladies." President Todd looked around her room, then back at the video camera projecting her image to the Pentagon and Whiplash. "We will proceed with the Whiplash plan as outlined. The bombers will be on standby. If the mission fails, they will proceed on my order. On my order only," she repeated.

There were murmurs of assent. The chief of

staff's face, which was centered in the feed from the Pentagon, reddened as he nodded.

"Let's get to work," said Todd, and the feed died.

Breanna rose, glancing at her watch. She had exactly sixty seconds to authorize the launch. She strode from the room, moving toward the command center down the hall. The entire team was there, waiting.

So was Ray Rubeo.

"Problem solved?" she asked.

"We have a solution," said Rubeo tersely.

There wasn't time to ask him to elaborate. "I am authorizing launch," she announced. "We may have to go with Plan B on the download, but we're moving ahead with the attack."

20

Iran

THE ROCKS GOT SMALLER AND EASIER TO GET OVER, but the slope steepened. Turk wondered if they couldn't simply stop. He didn't have to be in line of sight to get the download or guide the aircraft. But with Grease pushing ahead, he couldn't give up. He kept climbing, finally resorting to all fours, moving up slowly under the growing weight of the ruck.

"Just a little bit," said Grease every few feet. "Keep coming."

"Man, you're inhuman," said Turk finally. "You're a machine."

"No, but I ain't giving up."

"Neither am I."

Grease had to stop and wait for him every few moments. Finally he scrambled ahead, disappearing into the darkness.

Hell of a place to die, Turk thought. Somehow, he'd never believed he would collapse from a heart attack; going down in a fireball seemed much more likely.

And somehow more hospitable. He kept pushing, practically crawling now.

Why the hell didn't you eat?

When was the last time you had water?

It was Breanna's voice, upbraiding him. The real problem was sleep—he needed it. His mind was starting to float away from his body, swimming in some sort of disjointed consciousness.

When this was done, he was sleeping. No matter what. Let the damn Iranians kill him; he didn't care.

Sleep.

Something started to lift him.

"What the hell?" he said, spinning around to sit up.

"I'll take the pack," said Grease. "It's only about fifty feet to the ledge."

Turk held his arms up, as if in surrender. Grease lifted the pack, slung it on his shoulder, then reached his hand down. Turk took it and heaved himself to his feet.

"You think we'll make it after all this?" Turk asked.

"Damn straight," said Grease. "We've put too much into this now to fail."

"Yeah. Absolutely."

21

Over Iran

PARSA VAHID POINTED THE NOSE OF HIS MiG UPWARD as he left the runway, feeling the press of gravity against his chest. No matter how many times he flew, what he flew, or why he flew, the initial boost off the runway still gave him a thrill.

When his wingman Lieutenant Kayvan checked in—he'd taken off right behind him—Vahid told the control tower they were heading north. He banked slightly, coming to the proper course, then checked in with the controller. He needed special permission to fly in the Exclusion Zone; this had already been granted, and he was handed off to the special zone's controller, who used a reserved and scrambled frequency for even the most routine communications. The officer informed him there was one other flight already working the area, a small plane that Vahid knew would be practically useless in a night search. The controller gave him the flight's contact information; Vahid dialed in and hailed the pilot, who was currently near Qom.

"We'll go north of that," said Vahid. "We're available for support."

The other pilot thanked him. He sounded like an amicable sort; Vahid guessed from his voice that he was an older man, probably pressed into service for the Guard.

"God is great," said the man.

Vahid echoed him and signed off.

A few minutes later the controller told him to stand by for a communication from Colonel Khorasani. The colonel came on the radio within seconds of Vahid's acknowledgment.

"One of our units has had an incident," said Khorasani without any preliminaries. "A truck has been stolen. The unit is approximately nine kilometers south of the cave where the truck was discovered. It is headquartered at Kushke Nosrat Airport."

"Manzariyeh," said Vahid, almost in wonder— that was the military name for the airport. Once an air force base, it was now directly controlled by the Pasdaran. It was an open secret that it played a critical role as a transport hub for the nuclear program in the area. No planes were kept there, a calculated tactic to keep it from being targeted by the West. But there were healthy antiair missile defenses in the vicinity, and even though it was in the zone he'd been cleared to patrol, Vahid decided he could take no chances.

"Colonel, you'll have to alert the forces there

that I'm in the vicinity," he said. "Or they will shoot me down."

"That's being taken care of. The unit whose vehicle was stolen is conducting a thorough search, as are other units. The controller will be in constant communication with you."

"Understood."

"Captain, there is one other matter that you should be aware of. Five minutes ago we received word from one of our sources that an American bomber was taking off from Incirlik, Turkey. We do not have it on radar, and we may not have them on radar until a critical point."

"How many planes?"

"One is reported."

"They've done that before," said Vahid. One would be far less than the number needed for an attack.

"Yes, the other night, before the incident occurred. Be prepared for anything."

22

Iran

TURK LAY ON HIS BACK, DRIFTING. IF THEY'D CLIMBED Mount Everest, he wouldn't have felt as if he'd accomplished more.

But they were hours from their mission, and then days from getting out.

Maybe two days, he thought. Even less. They'd take the truck, go north, hopefully hook up with a new reaction force.

"Aren't you supposed to check in?" asked Grease.

"Oh shit. Yeah." Turk's chest muscles groaned as he got up. These pains were new; at least his body was trying to be original.

He took the satcom from his pocket. They were on a ledge facing south; the ridge rose several hundred feet above the road they'd left, but it was far from the highest point in the area; even in the dark he saw higher peaks to his left and right. The ledge itself was about the width of three bowling alleys, and maybe twice as long. The back end, which faced west, formed an irregular wall from three to five feet high as it ran north. There was a path down the east side that they hadn't seen in the satellite image, or at least not recognized; Grease had scoured the area for signs of someone else but found none.

"This is Tiger, checking in."

Breanna answered. "Go ahead, Tiger."

"We're ready for the download."

"We missed the 2300 mark," she said.

Not by too much, he thought, but she continued before he could protest.

"It's all right. We understand all your difficulties. We have a new arrangement. We're going to connect two hours before the attack. It'll be a longer download, but it will be fine. You won't need to do anything, as long as you're in position and the unit is on."

"Good," Turk told her.

"The parameters—your instructions for the attack are going to be a little more complicated than originally planned. You're going to do more flying than we thought."

"Hey," said Turk, suddenly perking to life. "Complication is my middle name."

"Good. Whiplash, off."

Turk looked over at Grease, standing with his arms crossed over his rifle.

"Complication's your middle name, huh?" said the sergeant. "Now what the hell are they throwing at us?"

"I don't know. It has to do with flying, though. I can handle it."

In fact, it would be welcome.

THE HOURS PASSED SLOWLY. THE MOON DISAPPEARED. Turk completed the download without a problem. They still had a little over two hours to go before the attack would start. Until then his biggest concern was keeping his fingers from turning numb with the cold.

Grease continued to scan the ground below with his glasses. Turk secured the control unit, making sure it was ready before it went into standby state.

"Do your legs cramp?" he asked Grease when he was done.

"Say what?"

"Your legs. Don't they get tired? Cramp?"

"No. I'm used to using them."

"So am I, but climbing and everything."

"Yeah, I guess. We train pretty hard."

"So I saw."

"You don't know the half of it."

Turk went to Grease's pack and took out one of the water bottles. "Were you trying to get me to quit?"

"We were trying to toughen you up."

"Quitting wasn't an option," said Turk.

"Good," said Grease, unmoved. "Don't drink too much of that water. Hard to say when we'll get more."

There were three more bottles in the pack, but Turk didn't argue.

"Lot of traffic out there." Grease gestured. "They're moving units around."

"They must be looking for us."

A stupid thing to say.

"They didn't tell me I was blowing up nukes," Turk added, more to change the subject than to impart information. "They only said we were blowing up equipment."

"Maybe they didn't know." Grease continued to gaze into the distance.

"No. They didn't tell me because, if we were captured, they didn't want the Iranians to know what they knew. It all makes sense now. I mean, we were expendable, right?"

"Always are."

"Even now, I imagine they won't say everything."

Turk stared south. Qom, the holy city, lay somewhere in the distance; he thought it was the glow of light at about ten o'clock, but he couldn't be sure. The Iranians had deliberately set their program up near the holy site to make America hesitate before attacking it.

The city would survive. From what he'd seen of the first attack, only the immediate area above-ground was affected; belowground might be a different story, though he had no way of knowing.

Still, to risk not only your own population—a million people lived in Qom—but a shrine holy to your religion—what sort of people did that? What religious leader could, in good conscience, approve such an idea?

The same kind of leader, perhaps, that would dream of wiping out another people because their God was not his God. Turk couldn't begin to comprehend the hatred, the evil, it involved.

"Trucks down there," said Grease, pointing. "See them?"

Turk went over and looked. The vehicles were driving northward in roughly the area where they had left the road. For a moment they appeared to stop, but it was an optical illusion, or some trick with his mind: the vehicles were still moving.

"I don't think they'll look for us up here," he said. "We're pretty far from the labs. Five miles— that's pretty far."

"Yeah."

"Once we hit them, they'll be so confused we'll have an easy time getting away," said Turk. "It'll be like the other day."

"You think that was easy?"

"Wasn't it?" Turk knew he was just rambling, trying to find something that would reassure himself, not Grease. He felt a need to talk, to do something, but at the moment all he could do was wait for the download to complete.

"Airplane," said Grease.

Turk heard it, too. It was coming from the south. He listened for a moment.

"Jet," he told Grease. "They'll never see us."

23

CIA campus, Virginia

"AIRCRAFT ARE AWAY. AIRCRAFT ARE TRACKING," declared Teddy Armaz, the head of the nano-UAV team. "Exactly sixty minutes to ground acquisition at my mark . . . Mark."

The screen at the front of the room showed the swarm's position over the Andaman and Nicobar Islands, southeast of the Bay of Bengal. They were gliding bricks at the moment, hurtling toward the earth at about Mach 5. In about twenty minutes the swarm would split into several subgroups. From that point they would fly a set of helixlike paths toward the target area, following the elaborate plan Rubeo's people had worked out to optimize the attack on the two sites.

When Breanna first saw the rendering of the flight paths, she had trouble making sense of it. The composite diagram looked like a piece of multicolored steel wool, pulled out at the top and twirled to a point at the bottom. Several of the individual loops looked like the path hailstones took in a storm cloud.

The complexity worried her greatly. What Rubeo saw as a set of mathematical equations, Breanna viewed as a collection of potential disasters. If just one of the aircraft deviated from its course at the wrong moment, it might collide with two others; the trouble would quickly mushroom. While the systems had been checked and rechecked, there was *always* some bit of random, unforeseeable chance, some oddity of fate that could interfere and throw everything into a mucked-up tangle in the blink of an eye.

Rubeo, standing at the back of the room, arms folded, didn't believe in chance or luck, at least not in that way. Breanna glanced back toward him, watching for a moment as he stared at the progress screen at the front of the room. He didn't move; he didn't even seem to breathe. He just stood ramrod straight, observing.

"Flight indicators are all in the green," said Armaz.

"Very good," Breanna told him.

"Turk is checking in," said Paul Smith, the team liaison handling communications. "You want to talk to him?"

Breanna touched the small earbud hooked into her right ear. It contained a microphone as well as a speaker.

"Channel B," she said, and the computer connected her into the line. She listened as Turk finished describing their situation to the controller.

They were camped on a ridge almost exactly five miles from each of the targets. The sun had just risen.

"Turk, how are you doing?" she asked when he finished.

"We're good," he said. His voice sounded faint and tired.

"You're doing a good job."

"Yup."

Shouldn't she say something more? Shouldn't there be a pep talk?

The words didn't come to her. "Good luck," was all she could think of as the silence grew.

"Same to you," said Turk. Then he was off.

"NASA asset is airborne and on course," reported Armaz.

"We have a heat indication in Aircraft 5," said Bob Stevenson, monitoring the swarm's systems. "The system is moving to compensate."

"Please isolate the image," Breanna said.

The tangle of flight lines on the screen disappeared, leaving one blue line near the center. The line was evenly divided between solid—where the aircraft had gone—and dotted, where the plane would fly. A new line, thicker, but in the same color, appeared on the screen. This showed the actual flight, making it easy to see the variance between what had been originally programmed and what the flight system aboard the nano-UAV was now doing to compensate for the high heat.

"Can we override that?" asked Rubeo from the back.

"Still in a plasma blackout," said Armaz. The

aircraft had, in effect, a speed-and-friction-generated shield around it that prevented communication.

"You should add the general flight-flow vector to your image," said Rubeo.

"Go ahead," said Breanna.

The line showed the overall pattern of the swarm, ghosting it over the screen. The errant UAV, being tracked by radar aboard the ship that had launched her, moved parallel to the lower line, getting neither closer nor farther.

"What's going on?" Breanna asked Rubeo.

"The indicator malfunctioned, not the aircraft," said Rubeo. "The computer tried to compensate, but it still got the incorrect signal. It's still trying to compensate, and still being told it's not working."

"What's going to happen to it?" Breanna asked.

"I'd have to work the math," said the scientist. He touched his ear, a tic Breanna knew meant he was suppressing nervousness—she guessed he had already run the numbers in his head. "But my guess is that it will end up well to the south of the target area by the time the plasma effect dissipates. At that point it will attempt to recorrect. It will be late to the party, if it doesn't self-destruct."

"Can we still accomplish the mission?"

"You can lose two more," said Rubeo. "If they're the right ones. Of course, nothing is guaranteed."

24

Iran

Turk rubbed the temples on both sides of his head. The download had finally finished and he was reviewing the plan to strike the sites. It was incredibly complex.

"I can't decipher some of these flight patterns," he told Sara Rheingold, who was going over the procedure with him from Whiplash. "I just can't."

"You don't have to, not until that very last set."

"I have to know that they're moving correctly."

"If there's a problem, you select the alternatives, based on what you've seen." She paused, then came back on the line. "Stand by for Dr. Rubeo."

"Captain Mako, you have reviewed the overall plan?"

"Yeah, but—"

"The procedure until the final attack is no more difficult than the first attack you rehearsed. When the time comes for manual control, the final speed of the aircraft will be well under one hundred knots. You will have an easy time guiding them."

"Well—"

"The flight control computer aboard the aircraft can slow their speed down to twenty-one knots if necessary. That's the last command stored. You will have an easy time taking them over. You fly them in stages. The other aircraft have been programmed to orbit or stand by in a way that preserves their flight energy until given an order to proceed. Each XP-38 UAV will be ready for you when you need it."

"Unless something goes wrong."

"Captain, may I suggest that you spend the next thirty-eight minutes going through whatever points you are confused about with my staff, and review the diagrams of the target sites. You really don't have much time to waste fretting over things you can't control."

25

Over Iran

Vᴀʜɪᴅ ᴛᴜʀɴᴇᴅ ᴛʜᴇ MɪG ɴᴏʀᴛʜᴡᴀʀᴅ, ᴍᴏᴠɪɴɢ ɪɴ ᴛʜᴇ general direction of the ground team that had just contacted him. He'd crisscrossed the area so many times in the past hour that he had lost track. Both he and Lieutenant Kayvan, his wingman, had landed once and refueled "hot"—waiting on the runway as fuel was pumped into their planes so they lost little time. They were once more getting close to their reserves, without any tangible results.

"We'll run into one of the mountains before we find anything," said Kayvan.

"You better die if you do," snapped Vahid.

"At least it's getting light. Maybe I can see."

Vahid nosed Shahin One through a thousand

meters, looking for the ground unit he was supposed to be in contact with.

The unit had responded after another driver reported seeing a truck on the hillside. The report was vague and the location and descriptions haphazard at best. The ground troops as well as the MiGs had looked over dozens of hillsides without results. Granted, it was dark and the terrain rugged, but the MiG's radar—reverse engineered from Russian equipment by the Iranians themselves—could detect a ground target the size of a truck or tank at some thirty kilometers. Nothing had appeared all night.

It didn't help that he had never trained to perform a night search. His wingman had barely practiced ground attack at all, and Vahid wouldn't have been terribly surprised to find that Kayvan couldn't effectively handle the radar. He was hardly a gifted pilot; he'd gotten his spot in the air force solely because he was the son of a member of parliament.

Vahid scanned outside the cockpit, peering down at the bluish earth. The terrain looked like a blanket slung over a child's bed. Here and there small tufts of black—rocks and bushes—poked from the fabric.

A narrow crevice appeared in the blanket. It widened slightly, spreading north.

"Ground Two, I am over the road," he radioed. "Can you hear my engine?"

"Negative."

"I am flying right over the road," he said.

"We do not have a visual. Sorry."

"Repeat your position."

Vahid climbed, trying to locate the ground unit. He was at the coordinates they had given him; obviously, they were mistaken.

Idiots.

They were some fifty kilometers from Qom; the Tehran-Qom Highway was on his left as he came south.

Maybe the jerk was reading the coordinates backward, giving what should be the second set first. Vahid made the mental correction and changed course. Before he could resume his search, the radio bleeped with a call from the Pasdaran colonel, Khorasani. Vahid gave him as diplomatic a report as possible, before adding that he and his wingmate were very low on fuel.

"You are to stay in the area as long as the ground unit needs you," said the colonel.

"I may need a divert field."

"What does that mean?"

"A place nearby to land."

"The closed air base—will that be suitable?"

"At Manzariyeh?"

"Yes."

"That would be fine."

"We'll make the arrangements." The colonel snapped off the radio.

"Shahin One, are you still with us?" asked the ground team. It was headed by a lieutenant whose voice seemed to crack with every other word. Usually the Pasdaran units were led by older men; this one seemed to be the exception that proved the rule. "We have been ordered to proceed immediately."

"We are here but cannot find you," said Vahid. "You're going to have to fire a flare."

"The enemy may see us."

"If the enemy is there, that is true," said Vahid. "But then I and my wingmate will know where you are and will be able to help you."

When he finally persuaded the lieutenant to fire the signal flare, it was Kayvan who spotted it—several kilometers east of even the reversed coordinates, and nowhere near the location the lieutenant had given him earlier.

"Idiot doesn't know his east from his west," complained Kayvan.

Though inclined to agree, Vahid said nothing. He corrected his course, then finally spotted the two trucks by the side of the road. They were about seven kilometers south of the former Manzariyeh air base, alternately known as Kushke Nosrat Airport. The field was off limits except to certain aircraft connected with the nuclear program.

"The vehicle up the hill," said the lieutenant. "Do you see it?"

"We're still too far," said Vahid. "It should be in sight shortly."

"Can you bomb it?"

"Are there enemy soldiers there?" asked Vahid.

"Unknown at this time."

"Are *our* soldiers there?"

"I'm sure this vehicle must be the one stolen by the enemy," said the lieutenant. "We need you to attack it."

"Stand by. We have to locate it first."

"Complete idiots," grumbled Kayvan. "We're probably blowing up the jackass's father-in-law."

26

Iran

Turk saw the flare just as the nano-UAVs came under his control.

One more thing to worry about, except he couldn't—he had to focus on the Hydras.

Site Two, the more likely bunker to hold the bomb, was first up. The entry point was an air exchanger unit shaped like an upside down U that sat on a concrete pad at one end of an agricultural field. The exchanger was housed in a large metal unit that sat next to an irrigation pump; the property over the bunker entrance had been turned into a working farm to help camouflage the facility.

Screens guarded the air scoop to keep birds and large insects out. The first UAV to arrive blew them both, extending its winglets like fingers to drag much of the screen with it. Two nano-UAVs flew right behind, swooping down, then taking a sharp right into a long air tunnel. They were moving at a hundred knots, considerably slower than the aircraft in the first attack but still beyond Turk's ability to physically control them in the twisting tunnel.

He didn't have to, at least not yet. The first aircraft blew a small hole in one of the filtration units; the second shot through, scouting the tunnel for the rest of the swarm. Turk glanced quickly at the performance stats. The computer recorded no problems. Then he clicked the main screen over to the swarm attacking Site One.

The plan was to enter through a straight pipe that had been identified as a utility exhaust at the southern end of the facility, one of several pipes clustered amid rusting machinery behind a shed attached to a cemetery. The facility had been built under the cemetery; the main entrance was through a large mausoleum set at the back of the property, with a secondary entrance in a storage shed near the road. Though deeper than Site Two, the facility was smaller and considered less likely to hold "the treasure," as the briefers referred to the atomic bomb material.

The initial entry was easy, but the UAVs had to execute an extreme turn west, plunge again, and take another turn to get into the shaft that led to the bunker's work area. Turk could not have flown the UAVs through the maneuvers except at extremely low speed, which would have robbed the planes of the momentum needed to strike the target. The computer handled them perfectly, and the lead Hydra blew itself up as it reached the interior exhaust turbine, making a perfect hole for the rest.

So far, so good. Turk switched his view back to Site Two. A trio of UAVs had entered the long utility chamber that ran to the main elevator shaft. The first UAV blasted a hole through it; the next group descended the shaft to the main level.

A warning flashed on the screen; the elevator had started up. The two UAVs reversed course, but it was too late for the leader; it was caught by the gondola as it rose and exploded.

The power to the elevator should have been shut by the earlier explosion; that would have sent the elevator automatically to the bottom.

It didn't. The intelligence was incorrect, or at least lacking. What else was wrong?

The explosion had minimal effect on the elevator, which continued to rise up the long shaft. Turk had to intervene.

"UAV 6, strike Power Nodule Two," he told the computer. The small craft, now traveling barely faster than the elevator, continued upward to a panel near the cable and gear mechanism. "Detonate," said Turk as it arrived.

He switched over to the feed from the NASA spy plane for a sitrep visual. The explosion had worked: the elevator was moving downward at a good rate.

Turk clicked the master control and slowed the next group, adding ten seconds to their flight plan.

"How we doing?" asked Grease from the edge of the ravine.

"Getting there." Turk lowered his head closer to the screen. He needed to concentrate.

"We got some trucks moving around down there. You hear those planes?"

"No," Turk said. "I gotta focus."

The unplanned destruction of the two UAVs

meant he had to change the priorities slightly for the remaining eight in the swarm. One had carried an infrared sensor, another a highly sensitive gamma measuring tool.

According to the plan, the UAV with the infrared sensor would have led the way into a dark utility tunnel that emptied into the elevator shaft. After detecting a spot in the shaft where water pipes cut through a hole, the aircraft would enter the pipe chamber and fly about twenty feet, where it would blow a hole through a thin wall into a ceiling space above the main laboratory chamber. The UAV carrying the gamma detector would then check the entrances at the far end of the lab, selecting the one with the highest residual radiation; presumably the corridor containing the room with bomb material. The rest of the swarm would follow, using the positioning coordinates radioed by the lead UAVs for their maneuvers. The next two had optical sensors that would inspect the area with the material. The swarm's distributed intelligence network would attempt to spot certain key images indicating as much. The rest of the drones would then destroy either the bomb or, if there was no bomb, the machinery or gear in the laboratory chamber, massing their explosions to cause a cave-in and further damage.

Turk faced a quandary. If he used the next two—UAVs 7 and 8, both equipped with optical sensors—in the slots where 5 and 6 were to have been, he'd be short an aircraft with visual sensors to make the final confirmation. That would mean taking a unit from the swarm meant to strike the other site, or possibly attacking blind.

He checked the location of the rest of the swarm. The nearest Hydra, UAV 9, was thirty seconds from entering the facility.

He slid it ahead in the next mission slot and directed the computer to reduce flight speed to the slowest possible. The computer warned that the command would reduce their flight energy to dangerous levels. Turk ignored it, zooming the image being projected from the NASA aircraft and focusing on the location of the two drones. He superimposed the schematic, looking for the weak spot.

He couldn't see the spot itself but knew it must be near where the pipes came out into the elevator shaft. He took direct control of UAV 7, and told it to strike the plotted position on the map.

He barely had time to select the IR feed from the aircraft before it blew up.

The computer flew UAV 8 through the hole into the main laboratory area, a large, irregularly shaped room over 6,000 square feet. Rather than allowing it to fly on its preprogrammed route, Turk instead used the bulk of the microengine's fuel to boost speed to fifty knots. He placed the aircraft in an orbit at the ceiling, flying parallel to the walls.

The room was lit; at least he had that.

He also had activity in it, which was unexpected.

The last six UAVs had already started downshaft.

Turk now had to locate the entrance to the test chamber. While the images were being analyzed, he spotted a room with a red door and a number of warnings in Arabic and, surprisingly, English.

That had to be it.

There were four or five people in the main lab, and he saw one pointing at the aircraft as it swung around.

"Unit 8, Destroy Door ID 2-3," he told the computer. The screen view changed, blurring to red, then a cloud of gray, then black.

An infrared image of the shaft above replaced the feed automatically as the control unit shifted the lead view to UAV 9. Turk had the swarm orbit the main lab room, then selected UAV 10, the aircraft with the gamma detector, and sent it and UAV 9 into the room behind the destroyed red door, a triangular-shaped chamber nearly 350 feet long and about fifty wide.

There was no indication from the detector. Aside from a few crates, the room appeared empty.

Fortunately, it was big enough for the UAVs to orbit in a holding pattern. Turk gave that command, then directed UAV 11, another infrared sensor robot, to destroy the other door, back in the main lab, this one green. He returned UAVs 9 and 10 back to the main room. As UAV 10 entered the room with the green door, it picked up trace radiation.

Not enough for material. In fact, it was so low it could have been a trace residual—the lingering radioactivity of workers who'd been near a small amount of material.

The green-door chamber was a rectangle that sank about a hundred feet farther into the earth. The floor area was approximately two hundred by five hundred feet wide. At the center Turk saw a cluster of workbenches; a spiderweb of shelving lined the west wall. Catty-corner to these shelves were a set of laboratory hoods and what in the infrared looked like stacks of small ovens and television sets.

"Analyze," he told the Whiplash computer, which was receiving a visual feed from his unit.

"Chemical mixing facilities, baking and shaping frames noted," declared the computer a few seconds later. "Explosive manufacturing."

The construction area for the explosive lens needed to construct a bomb?

"Calculate optimum explosion to destroy lab area Subbase 5-D," he told the computer. "Execute."

The swarm, which had been moving up and down in the room, suddenly retreated, flying back up into the main lab.

"What the hell?" yelled Turk, as if the control unit were human.

In the next second, he saw the lead nano-UAV darting toward a large round cylinder. Then the screen flashed white.

The feed from the NASA plane showed him what had happened—the UAVs had caused a massive explosion on a supply of bottled gas in the main lab area, which in turn caused secondary explosions throughout the rest of the facility. The pressure from the chamber where the explosives were manufactured ruptured one of the support girders above the lab, then the entire facility collapsed.

A perfect hit, except that they hadn't found the nuclear material they were looking for.

27

CIA campus, Virginia

Breanna watched the feed from the WB-57, which was focused on the area above the Iranian weapons lab known as Site Two. What looked like a puff of white smoke rose from the area where the UAVs had entered; it turned into a steady stream, something approximating a faucet. Two clouds appeared, at what had been the doorways to the facility. Then the ground between them cratered.

"Seismograph?" she asked.

"Not a nuke," reported Teddy Armaz. "Site Two is completely destroyed. Attack on Site One is under way."

"It was only an explosives lab," said Rubeo, standing next to Breanna. "They'll rebuild it in a month."

The surveillance aircraft shifted its flight pattern, extending its figure-eight orbit farther west. Breanna looked at the screen at her workstation, where the remaining UAVs were cataloged. All but the Hydra lost early on the mission were accounted for and in good shape.

Turk had done an excellent job improvising on Site Two; she felt confident he would do well with Site One. Some of the bands of tension that she'd felt tighten around her chest began to loosen. They were going to do this; he was going to get out.

"NASA asset has trouble," said Armaz up front.

"What's going on?" Breanna asked.

"RWR—stand by."

RWR stood for "radar warning receiver"—the aircraft was being tracked by Iranian radars. That in itself didn't mean anything, but it presaged Armaz's next warning.

"System 300 tracking them—there's a flight at long range. Two MiG-29s coming from the west."

"They're not in Iranian airspace."

"They're being challenged."

The unarmed reconnaissance aircraft was out of the range of the System 300, a sophisticated Russian antiaircraft missile system that had been acquired with Croatia's help. But the MiG-29s were another story. Though flying very high, the WB-57 was vulnerable to their radar missiles once they neared the border. The ground radar would direct the interceptors to its vicinity; once close, they would be able to fire.

"He's going to have to get out of there," added Armaz. "The MiGs are already looking for them—their attack radars are active and they are closing fast."

Breanna glanced at Rubeo. Turk had relied on the feed from the WB-57 to improvise the attack on Site Two. The next attack was even more complicated—and that was if everything went right.

"Those MiGs are attempting to lock on," said Armaz. "They're only a few seconds away."

"Get him out of there," Breanna said. "Give me Turk."

28

Iran

Tᴜʀᴋ ɢʟᴀɴᴄᴇᴅ ᴜᴘ, ᴍᴀᴅᴇ ꜱᴜʀᴇ Gʀᴇᴀꜱᴇ ᴡᴀꜱ ꜱᴛɪʟʟ ᴀᴛ the edge of the ledge, then turned his full attention back to the attack on Site One. Two UAVs had already blown through the preliminary barriers; he had fifteen left.

The plan required fourteen. One for good luck, he thought.

Something was wrong with the WB-57; a message declared the feed off-line.

"Turk, Ms. Stockard wants to speak to you," said Paul Smith, who was handling communications back in Virginia.

"Go ahead."

"Turk, we're taking the radar plane off-line temporarily," said Breanna. "He's being attacked."

"OK. All right."

"We're working on it."

"OK. I need to go." He switched off the coms

and took stock of the UAV swarm. In addition to the fifteen now hurtling toward the facility, there was one more at the far edge of the screen, designated as UAV 18, not yet under his control. He wasn't sure why it was so far behind, but he made a mental note and went back to the attack swarm.

The lead UAV descended through the air exhaust vent, plunging toward a chamber that had been identified as a cafeteria space earlier. Designated UAV 3, it hit the grill protecting the space, but did not explode; Rubeo's people had calculated it could get by the grill without needing to do so. It zipped across the room at high speed, banking so it could enter a corridor that led to another passage downward. Here, it struck a machine that worked an air-conditioning zoning mechanism. As it exploded, the vents connected to the unit sprung open, clearing the way for the rest of the swarm to enter through a different passage just above the cafeteria space.

The UAVs shot downward, entering a utility space populated by wires and pipes. The fit was excruciatingly tight, with bare millimeters of clearance at two points, plus a pair of tricky turns that looked like V's with an extra leg curving down at the end. Turk knew he could not have flown this himself, but the tiny aircraft navigated the passage with ease, emerging in a large, empty chamber apparently designed for ventilation and heating equipment, but not used.

The lead nano-UAV curled upward as it reached the end of the long space, exploding just before touching the top. The force pushed down a second UAV, which had followed, adding momentum to its attack on the thick metal access panel that formed the floor. The explosion blew a hole in the panel, but unfortunately, the hole was not quite large enough to allow the next UAV to pass. The aircraft tangled its wings against a shard at the edge. Before Turk could react, it had blown itself up, enlarging the passage.

That had been one of the trouble spots Rubeo had warned of, a place where he feared they might lose one of the designated aircraft and have to rely on the backups. Two more lay ahead.

UAV 5 was now in the lead, projecting its infrared image to Turk as it passed through an open doorway and started down a ramp area, passing someone walking up the ramp. The Hydra twisted on its axis, completing a hard turn to its right to enter a work area roughly the size of a football field.

The screen blinked. A new set of words appeared at the bottom of the image: UPDATE: PROCESSING AREA.

A small forest of silver cylinders that looked like stacked coffeemakers sat on the south side of the large room. They were centrifuges, used to refine weapons-grade uranium.

That was a significant find, but Turk had not been briefed on it.

The next area contained a large bath, built to hold fuel. The site they hit the first night had a similar area.

This was starting to look like the place.

The swarm moved into an orbit at the top of the

lab room, slowing while they formed themselves into two groups for the next leg of the assault. Turk debated whether to override—he could use one of the UAVs to destroy the centrifuges—but decided not to. If the attack was successful, they would be destroyed in the explosion.

UAV 5 tucked toward the floor, blowing out a stamped metal plate that covered an emergency drain. Seconds later the rest began to descend in a single line—until UAV 11, which struck something over the pipe and exploded.

UAVs 12 and 13 were caught in the explosion; there was a secondary explosion, and gas began hissing into the space. Fire destroyed UAV 14, and then UAV 15, disoriented, crashed into a centrifuge assembly.

Meanwhile, UAVs 16 and 17 plunged down the drainpipe unscathed, dropping toward the large holding tank at the east side of the facility. The tank had been punctured by UAV 6, opening the way into another large work space, about three-quarters the size of the centrifuge and pond area. The plan called for the swarm to move down another corridor into a lab area and from there to a second room that might be an assembly area, but Turk temporarily suspended it, putting the aircraft into a quick orbit around the top.

He closed his eyes and bent his head back, stretching his neck in a gesture of both prayer and despair. He didn't have enough UAVs to complete the mission, and he had no idea how to improvise around the problem.

29

Over Iran

CAPTAIN VAHID SLOWED HIS MIG DOWN FOR A SECOND run near the hillside. The ground unit was on his left, the vehicle somewhere on his right. He hadn't seen it on the first pass, though the soldiers on the ground claimed he had gone right over it. The rocks it was parked near—assuming it was there—obscured it on the radar.

He stared at the silvery ground, but it was just a blur.

"Fire a flare at the vehicle on my signal," he told the Pasdaran commander. "Copy?"

"They will know they have been located."

If they don't know that by now, they are true imbeciles, thought Vahid. He told the commander to do as he'd asked.

Banking the MiG, Vahid told his wingman what he was doing and then began his run.

"Fire," he radioed. A finger of red shot from the scratch road where the Pasdaran unit had stopped, leaping up the hillside into the rocks. Vahid saw something there, boxy, not moving.

The truck.

"Are you sure you want me to bomb it?" he asked. "You are very close."

Surely it would make more sense for them to go up the hill and inspect it themselves. But Vahid guessed that the commander wasn't willing to take that risk. If the truck was destroyed, there would be no way for the Israelis—or whoever was near it—to escape. He could wait for morning.

That was undoubtedly the idiot's logic. He didn't seem to calculate that whoever had driven it there was undoubtedly long gone, since the Pasdaran unit had not come under attack.

"Affirmative."

"Pull back, then," Vahid told them. "Radio when you are a safe distance away."

"A waste of bombs," said his wingmate. "But good practice."

30

Iran

TURK STARED AT THE CONTROL SCREEN. THE SIX UAVs he had left were circling at high speed in the water overflow chamber, an unfilled water tank that was part of the cooling apparatus for a system designed to hold hot uranium rods. The gear was left over from an earlier, ultimately abandoned phase of the project's experiments.

The UAVs were supposed to exit the massive tank through a small pipe, flying an intricate pattern through an emergency drain system and ventilation ducts before reaching the suite where the targeted lab was located. There, they would enter an air shaft, blast through a pair of ventilating fans, and invade the suite where the work cham-

ber was located. It would take four UAVs to clear
the way that far.

Once they had done their job, Turk would take
direct control and fly the remaining UAVs to the
target area. The chamber itself consisted of several small rooms. Turk would take the UAVs into
a corridor through the opening in the ventilation
shaft. He would then blast his way through a set
of double doors and enter the targeted space. It
would take three UAVs to clear the way. The last
would strike the target at a point the Whiplash
system calculated to do the most damage. Turk
worried about this; even a slight delay from the
computer as it relayed the information—or a
problem with the link—might complicate the
final task. Worst case, there might not be enough
momentum left to initiate an explosion.

Unless the doors were open. If so, he could save
several units and mass for the attack.

Turk hit the button at the bottom of the screen
to bring up the view from the WB-57. The plane,
under attack from the Iranian MiGs, was too far
away to provide a live image. The screen warned
that he was looking at a view frozen several minutes ago.

One door was open in the image, a technician
passing through it.

Turk touched the screen and twisted his fingers, enabling a 3-D schematic view constructed
from earlier radar penetrations. He moved it up
and zoomed, looking at the area of the pipes.

The computer beeped at him, warning that the
UAVs were getting close to the point where their

flight momentum would no longer be enough to complete the mission.

Turk looked for another way into the final chamber. The ventilation shaft ran close to a utility closet at the end of the suite. It would take two UAVs to get there, then a third to get into the closet, and a fourth to blow out of the door.

Leaving two to get through three doors.

He moved the diagram, saw the utility closet at the base of a long chase of wires and pipes that ran up parallel to the chamber. If he blew into that chase, then had the UAVs descend, he'd use only five to get to the final target.

Why hadn't the planners chosen that option? He zoomed the image of the chase. The passage was tight, with two elbow turns and a final V before the closet.

They must not have trusted him to guide them through the tight space. Not that he blamed them: the middle turn was ninety degrees. He'd never make it unless he was going very, very slow. And that wouldn't leave enough flight energy to guarantee time to scout the final chamber.

But he only had to make it once. Or rather, he only had to make each stage once, then use the onboard follow function.

Turk aimed UAV 7 directly at the spot where the metal chase touched the wall of the tank. The explosion sent a shock wave bouncing through the chamber. The other aircraft fluttered but adjusted well, remaining in their pattern.

Turk next slowed UAV 8 and tucked into the chase. The speed dropped under thirty knots—

slow for the craft but too fast to make the turn perfectly. He clipped the top right wing but managed to keep it intact and moving into the next elbow turn. By the time he was halfway through the elbow, his speed had dropped below stall speed, and the nano-UAV headed toward the bottom wall of the chase. Turk used his small microburst engine to propel it upward, past a twisted artery of wires and to the final V turn. He used his last bit of power to start the maneuver, then leveled off quickly to get into position to drop into the closet. But the wing had been damaged by the earlier bump, and the UAV started to spin. He managed to push the nose forward, sending the aircraft sideways toward the top of the closet wall. He pressed the self-destruct button as the right wing slapped against one of the steel members framing the door.

He wasn't sure he had a hole. Worse, he couldn't use the autofollow, since that would risk having the computer follow the crooked maneuver at the end. He'd have to try the maneuver again.

UAV 8 had optical sensors rather than IR. The chase was too dark for it. He selected UAV 9, circled several times to cut his speed to ten knots, then started through.

This wasn't like flying an airplane, or even like commanding a normal UAV. This was flicking your wrist back and forth, reacting to little bits of light and dark that flashed before your eyes. This was remembering what you had seen. This was motor skill and intuition, putting everything out of your mind but the little dot of UAV that flicked behind the screen.

The image blurred from gray to gray to gray and then light, vigorous light—he was out in the corridor—and the door ahead was open.

Go. *Go!*

"Swarm, follow," Turk commanded.

The swarm descended at high speed. In the meantime, he pushed UAV 9 up through the corridor with the last of its fuel, moving through the still-open door. The frightened face of a technician appeared, then disappeared as the aircraft sped to a door on the far side.

Closed.

The UAV exploded. But the rest of the swarm was now in the long hall outside the targeted chamber.

"Safe orbit," he commanded.

Turk caught his breath. He had four UAVs left. He'd need one to blow out the door; the rest to get his target.

UAV 16 had a radiation detector. He selected the sensor panel. The radiation was at the high end of the gauge.

He was in the right place, at least.

He got a warning from the control unit—UAV 10 was overheating.

Turk took control of the tiny plane and smashed it through the door to the targeted chamber. The unit that followed flashed video from the room: massive gridwork filled the screen, silver and red.

They were cages, with tigers in each, snarling and turning to dragons.

It was an optical illusion, caused by the lingering effects of the explosion and the rush of light. But it was an illusion built on reality—there were two large sets of metal struts and scaffolds at the far end of the room, beyond three sets of low walls made of sandbags.

Two bombs, each in its own holster.

"Calculate explosion point."

Seconds ticked by. They passed quicker than Turk expected—the solution, said the computer, was easy. It posted a crosshair between two pieces of metal on the assembly at the left, a tiny little spot big enough for one UAV only.

And that's all that was needed, it declared.

Turk took UAV 16 and directed it into the assembly. "Target spot, ignite," he said, directing the aircraft to ignite the explosive and detonate itself. He felt his body begin to relax as the aircraft zeroed in. The screen blanked with a flash of light.

Then the feed from UAV 9 replaced the image. That was impossible—the bomb explosion should have obliterated everything.

Except it hadn't. The computer had miscalculated, or there was some sort of flaw in the Iranian design, or the UAV hadn't struck it right, or any of a dozen different explanations that made absolutely no difference now.

The explosion had done something: part of the cradle holding the unfinished weapon up had fallen away. The bomb tipped over but remained intact, at least to the naked eye.

UAV 9 and UAV 15 were left, still orbiting at the top of the chamber though now at low speed, nearing their stall points. Lights flashed in the chamber—an alert.

Do something, Turk told himself. Do it.

But what?

Rubeo's people had identified a bank of small acetylene gas tanks at the north side of the room that could be detonated if no bomb was found. This would cause a partial collapse of the chamber roof, which should set up a chain reaction from above. The result would bury the chamber.

But not destroy it.

Better than nothing. And he was running out of time, as the UAVs were running out of energy. Turk took UAV 9 over directly, locating the tanks, which looked like a set of lockers at the end of the room. He was about to put UAV 15 into follow mode when he got a better idea. He told the computer to hit the acetylene with UAV 9, then steered UAV 15 toward the bomb he hadn't struck, aiming for the wired mechanism similar to the one he remembered from the other day. There was no time to calculate any more; he had to aim it himself.

UAV 9 struck the gas tanks. Fire flashed through the room, catching in the oxygen-enhanced atmosphere in a flash. UAV 15 wavered. He pushed hard on the flight stick, picking its nose up and plowing into the bomb assembly as his control unit's visual screen went blank.

A second later he felt the ground shaking beneath him, a gentle roll that quickly blossomed into a harsh jerk up and down.

He had ignited the nuke, and its shock had exploded the other one as well.

ORPHAN

———

1

CIA campus, Virginia

NO ONE SPOKE. BREANNA STARED AT THE MAP SCREEN at the front of the control room. Turk's position flashed on and off, on and off, a lonely green dot in a mass of gray and black.

"Seismographic data, confirmed," said Teddy Armaz finally. "We have a nuclear explosion—odd pattern—two maybe? One partial? Looks like, uh, four and a half total megatons. Uh—"

"Judging from the wave patterns, there were two weapons," said Rubeo. "These are only partial explosions. Whether because of our attacks or their design will require further analysis. Interesting."

Another brief moment of silence followed, no one speaking or even breathing. And then the room exploded with a cheer.

Breanna turned to Reid. He was smiling. "We did it."

"Yes," she told him. "Yes."

Reid picked up one of the handsets to call the White House. Breanna noticed Rubeo behind him. He was staring at one of his laptop screens, his face cemented into a frown.

Someone in the front yelled, "Yeah!" The cheering crescendoed, culminating in a round of applause that would have shaken a football stadium.

They deserved it. Iran's nuclear program had been critically disabled. It would take at least a decade for the Iranians to reconstitute the human and mechanical infrastructure; by then, all manner of things would have changed.

Still, they weren't finished.

"All right," she told the room. "Settle down. We need to get our people home."

2

Iran

TURK LAY ON HIS BACK, CONFUSED AND DISORIENTED. The control unit, still in his hands, had fallen onto his chest, but for a moment he didn't realize what it was. He was so tired that his brain was scrambled and his eyes physically hurt; dizzy, he thought he was falling from his bed in a dream.

His confusion lasted only a second. A jet passed somewhere above, nearby and low.

"Grease!" Turk sputtered.

Grease pulled him up by his shirt. "We have to move," said the sergeant. "Come on."

"Yeah, yeah, yeah." Turk started putting the control unit into the pack.

"Let's destroy it," said Grease. "We don't need to carry it."

"There's still one more UAV overhead," said Turk. "Which way is the truck?"

"We can't get it. There are troops watching it," said Grease. "We'll circle around and take one of their vehicles." Holding his rifle in one hand, he started down the slope, half sliding, half walking.

Turk strapped on his ruck and followed. After a few yards he found the slope so steep he had to dig his feet in sideways against the dirt. He leaned his whole side into the hill, trying to keep some control as he started to slide. Digging his heels in didn't work; he pushed with his elbow and finally turned his whole back against the earth, barely slowing until he slid into Grease's back.

The soldier said nothing, pulling him off silently, then tugging him to follow down a much gentler incline to a nearly flat path that tucked south. Bisected by a wide but shallow creek bed used by runoff during downpours, the path straightened as they went, moving along what Turk guessed was once a farm field, abandoned years before.

After they walked for a few minutes he spotted a building and what looked like a working farm, or at least a place where underground water allowed trees to grow. It was too far away to see what sort of orchard this might be. The trees looked thin, almost disintegrating in the early sun as they formed a narrow column roughly parallel to the path. Grease and Turk walked past the farm quickly, continuing until Grease, moving by instinct rather than map or GPS, turned sharply to the right.

"Stop," he said, after they'd gone another hundred yards.

Turk obeyed, lowering himself to his haunches while Grease continued forward. It was quiet, eerily so; Turk knew that they had succeeded, yet the lack of a response seemed to contradict that.

No, he thought. They were five miles from each site, too far to see what was going on at either. And it would be impossible for the Iranians to respond quickly, even if they knew what had happened.

The Iranian jet took another low pass near the hill. If it weren't for the plane, he might have thought this was all a dream.

3

Iran

CAPTAIN VAHID CHECKED THE MIG'S FUEL. HE WAS perhaps five minutes from his reserves, though he had more leeway now that he could use the Pasdaran base. It looked like he would need it: the ground commander had put the attack on hold, deciding at the last moment that he needed clearance not just from Colonel Khorasani but his own commander to make the attack on the truck.

The delay was excruciating. He widened his orbit around the search area, moving up and down Highways 7 and 71, which twined around each other from Tehran to Qom. The great salt lake, Hoz-e Soltan, sat to the east of the highways, a vast flat mirror of salty water so shallow it could be walked across, even in the rainy season.

Hoz-e Soltan was famous in Iran, and Vahid's older sister had told him stories about monsters in the lake when he was a young child. Bad children were led there and made to walk along the edge, where they slowly sank into the marshy edge.

But not all the way. When only their heads were above the surface, birds would come and build nests on their hair. The salt would preserve them forever as waterlogged mannequins, swelled and wrinkled by the saltwater.

On Vahid's first visit as an adult, he was surprised to see shapes rising from the salt bed in the distance. They looked like heads and nests, and for a moment he felt the same horror he'd felt listening to his sister. It was only when he drew closer that he realized they were large mounds of salt crystal and cakes of salt packed tightly like concrete, the afterbirth of the receding water.

"Do they want us to bomb this truck or not?" asked Lieutenant Kayvan finally. "Five more minutes of this and we are walking to base."

"We have more time than that," said Vahid, though he agreed with Kayvan's point. The idiot Pasdaran should hurry up and decide whether they wanted their truck shot up or not.

"Shahin One, can you hear me?" Colonel Khorasani's voice exploded in his helmet, sharp and angry.

"I hear you, Colonel."

"What is your status?"

"Colonel, the ground commander is waiting permission to destroy the truck."

"I already gave the order."

"Yes, Colonel, but the ground unit—"

"Destroy that vehicle immediately. Destroy anything near it. Do it quickly. Destroy anything that moves. Use every weapon you have. Do it now, Captain."

"Colonel, there are friendly units within a few hundred yards," said Vahid.

"You have my orders."

"Shahin One acknowledges."

"Whoa," said Kayvan. "What bit his ass?"

"Line up with me."

"Did he just give us permission to wipe out the Pasdaran unit?" Kayvan asked.

"Follow me in, and watch out for friendlies," snapped Vahid, switching to the ground unit's frequency to warn them.

4

Iran

PACING ON THE HIGHWAY A MILE NORTH OF QOM, Colonel Khorasani shook the handset of his satellite communications system as if it were a rattle before handing it back to Sergeant Karim in the command truck. The jets were some thirty kilometers north, much too far for him to see or hear.

"Has Fordow 14 checked in?" he asked his aide.

"No, sir. We're working on it."

"Work harder." Khorasani folded his arms in front of him and began pacing. Occasionally he glanced at the dusty skyline of the holy city on his right, but mostly he kept his eyes in the direction of Fordow 12, which had reported an "incident" nearly twenty minutes before.

The report was sketchy, but alarming: the captain of the Guard unit stationed there had reported a blast followed by a fire in the main underground bunkers. It had been severe; he reported there was a massive cave-in, with smoke and debris still spewing from the ventilation shafts. The access elevators were off-line; he had sent two men from the security team down the secondary stairways to find out what happened.

The men had not yet reported back. It was, after all, a long way down.

Khorasani had questioned the captain personally, asking about aircraft. There had been no sign of any, nor had the local radars picked up bombs or missiles approaching.

Sergeant Karim bent to the phone.

"A policeman near Baqeraba reports he felt an earthquake a few minutes ago," he said, looking up.

"Take his name."

"There was another report—"

"Don't bother me with trivia, Sergeant. Record the names. We'll have someone talk to them."

Khorasani had felt nothing, but the reports were ominous. When Karim hung up, he told him to try Fordow 14 himself.

"Colonel, I did try."

"Try again. And then I want you to contact Saiar in the Tehran office."

"The scientist?"

"Yes, you idiot. Tell him—ask him if there has been an event similar to the other day."

"It's still early."

"Call him at home if you have to. Find out."

"Right away, Colonel."

By now Khorasani knew it was highly likely that there had been another explosion, or perhaps two, similar to the one at Natanz D. One such incident might be a malfunction, but two? This could only be a deliberate attack.

And that spelled great trouble for him. He was sure to be blamed for not moving quickly enough to prevent further attacks.

If they were attacks. Surely, they must be due to flaws in the weapons or the procedures for handling them.

"Air General Shirazi for you," said Sergeant Karim, leaning out of the truck. "He wants to know what's going on."

Khorasani took the handset. "General, are we under attack?"

"You are asking me?"

"There has been an explosion at one of the laboratory facilities north of Qom, near Fordow. We expect many casualties," said Khorasani. "And I cannot contact another of our sites. There had been—some people have felt an earthquake in the region."

"That is why I am calling."

"Has there been an air attack?"

"We have seen *nothing*."

"Are you sure?"

General Shirazi cut the line, clearly angry. Khorasani had not meant that as an insult, only a question. The American stealth bombers certainly had ways of launching sneak attacks, and even a cruise missile might be undetected before it struck.

Why were there commandos and spies in the area, then?

Who said they were commandos? Just smugglers—a coincidence.

Khorasani had to consider the situation carefully. It could be an accident. Three accidents.

Blame it on the air force. No, more subtle: set it up so the air force would take the blame. He himself would say nothing.

Hints, only. Subtly.

If it *was* a ground attack, he had to capture the men who were responsible. If someone else captured them, they would be tortured and admit what they had done. They might even brag about it.

Americans surely would brag.

5

Iran

THE DEEP BASS OF THE JET'S THRUST SHOOK THE FLOOR of the desert as it dove toward the vehicle parked on the slope. A cannon thumped, the sound more like a runaway sewing machine than a gun. There was an explosion, then a sharp, loud *crack*.

Three *thrp-thrp-thrps* followed. The two men who had been guarding the vehicles on the road fell to the ground.

"Go!" hissed Grease.

Turk jumped to his feet as Grease ran toward the nearest truck. The aircraft was turning north, lining up for a second run. Iranian soldiers were some fifty or sixty yards away, beyond the farthest vehicle and close to the hill. The rest of the troops were strung out along the road and hillside, waiting for the jets to complete their attack.

Turk ran up along the passenger side of the vehicles. The straps on the rucksack with the control unit had loosened, and the pack bounced against his back. Its metal base punched his kidneys in an unsteady rhythm, a drunken boxer who knew where his mark was but couldn't quite find a steady pace for his hooks.

Suddenly the cab in front of him opened. Turk couldn't believe it—there wasn't supposed to be anyone here, and if there was anyone, surely Grease would have killed him.

The man had a gun.

He fired.

So did Turk.

The man fell. Turk kept running. When he reached the cab, he pushed the AK-47 inside, fired a burst, then looked in. The truck was empty.

"Go, go, go," hissed Grease, running from the head of the column. He'd killed the other guards.

Turk jumped behind the driver's side.

"It's running," he said, starting to back into a three point turn.

"Yeah. Just go."

Turk saw the fighter pull up beyond the hill. Its wingmate was above, circling out of sight, though he could hear it.

"I just killed someone," he said as he finished the turn.

Grease didn't answer. He was leaning out the window, making sure they weren't followed. The sound of the jets flashing overhead had muffled the gunshots.

Was it really that easy to kill someone, Turk wondered, so easy that he didn't even have to think about it?

Yes, it certainly was. It was easy to live.

WHEN THEY'D GONE A MILE, GREASE INSISTED THEY change places. He took the wheel and headed south. They were doing over a hundred kilometers an hour by the time they reached the highway, dirt furling behind them.

"We're headed toward Qom," said Turk as they turned onto the well-paved and marked road.

"No shit."

"You think that's a good idea?"

"I'll turn west as soon as I can. We have another safe house out in Lorestan. We should be there before morning, if we don't get stopped."

Hɪɢн ᴀʙᴏᴠᴇ Qᴏᴍ, Vᴀʜɪᴅ ᴄʜᴇᴄᴋᴇᴅ ʜɪꜱ ɪɴꜱᴛʀᴜᴍᴇɴᴛꜱ and got ready to return to base. He, too, was now low on fuel.

The truck had been completely destroyed; not even dust remained.

"Shahin One, are you reading us?" It was the ground unit they had just assisted.

"This is Shahin One."

"One of our vehicles has been stolen. We require your assistance."

"What the hell?" snapped Kayvan on the squadron frequency. "What are these idiots doing?"

"Silence," commanded Vahid. The ground unit gave the description of the vehicle—one of their small tactical utility trucks, a Kaviran. They had seen it heading south.

Vahid acknowledged and tucked his wing, rolling downward toward the dark earth. They were nearly twenty kilometers south of the truck he had just destroyed.

"I am on your six," said Kayvan, sounding chastised. "I am low on fuel. Ten minutes, maybe."

"See anything?"

"I have the highway—Freeway 7. I can see it clearly."

"Traffic?"

"No traffic."

Freeway 7, also known as the Persian Gulf Highway, was on Vahid's right.

"I have a car," said Kayvan.

"Not a target," said Vahid. "Keep looking."

"Something ahead."

"We'll go past and then sweep back around," Vahid told his wingman, realizing he was moving too fast to get a good look at the vehicle or shoot at it. "Stay with me."

"THE PLANES ARE OUT OF BOMBS," SAID TURK AS THE aircraft passed. "Probably out of ammo, too. They don't carry much."

"They'll be spotting for the ground units," said Grease. "Dig out the map. We'll have to look for another route."

Turk dug the map and GPS out from Grease's pack, on the floor between them.

"So what's the general plan?" he asked.

"Get the hell out of here. Go to Lorestan."

"Then what?"

"North to the Caspian."

"Five or six hundred kilometers."

"There's fuel at Lorestan. We can get there in two hours."

"In broad daylight?"

"You got a better plan, I'm all ears."

Grease's sharp retort felt like a slap across the face.

"We'll figure it out at Lorestan," said Grease, his voice softer. "Do you have to check in?"

"They'll have picked up the rumble. From here it's silent coms, unless we get into trouble," said Turk.

"Yeah. Unless."

"IT'S A KAVIRAN," said Kayvan. "DEFINITELY."

"You didn't see anything else north?" Vahid asked.

"Nothing."

"How's your fuel?"

"Well, I have to land soon."

So did Vahid. "We'll use the Pasdaran airfield," he told his wingmate.

"Even so—maybe five minutes?" Kayvan's voice made it clear that he was being extremely optimistic, and even at five minutes, his fuel stores would be even lower than Vahid's.

"Let's do this quickly," replied Vahid. "Take a run and head toward the base. Stand by while I talk to the ground unit."

The commander of the Pasdaran unit was in his own truck, coming south. Worried that he had mistaken the vehicle, Vahid told him to pull off the road immediately and fire a flare. He hunted around in the air for several seconds before he found the signal well to the north.

"Stay where you are until we clear," Vahid told him. "We're making our run now."

TURK HEARD A LOUD SCREECH, THE SOUND OF METAL ripping, then nothing; the world had gone silent.

The truck disintegrated around him, whirling him into the darkness at the side of the road. The next few moments were lost in a cloud of metal haze and fire. He crawled across the dirt, a black cowl around his head. He choked. His eyes burned. Finally he got to his feet and took a few tentative steps, moving toward clear air.

Grease—where was Grease?

Turk turned back toward the expanding fist of smoke that marked the road. He still didn't comprehend what had happened. They'd hit a bomb or something.

"Grease!" he yelled, starting forward. "Grease!"

The putrid air drove him to the left. He crossed the road and saw the front end of the truck sitting a few yards away. It looked as if it had been sawed in half, then quartered. The cab was nearly intact, propped on one end by the wheel.

Grease was still inside. Turk ran to the door, grabbed his shirt and pushed it between his fingers and the handle to act as an insulator if the metal was hot. But the latch was cool, as was the rest of the cab; it was the back of the truck that was on fire.

Turk pulled the door open. Grease was slumped forward against his restraints, hanging a few inches from the steering wheel. Turk undid the belt, fingers fumbling. He pulled at Grease, and though the sergeant's eyes were closed, somehow expected that he would follow him from the truck. Instead, his companion and protector sprawled out the door, face first against the ground, his feet wedged under the damaged dashboard.

"Come on," said Turk. He hooked his arm under Grease, pulling him up and out. He started back in the direction that he had come, circling back to the spot where he first emerged from the smoke.

It didn't occur to Turk that Grease might be dead until he put him down. He couldn't hear anything, and despite the full sunlight could barely see. His ears had been blown out by the bang of the explosion, his eyes unfocused by all that had happened.

"God," moaned Grease.

The word restored Turk's hearing. But it worked too well. Now he heard everything: the drone of planes in the distance, the rumble of trucks far away, the sizzling hiss of the fire continuing to burn.

He needed a gun. And the control unit. And Grease's ruck. But where were they?

"Stay here," Turk told Grease, letting him down as gently as he could manage, then ran back to the destroyed truck. The AK-47 and the control pack sat in the dirt a few yards from the front of the cab.

Looping the backpack strap around his right shoulder, Turk picked up the gun. He could hear a truck engine whining in the distance.

Grease curled himself into a little ball, moans and grunts coming from the recesses of his abdomen. He started to cough, and didn't stop until Turk lifted him to a sitting position. "We have to get to cover," Turk told him. "Can you walk?"

Grease groaned something in response. Turk twisted himself around to lever Grease upward, trying to be gentle as he propped the wounded man onto his back.

"We're going, let's move," said Turk, commanding his feet and the rest of his body to cooperate. He decided he couldn't get the gun or the control ruck without losing his balance; he'd have to come back for them.

Turk began walking away from the road, his first goal simply to get as far away as possible. Blood and adrenaline rushed to his muscles. He felt strong.

"We're getting the hell out of here," he told Grease.

Grease, draped over his side and back, didn't answer. He moved, as if trying to walk.

"I got it," Turk told him. "Let me do it."

A clump of gray and green loomed before him. At first glance it looked like a large body, laid out on the ground. Turk pushed that image away, stubbornly insisting to his brain that it couldn't possibly be a body. He was right; within a few yards the shadow had broken itself into several small trees and a cluster of rocks. He walked steadily toward it, Grease's weight pushing him closer and closer to the earth.

The rocks were the far side of an open pit that had been bulldozed sometime before, then abandoned. Turk walked to the rocks and put Grease down as gently as possible. Taking off his own shirt, he fashioned it into a narrow pillow and placed it under Grease's head.

"I'll be right back," he told his friend. "I have to get our stuff."

Grease said nothing. Turk took a step away, then remembering that he wasn't armed, reached down and took the sergeant's handgun. He held it in his hand as he ran back in the direction of the road.

6

Iran

"TRUCK DESTROYED," CAPTAIN VAHID TOLD THE ground commander as he headed for the airfield.

"Are there survivors?"

"I don't think so," said Vahid. "I took a pass but the smoke was so thick I couldn't see anything. The vehicle split into several pieces."

"Acknowledged, Shahin One."

"I'm rather low on fuel," said Vahid. "I've already sent my wingman to make an emergency landing."

"We'll proceed to the site. Thank you for your help."

"I can do one last run if you want."

"Negative, Captain. Thank you for your help. God is great!"

"You're welcome. God is great!" he repeated, with more enthusiasm than he had mustered in some time.

7

CIA campus, Virginia

"THEY DON'T SEEM TO BE MOVING ANYMORE," SAID Breanna, staring at the screen where Turk's position was marked. "They're only a few miles south of Qom—are the Guard units responding there?"

"The Iranians are still trying to figure out what's going on," said Jonathon Reid, who'd gone over to the console where a digest of NSA intercepts were being displayed in near-real time. "They're very confused."

The intercepts, compiled from a variety of sources, were translated by machine and color-coded for source. A program in the network applied various filters, showing Whiplash only the information that corresponded to a set of keywords and geographic locations. The sheer volume of the intercepts as well as the Iranians' own confusion made it doubly difficult to figure out what was going on.

"What about that Pasdaran colonel who was assigned to handle the investigation into the first attack?" asked Breanna. "Where is he?"

"I'm not sure at the moment," said Reid. "We're working on it."

"There's one nano-UAV remaining," said Teddy Armaz. "It was the unit with the malfunctioning sensor. It has about five minutes of flight time left."

"Can we self-destruct it?"

"No. The X-37B is well out of range." Armaz looked over Bob Stevenson's shoulder at the status panel. "It should destroy itself on its own in about five minutes, since it hasn't had a command."

Breanna nodded. The self-destruct protocol was one of several safeguards that had been instituted throughout the military's UAV fleet following an accident in 2012 that allowed a Stealth drone to descend into Iran practically without damage. Ironically, the capture of the drone and the subsequent sale of its technology to China had spurred the development of several more advanced American UAV projects, including the Hydras. Iran would have been better off simply letting the Stealth UAV alone.

"I don't like the fact that Turk's not moving," Breanna told Reid.

Reid was concentrating on the screen. "The WB-57 pilot has been recovered. Well that's one of ours back, at least."

"What about Turk?"

"He's moving in the area," answered Reid, zooming his screen. "He's still alive. For how long is anyone's guess."

8

Iran

TURK HEARD THE VEHICLE COMING AS SOON AS HE reached the rifle. He grabbed it and the ruck with the control unit and ran back to Grease.

The sergeant was lying exactly as Turk had left him. His eyes were closed. If it weren't for his groans, Turk would have thought he was dead.

The truck was just reaching the wreckage. Rather than stopping, though, it kept going. Turk felt a slight bit of relief, then remembered the airplane was still above somewhere.

He had one more nano-UAV, didn't he? Where was it?

Pulling the control unit from the backpack, he unfolded it and turned it on. The Hydra was circling above, descending in a gradually tightening spiral. Because it hadn't been contacted in a half hour, it had begun its self-destruct sequence. In twenty-eight seconds it would blow itself up.

"Computer, establish direct control," said Turk. "UAV 1."

"Control established."

The destruct panel cleared. Turk checked the aircraft's status. It was in perfect order, except for the defective gauge, which still indicated it was overheating.

The aircraft had an infrared sensor. Turk scanned the feed, looking for the Iranian aircraft.

But the sky near the Hydra was clear; the MiG had moved on.

The sound of the truck interrupted him. He crawled to the side of the small mound of dirt, squinting into the distance as the vehicle stopped near the wreckage. Men appeared from the truck, casting long shadows as they stepped in front of the low sun. There were six. They split up and moved around the wreckage methodically.

Turk calculated his odds with the AK-47.

He had only one magazine. One three-round burst per man—he'd have to be incredibly good—and lucky.

The shadows of the men danced wildly. They ran to the vehicle.

They've missed me, thought Turk.

Then he saw the truck back up and turn in his direction.

Turk turned around and looked at Grease. The Delta sergeant was in no shape to move.

"I'm not going to abandon you," said Turk, patting Grease's shoulder. "I just need a better vantage point to fight from."

Six against one? Even Grease would have trouble with those odds.

Turk started to go back to the side of the hill, thinking he would ambush the men when they got out of the truck. Then he had a better idea.

He pulled over the control unit and took command of the UAV.

"Target vehicle," he said. "Destroy."

Turk looked up from the screen. The UAV was 3,000 feet above, banking around in a turn. He strained to see it, but the bright sky wouldn't give it up.

He raised his rifle, steadying his aim on the truck. Suddenly, an ear-piercing whistle broke the silence. As the shriek grew unbearable, it was overrun by a sharp crack. The UAV exploded point-blank in the cab of the truck rushing toward him.

Turk grabbed the rifle and ran forward, gun hard against his side, legs churning. The truck was on fire. Someone stumbled out of the passenger side. Turk raised the nose of his gun and fired.

The man fell.

Running to his right, Turk circled the truck, finger ready against the trigger.

There was no one to shoot. There'd been six in the vehicle; five died in the explosion and fire. The lone survivor lay gut-shot on the ground nearby, dead by Turk's burst.

Something popped. Turk dropped to his haunches, spinning toward the road.

Ammo cooking off.

There'd be more. He looked for another weapon but saw none.

Best to go, he told himself, best to get the hell out of there before their friends come.

He ran back to Grease.

THE SERGEANT HAD PROPPED HIMSELF UP ON ONE elbow by the time Turk returned. Only his left eye was open.

"Grease," said Turk, lowering himself next to him. "Hey."

"I screwed up," said Grease.

"No. We got them. We got them. Their labs are destroyed."

"You did that. That was your mission."

"No. We both did it."

Grease coughed. "I . . ." His arm slipped and his head collapsed to the ground. He was having trouble breathing. "I . . ."

"It's all right," Turk told him. "Save your strength."

"I didn't complete mine." Grease's voice was a hoarse whisper. "I'm sorry."

"We'll get out. Don't give up."

"I . . ."

"We're going to make it, Grease. I'll get us to that next safe house or whatever you mentioned. Then tomorrow night we'll go to the coast. We'll make it."

"I was supposed to kill you," muttered Grease. "I just . . . supposed to . . . can't, but . . . I just . . . I . . . failed . . . I failed. I'm too weak . . ."

Turk jerked back, a shudder running through him. By the time he recovered, Grease was dead.

REFUGEE

———

1

The White House

IT WAS, IN MANY WAYS, A PHILOSOPHICAL QUESTION.

Was it better to leave some portion of doubt in your enemy's mind, or did you enhance your position by taking full credit for their turmoil?

Christine Mary Todd had never been a devotee of Sun Tzu, the Chinese philosopher on warfare, who would have counseled doubt. She did, however, know her Machiavelli. The early fifteenth century Italian writer counseled judicious use of both brute force and deception, a philosophy with which she agreed.

Barely an hour had passed since the second lab and its weapons had been destroyed, but already there had been two reports about earthquakes in the region. It would soon be well known that the seismographic signal indicated these were not earthquakes; from there, even the dimmest reporter would connect it to the still unexplained incident a few days ago and declare that *something* was going on with the Iranian nuclear program.

The only question was what.

Todd feared that the Iranians, realizing their program had been destroyed, might attempt to claim they had tested a bomb, and make some geopolitical hay out of that, perhaps bargaining for a full lift of sanctions in return for "dismantling" the now destroyed program. The calculated yield would indicate that if it was a test, the bomb had not lived up to its potential, but an atom bomb was still an atom bomb.

"My feeling is that we must declare that we did it," Todd told the others gathered around the conference table in the White House basement. "The question is how many details to give."

"Tell them," said the Secretary of State, Alistair Newhaven. "Demonstrate the aircraft. If you don't go into enough detail, it's very likely the Iranians will claim that we used nuclear weapons on them."

"The scientific data will show that the explosions were too small to be our nukes," answered Blitz, the national security advisor.

"Not the second one," countered the Secretary of State. "And they might claim that the explosions came from our warheads. Frankly, I'm amazed that the Iranians haven't said anything yet. We've been lucky."

"They're too confused. As I predicted," retorted Blitz. "I'm still against making *any* statement. It's an invitation to be attacked. And even the most generic remarks may give away secrets. Why give the enemy information when there's no need? I say, no announcement at all."

"We went over this weeks ago," said Newhaven,

frustration creeping into his voice. "They will simply assume it was us in any event. If you were worried about retaliation—a valid fear, I might add—then you should have been against the attack in the first place."

"Enough," said Todd. "We will say that we conducted a series of covert operations using technology that was designed to minimize casualties. I believe that's bland enough to get the job done without going into details. And there will be *no* details."

She looked at the Secretary of Defense, whose staff she was certain was just dying to go off the record to polish their boss's image. He was sure to be one of the candidates to succeed her.

He was as vain as he was indecisive. He would make a particularly lousy President. She had to keep him from that.

"Is that understood?" Todd said pointedly.

"I have an informational question," said the Secretary of State. "Are our people safe?"

Todd realized that Newhaven was actually asking whether the Iranians might capture the team and use them for their own propaganda purposes.

"I'm told that all efforts to recover them are proceeding," said Todd, keeping to herself for now the fact that only two were still alive. "Are you arguing that we wait until they are recovered?"

"No, it makes no sense to wait," said Newhaven. "Not in the scheme of things. I'm just . . . concerned."

It was amazing how many platitudes and clichés could be rolled out, Todd thought, when you were trying to justify sacrificing your people.

Fifteen minutes later President Todd entered the Oval Office. A pool camera had been manned after the news and cable networks were alerted that an important announcement was coming from the President. Reporters were waiting in the hallway to witness her statement. They'd been told it would be very brief and she would take no questions afterward.

David Greenwich, her chief of staff, was waiting near her desk.

"Mr. Reid and Ms. Stockard need to have a word," he said.

"Good. I need to speak to them as well," she said, sitting. Todd picked up the phone and told the operator to put the call from Whiplash through. "You have an update for me?" she asked.

"We still haven't been able to contact Captain Mako," said Breanna Stockard. "He's moving."

"I see. And Sergeant Ransom?"

"We have no other information."

"Are they likely to be captured?" asked Todd.

Reid cut in. "As I said earlier, the odds on any of the team making it out alive are very long."

"But Captain Mako is definitely alive?" asked Todd.

"He's definitely moving," answered Reid. "That's as much as we can say. We're reluctant to call him, since we don't know the circumstances. It may give him away."

"His capture would not be optimum," said Todd.

"Absolutely not. We are pursuing our final alternative."

"I would certainly prefer that he escapes alive," said the President. There was no need to continue. Todd drew a deep breath. "Let me reiterate—job well done. Both of you."

"Chris, I assume you've decided to announce that we were responsible," said Reid. Even if he hadn't used her first name—a severe break in protocol—she would have known from the shift in his tone that he was making a plea based on their long friendship. "I— It would be better for our people if there was no announcement yet."

"I understand. Unfortunately, if we let the Iranians announce the attack, there will be other repercussions. I'm sorry."

"Thank you, Madam President," said Reid stiffly.

Todd hung up the phone and looked up at David Greenwich, near the door. "Ready?"

"That's your call, ma'am."

Todd took the paper with her statement from the folder and looked at it. There hadn't been time to put it on the teleprompter, but that was just as well—better, she thought, to do this the old fashioned way. It would give things a formal feel.

She reached into her bag and took out her reading glasses. She didn't actually need them to see the statement, but they were a useful prop.

"You can let them in," she told Greenwich. Then she leaned back in the seat, folding her hands together in her lap. She gave a smile to the technicians and the press corps as they entered— her "schoolmarm smile," as her husband put it.

The reporters and technical people came in and began milling around, checking equipment and taking their places. Finally, all was ready.

"The light will come on, and we'll be live," said the technical director. He was actually a White House employee who worked for the communications staff. He pulled the headset on, adjusted the microphone, and told the man coordinating the network connections that they were ready to go.

"My fellow Americans, I come to you tonight with important and serious news." Todd felt the slightest tickle in her throat as she started, but pressed on. "As you are aware by now, Iran has moved forward with its program to develop nuclear weapons, despite sanctions and universal disapproval from the international community."

Todd paused. She was looking straight into the camera—the statement was brief, and she knew it by heart, not least of all because she had written it herself.

"What you don't know," she continued, "is that the Iranian program was much further along than most people have speculated publicly. A few days ago I learned definitively that the Iranians had constructed a small number of devices and were planning to make them operational."

She paused again. There was no smile on her face now. Her mouth was set, her gaze determined.

"Realizing how grave the situation was, I authorized our military to conduct a measured attack to destroy the bombs in their bunkers. Those operations have now been carried out. I am sure that you will understand if I do not give the exact details of those military operations, but let me assure you, and the world, that we did not ourselves use nuclear weapons in the process."

Todd took off her glasses.

"The fruits of the Iranian program have been destroyed. Rest assured that we will continue to monitor the Iranian government's actions, and take whatever corrective or punitive measures are necessary. We have no argument or dispute with the Iranian people themselves, as I hope they will realize from the pinpoint precision and limits of our action. But we will not allow nations to violate international law or go against the wishes for peace by the world at large."

Todd, face still stern, practically glared into the camera.

"We're off," said the director.

As she rose, the press corps began asking questions.

"We'll have a full statement in an hour at the regular briefing," she told them. "Until then, I'm afraid I have quite a bit to do, and there will be no further statement from myself or my staff."

2

Over India

MARK STONER LISTENED TO THE SILENCE OF THE MA-chine. It was not like a human silence, nor was it an absolute absence of sound. It was more a very soft hum, filtered through wires and circuit boards.

He heard the same silence in his head some-times.

"Download is complete," said the machine. "Awaiting instructions."

"Proceed with separation sequence as prepro-grammed," said Stoner. "Prepare to launch."

"Affirmative. Proceeding."

Six and a half minutes passed. Stoner watched them drain off the counter in his visor. He could tap into any number of different sensors, display-ing them on his screen in dozens of preconfig-ured combinations. But he preferred not to. He preferred the gray blankness of the screen. And so the only thing he saw were numbers, draining slowly in the left-hand corner of his vision.

The computer announced that they were reaching the final launch checkpoint. Stoner had not received an order to abort, and so he told the computer to proceed. He was past the point of no return for this orbit. If he didn't go, he'd have to wait roughly two hours before being in position again. And there was no sense in that.

One hundred twenty seconds later the computer announced that it was starting the separation countdown, beginning with sixty seconds. Stoner took a long, slow breath when the numbers on the computer reached ten.

Lying facedown in a pod attached to the belly of a hypersonic X-37B, Stoner at that moment was above the Bay of Bengal, moving at several times the speed of sound. His launch capsule was considered highly experimental, and doctors had not cleared it officially for human use due to the high g stresses and temperature variations it subjected its passengers to. Stoner was not immune to these— one could not flaunt the laws of gravity entirely— but his body could deal with stresses well beyond those of the average human. In a sense, he was an athlete's athlete, though no athlete would have accepted the trade-offs it had taken for his body to reach such a state.

Tucked into the belly of the X-37B, Stoner's capsule was as lean as its passenger. From the outside, the vehicle looked like a flattened shark, with faceted, stubby wings and no tail surface. From the inside, it looked like a foam blanket, squeezed tight against Stoner's body and equipment packs.

He was some 2,200 miles from his tentative landing target. It was time to launch.

Three, two, one . . . Stoner felt a thump, but otherwise had no sensation of falling or even slowing down. Encapsulated in his pod, he was still a satellite moving close to eight times the speed of sound.

The exterior geometry and the coating made the pod difficult to track from the earth, especially in the shadow of its mother ship above. Within seconds the pod had steered itself toward a keyhole in the Iranian radar coverage, taking a course that would avoid the country's few radars capable of finding high-flying aircraft and missiles. It aimed toward a point the mission planners called Alpha, where the pod ceased being a satellite and turned into a flying rock, plummeting toward the earth.

Stoner didn't know the specifics about the radars he was avoiding or the maneuvers that the craft would take. To him, Alpha was just a very sharp turn down, one that would press his flesh against his bones. He readied himself for the maneuver, slowing his breathing further, until even a yogi would have been envious. The pure oxygen he breathed tasted sweet, as if his lungs were being bathed in light honey. He saw a white triangle in his mind, a cue that told his body to relax. He had worked hard over the past several months to memorize that cue—relaxing was the hardest thing to learn.

"Ten seconds to Alpha," said the computer.

Physically, Stoner couldn't move. In his mind he leaned forward, welcoming the plunge.

The craft tipped and spun sharply. Now he was a bullet, plunging to earth. The gauge monitoring the hull temperature appeared on the information screen as the friction spiked. The temperature was yellow, above the safe area.

"Faster," he whispered, and pushed his thoughts ahead.

"Leveling," declared the computer a few seconds later.

The pod became an airplane, extending its stubby wings as far as they would go. It was now over central Iran.

Stoner got ready for the next phase of his flight—leaving the pod.

"Countdown to separation beginning in ten seconds," said the computer.

Stoner started to exhale. As he pushed the last bit of air from his lungs and contracted his diaphragm, the floor below him swung back. He fell immediately, the capsule maneuvering to increase the force pulling him away.

He pulled his arms tight against his body, falling into a sitting position as he descended into the night. He was still relatively high—sixty thousand feet—and had he not been breathing pure oxygen would have passed out. He saw nothing, just blackness.

"Helmet," he said in as strong a voice as he could manage.

The visor image snapped to a synthetic blue, then flashed and gave way to a panoramic view of the ground he was falling toward. The optical image was captured by one of the stereoscopic cameras embedded in the shell. A small GPS guidance indicator and an altitude ladder appeared at the right. The numbers said he was falling at a rate of 512 knots, not quite supersonic.

Slower than he had in practice.

The sun was brilliant. The cloud cover looked like a tufted blanket below him.

Stoner tucked his head toward his chest like a diver and rolled forward until he was head first, his legs behind and slightly above him. As he pushed them upward and sharpened the angles of his descent, he slowly spread his arms. The thick webbing that had been folded between them and his chest fanned out. Then he extended his legs, stretching the carbon and titanium webbing between them.

Mark Stoner was now a human parachute. Or, as one of his instructors had once quipped, a breathing brick with stubby wings.

He pushed his body around, aiming to get in the general direction of his target. To avoid the long-range radars, he had dropped south and west of his preferred landing zone. Now he needed to move back north. The course change took some time to accomplish.

His landing zone bordered an area well protected by the radar. His smart helmet had radar receiving circuitry—a "fuzz buster" that could detect and alert him to radar waves. Slightly more sophisticated than the latest circuitry in fighter jets, the miniaturized radar detector indicated the closest radar signal was well off to his right.

Stoner shifted his body. The suit he was using had been pioneered by Danny Freah in the 1990s. Working with Freah on the newer version, he'd received quite a number of tips on how to get the most from the lightweight titanium rods and their small motors. Without them, even Stoner's overmuscled body would have found the fall exhausting.

The visor display highlighted Istgah-E Kuh Pang, the closest named village to his landing target. It was built along a railroad; the only roads were hard-packed dirt and trails through scrub and rolling desert bordering it.

"Locate target subject," he told the computer.

The screen flashed, put up a map, then zoomed back. The Whiplash locating system showed his position and that of Turk Mako's. Turk was sixty-seven miles away, across chalky, uneven hills, and several valleys that passed for fertile in this arid land.

Still roughly where he had been earlier.

This will be easy, Stoner thought.

The edge of a radar coverage area was to his right, barely a mile away. The arc extended forward—Stoner maneuvered left to avoid it.

The computer advised him to lower his speed. He pushed his elbows out, increasing the resistance. He had to begin bleeding off speed now if he was to survive the landing without broken bones. He dipped his left arm gently, banking in the direction of an open valley, then dipped in the opposite direction, lining up toward the town. But there was another radar, and then suddenly the display began flashing—he was being picked up by an aircraft, extremely close, flying in the shadows of the mountains.

Stoner pressed his head down, moving a little faster.

"Visual," he told the computer.

The hills popped into view.

"Eight times magnification," he told the computer. Stoner wanted to see details of the terrain he was flying over. "Locate aircraft."

"Aircraft ten miles south," said the helmet, calculating from the RWR; it was too far for the infrared viewer to pick it up.

"General course?"

"South by southwest."

Not something to worry about, he decided, moving his arms out farther to slow his descent.

The suit flapped slightly at his shoulder where it was fitted beneath his backpack, but otherwise it was a snug, tight fit. He felt good, in control through 20,000 feet, though still moving a little faster than he should.

Stoner tilted to his left and pushed his legs out, intending to begin a wide spiral to slow his momentum before dropping into the target area. With every second, he got closer to becoming an ordinary flying human.

He turned through the circuit a second time, his altitude passing through 15,000 feet above ground level. The radar warning detector began to bleep urgently. Red blossoms appeared on his screen.

Tracers.

He stared at them. They were red—Russian-made ammunition, slightly different than the orange typically used by Americans and NATO. They looked like fountains, sputtering and then dying.

They thought he was a plane. A line of red appeared in front of him, a slash in the sky revealing blood.

Now great bursts of red pummeled the thin blue around him. Angry fingers groped toward his body.

He was being fired at. And the bullets were coming from the direction he needed to go through to reach his target.

3

Manzariyeh Air Base, Iran

"You idiots! I am an Iranian plane! I need to land! Stop your idiotic shooting."

Parsa Vahid screamed into the radio as the antiaircraft batteries continued to fire, seemingly in every conceivable direction. A radar installation near Qom had reported an unexplained contact— very likely Vahid or his wingman—and sounded an alarm that caused every gunner in the western half of the country to see if his weapon worked. At least no one was firing missiles.

Yet.

An ominous fist of black and red reached for his aircraft.

"Controller! I need these guns to stop!" Vahid radioed to the Pasdaran controller at the former Manzariyeh air base.

"We are attempting, Captain. Please stand by."

Vahid couldn't stand by: he had only a few pounds of fuel left in his tanks. He lined up with the airfield and held on, just ducking under a fresh wave of flak as his wheels touched the ground.

"The gunfire is being extinguished," said the controller as the plane rolled out.

Too late now, thought Vahid. Let them fire all they want.

He had cut it close—too close. The MiG's engines sputtered and shut down. Vahid coasted to the apron and onto one of the access ramps. Aiming for the hangar area near the headquarters building, he ran out of momentum just shy of the parking area near the civilian terminal building.

Kayvan, who'd landed some minutes before, ran toward his plane. Vahid got out, tossing his helmet back into the aircraft in disgust.

"We need fuel," he told the wingman, jumping down. "Where are the fuel trucks?"

"A visitor is on the way." Kayvan pointed to an SUV driving up from one of the dirt access roads. Two military vehicles were following it at a distance.

"It's the general," added Kayvan. "I think we're in trouble for landing here."

It took a moment for Vahid to realize the general Kayvan was talking about was the head of the air force, General Shirazi. He had no idea why Shirazi was here rather than in Tehran or Omidiyeh, but he suspected whatever accident of fate had brought him was going to turn out to be a poor one for himself.

"Do we have facilities inside?" he asked Kayvan.

"The Pasdaran haven't even sent anyone to greet us," said the lieutenant.

"Great." He stripped off his survival gear, disgusted, awaiting his fate.

The general's vehicle came to a stop a few meters from him. The rear window rolled down.

"Captain Vahid," General Shirazi called from inside. "You'll ride with me."

Vahid walked over to the SUV and got in the other side. Kayvan stayed behind.

"What happened?" asked the general. They remained parked.

"I was asked to strike a vehicle that the Pasdaran said had been stolen," said Vahid. "There were two vehicles, excuse me. One was on a hillside. The other was moving. We destroyed both of them."

"They admitted the trucks were stolen?"

"They said—"

"Why would they do that? Only to shift suspicion," said Shirazi, adding his own explanation. "It makes them look bad, so whatever they are hiding is worse. Ten times worse. A traitor. Several traitors."

The general's tone made it clear that the subject was not one for debate. He asked Vahid to recount everything that had happened on the sortie, starting with his takeoff. Vahid did so, including even the most mundane details, even his debate over his fuel reserves. The general began humming to himself. Vahid wondered if he was aware of it, but thought it best not to ask. He had never seen or heard of this eccentricity, but stress often brought out odd quirks.

"Enemy troops infiltrated the area," said the general finally. "That is the only explanation that can be given. Bombers would have been detected and shot down."

"General, I thought there had been—you said the other day that there had been an accident."

Shirazi gazed at Vahid as if he were the dumbest student in a class of idiots.

"The official explanation," said the general finally.

"Yes, General."

"Do not contradict me."

"No, General. I personally do not know what happened. My role was to follow orders."

"Exactly."

Shirazi was clearly contemplating something; surely it had something to do with how to use the incident to improve his position with the government. But it was not of immediate importance to Vahid—what he had to do was keep his head down.

"Your wingman," said the general, "can he be trusted?"

"Uh, absolutely."

Probably not, thought Vahid, but certainly that was not what he should answer.

What would One Eye say to this? The old flight instructor would warn him away from politics—warn him away from all of it.

But if he didn't toe the general's line, what would happen to him?

"I am glad to hear that the man is a worthy officer under your command," said the general. "You will do well as a squadron leader."

Even though Vahid knew he was being flattered, he couldn't help but feel a twinge of pride and some anticipation.

"Not today, but soon," added the general, deflating him a little. "In the meantime, write up what you have told me in a report. It is to come directly to me."

"Yes, General."

Shirazi turned his gaze to the window. "A nice air base, don't you think?"

"Yes, General."

"We should have it back. Many people feel that way. Getting it back in its rightful place . . ."

Shirazi trailed off, but Vahid could easily guess what he was thinking: the man who restored Manzariyeh to the air force's portfolio would not only win unlimited honor from his fellow service members, but would be seen as someone of great power, able to deal with and perhaps even best the Pasdaran.

"I am glad you landed here. An accident perhaps," added the general, "but a fortunate one. We will do everything we can to continue your operations here—it is very necessary."

"Yes, General."

"You may go," said Shirazi. "We will have trucks and maintainers sent. But remember this—Colonel Khorasani, the man you have dealt with?"

"Yes?"

"Be very careful with him," warned Shirazi. "If he asks to speak to you, tell him you must speak to me first. Route things through my office. In the meantime, do your report and return to the air as quickly as possible. We need all aircraft to protect Iran."

"Yes, General."

"Off with you now. I will send maintainers to you shortly."

4

Iran

STONER'S FIRST INCLINATION WAS TO SIMPLY STAY ON course. The tracers were exploding below him, and while there was a slight chance of being hit by the shrapnel, he thought it was worth the risk to get as close as possible to Turk Mako and complete his assignment. But when a flourish of shells exploded a half mile ahead, he realized they were exactly at his altitude. With the gunfire spreading before him, Stoner ducked left, just barely avoiding the fusillade that followed.

The sharp maneuver allowed him to change course, but it presented a problem with his stability. He began dropping at an extreme rate, accelerating as he pushed his arms and legs out full. Within seconds his body began to rotate, and he realized he was heading toward a dangerous flat spin, impossible to recover from.

With the cue in his helmet indicating his body was oriented in a level position parallel to the ground, Stoner pulled in his arms, then tucked his head toward his chin, closed his legs and threw them back, trying to pitch into a downhill posture. Once he achieved that, he gradually re-opened his arms and legs, remaking himself into a stable airfoil moving in a direction he could control.

Wind raged at his body, upset that it would be used to defy gravity and the natural order of things. Men didn't fly, and they shouldn't attempt it. Buffeted up and down, Stoner strained to hold his limbs in position. When he hit 5,000 feet, he banked, this time gently, turning back north.

The gunfire was well off to his right and slightly behind him. According to the GPS, he was forty miles from his target, with little hope of getting there before reaching the ground.

Stoner steered himself farther east, deciding that since he would never reach the target, he would be better off landing in the soft desert plains. He cleared his mind. His forward speed had slowed to about seventy-five knots: still far too fast for a landing, but at least slow enough that he could set up for one.

He continued to coast, heading over a set of rocky crags. The edge of the desert came into view as he skimmed below 2,000 feet. Tucking his chin down, he did a flare to slow himself to landing speed. He quickly lost forward momentum. He flared wider, then tipped his upper body forward. As he did, he released the small chute at the back of his neck. Far too small to hold him, the chute provided enough extra resistance to get him to walking speed as he came through three hundred feet.

There was a rock outcrop directly ahead. Stoner

struggled to keep his momentum up. He was a little awkward, not having had enough practice with the rig, and with a good hundred feet between him and the ground he started to fall. He pushed forward, then swung his legs out and did an awkward tumble into a barley field. He managed to curl his body at the last moment, tucking into a roll as he hit.

The blow knocked him semiconscious. He rolled onto his back, disoriented.

What am I doing here? What is my mission?

He knew there must be an answer, but his mind refused to give it. All he could do was stare into the never-ending blackness that enveloped the earth around him.

5

Iran

COLONEL KHORASANI TOOK ANOTHER WALK AROUND the wreckage of the command truck. He needed space to think this through, space and time, but there was little of either.

There was no doubt that the vehicle destroyed on the highway had belonged to the Pasdaran unit, stolen out from under their noses while they twiddled their thumbs aimlessly around the vehicle they found on the hillside. They had proven themselves idiots of the highest degree—typical,

Khorasani thought bitterly, of the bumpkins assigned to the Guard in this region. That fact did little to help him.

The company commander had been killed when his vehicle exploded. The battalion commander came to investigate; he was in something close to a catatonic trance by the time Khorasani arrived.

Under other circumstances the commander would have made a useful scapegoat, but he was related to a high-ranking member of the clergy. Khorasani therefore had to worry about saving the battalion commander's hide as well as his own.

But there were more immediate problems. He needed to find the person who had fired the projectile that blew up the truck. Presumably, they were the same people who had stolen both vehicles.

Were they responsible for the "incidents" at the bunkers? Khorasani doubted it, and yet, what other explanation was there? Would a wild smuggler bound for Iran have been nearly so bold, or effective? It had to be the Mossad. It simply had to be.

But ground troops would never have been able to enter the labs. So what had happened there? Unrelated accidents? Raids by as yet unidentified bombers? In either case, how would the Israelis be explained?

Colonel Khorasani kicked at a clod of dirt. He needed to construct a coherent explanation of what had happened that passed blame away from the Guards—and away from himself. But he also had to figure what *really* happened. For without knowing that, he might say or do something that would unravel whatever official story he constructed.

The infidel bastards were at the heart of this, certainly. He had to tamp down his hatred—it would make him irrational, and he needed a clear head now more than ever.

"Colonel," said Sergeant Karim, approaching cautiously, "one of the teams has found something at the edge of the soil mine."

Khorasani caught the grim look on Sergeant Karim's face. Karim didn't speak of it, but scenes of death turned his stomach. His face always blanched a shade or two when they spoke of it, and the colonel thought he must be struggling mightily to suppress the bile now.

"Where?" he asked Karim.

"Follow me, sir. It's best on foot."

They walked through the field and up a small incline. The sun was just warming the day, but it was already seventy degrees. It would be over ninety by noon.

He would need to make a full report to the ayatollah by then.

"Maybe they were deserters," he said aloud. "Panicking and desperate to leave because they caused the accident. Renegade scientists. Traitors. Or fools. Fools are better. Easier to explain."

"Excuse me?" asked Sergeant Karim.

"Nothing," said Khorasani.

Karim led him in silence to a cluster of brush. There was a body in the weeds. A man had crawled here, curled up like a baby and died.

"It's not a member of the Guard unit," said Sergeant Karim. "I had one of the sergeants look at him." He gestured to a man smoking a cigarette a short distance away.

"Turn him over so I can see his face," said Khorasani.

When Karim hesitated, Khorasani did it himself. Looking at the dead didn't bother him.

Dressed in what looked like Pasdaran fatigues, the man was large and in good shape. He looked more Arabic than Iranian, but he could be an Israeli or an American.

That's the sort they would choose, wasn't it? Someone who looked the part.

Khorasani let his mind wander as he looked at the man, thinking of how such an operation would run. You might try infiltrating the bunkers with the help of a few traitors; in that case, what would this man and whoever was with him be doing? Maybe he'd brought material for the attack and was on his way out, or to another target.

Or maybe he was supporting an air attack, directing it with a laser device.

Or maybe he was recording what happened. Their satellites were limited. The Americans were always delivering boasts about their technology that proved to be empty.

The colonel searched the body. The man had no weapon aside from a combat knife, and no ammunition. He had no papers either.

But what was this, taped to his chest?

Money, and quite a lot of it—10 million rial checks, along with 100,000 rial notes.

There were euro notes as well—fifty-three of them, each a hundred euro note.

Khorasani rose. The money would be considerable anywhere, but especially in Iran. It could get him to exile, if he wished.

He handed it to his sergeant.

"Count this," he told him. "Make sure there is a record."

Sergeant Karim took it quickly. Apparently, money made it easy to overcome his aversion to death.

How many others had been with this man? Khorasani walked a few meters, examining the area. The ground had been disturbed by the units that responded after the attack, so there was little hope of getting a read on how many there were.

A small handful. Was there another truck?

Which way would they go?

Either they would attack another lab or they would seek to escape.

They would have to wait until nightfall in any event. Traveling during the day was too dangerous—as Khorasani had just proven.

Where to hide? The barren lands nearby were less than ideal, since they could be scouted by air—and would be.

Kaveh Industrial City was twenty-one miles away, due west. There were many buildings there, including several dozen that were abandoned. It would be an ideal place to hide.

Could they reach it on foot?

Too far.

"What's the town in the distance?" Khorasani asked one of the soldiers standing nearby.

"Istgah-E Kuh Pang."

"Is it big?"

"No, Colonel. A few buildings. The train runs through."

"Find your sergeant and tell him I want an immediate report. I will be at my car." Khorasani walked down the hill to his vehicle, where Sergeant Karim had just finished counting the money. "Find me a map of this place Istgah-E Kuh," he said. "See what units are in the area. Have them secure it and wait for our arrival."

"Yes, Colonel. Air General Shirazi wanted to speak to you. He said it was urgent."

"Urgent." The word seemed like a spoon of bitter medicine in his throat. Khorasani considered blowing him off, but decided it would be more useful to know exactly what the general was thinking.

"Get him," he told the aide.

Khorasani braced himself for an argument when the general came on the line, but Shirazi surprised him by apologizing.

"It was wrong of me to hang up on you," said the general. "We both have the same goal. The pressure, of course, is on both of us."

"The air force especially," said Khorasani sharply.

"I have spoken to all of my squadron commanders personally. We have seen no aircraft. The radar data backs this up, as do our allies."

Allies meant Russia, which had loaned Iran

radar technicians some months before. The technicians were low-level people, and not necessarily the most savory characters, Khorasani knew, but they did lend some credence to Shirazi's contention.

Khorasani, however, was not ready to back down.

"The American planes are stealthy and launch from great distances," he said. "They could easily have launched this attack."

"Nonsense. I've already seen the damage at Fordow 12. There is no bomb crater—the attack was done from the inside."

"Doubtful."

"You've already completed your investigation? Of an attack that is less than a few hours old?" said Shirazi.

Khorasani rubbed his cheek. "What is your point, General? Why did you call?"

"My point is that you should be looking for infiltrators and spies," said Shirazi. "As the air force is."

"I am doing everything I am supposed to do."

"You are in pursuit?"

"We are not sure what happened," said Khorasani, unsure what the general wanted. "We are leaving nothing to chance."

"I understand several vehicles were stolen from Guard units."

"And?"

"I have reconnaissance aircraft that could assist in a search. The planes that we have in the area now are needed for defense, in case the Americans do launch an attack. I am proposing that we work together to discover what happened."

The general explained that he had a squadron of F-4 Phantoms, which were used for reconnaissance. He could transfer them to the area to aid with the search. He didn't need Khorasani's help or permission, he added, but if they were working together, they should coordinate their efforts.

Still wary, Khorasani let the general ramble until he came to what seemed to be the point: he wanted to base the reconnaissance planes at Manzariyeh and establish a support unit there.

"The planes could help you search for guerrillas," said Shirazi.

"The base is under Pasdaran control."

"And so it would remain. We need only a small place for those planes. And their escorts."

"Escorts?"

"The planes that assisted you. They were short of fuel."

"Yes . . . I would appreciate your help," continued Khorasani, choosing his words carefully. "The search efforts need to be . . . discreet."

"Understandable. And this is my point. If the planes are based at a regular air base, there will be rumors," continued the general. "If, however, they were at a base near the attacks, such as Manzariyeh, things would be easier to coordinate. We find the true cause of these incidents."

Shirazi was angling to reopen the air base, obviously, and who knew what else.

But cooperation might be useful, Khorasani

thought. For one thing, he could use more air patrols to survey the area.

"I see the logic," he told the general. "How soon can you arrange the flights?"

"Within a few hours," Shirazi told him. "I'm sure you will find the pilots cooperative and our alliance fruitful."

6

CIA campus, Virginia

"FIRST SATELLITE IMAGES ARE JUST COMING IN NOW, Ray," Breanna told Rubeo. "A big crater—it looks like a meteor strike. Much deeper than the first site."

Rubeo tapped the display area of the table, then toggled down to the incoming intelligence report. The preliminary analysis indicated that the designs were not particularly efficient. But how efficient did a nuclear weapon have to be to be considered a success?

The Hydra attack, on the other hand, had been a complete success. They had saved hundreds of thousands of lives.

And yet, the scientist felt uneasy. If the Iranians had come this close, undoubtedly they would try again. They would learn from their mistakes, making their bunkers even more formidable.

The conflict would never be over.

Science could do so much good, and yet be put to so much evil.

"Ray?"

Rubeo glanced up and saw Breanna staring at him, a quizzical look on her face.

"I'm sorry, I didn't hear," he said.

"Turk's satellite phone hasn't been on since shortly after the attack," said Breanna, repeating what she had said. "There was an error code that might indicate it malfunctioned or was damaged."

"Thomas can help you," he told her. "He's the expert on the system."

"Thank you. He's still alive," Breanna added hopefully. "He's moving. Very slowly."

Rubeo nodded. They had already determined that the sergeant with him, who also had an implant, was dead.

"Do you want to go home and take a nap?" asked Breanna.

"There's much work to be done, analyzing this and checking our performance," he said, tapping the display area to close it. "I need to get started on it without delay."

7

Iran

TURK RESTED AGAINST THE POWER LINE POLE, TRYING to fight off the fatigue that was pushing down his eyelids. The pole rose from a ditch, sheltering him on two sides; he sat in the shadow against a jumble of rocks, willing himself invisible.

The worst thing was the urge to sleep. He knew if he fell asleep, he'd wake up either under arrest or dead, assuming one could be said to wake up in the afterlife.

A small Iranian village sat to his left behind a low hill, barely discernible in the rising haze of heat. In front of him, perhaps twenty feet away, were train tracks. When Turk first spotted them, having walked along the power lines for a short distance, he thought he might hop aboard a passing freight train and escape. It was something he had done often as a teenager, running alongside a boxcar and leaping up the ladder at just the right moment. But after watching awhile, he realized it was hardly a plan at all. He had no idea where the train would go, nor could he expect to remain unseen on it.

And besides, no train seemed to be coming.

He needed a plan, something more than the vague notion that he would escape.

Guns sounded in the distance, firing at random intervals. It was antiaircraft fire, undoubtedly the product of overanxious, nervous minds. The Iranians didn't realize yet it was too late for all that.

Turk regretted having left Grease for dead. It seemed weak and foolish, a surrender that he shouldn't have had to make. Logically, he knew he had no choice. Grease would have been too heavy to carry very far, and there was no way he could even have gotten here, let alone go on. But it still felt, it still was, terribly wrong.

Whiplash would be tracking him. They might send someone to rescue him—the SEAL response team or maybe even another Whiplash unit.

But if they had assigned Grease to kill him, would they bother?

Maybe Grease meant he'd been assigned to kill him if they were going to be captured.

Surely that's what he meant. Turk could understand that. He knew too much about the program, about a lot of things. And the Iranians would torture him to death anyway. Being shot by Grease would have been merciful.

Shoot me, Grease. I deserve it for leaving you behind.

He had the sat phone but dared not use it, afraid that the Iranians would monitor transmissions in the area.

He needed clothes. The ones he was wearing were torn, dirty, and covered with blood. He'd steal clothes, then find a place to hide. Rest. At night he would start walking to the Caspian, or at least in that direction.

Turk had taken Grease's ruck with him, knowing he'd need some of the gear. It didn't have much in it besides ammo and first aid equipment. That made sense, but he knew he couldn't take much with him. He needed to stay as light as possible. As precious as the ammo would be in a fight, it would slow him down too much. Besides, he could never really count on fighting his way out; he wasn't Grease.

Grease!

The control unit was the real weight. But he couldn't just leave it. Simply breaking it up wouldn't do. He'd have to smash it to smithereens.

Who out here would have the faintest notion of what it was?

The sun continued to move up in the early morning sky, robbing Turk of the shadows he thought protected him. He needed another hiding place.

He got to his feet, then struggled with the backpacks before finally hoisting them to his shoulders. He started along the trail beneath the power lines, heading toward a set of low-slung buildings at the edge of the desert, beyond the far end of a village. In the distance he heard noises, vague murmurs of people going about their business.

The trail angled away from the train tracks. He decided to follow it, and as he got closer, realized the low-slung buildings weren't buildings at all but old ruins, hard-baked by centuries of sun. Still, he approached cautiously, balking at accepting his good luck. But the ruins, a small fort and houses eons old, were completely empty.

An excellent hiding place. He shuffled around until he found a building that was small but mostly intact, except for the nonexistent roof. Constructed of large bricks, its floor was completely covered by sand. Turk took off the rucks. Rifling through Grease's, he sorted out what he thought he could carry in his clothes: two spare magazines in his pocket, three for the pistol, which he strapped to his waist.

The paper map. The GPS. Grease's phone, similar to his. And two bottles of water.

He slid the ruck down behind the rocks. It didn't look like much, and even if it was found, wouldn't tell anyone anything—ammunition for AK-47s had never been a state secret anywhere in the world.

The control unit was different. He needed a better hiding place for that. Turk took it under his arm and slipped out through one of the windows, treading carefully along the stone walls.

How long ago had the place been abandoned, he wondered. It seemed to go on forever. Most of the ruins were no higher than his knee, but enough of the rest remained to convince him that this was once an important place.

Finding a building where a wall had recently collapsed into a haphazard pile of stones, he moved some of them aside, then carefully placed the control unit beneath them. When he was finished, he rose and memorized the place, promising himself he would come back and recover the unit. Then he continued to explore, working his way in the direction of the railroad tracks. He carried the rifle in one hand, down at his side. He held his left arm out, not so much for balance as a guide, pointing the way he was walking.

The ruins were so extensive that when he entered the yard of a house that was still occupied, he didn't realize it until he heard noises from the back courtyard: a woman calling to her children.

Turk froze, not sure what to do. The woman was standing behind the wall barely twelve feet away. He could just make out the back of her head.

He was about to back away when he saw something fly up in the air.

Clothes. She was hanging things out to dry.

Turk went down on his haunches. As the woman continued to hang up the wash, she began to hum gently to herself. He waited, turning left and right every so often, making sure he was alone. Finally he heard her moving away, back toward the house, calling again to the children.

He edged to the wall, muffling his breath in his mouth. If someone came, he would kill them.

The woman?

He would have to.

The child?

He couldn't. Probably not even the woman.

Wasn't he at war with these people? Hadn't these people built several nuclear bombs? They wanted to kill thousands, even millions of innocents. Shouldn't he want to kill every single one of these bastards?

If he had to. He didn't seek war but now that he was here, now that he saw what they had done, what they had all done, he would kill every single one.

Except the child. And probably not the woman.

Turk leaned over the wall. There was a forest of clothes of different varieties, colors, and shapes. He saw a pair of dark pants and a longish shirt. Men's clothes. They were hung almost against the wall. He leaned just far enough to take them, and whisked them over to him. The material was damp but not as wet as he expected.

Holding them in his left hand, he backed out,

rifle ready, then scrambled as quietly as he could back to his hiding place in the ruins.

8

Iran

WHAT AM I DOING HERE? WHAT IS MY MISSION?
I'm lost. I am an assassin. My job is to kill.
I have killed many. In Romania. In Hungary. In the Czech Republic. In France. In Greece. In the States.
Not the States.
Turk Mako. Locate. Neutralize.
And then?
Return.

Stoner rose to a sitting position, gathering himself and taking stock. His legs and side were bruised but he was all right.

Still wearing the helmet, he took off the suit and rolled it into a ball. From the fanny pack at his belt he removed a small incendiary device and placed it in the middle of the ball. Then he walked over to an irrigation ditch at the edge of the field. There was a trickle of water in the bottom, but that was no matter—he placed the bundle down on some rocks, then pulled the ring on the device. It flared and began to burn.

Stoner unhooked the small ruck on his back and unzipped the rear compartment. Inside was a broken down M-4 with customized parts, including a compact upper assembly and a scope made by L3 EOTech that synched with a targeting system in his helmet. He assembled the gun, then checked his location and that of his subject.

Turk had moved since Stoner had begun his descent. He was in a small village near railroad tracks some twenty-five miles away.

It would take him four hours to run there. Or he could steal a car.

Stoner preferred speed over safety. He began looking for a vehicle. In the meantime, the words describing his mission played over and over in his head:

Turk Mako. Locate. Neutralize.

9

Istgah-E Kuh Pang, Iran

THE PANTS WERE TOO SHORT AND THE SHIRT A LITTLE too wide for Turk, but they were better than what he had. The dampness actually felt good, soothing and cooling his strained and bruised muscles.

As he balled his old clothes up, Turk formulated a tentative plan. It was simple and bare, yet it seemed to take the greatest mental exertion to construct. He would rest here until the sun set. Then he would set out along the railroad tracks, heading north with them as far as he could.

It was some 112 miles in a straight line to the

Caspian. Much of that was over mountains—but that was good. Mountains meant cover. They also meant there would be plenty of places to rest.

The most difficult part was a stretch of twenty miles or so through a desert. That would take him at least five hours—a whole night, he thought, for it would be too dangerous to travel during the day.

Turk slid his satellite phone from his pocket. No one had tried to contact him. But that wasn't unusual. Protocol called for him to contact them, since they couldn't know whether he was near someone or not.

He raised his finger to unlock the phone, but then stopped, not because he was afraid the Iranians would home in on the signal, but because he was suspicious of Breanna, of Whiplash, Reid, and the others. They'd assigned Grease to kill him. Who knew what they would do now?

Maybe the phone had a bomb.

He stared at it, knowing he was being paranoid. But he couldn't call. He just couldn't.

What would he say if he did? Help? Would he cry like a baby? What was the sense of asking them for something they wouldn't give?

Better to put the phone away and do this on his own. Or die, if that was the option. Because the only one he could really count on was himself, not them, not even Breanna.

He understood Grease now. From the very beginning Grease had tried to maintain distance. He was trying to avoid forming a bond, to make it easier to kill him. But they'd bonded anyway. It was impossible not to, in war.

That was what Grease was trying to say at the end. He thought it was a failing, a fatal weakness.

It doesn't negate who you were, Grease. You were still a hero.

My hero.

I'm going to get out of here. On my own.

Turk slid over to the corner of the ruined building, leaning against the walls. Without trying to, he fell fast asleep.

HE WAS IN OLD GIRL, PUSHING THE STICK AROUND. IT was his last mission back at Dreamland, flying with the admiral.

Except it wasn't. He was lower, treetop level, looking for something.

Trees, not the open terrain of Dreamland.

There *was* someone with him in the backseat, though he wasn't sure who.

Grease.

They were doing a recee, looking for the rest of the patrol. He saw the bus, moving along the highway. He pressed his mike to tell Grease.

It didn't work. He turned his head and could see him staring from the backseat, no helmet on, dressed in the Iranian fatigues they'd worn.

It was a dream, a dream! I am dreaming!

A sense of horror came over him as he stared into Grease's face.

Grease!

You abandoned me!

But you were going to kill me!

You abandoned me!

Turk jerked his head up, fully awake, back in the cellar of the ruins. Something loud passed overhead.

An airplane. Two airplanes.

He got up and went to the open window at the rear of the building. The planes were nearby.

They were Phantoms, their smoky contrails lingering as they climbed about three-quarters of a mile to the north.

Phantoms?

The sun was still fairly low in the sky—nine o'clock, he calculated. When he looked at his watch, it was 0921. He'd slept for a little under two hours.

The jets took another pass, this one from the north, riding down the railroad tracks. They were Phantoms, all right, not U.S. planes but Iranian, vintage craft held together by duct tape and ingenuity, as the saying went. Turk saw a reconnaissance pod hanging off the nearest plane. It had air-to-air missiles as well, but no bombs. Dressed in a tan, brown, and green camo scheme that reminded Turk of the Vietnam War era, the planes flew south, staying with the tracks for several miles, vanishing in the distance.

He heard them coming back and waited, pressed against the wall in their direction. They passed almost directly overhead and he watched them stride into the distance, then bank into a circling turn. As they came around north of him, he saw their landing gear beginning to deploy.

They were landing.

For a moment he was confused—why land in

the sand? Then he realized they must be using the air base where he and Grease had stolen the vehicle the night before.

Turk stared into the haze until the planes were well out of his sight. He slipped back to the corner then, sliding his back against the ancient stones, intending to sleep some more. But he'd no sooner hit the dirt than he heard vehicles nearby.

"Damn," he muttered, grabbing the assault rifle. "Damn."

10

Iran

STONER FOUND NO VEHICLE WORTH TAKING IN THE hamlet of a dozen houses near where he had landed, and the only thing with four wheels in the next town was a farm truck so old and rusted he doubted it would last more than a mile. He ran for a while instead, moving through the foothills and skirting the village of Saveh, since he was making decent time and there was no need to risk being seen. He checked on Turk's location every half hour, using a radio device that tapped into the Iranian cell phone network and from there a Web site where Whiplash was relaying the data. While the Web site could be found and his cell phone intercepted, as a practical matter he was following the theory behind Poe's famous *Pur-*

loined Letter—hide in plain sight, and no one will see you.

Some nine miles east of Saveh, Stoner came to the outskirts of another village, this one large enough, he reasoned, to have a good choice of vehicles. It had taken nearly three hours for him to get this far; he reckoned that it would take another two to get to Turk. Taking the vehicle now was insurance against needing one later; getting away from the area after dispatching Turk would be best done quickly.

The place wasn't particularly large, and with a few key exceptions—one being the lack of pavement on the streets, another the two minarets—it looked like a rural hamlet in the southwestern United States might have looked in the late 1940s. As Stoner got closer, he noticed a curious set of low-slung brown structures near the older houses.

He stopped. Focusing his eyes—his augmented vision let him see about as well as a good pair of field glasses—he examined the huts. At first he thought they were barracks and that the village had been turned into a military town, something not unheard of in Iran. But as he watched, he saw people emerging. After a few minutes of observation, he realized the structures were hovels constructed for the poor by the government, or some local charity. The town was filled with them. Many of their occupants worked at the small factories on either end of the village or tilling the fields that surrounded it.

Stone moved around the outskirts of the village cautiously, staying just beyond the edge of the cultivated fields. His smart helmet was slung over the top of his narrow rucksack; his gun was over his shoulder. The dark green jumpsuit he wore was patterned after clothes Pasdaran mechanics used. If he went into town, he would stash his gear and keep his mouth shut, hoping that between the coveralls and his frown he would look both sufficiently ornery and ordinary to be left alone.

Stoner found a group of fallow fields separated by a narrow, weed-strewn lane. He walked down the lane, trying to see beyond the farms at the village boundaries. There weren't many people on the streets; most people were either at work or school this early in the morning.

A pair of cars were parked in the courtyard beyond the fields. He walked toward them, considering which of the two would be easier to steal. He had just decided on the car on the left—it looked like a '70s Fiat knockoff—when he spotted something more enticing leaning against the barn wall: a small motorcycle, twenty years old at least, but with inflated tires and a clean engine.

Stoner walked to the bike. Everything in his manner suggested he was the proper owner. He put on his helmet—rare in Iran, especially in the countryside, but appropriate—then reached to fiddle with the ignition assembly.

He didn't have to. A pair of wires hung down from the keyed ignition, already used as a makeshift hot wire. He connected them, then launched the kick start.

He kicked the metal spur so hard it stayed down for a moment. The bike caught in a fit of blue smoke and a backfire. He eased it toward the dirt road that separated the fallow and productive fields, gradually picking up speed. He didn't look back.

THE MOTORBIKE STONER FOUND WAS IN NEED OF A tune-up; its clutch stuck and the brakes grabbed only on whim. But these were considerations rather than impediments as far as Stoner was concerned. He nursed the vehicle north through a series of low hills, occasionally cutting back to make sure he wasn't being followed. He'd gotten clean away. No one was following him.

He wasn't sure he could say the same for Turk. As he approached the village where Turk was hiding—its name according to the GPS map in his smart helmet was Istgah-E Kuh Pang—he saw a pair of troop trucks rushing along the dirt road that paralleled the railroad tracks. Two jets, Phantom F-4s, streaked across the sky so low that it seemed he could have spit on their bellies.

It would be more difficult if the Iranians found him first. But only a little.

Stoner let the little bike putter along at four or five kilometers an hour, easing it over a dirt road that veered eastward away from both the railroad tracks and the village. Old ruins lay dead ahead, their red-tan bricks already growing warm with the morning sun.

Troops were going door-to-door in the village. They'd cordoned it off for a search. But they hadn't reached the ruins yet.

The motorcycle stalled as Stoner took it up an incline. He coasted to a stop, then pulled out the cell phone to find out where Turk was. He'd just hit the button for the locator app when something whizzed over his head.

He threw himself and the bike to the ground, instinctively knowing he'd been fired on before the actual thought registered in his conscious mind.

11

Istgah-E Kuh Pang

COLONEL KHORASANI JERKED HIS HEAD AROUND AS the rifle fire began.

"What are they shooting at?" he demanded.

Sergeant Karim, who was no closer to the action than he was, nonetheless answered in his usual authoritative voice. "Someone near the ruins, Colonel. On a motorcycle. They called to him and he didn't stop. The villagers say he does not live there."

"I want them alive," he commanded. "I want them alive so they can be questioned."

"They may get away, at least temporarily," said the sergeant. "Would you prefer that?"

The sergeant's tone was halfway between condescending and informative; Khorasani couldn't quite decide whether he was being mocked or not.

He decided to give the sergeant the benefit of the doubt. They'd had a long night without any sleep.

And now that he thought of it, wouldn't it be better, and simpler all around, if they just shot the bastards? In that case, the matter would be much more easily settled. He could huddle with his superiors, and then with Shirazi. They would concoct a story that would minimize the damage. There would still be great danger, and undoubt-edly more complications, but at least he wouldn't have to worry about someone getting hold of the prisoners and reinterrogating them.

"On second thought, Sergeant, tell them to attack with extreme prejudice and vehemence," commanded Colonel Khorasani. "The sooner we dispose of these pests, the better."

Stoner saw the two men who'd fired moving down along the rocks. He could take them easily; the question was what to do next.

Turk was in the ruins due west of him. To get there he would have to get past another group of soldiers coming down a road at the far end of the village.

He could retreat south, then swing back, hoping they didn't have time to span out along the flank. Some would follow him; those he could ignore. The others between him and his target could be picked off one by one.

Better to move ahead now, while the size of the force was still manageable and the initiative was still in his favor.

Stoner rose and fired two bursts. The men who had shot at him fell. He picked up the bike and pushed it to the left, coasting with the hill until the engine caught. Steering down the dirt road, he angled toward the ruins.

The dirt in front of him began to explode in tiny volcanoes of dust.

More bullets. There were men nearby he hadn't seen.

TURK PUSHED AGAINST THE SIDE OF THE RUINS AS THE gunfire stoked up. It was coming from the western end of the hamlet, up near the tracks.

They weren't shooting at him.

Was it Grease?

Grease was dead.

It had to be Grease.

Dread? Curtis? Tiny? Captain Granderson? Gorud?

All dead. He knew they were dead. He'd passed the truck. So it could only be Grease.

A fresh wave of guilt and shame swamped him. He'd abandoned his companion, even though he was still alive.

Turk started through the window, then stopped, catching a glimpse of a vehicle moving from the far end of the ruins, down the dirt road at the eastern edge of the desert. A half-dozen men trotted behind.

There were too many. Too many for one man, and even two.

Too many even for Grease.

Sᴛᴏɴᴇʀ ᴘᴜᴛ ᴛʜᴇ M-4 ᴏɴ ʜɪs ʜɪᴘ ᴀɴᴅ ꜰɪʀᴇᴅ ᴀs ʜᴇ drove, hoping to chase back the men coming down from the village on his left. It worked, but he faced a more difficult problem ahead—a troop vehicle had stopped at the far end of the ruins, and soldiers were using it for cover. From their uniforms, he guessed they were Pasdaran, Revolutionary Guards.

He got off two bursts, taking down three or four, and was aiming a third volley when the bike began slipping out from under him—someone had managed to get a bullet into the tire. He let it go as gracefully as he could manage, putting his weight on his left foot and swinging his right out as the bike hit the dirt. As he started to run, something hit him in the chest, just above his heart.

The slug was stopped by the thin, boron-carbon vest he had under the coveralls. He barely felt it.

Stoner sprinted to the left, running toward a low wall. As he neared it, he rolled on his shoulder, turning and facing the men who had fired at him from above. He saw three men; all of them fell with a tight double-pump on the trigger.

Stoner checked his breathing, slowing it to retain control. He could feel blood vibrating in the vessels at his neck, and knew adrenaline was coursing through his veins. For years he'd been pumped with artificial stimulants, every bit of him altered and manipulated. He'd been the slave of monsters who used him as their weapon, primed him to kill, hired him out as a high-profile assassin.

And now he remembered not the details of that time, the horror of being controlled, but something deeper: excitement. Danger. Life.

He loved it. It was oblivion.

Stoner saw two more men coming from the direction he'd just driven. He aimed and fired, got one, but missed the next, leading him rather than simply squeezing off a bullet into the man's chest.

It was the sort of error one made in haste. It was emotion-driven, adrenaline-fueled. He would not make it again.

The man had ducked behind a wall. Stoner took a very long, very slow breath, switched the gun to single fire, then waited for the man to rise.

He took him with a shot to the head.

"Infrared," said Stoner, telling the smart helmet to switch on its infrared sensors. "Count."

The smart helmet calculated five targets moving along the edges of the ruins behind the men he'd just killed. They were obscured by the terrain, but their heat signatures were visible.

Stoner looked left and then right, gauging the area and its potential for cover.

They'll expect me to be in the ruins.

If I retreat to the low run of buildings behind me, I can crawl into the weeds on my left. Then I'll have a clear shot at the group coming up in front of me now.

I'll get Turk Mako when I'm done. If they don't find and shoot him first.

TURK REALIZED HE WAS GOING TO DIE. BUT RATHER than scaring him, the knowledge freed him. It

told him that he should take out as many Iranians as he could. In that way, he would atone for
having left Grease.

He had to be smart about it. Going kamikaze
was foolish, and an insult to all Grease and the
others had taught him.

Slipping out the window of the ruined building,
Turk slithered to the ground like a snake. Automatic rifle fire boomed left and right; it sounded
like he was on a firing range.

Move out!

He crouched down, keeping himself as low as
possible as he moved along the ancient alley between the ruins. The loose sand and dirt were
slippery, and with his weight bent forward, it
wasn't long before he tripped, sprawling forward
in the dirt and landing hard on the rifle.

Once, this might have discouraged him, perhaps even sending him into a depressed spiral that
he'd never recover from. It would have reminded
him that he was a pilot, useless on land, awkward
and vulnerable. Now it was only something to
work through, even take advantage of: he had
become adept on the ground as well as in the air,
a true warrior.

Turk crawled along the ground, knowing that
in his final moments on earth he was going to kill
as many of his enemies as he could. He kept going
until he reached an open spot between the walls
where he could see the nearby ruins. Something
moving on his left. He raised his rifle but before
he could aim it was gone. He watched along the
top of the old stone wall, saw one, two shapes

briefly passing, then nothing as the wall rose a little higher.

Two men, a pair of Iranians trying to get down along the side of the ruins.

Turk started forward, then stopped. It would be better, he realized, to retreat to the remains of the building on his left and a little behind him. Then he could go around and come up on their rear.

He'd have to be fast.

Up, he told himself, and in a moment he was on his feet, running.

SEVEN TARGETS APPEARED ON STONER'S SCREEN, IR ghosts that moved across the darker rectangles of the ruins. Lying prone in the dirt amid a few clumps of scrub weeds, he waited until they stopped near the edge of a building that was nearly intact. Switching to burst fire, he moved his rifle left to right, shooting into the scrum until all but one of the men were down. The survivor retreated up one of the alleys, disappearing behind a low run of tumbled-down blocks and stone.

Two or three of the men he'd shot were still alive, trying to crawl to safety. Stoner dispatched them, then changed the magazine and started after the man who'd escaped.

Two vehicles appeared in the distance on his left, both Kavirans. One winked at him—a machine gun was mounted in a turret at the top, Hummer style. Stoner went to a knee, zeroed in on the small area of glowing flesh at the top of the flashes, then fired.

The Iranian fell off the top of the vehicle. The passenger-side door opened. Stoner waited, then took the man as he tried to climb up to the gunner's spot.

Stoner shot down two more Iranians, one from each truck, before they decided to retreat. Then he shot out the tires on both vehicles. It slowed, but didn't stop, their retreat. He turned back toward the collection of ruins to follow the man who'd gotten away.

Something moved at the corner of his vision as he neared the closest ruin. He spun and found two Iranians taking aim.

He emptied the mag, dropped the box and pulled up a fresh one. In the half second it took for him to grab the fresh bullets, something turned the corner on his right. Two men, shooting— Stoner threw himself down. But before he hit the ground, the gunfire abruptly ended. Both Iranians keeled forward, blood pouring from their shattered heads.

Behind them stood Turk Mako.

I T WASN'T GREASE. TURK STARED AT THE FIGURE IN THE field, the man he'd just saved. He had the faded camo uniform of the Pasdaran Guard, but he was wearing a Whiplash smart helmet.

Grease really, truly, was dead.

"We have to get out of here!" yelled Turk. He pointed left and started to move. "Come on."

STONER STOOD, FROZEN TO THE SPOT. TURK MAKO was there, not fifty feet away.

Assassinate.

He raised his gun, then hesitated. Turk had just saved his life; at that range, the Iranians would have had good odds of hitting him somewhere.

A strange emotion took him over: doubt.

What was his job, exactly?

Find and eliminate Turk Mako. He had been sent precisely because he wouldn't feel.

Stoner hesitated as Turk ran. Killing him was trivial. He raised his weapon.

What was his mission? They wanted him eliminated.

Stoner was a killing machine, turned into something less than human. He hesitated. He had a memory of something else, something deeper.

Turk Mako had just saved his life. He was an American. Turk Mako was on his side.

A man's heat signature flared in the corner of his screen. Stoner turned, saw that he had ducked behind the wall.

He waited until the man peeked out again, then fired, striking the Iranian in the head.

Assassinate Turk Mako.

Save Turk Mako.

Stoner moved methodically up the row of the ruins, reaching the dirt road that ran along the edge of the city. A dozen buildings sat between the road and the railroad tracks, strung out in a long line between clusters of buildings at either end. The Iranians had moved two large troop trucks near the tracks at the exact center of the road and the city; a half-dozen men were standing in disorganized clumps around the vehicles.

Poor discipline, thought Stoner, switching his weapon to single fire to snipe them, one by one.

T URK REACHED THE SLOPE OF ONE OF THE FIRST HILLS overlooking the city before realizing he was alone. He climbed up, some seventy or eighty feet, and looked back in confusion. The Whiplasher was in the center of town, walking near the vehicles parked there, methodically eliminating soldiers.

Turk watched in wonder as the trooper single-handedly took on what had to be a platoon-sized force. The enemy didn't gang up, and the groups of soldiers east and west at either end of the village remained where they were, but it was still an impressive, almost superhuman show. Even Grease couldn't have accomplished it.

Was he just lucky? Could he keep it up?

Turk climbed to the rounded peak and surveyed the area behind him. Hills poked out of the desert like measles. There were clumps of vegetation, mostly in the valleys between the hills.

A pair of jets passed to the southeast. He started to duck, afraid they'd been sent as reinforcements, then realized they were in a landing pattern.

The same base as the Phantoms he saw landing earlier, he thought. The base that had been empty.

Wɪᴛʜ ᴛʜᴇ ʟᴀsᴛ ᴏꜰ ᴛʜᴇ Iʀᴀɴɪᴀɴs ᴅᴇᴀᴅ, Sᴛᴏɴᴇʀ ᴄᴏɴ-
sidered taking one of the vehicles. But it would be
easily spotted, especially from the air; he'd heard
aircraft and decided that he would do better, at
least in the short term, on foot. So he turned and
ran back toward the ruins.

"Map subject," he told the computer in the
smart helmet.

A map appeared in the lower left-hand corner
of the visor, showing Turk's location and his own.
Turk Mako was several hundred yards away, on
the top of a hill.

Kill him now.

Stoner heard the order in his head, and recognized it as a remnant of the person he'd been—the
assassin created as the ultimate weapon, guided
by hypnotic suggestion.

He was no longer that person. He was Mark
Stoner—not quite the man he'd been before the
accident, but more himself than the robot he had
become. He decided what he did, not some human
programmed with designer drugs.

He would bring Turk Mako back alive.

Tᴜʀᴋ ᴡᴀᴛᴄʜᴇᴅ ᴛʜᴇ Wʜɪᴘʟᴀsʜ ᴛʀᴏᴏᴘᴇʀ ʀᴜɴ ᴛᴏᴡᴀʀᴅ
him, moving faster as he approached. He was a big
man, thick at the shoulders though not the waist.
Dirt and dust trailed behind his feet. He ran like a
sprinter, but faster. Turk had never seen a man run
that fast, not when he was training with the Delta
team, not when he was a high school athlete.

The two remnants of the Guard unit were still back at the village, split in two and separated by nearly two miles. They weren't moving to pursue. Perhaps they didn't even know what had happened.

Turk let his rifle slide down by his side as the man came closer. He was starting to feel tired again, starting to feel the aches in his muscles.

The man ran up the hill, his rifle pointed directly at him. Turk felt his throat tighten; his heart clutched, contracting with a long beat.

What was this?

The man stopped, gun still pointing at him. "Captain Mako?"

"Yes."

"Stoner. Let's go."

Stoner turned to head north.

"Wait," said Turk. "Not that way."

The trooper turned back.

"I have an idea," said Turk. "I think I know how we can get out of Iran quickly."

12

Pasdaran Base 408
Kushke Nosrat, Iran (Manzariyeh)

CAPTAIN VAHID WATCHED THE TWO F-4 PHANTOMS SET down on the closer of Manzariyeh's two runways, then bump along the access ramps and head for the apron adjacent to the terminal building. The uneven concrete pavement was one of several signs of neglect only visible up close. With Qom closed to foreign pilgrims and the air force evicted, the Pasdaran troops quartered here had little incentive to keep the place in top shape. They didn't even keep the name: known to the air force as Manzariyeh, the few men they had met here on the ground used the civilian "Kushke Nosrat" and stared blankly when he'd said "Manzariyeh."

"More planes," said Kayvan. "But no maintainers."

"Yes."

"They can't expect us to fly without fuel."

"It's supposedly on its way." More than a little of Vahid's frustration slipped into his voice. They'd been here for hours, told to stand by and join the Phantoms on reconnaissance but given no support—not even a place to sleep.

The Pasdaran were ignorant animals and idiots.

"I wonder what we did to deserve this punishment," added Kayvan. "Escorting old ladies."

"It's not punishment," said Vahid. "It's an honor."

"An honor, flying with Phantoms? What are we protecting them from? The scientists' own errors blew up their labs."

Vahid whirled. "Shut your mouth," he told the lieutenant. "Just shut it."

"Why? You know the Americans didn't send bombers. We would have seen them. Even the B-2s aren't invisible."

"Shut your mouth, Lieutenant. Keep your ʼminal thoughts to yourself."

"Don't worry, Captain. I won't hurt your chances for promotion."

Vahid just barely kept himself from decking the man.

"I'm going inside to see if I can find something to eat," he told Kayvan. "Stay with the planes."

"But—"

"Stay with the planes, Lieutenant, if you know what's good for you."

Where the hell was their fuel?

13

Istgah-E Kuh Pang

COLONEL KHORASANI COULDN'T UNDERSTAND WHAT the major was telling him.

"Half of your company?" said Khorasani. "Half your company is *dead*?"

"Twenty men," admitted the major. "But the enemy has not escaped. They are still in the ruins. Hiding."

"How many?"

"Two dozen at least. Maybe more."

The major described how his unit had surrounded the village, then been ambushed from the site of the ancient city at the edge of the desert. By the time the major finished, the enemy force had increased twofold.

Khorasani was split between disbelief and awe.

How had such a large force managed to get inside Iran, let alone avoid notice over the past two days? Even allowing for some exaggeration—the major, whose shirttail was askew, was clearly not the most competent officer in the Pasdaran—the enemy force must be considerable. By the time Khorasani arrived, the enemy force had retreated, though there was still some scattered automatic rifle fire near the ruins.

One or two enemy soldiers—even a dozen—might be dealt with. But there would be no explaining away something this size.

On the other hand, the regular army was responsible for dealing with conventional enemy forces. They would be the ones to blame.

"I've called for reinforcements," continued the major. "We should have more forces soon."

"Send more people south," said Khorasani, "so they can't escape from the ruins."

"I have sent two squads into the hills. I will send more when I have them. They won't escape."

"Good."

"I was wondering, Colonel—should I call the army for reinforcements? The air force has flown over a few times, but they do not yet—"

"The army is not to be involved," snapped Khorasani. "Our forces only. Keep me informed."

The colonel's shoulders drooped as he walked back to his command car. There was very little he would be able to do to shield the Guard from some blame, at least.

They had to neutralize the enemy force, kill all its members. That was the first priority. After that he would construct the story of what had happened.

No matter how creative he got, there would be serious repercussions. The Pasdaran could well end up decimated.

As for his own career, that clearly was ruined. Whether he could save his life or not remained to be seen.

14

Iran

STONER LISTENED TO TURK DESCRIBE HIS PLAN TO GET to the airport and take a truck, the words triggering a cascade of images in his mind. Half were specifically related to the mission—he recalled the map of the area, the airport layout, and the general disposition of the forces, all of which had been briefed.

Half of the rest had nothing to do with the mission, and were neither benign nor comforting. He saw explosions, cars and buildings, a head bursting as a bullet hit, a vehicle veering straight into a bridge abutment.

He had no idea where they came from. There was no caption material, no explicit connection or explanation, no context, just seemingly random images interfering with the matter at hand.

The pilot's plan made some sense—they would

go to a lightly held base and steal a vehicle. The base was some eleven miles away.

Two hours. Less if he ran flat out, which he would.

Stoner looked back at the village. He couldn't see everything that was going on, but he heard more vehicles arriving, and guessed that the Iranians were reorganizing. They would try to surround the area next. They would concentrate on the north, since it was easiest to travel in that direction. Going east meant crossing the desert hills. It was also the direction of the air base, which the Iranians would assume was an unlikely destination for the men they pursued, since it was their own stronghold.

Turk's plan was their best bet, definitely.

"Let's do it," said Stoner, starting to run.

Sᴛᴏɴᴇʀ's ǫᴜɪᴄᴋ ᴀᴄǫᴜɪᴇꜱᴄᴇɴᴄᴇ ᴛᴏᴏᴋ Tᴜʀᴋ ʙʏ sᴜʀprise. He hesitated a moment, then started to run after him. By the time he was halfway down the hill, Stoner was some ten yards ahead. The distance between them increased rapidly, until finally Turk had to yell to the other man to stop.

"Hey!" he yelled. "I can't keep up. Hey!"

Stoner turned and stopped, waiting for him. Exhausted from the sprint, Turk slowed to a trot; by the time he reached Stoner he was walking.

"You have to move faster," Stoner told him. His voice and affect were so flat that under other circumstance, they might have been comical.

"I'm sorry."

"Here. Give me your gun."

Turk hesitated. "But—"

"Give me your gun and get on my back."

"On your back?"

"I will carry you. Let's move. Come on."

"I'm keeping my gun," said Turk, still unsure this was going to work. But he decided it was silly to resist, and so when Stoner turned around, he climbed on, piggyback style. Stoner began running, slowly at first but quickly gathering speed. Turk guessed he was going as fast as he had been before, maybe even faster.

They ran like that for nearly forty minutes, Stoner keeping the same pace over the rocks as he did over level paths. Turk knew of Stoner's rescue by Danny and the others; he'd heard a small amount of his history. But he hadn't spent any time with him, and he'd thought, quite frankly, that some of the tales of his prowess and strength were exaggerations. Clearly they weren't. He was amazed at the man's strength and endurance, which not only was superior to his own but far exceeded even that of the Special Forces soldiers he'd been with.

They stopped to rest and scout their position on the eastern side of a hillock, in a bend in a trail. The base was four and a half miles away; Turk could make out the concrete expanse of the runways in the distance.

He'd told Stoner they would steal a truck at the base, not a plane. He was afraid Stoner would think taking a plane was too wild, too crazy. To a person who didn't fly, it probably was. But the more Turk considered it, the better the odds seemed.

"They don't man the perimeter," said Stoner, gazing in the direction of the base.

"They didn't the other night, but there are posts and—"

"No one is in them."

"You can see that far?"

"Yes."

"What are you, Superman?"

Stoner stepped back, glaring at him.

"I didn't mean that as an insult," said Turk. "I'm just amazed you can see that far. And hell, you're—strong."

"There were operations. There are downsides and costs."

"Yeah?"

Turk waited, but Stoner didn't explain.

"I don't think they're following us," Turk said finally.

"They will." Stoner turned back in the direction of the base. He pointed. "If we go north and then follow the pipeline, they won't see us, even if they do man the closest lookout. There is more cover farther east, along the main line. We can move behind it, then around into the facility from the north. It is in our interest to move as quickly as possible," he added. "Get on my back."

AN HOUR AND A HALF LATER TURK AND STONER crawled on their hands and knees behind the scar of the pipeline, moving to an access road on the north side of the base. The nearest observation post was five hundred yards to the west, and it would be difficult for anyone to see them as long as they stayed low to the ground.

Even crawling, Stoner was fast. Turk followed as quickly as he could but still fell behind. The piles of dirt were of different heights, jagged both at the top and the sides, and Turk found himself wending around them like a caterpillar. Losing sight of Stoner, he resisted the temptation to stand, continuing in the dirt until his stolen pants were worn through at the knees. Finally he twisted around a fat mound of sand and found Stoner studying the fence and the facility beyond.

They were near the point where he and Grease had gone in before. A truck was parked about twenty yards up the road, facing the eastern end of the base and away from them.

"Sorry it took me so long," said Turk, scrambling up behind Stoner.

"Mmmm."

Stoner stared at the truck. It seemed to Turk that he was gauging whether to take it. Turk turned his gaze toward the rest of the base, scanning the runways. He'd been right about the aircraft he'd seen earlier; they had landed here.

A chime sounded—a wristwatch alarm on Stoner's arm. The Whiplash operative reached into one of his pockets and pulled out a small cardboard container about the size and shape of the matchboxes that bars and restaurants once gave away. He slipped it open and dumped the contents into his mouth.

"What are you doing?" asked Turk.

"Meds."

"What kind?"

"All kinds."

"Is that alarm to remind you?" Turk pointed at the watch.

"Every day. Sometimes more."

"What's in them?"

"Different things." Stoner shrugged. "It's how I live." He pointed at the truck he'd been watching. "We can get it from the back. We'll break through the fence there and keep going."

He started to rise.

"Wait," Turk told him, grabbing his arm. "You see over there? The planes? They're F-4 Phantoms. They're being fueled on the apron, at the end of the north field."

"Yes?"

"They're two-seaters. We could take one. It's farther than the truck, but if we go straight across the field here, we can get there before anyone sees us."

"There is someone with binoculars on the building," said Stoner. "They'll see us."

"We'll be at the planes by the time they send someone to get us," said Turk. "Look, they're being refueled. We can fly out. We'll take one right to Kuwait. It's what? Forty minutes, max. We'll be home free."

"You can fly it?"

"I can fly anything."

"What about those?" Stoner pointed to a pair

of MiGs parked on a second apron closer to the buildings.

"They're better planes, but they're one-seaters," Turk said. "So unless you can fly, too, we want one of the Phantoms."

"We will have to run across open land," said Stoner. "It will take time."

"Me, yes. Not you."

"Go!" was Stoner's answer, jumping up and dashing toward the planes.

THE FIRST OF THE PILLS WAS JUST STARTING TO TAKE effect as Stoner began to run. He could feel the stitch in his side melt. The dark blanket that had begun to descend on his head evaporated. The pills counteracted some of the remaining poisons in his body, but also replaced the hormones he could no longer manufacture. Most important, the drugs supplied part of the boost his organs had been trained to need.

No one had ever asked what was in them before. Stoner himself didn't know.

Four men were near the planes. One was over-seeing a fuel hose by the wing of the lead plane. Another was back by the fuel truck. The last two were loading something beneath the plane—a bomb, Stoner assumed.

There were other men and vehicles back near the hangars, half a mile away, working on the MiGs.

If something went wrong, he would blow up the

tanker truck, then go and get the security vehicle sitting back by the terminal. Most likely they would come to him, responding as soon as they saw the attack.

Stoner felt his energy increasing with every step. He ran as fast as he had ever run, the wind whipping past his helmet.

The man near the tanker truck spotted him and raised his hand to warn the others. Stoner brought his gun up, zeroed on the cue in the visor and fired. As the man fell, Stoner turned the barrel toward the man under the wing with the fuel hose and shot him from two hundred yards; the man dropped the hose and took a step back. Then he staggered forward, falling facedown onto the cement.

Fuel squirted out for a moment, then stopped, shut off by the safety device at the nozzle.

The two men who'd been working on the bomb took off on a dead run in the direction of the MiGs. Stoner changed direction to follow. He could feel his legs get stronger, the muscles thickening with each step. Hate filled his head. He wanted to kill these men, crush them like ants, pound each skull against the tarmac. Hatred and anger built exponentially. He felt his head warming, his heart racing.

Why was he so angry?

Anger was an excess emotion, something that clouded his vision and his judgment. He could not be angry.

And yet he was, beyond all measure.

Tᴜʀᴋ's ʟᴜɴɢs ꜰᴇʟᴛ ʟɪᴋᴇ ᴛʜᴇʏ ᴡᴏᴜʟᴅ ᴄᴏʟʟᴀᴘꜱᴇ ʙʏ the time he reached the first runway; by the second, his legs were cramping. He willed himself forward in a delirium of broken energy but desperate and wild hope.

Do it! Go!

Stoner was far ahead, running after the two men who had retreated from the Phantom. Turk started to follow but realized Stoner would catch them long before he caught up to Stoner; he was better off going to the planes.

The scent of jet fuel nearly overwhelmed him as he ran onto the apron. When he got to the first Phantom, he saw why—some of the bullets that had killed the man closest to the tanker had punctuated the tank as well. Two narrow streams of fuel spurted from the truck, crisscrossing as they dropped toward the pavement. The fuel ran in a large puddle toward the second plane. He turned to the first, which was the one being prepped when they attacked.

Go, Turk told himself. *Get the plane started and go.*

Hᴏᴡ ʜᴀᴅ ᴀɴɢᴇʀ ʙᴇᴄᴏᴍᴇ ᴀ ᴘʜʏꜱɪᴄᴀʟ ᴛʜɪɴɢ? Hᴏᴡ had it become so overwhelming?

Stoner saw himself grabbing the nearest man by the back of his mechanic's coveralls and dashing him to the ground. He saw the blood bursting from his skull, the front of the man's leg turning ninety degrees forward. Stoner floated above his body and saw himself grab the second man, throwing him to the ground and then kicking him, pounding him to unconsciousness with two blows from his foot.

The hatred was irrational. The hatred felt incredibly good. It felt familiar. He had felt it many times before.

That was the man they had made him, the angry man. That was the purpose of the experiments and additions to his body, the manipulation. Create the perfect assassin. Create the angry man.

That was not who he was now. Zen and Danny had rescued him. He was no longer the angry man. Drugs or not, he was Mark Stoner.

He stopped kicking the Iranian and turned to go back to the planes.

When he was about two hundred yards away, something told him to stop and turn. He spun and saw an Iranian Hummer moving out from the terminal building. Dropping to a knee, he took aim at the windshield of the vehicle. He fired a three-shot burst into the driver's head. The vehicle slowed to a stop.

More men were coming, these on foot, running from a building on the left. Fighting back the rising anger, Stoner calmly flicked the gun's shooting selector and began picking them off as they ran, firing center mass on each Revolutionary Guard, taking down four of the five.

The last man, seeing his friends go down, threw himself on his face. Stoner got to his feet and fired a single bullet, striking the cowering man on the top of his skull.

It didn't make him feel better to have killed the man.

Progress, he thought.

As he turned toward the Phantoms, Stoner saw the jet fuel leaking from the truck. He headed straight for the truck, splashing the last few yards to the cab. The vehicle's engine was still running; he put it into gear and drove to the edge of the ramp connecting it with the rest of the airport's ramp network. He hopped out of the truck and ran to the stream of jet fuel spitting out of the side.

Reaching to the lower pocket on the leg of his pants, he took out a plastic bag with a lighter and kindling. He lit the bag and tossed it toward the stream of fuel. Before he could back away, the stream exploded into a fireball that consumed the tanker.

WORRIED THAT THE LEAKING FUEL TRUCK WOULD catch fire, Turk had taken the plane up the apron before bothering to start the Phantom's second engine. When he was a safe distance away, he stopped and glanced back for Stoner.

A wall of fire erupted on his left, blocking off the plane from the rest of the airport. It was so hot that he felt a sudden rush of heat.

He was going to die.

"Stoner!" he yelled. "Stoner!"

Turk pushed up in the seat, leaning over the side to look for the other man.

Leave! he told himself. *Go! Go!*

He was sent to kill you. He'll kill you still—that's what he's doing. Go!

Turk looked at the terminal building. There was a truck there, but no movement. He craned his head, looking at the burning fuel truck.

Where was Stoner?

"Stoner!" he yelled again.

"Here," shouted the other man, clambering up the wing on the right side of the plane, away from the fire. "Let's go."

"Yeah. OK." Turk blinked; Stoner really *was* Superman.

"Strap yourself in," Turk yelled. "We don't have oxygen. Just hang on and we'll be home."

Without oxygen hookups or pressurized suits Turk would have to keep the plane low, or risk decompression sickness.

"OK," said Stoner, dropping into the seat.

Turk engaged the other engine, starting it and then ramping to full power. The Iranian F-4 was a lot like Old Girl, but it wasn't exactly the same; he had to stop and think about what he was doing. First and foremost, the instrument panel was *very* different—Old Girl had been modernized several times, and now featured a full glass cockpit close to state-of-the-art. This Iranian plane was all dials and knobs. The stick and throttle looked a little different as well, though in function they were fully equivalent.

Turk let off his brakes and eased the Phantom into a turn up the ramp, picking up speed gently as he lined up to start the takeoff.

Damned if the runway didn't look short.

Very, very short.

Too late to worry about that now. Too late to worry about a lot of things.

Turk jammed his hand on the throttle, making sure the engines were pushed to the max. They rumbled behind him, coughing for a half second on some impurity in the fuel, then shaking it off. They whined with a high-pitched, distinctive scream as the Phantom raced down the long bumpy stretch of concrete.

The plane wanted to fly. Her wings flexed with the wind, sinews stretching. The base and desert swept by in a blur.

And then they were airborne, the Phantom rising like a bird, a thundering, anxious bird, but a strong one nonetheless, knifing into an onrush of wind.

15

Pasdaran Base 408
Kushke Nosrat, Iran (Manzariyeh)

As soon as Vahid heard the gunfire, he ran from the lounge of the terminal where he'd been drinking tea, passing through the long hallway to the outside parking area. His first thought was that the Pasdaran Guards had had enough of his wingman and decided to shoot him.

Then he saw the fire.

"What the hell is going on?" yelled Vahid as two men came at him on a dead run. One was bleeding from the head. Vahid reached to stop him but the man charged past, blood streaming from his temple to his neck and from there to his shirt. He'd been hit by a fragment of some kind; if he would stop to stanch the bleeding, he would be all right, but in his panic he was going to bleed to death.

One of the Phantoms rose off the runway.

How? He'd left the F-4 pilots inside, waiting for a fresh pot to boil.

Vahid started for his own plane. If they were under attack, he had to get in the air.

Where was Lieutenant Kayvan?

Two figures were crouched near the rear of his MiG. One was one of the maintainers who'd arrived a short while before. The other was his wingman.

"The planes!" yelled Vahid, starting toward them. "Kayvan! We're taking off. *We're taking off!*"

16

Iran

TURK STEADIED THE PHANTOM AS HE CLEANED THE landing gear, coming off the runway a bit slower than Old Girl would have. He had more weight and weaker engines: two 500-pound bombs were strapped under his wings, and a pair of old model Sidewinders on the outer rails. But on the positive side, the plane was loaded with more than enough fuel to make Kuwait.

The first thing he needed to do was jettison the bombs. As he banked westward, he checked the armament panel—old school but easily operated. He reached to the switch to select the weapons so they could be jettisoned. Then he remembered the control unit, still hidden in the ruins near the village.

Why not drop the bombs there?

C OLONEL K HORASANI STARED AT S ERGEANT K ARIM AS he ran down the hill from the control car.

"Colonel, one of the teams searching the old ruins found a computer in the rocks," said the sergeant between gasps for air. "Electronics. Computers."

"Where?" demanded Khorasani.

"Platoon two," said Karim. He pointed to the left side of the ruins. "It would be in that direction."

"Go back and tell the commander to meet me," said Khorasani. "I'll walk."

He let his binoculars fall to his chest and began walking down the embankment. The reinforcements were still fanning out around the area, moving in slow motion. For all the braggadocio of its lower ranks, and all the connections of its leaders, the Revolutionary Guard was at its heart a disorganized bunch of rabble one step removed from the streets.

Khorasani was truly baffled about what had happened. While the carnage he'd seen indicated a large, efficient force, anything above squad size would have shown itself by now. Were the Americans or the Israelis fielding invisible soldiers now?

He would figure it all out later. For now, they must be destroyed.

The squad commander was a sergeant, an older man, fortunately. They were the only ones worth a whit in the Guard. The man raised his hand to salute.

"Where are the items that were found?" Khorasani asked.

A jet passed overhead, drowning out the man's answer. The sergeant glanced upward, but Khorasani ignored it—it was about time the air force got involved.

Another problem.

"The computer?" he asked as the jet banked away.

"We found it in that house below," said the sergeant, pointing. "It was under some rocks. We left it in case the positioning was significant."

On the other hand, the older ones knew nothing about computers.

"Let's have a look," the colonel said, starting for the ruins.

THE PHANTOM'S GROUND-ATTACK RADAR WAS WORKED from the rear seat, and there was no chance of getting Stoner to activate it without a lengthy explanation. But Turk figured he could do a dead-reckoning drop—point the nose and let 'em go.

He took a practice run first, getting the feel of the plane and his target. It wasn't as easy as he thought. He realized as he cleared that he would have overshot by quite a bit, and that was before gravity pelted him in the face and chest. He'd have to come in slower and wait even longer.

The soldiers on the ground would undoubtedly realize something was up. Next pass and go.

As he circled to take a second run, Turk tried to remember the last time he had done a dead-reckoning dive on a target. He couldn't remember doing it ever, though he was sure he must have practiced at some point. In fact, the only situation he could think of that was even remotely close involved a video game when he was thirteen or fourteen.

At least he'd been good at that.

Turk steadied his aim as he lined up, using the nearby house for reference and trying to calculate where momentum would put the bombs.

Five hundred pound bombs. All I have to do is be close.

He pickled and pulled off. The plane jerked upward, glad to be free of the extra weight.

Not like in a video game, that.

The Phantom continued over the city, passing the railroad tracks and the open desert to the west of Istgah-E Kuh Pang. More Pasdaran vehicles had arrived, and there were pools of men gathering at the center of town. Turk banked south, pushing the Phantom over the area where he had bombed.

Black smoke and pulverized brown rock lingered in the air. The corner of the building had been replaced by a double crater. There were bodies on the ground.

Mission complete. Time to go home.

17

Iran

VAHID STARTED THE MIG ROLLING. THE SMOKE FROM the fire made it impossible to see much of the airport in front of him, let alone where the attackers were. He guessed that they must be near the runway, but decided he would have to take his chances and try rushing by them. Staying on the ground would surely cost him his MiG.

The fire blocked the normal access to the runway. Instead, Vahid turned his plane along the narrow road in front of the terminal building. Meant to be used by cars, it was lined by light poles. Seeing the MiG's wing coming close on the left side, he pulled one wheel off the cement, riding cock-eyed all the way to the service access road before turning onto the ramp that led to the middle of the runway. Gaining speed as he went, Vahid turned right, trundled to the end and pulled a U-turn on the uneven and ill-repaired concrete apron before lining up to take off.

The F-4 near the fuel truck spit a fireball across the field. Flames licked across the wings and up the tail, small curlicues feasting on the paint.

Vahid heard One Eye shouting at him: *Go!*

He hit his throttle and rocketed down the white expanse, lifting into the morning air. Worried that whoever had attacked the planes on the ground had shoulder-launched missiles, he let off flare decoys, jerking the nose of the MiG upward, pushing the plane for all she was worth.

He started to breathe easier as he climbed through 5,000 feet. No longer worried about shoulder-launched missiles, he began a climbing orbit around the airfield, rising as he spun around looking for whoever had attacked the base. He didn't have much to attack them with—besides his cannon, there were a pair of radar missiles and another pair of heat-seeking missiles on his wings—but he'd at least be able to give their location to the units on the ground.

Assuming the ground answered. Vahid had taken off in such a rush that he hadn't even contacted the tower. He tried doing so now, only to belatedly realize he had inadvertently knocked the radio off when climbing into the cockpit.

One Eye would never have let him live that down. Vahid hit the switch and heard the controller practically screaming into his ear, demanding he respond.

"Shahin One acknowledges," he told the man. "I'm off the field and looking for the attackers."

"Be advised—someone has stolen Badr Two."

"Repeat?"

"Badr Two took off without authorization."

"Who took it?"

"Unknown. The pilots are on the ground. It may have been one of the Israelis!"

"Impossible," said Vahid. He turned out of the climb and circled toward the control tower, certain that the enemy forces had taken it over.

"Captain Vahid, are you receiving? This is Major Morad."

Morad was the leader of the Phantom squadron; they'd been joking over tea just a few minutes before.

"Major, where are you?" asked Vahid. "What's going on with the control tower?"

"Captain, I'm in the tower. I'm on the ground. We're all on the ground. One of my aircraft has been taken. Pursue it."

"I have it heading north," answered Vahid. "What are my instructions?"

"We're getting in contact with General Shirazi."

"Are you sure this isn't one of your pilots?"

"They are all here. It must be a commando, stealing our secrets."

That is very doubtful, Vahid thought.

"I am setting up an intercept," he told the major. "Stand by."

18

Iran

Turk pulled the harness against his shoulder, tightened it as far as it would go against his shirt. He felt naked, and in a sense he was—no pressurized suit, no survival gear, not even a "hat." While the Phantom's cockpit was pressurized, he knew he had to be careful not only about his altitude but his maneuvers—a sharp turn might knock him unconscious, perhaps permanently.

If he had to stay low and level, his better course out of the country would be north—get up and out through the Caspian, where the air defenses were far weaker. It was a little farther, but it was in the direction of the units that were supporting the SEALs. It also might seem counterintuitive to the Iranians; they'd expect him to go toward Kuwait.

Level at 5,000 feet, he turned north and moved the thrusters to max, winding the J-79-GE17 turbojets up like tops ready for a good spin. The Iranian Phantom gobbled fuel; Turk could practically see the needles dive toward empty. He backed off his thrust, deciding that 350 knots was a decent speed, a compromise that would conserve fuel while making good time. At roughly six miles a minute, it would get him to the coast before the Iranians could scramble their northern fighters. Once there, he could goose the afterburners for a few seconds and ride the wave to Baku in Azerbaijan.

There was one last problem: he had no way to use the radio. Breanna and the others were undoubtedly tracking him; he assumed—*hoped*—they would alert the authorities there as he approached. Landing itself would not be a problem. The runway had been built for Soviet military use and was more than long enough to get in comfortably.

He thought of using the sat phone. That might work.

Not now—he had too much to do and worry about in the unfamiliar plane at low altitude. He'd wait until they were over the water and out of Iranian territory. There was nothing they could do at the moment anyway.

Fifteen minutes to the coast, by his watch.

Turk rocked back and forth in the cramped cockpit, checking his gauges, studying the instrument panel. The main controls for the Phantom's radar were in the rear compartment, and while he had made sure the unit was on before taking off, he now had no way of doing much more than that. Against the Iranian air force, the Phantom's early X Band radar would still be a perfectly acceptable tool, but he had almost no control over it beyond the ability to lock a single target at relatively close range. The Pulse Doppler mode that had been preset was useful, allowing the pilot to "see" targets ahead as long as he could interpret the old-style screen. Targets moving "on beam" or at the side in the direction of the plane were essentially invisible, a problem if he was pursued from either flank. But the radar was fine for what he wanted; it would help him avoid problems. If he saw contacts ahead, he'd go around them.

For now, the sky was clear. Fourteen minutes to the coast. They were going to make it.

VAHID COULD SEE THE F-4 FLYING AHEAD FIVE MILES. IF it was being flown by an enemy, he wasn't being too obvious about it. He was relatively low, at 5,000 feet, and going only about 350 knots: not slow, exactly, but hardly running away.

He was going north, in the general direction of the Tehran air base where the Phantom wing was ordinarily assigned, which was a puzzle. It seemed more logical to Vahid that the pilot should be heading toward a safe haven.

But Major Morad was adamant that the plane had been stolen. He hadn't radioed back with additional directions; apparently he was still waiting on General Shirazi.

Vahid closed the distance to the F-4 slowly, aiming to draw in tight to the plane's left wing. The Phantom, meanwhile, made no move to avoid him.

It also didn't answer on the assigned radio frequency, or even the rescue band used for emergencies. That was suspicious, though not enough to shoot the plane down.

Vahid drew to about thirty meters of the Phantom, matching his speed as he pulled parallel to the aircraft. He could see two men in the cockpit. They didn't seem to have helmets.

The man in the rear looked at him. Vahid waved and pointed, motioning that they must follow him.

THE VIEW OUT OF THE COCKPIT WAS SO RESTRICTED and Turk was so focused on what was in front of him that he didn't even notice the MiG on his wing until it was practically touching.

When he did see it, his shudder shook the plane.

He drew a deep breath, trying to plot what to do.

Ignore it.

He held steady, deciding that if he acted non-chalant, the pilot would break off and leave him alone.

Unfortunately, that was pure fantasy, as the MiG soon demonstrated with a swoop over his front quarters. The other plane passed so close that the missiles on its undercarriage nearly hit Turk's right wing.

Two of those missiles looked like radar homers, Russian R-27 Alamos. The others were heat-seekers, early Sidewinders, from the looks of them. Any one of them could turn the Phantom into a dead hunk of tin in an instant.

Turk waited until the plane reformed on his left wing, then waved to the pilot, signaling that he didn't have a headset.

I'll stall for time, he decided. I'll get close enough to the coast to make a dash for it.

But the MiG pilot wasn't having that. He signaled adamantly that Turk had to follow him, pointing with his finger to the ground and gesturing violently.

"OK, OK," said Turk, feigning compliance as he gestured with his hands. "Where do you want me to go?"

The pilot moved his hand left. Turk pretended not to understand.

Turk thought he might catch the MiG by surprise if he went to his afterburners. If he did that, he might be able to get enough of a lead to outrun it, at least to the border. But there was no way that he could outrun the radar missiles, which had a seventy kilometer range.

THE PILOT IN THE PHANTOM SEEMED SOMEWHAT OUT of sorts, gesturing wildly, willing to comply but keeping his plane on the course it had been flying. Vahid guessed that the man was one of the mechanics who'd been working on the plane when it was attacked; he didn't have a helmet, and while he was doing a good job of keeping the airplane straight, he didn't seem capable of turning or even going very fast.

Major Morad's claim that the plane had been stolen seemed ridiculous. Even in Iran, the Phantoms were obsolete. Undoubtedly this was a story the squadron commander was concocting to cover up whatever was really going on.

Life in Iran was becoming unbearable.

Vahid radioed for instructions. Neither Morad nor the controller answered. Having the Phantom follow him back to the base they had just taken off from seemed like a foolish move if it was still under attack—a reasonable guess, given Morad's radio silence.

Vahid pushed the MiG slightly ahead, easing in front of the older plane by thirty or forty meters.

"Follow me," he said over the emergency radio frequency, even though the pilot didn't seem able to reply. "Take a turn slowly and gently—bank. Use your stick."

There was no answer from the plane. Instead, Morad radioed him, finally answering his earlier calls.

"I have spoken to one of the general's aides. We need you to switch to Western combat control." The major added the frequency and the name of the controller, a colonel whose name sounded like *arrr* as the transmission broke up. Vahid tried to puzzle out the name but couldn't work it against his memory, nor did the voice sound familiar after he found the frequency.

The colonel, though, seemed to know him, and immediately asked if he had the Phantom in sight.

"I have it on my wing," he said, glancing over his shoulder at it. "The pilot appears to be a novice. I think he is one of the maintainers who panicked when the base was under attack. He can fly straight, but otherwise—"

"You are to proceed to Tabriz air base," said the colonel, cutting him off. "We are scrambling fighters to meet you."

The airfield, located outside the city of the same name, was the headquarters for Tactical Squadrons 21, 22, and 23. But it was some 370 kilometers to the east; Tehran would have been much more convenient.

"I'm not sure how much fuel he has," radioed Vahid. "Nor do I think he can maneuver. I don't think he's much of a pilot. From the looks of him, he's a maintainer who panicked to try to save the plane."

"You have your orders, Captain. We will have escorts in the air within ten minutes."

"Roger."

"If the plane does not comply, you are authorized to shoot it down."

"Destroy it?"

"Affirmative. Attempt to do so over open land. But that should not be your deciding factor. Take it down at all costs if it doesn't comply."

TURK WAITED UNTIL HE SAW THE PILOT GESTURING FOR him to follow. The man seemed almost desperate, moving his hands vigorously.

He needed to wait until the last possible moment. It was a contest of time now; time and distance.

The odds were not in his favor. But when had they ever been?

Turk rode the Phantom steady, watching the indicated airspeed carefully. He felt a little light-headed, but was sure that had nothing to do with the plane—they were at 4,000 feet now, and even if the cabin were wide-open he ought to be able to breathe normally. So it was nerves, a problem he could handle. He slowed his breathing, relaxing his muscles as best he could. He leaned gently on the stick, nudging the Phantom so it seemed like he was turning in the direction the MiG wanted.

His other hand settled onto the ganged throttle, waiting.

The MiG pilot saw him moving and began his bank, aiming to lead him wherever it was he wanted to go. Turk started into the turn very slowly, then, as the MiG started to pull ahead, he killed his throttle, practically stalling the Phantom. The MiG floated into the middle of his windscreen. Turk hit the trigger, spitting a burst of 20mm rounds out from the plane's centerline.

The stream of fire missed, but he hadn't counted on knocking her down. What he did want was what happened: the MiG pilot, seeing tracers blaze by his windscreen, rolled out of the way. By the time he recovered, Turk had the Phantom's afterburners screaming. The F-4 jumped through the sound barrier, surging northward and moving as fast as she had gone in years.

Vahid's instincts took over as the tracers flew past. He ducked and rolled, spinning away from his enemy. Even though he calculated that he was too close for a successful missile shot from the Phantom, he let off flares, then jerked the MiG hard to the west. Right side up, he expected to see the F-4 pulling in front of him, caught outside of the tight turn as it moved in for the kill.

He couldn't spot it. He practically spun his head off his neck, making sure the Phantom wasn't on his six somewhere he couldn't see. What the hell?

The other plane was way out in front, moving north at a high rate of speed. Vahid armed his air-to-air R-27s, got a strong tone in his helmet indicating he was locked, and fired both. Only after the second missile was away did he radio the controller to tell him what was going on.

Turk expected the MiG would fire its radar missiles almost immediately. Under most circumstances in a modern American plane, that wouldn't be a problem: the weapons would be easily fended off by the ECMs.

In the Phantom, things were a little different. He had to rely on his guile.

He pushed lower to the ground, still picking up speed. The plane was equipped with a radar warning receiver, which ordinarily would tell the crew when it was being tracked by a radar. But the receiver hadn't worked earlier, when the MiG was coming up from behind, and it remained clean now, either malfunctioning or not activated correctly.

Turk assumed there was a problem with the RWR and decided to ignore it. He saw the encounter in his head, playing it over as if it were one of the scrimmages he routinely did with his UAVs. He saw the Iranian pilot recover, then launch the first missile. He'd look back at the radar, check for another strong lock, then fire again.

Or maybe he would wait and see what the first missile did. But that wasn't going to work now.

He counted to three, then pushed the stick hard and rolled into an invert, turning at the same time to beam the Doppler radar in the MiG and confuse the missile. He drove the Phantom lower, pushing so close to the ground that the scraggly brush threatened to reach up and grab the plane as it passed. A small city lay ahead; Turk went even lower, coming in over the rooftops. He kept counting to himself, knowing that the missile was behind him somewhere, and hoping it would run out of fuel.

The R-27 had a semiactive radar; it rode to its target on a beam provided by the MiG's radar. Turk's maneuvers had confused the radar momentarily, and his very low altitude made it hard for the enemy radar to sort him out of the ground clutter.

He saw a canyon coming up and decided to turn with it, hoping the close sides would shield him from the guiding radar. But the Phantom was now moving well over the speed of sound, and she wasn't about to turn easily or quickly. Worse, he felt a punch in his stomach as he tried to turn—the g forces were quick to build up. He had to ease back, and gave up his plan. Instead he stayed as low as he could over the open terrain, running toward the buildings ahead.

Sweat poured from every pore of his body, including the sides of his eyes; he could barely keep his hand on the stick.

Seconds passed, then a full minute. He let off on the gas and banked, more gently this time, aiming north.

Something shot in front of him, maybe a mile away. It was one of the missiles.

"Shit," he muttered.

Then he felt the tail of the Phantom lifting out of his hand, pitching his nose sideways.

The other missile had exploded behind him.

19

CIA campus, Virginia

Breanna watched as the signal indicating Turk's position jerked back northward.

"What the hell is he doing?" Reid asked.

"I don't know. Assuming he's in a plane, they may be ducking a missile." They could only guess what was going on; there'd been no word from Turk, or Stoner for that matter. It was clear from the intercepted Iranian radio transmissions that the Iranians had not captured them. The Iranian air force was scrambling after a Phantom that had left Manzariyeh without authorization; Breanna guessed that must be Turk, trying to fly to safety.

"Try to contact Stoner again," Reid told the communications aide. "Get him."

"Sir, I just tried. There's been no answer."

"Try again."

"He's heading north," said Breanna. "I bet he's going to Baku."

"Can he make it?"

"I don't know." She looked at the screen. The maneuvers indicated he was under attack. Off the top of her head she wasn't sure what the Phantom's range might be, and there was no way of knowing how much fuel it had. "We need to talk to the Azerbaijan air force," she told Reid. "He's going north—he'll be heading toward their air space."

"You're sure?"

"Absolutely. They have MiGs—can we scramble them?"

"I don't know if that will be doable, Breanna."

"Try."

20

Iran

VAHID CURSED HIMSELF. HE'D FIRED TOO SOON, SURE that the F-4 pilot wasn't much of a flier. Now he saw that was a mistake; the man was smarter than he'd thought, and at least knew the basics of dodging radar missiles.

No matter. He'd drive up close and put a heat-seeker in his fantail.

Once he found him. The radar was having trouble locating the Phantom in the ground clutter.

Maybe he crashed after all.

No. There he was—twenty kilometers away. Running north toward the Caspian.

Vahid juiced his throttle, opening the gates on the afterburners. The sudden burst of speed slammed him back into his seat.

He'd close on the F-4, get tight, then fire. He wasn't going to make the same mistake twice.

STONER SAT IN THE REAR SEAT OF THE AIRCRAFT, watching with detachment as the plane bucked and turned, jerking sharply in the sky.

They weren't particularly high. He could see the ground clearly out the side of the windscreen.

If we crash, he thought, Turk Mako will die, and my mission will be accomplished.

TURK STRUGGLED WITH THE CONTROLS, TRYING TO muscle the Phantom back level after the shock of the missile explosion behind them. If he'd been higher, he could have simply sorted things out in a long, sweeping dive, but he was far too low for that. He pulled the stick, straining as the plane skidded in the air. His airspeed had bled off precipitously; the Phantom was very close to a stall.

Get me out of here, Old Girl, he thought. Let's dance.

He pressed again on the throttle and jerked the stick back. He was dangerously close to one of the Phantom's peculiarities—the aircraft had a tendency to fall into a spin when the stick was muscled too hard at a high angle of attack. But the F-4 wasn't ready to call it a day; she managed to keep herself in the air and moving forward despite the pilot's nightmares. There was damage to the tail—he could feel the rudder lagging—but the old iron hung together.

The plane began gaining altitude. There was no question now of doing anything fancy; he would have to get away, straight line, balls out.

Water, then find the coast.

One thing he had going for him—the MiG pilot probably thought he'd splashed him with the missiles.

There were mountains ahead. Turk nudged the F-4 skyward, aiming to skim over them so close he'd chip paint.

VAHID'S RADAR FOUND THE PHANTOM AHEAD TO THE east, roughly a hundred kilometers from the Caspian if it kept on its present heading. He was over the Elburz Mountains and using them to good effect, tucking well below the peaks and hoping the irregular topography would make it hard to track him.

He was right, but Vahid realized he didn't have to stick too closely to his prey. It seemed obvious that the pilot was going north to the Caspian. He would simply beat him there.

Other fighters were scrambling now. The radio was alive with traffic and orders: shoot the enemy down.

Vahid blocked everything out, concentrating on his plane and the pursuit. The Phantom was fast, but his MiG was faster. He was also higher. He titled his nose back and climbed some more, planning how he would take the Phantom in their final encounter.

THE MOUNTAINS SEEMED ENDLESS. TURK HAD BACKED off the throttle, worried about his fuel supply, but he was still moving at over 650 knots, yet there seemed no end to the damn things. They were green, greener than anything he'd seen in Iran. The sun glowed overhead, the sky clear. He imagined there were vacationers somewhere below, enjoying the day and the sea.

Wherever the hell it was.

Hang in there, Turk told himself. Just hang in there.

He examined the dials in the cockpit. He still had a decent amount of fuel. The damage to the tail was light, if the controls were to be believed: the plane seemed ever so slightly slow as it responded to the rudder, but not so much that it wouldn't go where he wanted.

Come on, come on. Let's get there.

Nothing but green and brown below.

Damn!

And then there was sea, a green-blue sheet spread in front of him.

Free, he was free.

Except: there was the damn MiG, three o'clock in his windscreen, heading due west but pushing onto his wing in what Turk recognized was the start of a sweep that would end with the Phantom in the fat heart of his targeting pipper.

Vahid felt a rush of gravity as he pulled the MiG hard to complete the sweeping intercept. The Phantom, riding straight and true, rose into his screen as he put his nose down. He had the MiG dead on its enemy's tail. He had his gun selected; he was close to the other plane and wanted the satisfaction of perforating it.

The distinctive tail of the American built plane seemed to droop; Vahid edged his finger onto the trigger as it filled out his target.

Even as he fired, the other plane disappeared. Vahid started to pull up, then realized what the other pilot was doing.

It was almost too late.

Using its control surfaces like speed brakes while it throttled back, the F-4 had dropped below and behind the MiG in an instant. The hunter was now the hunted—Vahid tweaked left and right as a stream of tracers exploded over his right wing. He began a turn, then changed course, hoping to catch the Phantom overshooting him. But whoever was flying the F-4 was very, very good—he not only didn't bite on the fake turn, but managed to stay behind him long enough to put a few bullets across his right wing. Vahid rolled, trying to loop away, but that was nearly fatal—the F-4 danced downward, drilling two or three more bullets into his left wing and fuselage before passing by.

You underestimated him, One Eye would have said. *I didn't teach you that.*

Vahid pulled up, selecting his IR missiles. But

the panel indicated they wouldn't arm. Some of the bullets that struck the plane earlier had disabled the controls or the missiles, or both.

So it was down to guns, one on one.

Vahid leveled off, looking for his opponent.

T URK FELT HIS THROAT CLOSE WITH THE SHARP TURN. His head pressed in and his heart clutched. It was as if a huge hand had grabbed hold of him and squeezed with all its might.

Don't do that again. You'll pass out and crash.

He'd gotten bullets into the other plane. Enough to splash the damn thing, he was sure.

Had he? Where was it?

Head clearing, Turk began a climb. After only a few seconds a tiny shadow passed to his right— cannon fire from the MiG.

He steepened the climb and rolled, surprised to find the MiG practically alongside him.

Within seconds Turk realized they had managed to put themselves into a classically difficult position. They were two fighters locked in a deadly embrace. Neither could afford to accelerate or drop away; doing so would allow the other to slide behind him.

How long could they keep this up? Turk nudged his rudder gently, edging the plane right in hopes that he might be able to let the MiG spurt ahead. But the MiG pilot was too sharp for that—he came with him, rolling his wing around about a quarter turn just as Turk did.

Turk thought of various ways to break off. The

best seemed to be to mash the gas, turn tight and get his nose facing the other plane. The MiG would have to turn outside to keep from being thrown in front; Turk would be risking a quick missile shot but he was confident he could get his own shot in first.

The trouble was, he doubted he could stand the roller-coaster force needed to pull that maneuver. Nor could he afford to stay in the climb much longer; the thin oxygen would kill him.

The man flying the other plane had good instincts. Maybe he could use those against him.

Both planes were flying almost straight up, canopy-to-canopy, turning a tight, ascending scissors pattern in the sky. Neither could afford to stray.

Turk had an idea. As he turned his wing to start a twist, he pushed the Phantom closer to the MiG. In an instant, he jerked the nose forward and at the same time fired the gun.

His idea was that it would look to the other pilot as if the Phantom was trying to crash into him. Whether it did or not was impossible to tell, but the maneuver had the desired effect: the MiG spun off to the right.

Turk's own instincts were to follow. Everything he knew told him that he had the other plane where he wanted him. And certainly he would have if he'd had a flight suit and oxygen.

But he told himself his job now wasn't to shoot down the MiG. It was to get himself and Stoner home. And so instead he pushed the Phantom back around to the north and accelerated again, sure he was home free.

He'd barely caught his breath when a fresh set of tracers exploded ahead of his right wing. The Iranian didn't want to quit.

21

CIA campus, Virginia

REID RAISED HIS HAND AND GAVE BREANNA A THUMBS-up, indicating that the American military consul in Baku had convinced the Azerbaijan air force to scramble its forces. The SEAL command had already released the MC-130 in Baku; it was preparing to take off and fly over the Caspian.

She told herself that Turk was going to make it. Against all odds, he was going to make it. She hadn't sent him to his death.

22

Over the Caspian Sea

TURK FELT THE PLANE SHUDDER SEVERELY AS HE JINKED left and right, barely ducking the fire from the MiG. Between the old metal and whatever damage the Iranian had done to him earlier, the plane was starting to strain.

The MiG and the F-4 were still locked in a death dance, neither able to get an advantage. The MiG slid behind him, but Turk managed to push the Phantom just enough to stay away from his bullets.

Their speed dropped, moving through 220 knots. While the MiG was a nimbler airframe, Turk thought he must have done some damage to it, at least enough to keep it from trying anything too fancy. But its pilot was tenacious, clinging tightly.

Even if the MiG didn't nail him, the more maneuvers he did, the better the odds that he'd run out of fuel before reaching a safe airport. And parachuting wasn't an option. He needed to get away quickly.

Turk racked his brain for a way to get the MiG off his back. The only thing he could think of was a low altitude spin and a crash—not a particularly pleasant solution, even if the plane could take the g's.

Unless it didn't actually happen.

As another burst of rounds flashed over the canopy, Turk jerked the Phantom's stick, trying to make the plane look as if it had been hit. He backed off as his plane began to yaw, then pushed in on his left, tipping his wing down and holding his breath.

By now the MiG had stopped firing. He was still back there somewhere, though.

When the blue sea filled his windscreen, Turk held the Phantom's nose down for a three count. Then he pulled up on the stick, muscling it back as hard as he could while giving the plane throttle.

His head floated in the sudden rush of blood. The Phantom didn't like the maneuver either, threatening to fall backward in the sky. The control surfaces, confused by the contradictory forces working on them, bit furiously at the air, trying to follow the pilot's crazed instructions. The engines, suddenly goosed with fuel, roared desperately, pushing to hold the plane in the air despite the heavy hand of gravity.

And there was the MiG, right in front of him.

Turk fired, lying on the trigger even as he fought to get the Phantom stable. He got off a burst and a half, then the goosed engines pushed the Phantom ahead, whipping over the MiG close enough to scorch the paint.

He'd put a dozen bullets into the MiG's airframe, and this time there was no way they wouldn't have an effect: Turk saw a bolt of flame in the cockpit mirror.

If he'd been more confident of his fuel, he might have turned around to watch his enemy burn.

Vahid felt the blood draining from his head as the MiG began to disintegrate around him. Victory had been snatched from his hand in an instant. Not just victory—the tables had been completely turned, the pilot in front suddenly behind, the predator now the victim.

He needed to pull the ejection handle. He needed to get out of the plane.

Why? He'd been defeated. He was not the best, and would never be. He couldn't stand the humiliation.

Could he go home to his father, the war hero, and look him in the eye?

Get out of the aircraft, he heard his old instructor say.

One Eye's voice screamed at him.

Save yourself. Fly and fight another day.

Vahid's hand wavered over the handle as his mind battled. He thought of his mother, who would love him no matter what. He saw his father again, as he had known him as a young man, before the injury.

And then it was too late: a fireball erupted, consuming the MiG-29 and Iran's finest pilot.

STONER FOLDED HIS ARMS, WATCHING OUT THE SIDE of the cockpit as the Phantom leveled off and continued north over the sea. The plane flew steady; bullets no longer coursed over the wings or exploded in the distance. Whatever had been chasing them was gone.

So they were getting out. That was all right, wasn't it? He didn't have to kill Turk if he got him home.

The memories poking Stoner earlier had receded. They were like booby-traps in the jungle, waiting to swallow him if he stepped wrong. But he didn't know how to excise them.

Maybe one of the shrinks back home would.

The mission had been a good one. He liked it

tremendously. Everything about it, the sensation of adrenaline in his body, the feeling in his stomach when he ran, the crush of his fist against an enemy.

He hated the enemy. He hated people who wanted to hurt him, or hurt his people.

That was who he was. Whatever else they had done to him, whatever the drugs and biomechanical devices they'd put into him, that part was definitely his.

CLEAR OF THE ENEMY PLANE, TURK TOOK OUT THE SAT phone. He pushed the power button. Nothing happened. The damn thing was dead.

He reached into his pants pocket for Grease's. He remembered taking it from Grease's ruck. But he found the GPS, not the sat phone.

He reached into his other pocket, feeling a little desperate. The phone was there.

But it was a cell phone. Grease had the sat phone in his pocket or somewhere else, and he had missed it.

Have to do something else. Don't fall apart now.

Turk held his course due north for another five minutes before turning westward. He had only the vaguest notion where he was. While he still had a reasonable amount of fuel, he began to prepare a mental checklist of what he would do if Baku didn't turn up very soon. He would hunt for another airstrip. If he didn't see one, he could land on a highway—supposedly the Russians had built them long, straight, and wide for just such a contingency.

Better to find Baku. Much, much better.

A small fishing boat bobbed in the distance. The coast was just beyond it.

Another plane was coming down from the north. It looked like a civilian aircraft, an air-liner. As it came closer, he saw that it had four engines—an MC-130.

Oh baby, he thought, changing course to meet it.

SURVIVOR

———

1

The White House

CHRISTINE MARY TODD PUT DOWN THE PHONE AND looked over at her visitor.

"Our last operatives are out of Iran," she said. "It's a great day."

"Yes."

"We had to make the strike," continued the President. "It's too bad that so many Iranians had to die, but they were all involved in the program—the vast majority were involved in the program," she added, correcting herself. A handful of people had died on the ground during the team's attempts to get out. Some were undoubtedly civilians.

A number of Americans had also died—the entire team that had escorted Captain Mako, who by some miracle and his own ingenuity, along with the heroic efforts of Mark Stoner, managed to survive.

Truly, considering all that was at stake, the toll was extremely light.

"Are you going to explain how we did it?" asked her visitor.

"Absolutely not. Some will figure it out eventually. The Chinese, I'm sure, will have their suspicions. And the Russians. They'll be doubling their investment in nanotechnology, and UAVs, I'm sure. The Iranians, though—they haven't a clue. Why they wasted their resources in this way, building weapons they not only can't use but can't completely perfect—"

"I meant are you going to explain it to us."

"Eventually." Todd smiled. "Yes. In general terms, of course."

"There will be blowback," said her visitor.

"I expect it. We've already seen an uptick in communications traffic among the usual suspects." Todd glanced at the phone on her desk. Nearly every button was lit, even though she had told her operator and the chief of staff that she wouldn't be taking calls for an hour. The world, it seemed, was determined to spin on, with or without her.

"But back to the matter at hand," said Todd. "The presidency. Given everything I've said—would you consider running?"

"I don't know."

"I think you'd make a great President. And, since my medical condition will be . . . tiring, I don't think I should run for reelection. So, you would have a wide-open shot."

"I see that."

They were both silent for a moment.

"You don't want the job?" Todd asked.

"I'm, uh—I hadn't realized you were sick."

"Nor did I. And I don't feel it either." Todd smiled. Not today anyway.

"Why back me? We've never completely gotten along."

"Oh, I think we have, in the important areas. And frankly, I liked your opposition. It kept me honest. Besides, I think you'd make a great President."

"Well, thanks."

Todd rose. "Think it over, Senator. There's no need to give me an answer, but you will want to start getting your ducks quietly in place. These things take an enormous amount of energy and time."

"So I've heard," said Zen, wheeling forward to shake her hand.

2

Fort Benning

Turk Mako remained at attention as the bugler's notes faded. The ceremony honoring Grease and the rest of the team had come to an end.

Their bodies hadn't been recovered. The Iranians had been curiously silent so far, despite the President's statements and numerous analysts' pronouncements that the U.S. had managed to destroy the Iranian bomb program with weapons that it steadfastly refused to describe. Todd had promised that the details would be revealed when appropriate; Turk understood that to mean *never.*

They'd given him a place of honor at the front. He remained standing as the others left, nodding as people looked at him but remaining in his own cocoon. Soldiers, civilians, filed by silently.

Turk glanced at Stoner, standing toward the back. He hadn't seen him since the hospital in Bethesda when they'd returned. Stoner hadn't said much. Turk couldn't tell whether he was fighting some inner demon or simply a very quiet man.

Stoner had saved his life, not least of all by disobeying orders to kill him.

No one said those were the orders, but Turk knew they were. He wasn't sure exactly how to treat Breanna. She'd known all along that he was to be killed.

It was her job; he knew that. It was his job; he knew that, too. But it was hard to know what to feel about a person after that.

Turk's body had taken a beating, but the mission had done more than that to him. He'd changed. He'd been a cocky pilot when he started, sure of himself in the air. On the ground, he'd been a bit of a dweeb, awkward and timid at times.

Now he wasn't.

A pair of jets passed overhead. Turk glanced upward. They were F-35s, the latest multirole fighters in the U.S. inventory.

And maybe the last. A lot of people thought manned combat flight was over. Machines could now fill the gap, making their own decisions, flying more reliably than men ever could.

Had he proven them wrong? If he hadn't been there, the nano-UAVs wouldn't have succeeded. A human was still needed in the mix, and a good one.

Or was this just one last gasp? The next generation of aircraft, surely only a few years away, might have enough processing power to handle all decisions on their own.

Turk wasn't sure. He liked to fly, and he was very good at it, and that colored his opinions.

One thing he did know: true courage would never go out of style. It would just be harder to find.